P9-DEB-915

The Remarkable Book Shop
July 11, 1982

For Linda —
With so much appreciation
and love!
To actually buy it!
Bless you..
Jill

Also by Jill Robinson

NONFICTION

Bed/Time/Story

With a Cast of Thousands

FICTION

Thanks for the Rubies, Now Please Pass the Moon

Perdido

Dr. Rocksinger and the Age of Longing

DR. ROCKSINGER AND THE AGE OF LONGING

Jill Robinson

Alfred A. Knopf New York 1982

THIS IS A BORZOI BOOK
PUBLISHED BY ALFRED A. KNOPF, INC.

Grateful acknowledgment is made to the following for permission to reprint from previously published material:

Ice Nine Publishing Co., Inc.: Excerpts from *Casey Jones*, words by Robert Hunter; music by Jerry Garcia; Copyright © 1970 by Ice Nine Publishing Co., Inc.

Warner Bros. Inc.: Excerpt from "I Get A Kick Out Of You" by Cole Porter. © 1934 (Renewed) Warner Bros. Inc. All Rights Reserved. Used By Permission.

Library of Congress Cataloging in Publication Data

Robinson, Jill, [date]
Dr. Rocksinger and the age of longing.

I. Title.
PS3568.02898D7 1981 813'.54 81-47522
ISBN 0-394-50951-X AACR2

Manufactured in the United States of America

FIRST EDITION

FOR

Johanna Schary Robinson

AND FOR

Jeremy Zimmer

Life would be no better than candlelight tinsel and daylight rubbish if our spirits were not touched by what has been, to issues of longing and constancy.

—George Eliot, *Middlemarch*

. . . a new world of new dreams is a fierce and demanding thing . . . and lessons are hard to learn when one is breathless in a cold and active sea. But they must be learned nevertheless. For hardened hearts and dead souls are left to those who do not understand that we sometimes do grave damage to those whom we love. Hardened hearts and dead souls are left to those who harm an innocent and then do not embark upon a life of careful amends.

—Mark Helprin, *Ellis Island*

Dr. Rocksinger and the Age of Longing

1

The roads in Connecticut all look alike and never go the same way twice and I was lost.

"No wonder you have not come home," I said to my husband, to the Bill who was not here, who had been gone two months, "No wonder you are lost and now I am lost and talking to you, out of my mind. And I am lost because for all these years your face, your hands, your silent ways, you, just you have been my reference point and you are gone and I do not know how to do days without you."

I'd finished taping some of my radio shows in the city early. I'd worked. I'd tried. But with every word I felt my husband's absence running along behind like a taped shadow.

And on my way home, back to Medwin's Landing, I'd decided I would look for an apple orchard and I'd driven off on these roads and found an apple orchard. The mother who makes apple pies is reassuring; the apple pie is nothing if not confidence. And I had bought a lot of apples to make pies for my daughter and son—for Brynn and for Dylan. The mother who makes apple pies will not lose her mind. She will not leave you. She knows how to care for you. She rolls out this pastry. She takes this knife and she holds it carefully. And you watch and look at each other and take a breath as she picks up the apple and slices it neatly. She threatens nothing. She survives with grace.

I had not started out for apples. I had started out to search for Bill. Two months ago he had taken me to see *Farewell, My Lovely* and had held me in his arms all the whole night long and the next morning he'd said in his casual soft way that he was going out to pick up a new baseball glove and he never came back. But who knew how they might have changed these roads since he was a boy here, who knew how much more confusing it could be if you expected at least to know where you were going. I surely did not.

Perhaps this was foolishness to look for him but then chances are called chances because they are not expected. And I had surely not expected him to leave. You did not hate me, Bill, not when you slept around the curve of my body, not when you held me between your fine high-strung knees.

Now I collided with a sign: THIS ROAD IS TEMPORARILY CLOSED. Perfect.

I turned off my car and I picked up an apple from the bushel baskets next to me. I stepped out and pitched that apple into that black and yellow sign. I stood there in the middle of the road with my hands on my hips. "Rats to Connecticut!" I said. "I will die without you," I shouted, and hurled another apple. "You, oh you. I cannot be without you."

And I picked up one more apple. "You will not." I told myself. "Stop. You will take a deep breath. You will figure out how to get home. You will make pies." I perched on the edge of the front seat of this station wagon; this family car I'd believed in; the magic that would insure the perfect, ordered Connecticut existence. The husband and wife in the front seat. The children in the back. Now I sat there, the door open, my legs dangling out. "Eat the apple."

What I had intended most of all to insure was that this most favorite of all of my three marriages would last. Cleo, who managed the station and generally produced my show, had just shepherded me through taping and then cutting four interviews. We had tried to plan next week's programs.

"Maybe," I had said, "we should do one on How to Keep Your Marriage Together When He Is Gone." Cleo had reminded me that each of my marriages showed a startling gift for downward mobility. "Perhaps you could see this not as an ending, but as the beginning of a new trend. Sometimes I think your selection of husbands is that of a woman who's trying to prove to herself that marriage doesn't work."

I threw the apple core off into the bushes. "Become a tree," I said. I opened the glove compartment, where I found one pair of sheepskin-lined gloves, a flashlight, a jar of salted almonds, a spray bottle of Je Reviens, the Chevy handbook, a pocket illustrated *Field Guide to North American Birds* and no map.

I shook my head, and as I got back into the car I pulled the glasses on the top of my head back over my eyes. I looked at the leaves on fire. Ending is the cruelest season. It lasts your whole life long.

Stop that. Just start the car. Turn it around: north, you just keep going north, and perhaps a bit east, which is where it is getting darker. Wonderful that you know that. And this has to be north because the darker part is to the right. "Right."

It did not feel "right" because the road was turning now toward the darker part and downhill. Ah. A car was coming. Too fast—I couldn't catch the driver's attention. And it was not Bill. In every car, on every road, I expected to see him. I'd lie by the road and wait, curled under the snow, like Gelsemina with her trumpet, if I thought he'd come.

But you do not die of love in Connecticut. You carry on. Yes. You surely do. A truck whizzed by. I pulled over again onto the shoulder of the road. I got out. You do not lie down on bittersweet all tangling its drying vines with thornbushes. No matter how tragic. I picked a few strands. I'd come back if I ever figured out where I was, and pick so much—armfuls, sprays of it for everywhere, over the bathroom mirror, the headboard—and the house would be a bower for Bill to come home to. If the set was beautiful one could overlook the characters, the play. Yes: embellish, disguise. Deny. Another car came by: there; the charm—just like my third marriage. And the third car went by. Now an old black limousine, with fins, slowed up.

I ran out around my car waving my hand with the bittersweet clutched and trailing. A young man was driving, but it was the one in the back seat who rolled down the window.

"Do you need something?" He had hanks of long dark hair, and if anyone was in need of anything, he was in need of a comb. But then, look to thy own last, cobbler. Brynn and Dylan combed their heads with rakes—surely not with their lovely Mason Pearson brushes, which had not been removed from their original boxes.

"Yes. I'm lost." My eyes filled with tears; I could not stop. "I'm lost, my husband's gone, and it's hopeless, and I'm trying to get back to Medwin's Landing." And I could not hold on to myself.

"That's where we're just coming from. You sure got yourself real lost," he said. "Oh, wow." Very serious, sad eyes behind the smile.

"Really?" I asked. Somehow, amid all the wailing, there's the essential corner that knows what it's doing that is not *really* lost. I must now regroup. I must listen. I have two children. I must not let go. I wiped my eyes. I put the bittersweet into the car and brought out my notebook and a pen.

"Well, hear me on this, Gary," he said to the driver. "See, you're goin' in the wrong direction and what I want to do is get you back on the Interstate."

"Yes." I nodded. "That would be excellent. I was actually looking for an apple orchard, too, and took this road, and—do you want an apple?"

"Sure—crazy! Gary—an apple?"

Yes. Crazy. I picked out two apples from the bushel, handed one to him and another to the friend playing chauffeur.

"That's really neat. You give great apple," he said. He took a bite.

"I'll let that go right by," I said, fast. A smile came from nowhere. Oh, from somewhere: the place where you do your work anyway even when the sky is falling. Stop. "Just give me the directions, please."

"Cool." He switched on a short smile. "Sorry." He put back his serious expression. "You just turn around, then you'll come to this fork with three roads—there's the Bluebird Inn. Don't turn there, stay straight, right along by the reservoir, then you make a right on Route 161—they've got a sign that's a little beat up—and it looks like you go straight, but don't . . . and are you with me?" He grinned again. He would be cute for Brynn except Brynn pretended to dislike self-assured boys who talked a lot because I supposed they reminded her of Dylan.

"Yeah, I'm hangin' in," I said, talking in the way they do. "Now I turn right on one sixty-one, yes?"

The directions took a page of my notebook.

"I'm due up in Hartford to play a gig," he said, "or we'd turn around and lead you back home—but you'll be cool if you just take it easy, see where you're going, and uh, thanks for the apple." He looked at me again. "Are you sure you'll be all right?"

"Sure." I smiled again. I thanked them, and the limousine purred off. No matter how old, how large the fins, no ordinary car makes the limousine sound. Does the bereft woman-in-love give a moment's consideration to such things? There was the conflict; the lure I thought true love would surely override.

I took out my pocket watch. My parents had given it to me when I got my own radio show. It was inscribed on the back: *The Margot Fox Show*. And *Pace, darling*, it said. That had probably been my mother's idea, and it did not mean "peace" in Italian. Between her designing and his work in the theatre they knew all about timing.

It was late. No time to get pies done before dinner.

My mother had it both. True love and success. But was she happy? Perhaps the better notion was that true love does not override but will encompass all considerations.

Priorities. Yes. Go home and make the pies to reassure the children that you are not completely crazy. They will have actual homemade pies as a cozy midnight snack if not exactly as a proper dessert. There is always another way to see everything. You look. You take a little time and look again, and the meaning will have completely changed.

When she revealed she would not be able to see anymore, my mother had given me the splendid kaleidoscope my father had made for her. She had closed the door to her studio, spectacles with jetty black lenses already in place on her nose, and handed the kaleidoscope to my father. "You know how much Margot loved it and would have wanted you to give it to her." I am Margot. I was not dead then and am not dead now. But my parents always spoke with ceremony as if everything was a rehearsal for the deathbed speech. They talked as if the evanescence of life, and, therefore, of marriage, was unique to them and not of broad general application. If something happened to them—my God, it would be the end of love. When anyone talked about love, the love that is "bigger than both of us," I knew I was supposed to think of my parents and surely not of my own failed marriages.

This was fifteen years ago. My children were small, my father would be young forever, my mother was not blind. She looked at me sharply through the glasses. I interpreted her intensity then as hatred for me. Before shocking things began to actually happen to me, in the days when I would invent them to get out of doing other things, or to get attention, I had told everyone at school that my mother wore dark glasses because a rival designer had gotten jealous of my mother's Coty Award and had thrown acid in her face. No one has ever known what was actually wrong with my mother's eyesight, which comes and goes—it would seem to a hostile observer—at whim, but acid it surely was not.

My father had turned to me with his beaming smile, his soft eyes brimming, and handed me the kaleidoscope. Except for one other thing I didn't understand then that she had given me, this was the best present I'd ever had from my mother, although she had given it to him to give to me.

In the late forties and the fifties my mother had been a successful fabric designer. Millicent Balin Fox. The kaleidoscope had always sat on the light table in her studio behind their summer house in Southford, Connecticut. My father, the set designer Sylvan Fox, had fashioned the kaleidoscope out of a triangular tunnel of long, narrow mirrors. He'd wrapped these with velvet and at one end he had attached two disks of glass into which he'd inlaid petals of dried flowers, slivers of gems and tiny bits of fabric.

When I was a child I used to take the kaleidoscope from the studio and climb the apple tree under my bedroom window and watch my father playing tennis. The kaleidoscope fractured his distant white-dressed form into pieces of dashing light: periwinkle comets looping and darting through the ultramarine chips of glass. Years later I watched my son and daughter toddling on that lawn, bobbing and glinting through the gold leaf, through fading rose petals. Then they'd come starry as I'd hold the disk on a dappled pattern of mauve and silver, pale as old photographs of my parents when they were children, and it was not enough to watch. I'd run out, I'd run out on that lawn, and swoop them up and roll with them, tickling them with forget-me-nots and digging my face into their chubby forms, sniffing the smells of sun under their chins, and we'd lie there, and I'd have one arm tight over each of them, stay, stay, stay. And I'd hear them breathe next to me on that lawn. But it does not stay, time, just like this.

And in this same way, when I turn glances, sounds and touches over in my mind, when I reflect upon people, places and moments, the perspective of time and changing considerations performs like this splendid kaleidoscope. So my husband's disappearance seemed to be the most significant element in this period of life. Then, with some distance, I looked again, and I could see that the importance was in what his disappearance revealed.

And, with another twist, another period of time, I could see that new, yearning distractions I had invented were simply more disguises and cover-ups of a new fear, an apprehension of coming losses that would not be masked by the pursuit of a new career, the embrace of a different lover, or even truly eased by the reaching for a kind of faith.

2

From the front gate to Fitzgerald Packard's house on upper Main Street you could look down the hill, down through the curve of Medwin's Landing, past the peaked housetops, down to the wharf and right down to the river shimmering through the mist. And everywhere you looked, on any reasonably fair day, there they were.

They were everywhere. Hanging out of car windows, slinking along sidewalks, slouched against the walls, hunched on motorcycles, gum popping, doors slamming, tooth braces flashing. They sniggled, smooched, whistled, whirled, clattered and chattered, and two of them were mine and this was not what I'd intended for them at all.

I believed in the healing power of roots, hometowns and heritages, especially those which were not my own, and so I'd convinced Bill Spinning that he needed to move back to where he was born, to his Connecticut, not mine, not my roads, these. My childhood Connecticut was one step inside the stage door, where the theatre people performed their pastoral dreams in the easy season. Surely, everyone in Bill's Connecticut had actual happy families in colonial houses; my children would know happier children, the dog would know happier dogs. And in Bill's Connecticut there would be no open marriages, no swinging, no street corner drunks, no talking t-shirts, fit friends to say "Find Yourself." In Connecticut there would surely be no divorces. And people (Bill) would stay put.

I had waited one more week to see if Bill would come home and then I'd called Fitzgerald Packard, who was a private detective as well as the real estate broker here. Fitz had found the house we rented when we moved here last year from the city.

"A classic case of abandonment," Fitz had said to me when I had finally called and, in a voice with a stillness that alarmed even me, told him Bill was gone. I'd agreed to walk over and meet Fitz at his house and then we would stroll down and pay a visit to Judge Blanche Hutchins, who, Fitz said, had been most distressed to hear of my husband's disappearance. "But," he said, "she was not surprised." He did not elaborate. It was his way, I'd decided, of reminding me I was new, and had not understood the ways of the menfolk.

I'd come here the first time to interview Judge Hutchins, and she had, after one of our talks, introduced me to Fitz, who had offered to show me houses. I had fallen in love with the idea of this town, just as I had fallen in love with the idea (*my* idea) of Bill, this graceful, lonely former baseball player, eternally in search of old summertime triumphs. Fitz had asked me if I had children.

"Two," I'd said. Many years before Bill I had fallen in love with the idea (*my* idea) of a young airplane pilot who had become the father of my children. What he shared with Bill, and with an elegant publisher I'd briefly married in between, was a certain distant expression I took as a symptom of a deep melancholy I would make it my business to cure.

"Why," my mother had said, "do you always marry men who already want not to be there?"

"Because," I said, "I am already used to it then when they aren't."

"That," she said, "is not true." She was right. Which I would not tell her.

Fitz had asked, "And are these in fact children or are they

teenagers?" His eyebrows like circumflexes rose, then crouched down over his little black eyes. At least he had not pretended to like them.

As Fitz came out of his house now, he looked right past me at the three kids unwisely hanging around his fence, sharing one cigarette, passing it about to give the impression it was pot. "Rowdies and indigents," he said. "Malingerers." And then he tipped his hat to me. "My dear girl; such a tribulation!"

I touched his arm lightly. "No, no, I'm fine," I said.

"Well, we shall see what we can do." We walked down his path to the gate. He nodded to the boys, but did not shoo them away. I decided he enjoyed the aggravation. Probably was good for his circulation.

"Morning, boys," he said.

They nodded, they gazed, they leaned. Fitz sighed, exasperated, adjusted his plum bowtie, and tilted his gray tweed Irish hat just so.

Taylor's roofing company truck came up the hill. Teddy and Freddy, Frank Taylor's big blond sons, stood in the back in the down vests and the jeans.

"Good morning, Jennie, before you knock me down," Fitz said. We stepped back as two young girls tore out of a house, waved at the Taylors, smiled, yelled and clapped their hands over their mouths.

"Would you mind if I check to see if my car is ready?" Fitz said. He was already angling his direction toward the service station at the corner of Willow and Main.

"You know it won't be," I said. "They never are."

"That is true," said Fitz. "But I like to harass them. It doesn't work but it entertains them slightly and reminds them my car is still there."

We crossed to the service station. A pair of jeans ending in ragged sneakers slid out from under a car. It was my daughter, Brynn, lying on her back on a dolly upholstered in rose-covered carpeting.

"So we meet again," she said to me. She had left for school two hours ago. I'd assumed she was here because I'd seen our dog, Spike, frisking in the weeds behind the station where the wrecks were kept. She stood up, took a cigarette out of the pack rolled up into the sleeve of her t-shirt, which said "Eat Worms." Her careful attempt to look carelessly tough was not entirely successful. Although she'd slammed her fluffy blond hair back into tufts clasped by plain rubber bands, the hand with which she was tamping down her cigarette on its hard pack glimmered with tiny gold rings, and bordering the grimy sweatband around her wrist were several delicate gold bracelets.

"School out early?" I said.

"Long class break," Brynn said. She lit her cigarette with a steel Zippo. "I thought you were goin' down to the city to do those interviews you were workin' on last night."

"My plans changed," I said.

"Happens to all of us," she said.

Fitz watched us carefully. "Your mother must be very disciplined," Fitz said, making the sort of point they hear very clearly and dislike immensely.

"She always pulls her ideas out of what's going on. I can hear it now: The Obsessive Student: Is Your Child Hiding Her Heartbreak in Books?" She grinned at me. Then jerked her thumb in the direction of a dusty black '62 Chrysler. "That your car?" Brynn said to Fitz.

"I am afraid so."

She shook her head. "Well, see you, Mom. I got to do an oil change on this buggy." Like all the others who had lived here all their lives, Brynn now had jobs. It was never clear where hanging out left off and work began, but "the job" was of particular convenience in dealing with concerned parents who puzzled about one's whereabouts. One could always say, "I was working." "Workin'," they would say, or "on the job." Perhaps the Medwin's Landing school system ought to have been commended for adopting such a thorough interpretation of "work-study" programs usually found in institutions of much higher learning.

Clutter, jeans, coin machines, cars with doors, hoods and trunk lids angled open, never finished, never fixed, with grease enough and tools enough for every one of them to play with. Even if the kids figured out where they wanted to go so badly, the cars would never be ready. I watched Brynn stroll back with the rolling gait reserved for garage work and I wanted to rush over and hug her. Such sturdy young bravado. How she must quake inside. She'd snap my head off if I said I saw it and knew about it because I had it too. Had my mother? Does fear ever become so socked in that all you can ever show, ever, is aloof brash fury, never mind how masked it may be with wit?

"Do you mind if I pick up the paper and have some tea?" said Fitz. "We are a bit early to catch Blanche on her lunch hour."

"No. I'll have something," I said.

We walked past the window box of faded plastic chrysanthemums and into Chickens. Fitz bought *The New York Times* and picked up the local paper and sat down at the diner counter. Helena Sedakis put baked apples up on the glass shelf next to the half grapefruits.

"Good morning, Helena, my love," Fitz said. Helena's and George's diner was also the Western Union office, where parents rushed in to send money orders to kids in trouble out of town. Two days a week Helena was a drug and alcohol counselor at the hospital. And Jennie, their own daughter, had just been released, Fitz told me, after her second overdose in ten days. They were so aware, the parents, it didn't seem possible.

But then Jennie was involved with the dread Reilly, and, sweet as she was, perhaps she wasn't motivated enough. That was the thing about small towns and drugs—the lack of urgency. I'd thought that in Connecticut there would be real schools with serious New England schoolmasters and long, rigorous class schedules. Math at nine right through to science at three. ("And look," Dylan had said to me, "how helpful that was to *you*, paragon of self-discipline.")

Most of Helena's and George's customers were kids, sitting in the seats, knees up; Cokes for breakfast. The laughs coming so early from high up in their noses.

And here was Dylan. And why was I surprised? His tall, angular build gave him a look of enterprise and he had the authoritative manner of someone brought up in the city. He was passing by on his way out from the back and smiled at us very fast; they both had the same eager grin and, like all of the others, did not wish their friends to see them flash it at adults. One did not acknowledge more than a nodding acquaintance with adults in the presence of one's peers.

However, Fitz reached out. "Dylan, good morning to you. Might I ask you a question your mother cannot answer?"

Dylan stopped in midlope. "Sure. Hi, Mom, how's it going?" Dylan did not drop his g's. Possibly because not doing it gave him one more thing to torment Brynn about. And conversely, she could add his elitism to her own arsenal.

"Do you happen to recall the license number on the Buick Mr. Spinning has."

"N2-562," said Dylan, "but he won't have the car long—it never worked. But then neither did Bill." Dylan grinned at me, and then at Helena. "I think I need another jelly doughnut to go—just put it on my mom's tab."

"Uh, swinger—you pay like always." Helena flashed a smile right back at him. And he took the doughnut and dug into his jeans.

"My treat," I said, quickly. I put my hand out and touched his arm.

"Thanks, Mom," he said. He eased for an instant, looking very young. Then he shook Fitz's hand and straightened, toughened up again. "In case you run across Bill Spinning, you tell him from me," Dylan said to Fitz, "that no one does this to my mom and gets away with it." He strode out with a fast grin over his shoulder for a girl at the counter.

Helena looked at me carefully. "How are you doing?"

"Oh, I'm fine." I shrugged and smiled. She shook her head. "We'll talk sometime."

"I know," I said. You circle in slowly to some friendships and we both had known from these first careful exchanges that we liked each other. You know in advance: this will be a friend; this will be an acquaintance.

Helena served Fitz his peach yoghurt and tea. "Well, we have a fine day today. Not foggy. Perhaps that will convince us. Everything is wonderful for a day."

"Chilly though," said Fitz, helpfully for those of us who wanted not to be cheerful. "Wind coming up. It's going to be bad tonight." It was not at all chilly, but I think Fitz enjoyed being the old-timer with weather in his bones.

"Oh the first storm of the season," Helena said, balancing a plate on her arm as she flipped pancakes with the other hand. "Then George must go down to the river and see to the boat. We lost one already. Reilly, of course, out with that boy. No one can get you in trouble but yourself, of course, but it does help you start out if you have Reilly around."

Rafts, dories, rowboats, skiffs, summertime's traffic, lurking, drifting, hustling on the water. The kids fished for fish that were not there, listening to the speedboats of the rich they could not see in the fog. Reilly and another kid had wrecked Helena's and George's runabout last summer. They had collided with a police patrol boat on their way to a connection with a dealer from across the river.

Kids. There must have been at least as many in New York —but you didn't see them. That, I told myself, was because they are in school. But that wasn't true either: open schools, schools without walls, without doors, without hours—without my kids, most of all. So who was I to talk. Especially since as long as they were around and all right, what more did you need. This was very much the same attitude I had about husbands. I was more successful with kids. Kids. Three of them in blue jeans were hanging around the phone booth, one of them with a guitar slung around his back. I listened to the sound of them leaving. One on clogs, one on skates, the third in cowboy boots.

"Why," said Helena, wiping the counter, "are they not into sneakers? Why is it that our kids want only the noisy shoes?" She looked at me. "Let's have some coffee soon." I stayed a bit distant because I knew she was in A.A. People, like me, who used to drink, could sense it, I supposed. All the catch phrases those people used, the way they'd look at you as if they knew. Cleo's classy friend, St. Cheri, was in it too, and Cleo would sometimes hit me with one of their little slogans and I'd throw a little punch. I'd stopped drinking because I thought perhaps that was what made Bill so silent and sad. (It had to be something I could fix.) I was relieved I had, because when Bill left my mother said, in front of the children, "It's fortunate you're not like your Aunt Elise or you'd have died." Elise had thrown herself out of a window after her second husband left. But I'd reminded my mother quickly, "I'm already not like Elise because he was my third husband and I stopped drinking two years ago."

"She was not an alcoholic," my mother said. "You should not imply such a thing. She had tragedies. Who would not drink?" I prayed, please God, that I would not. Have tragedies. Or drink again.

Fitz finished his tea and walked down Main past the Theodore Lane Congregational church, high above the street, oaks gold against the white steeple and the steeple bright against the gray sky.

"Helena and George go to their A.A. meetings in the old stable behind the church," Fitz said a little too cozily, although they didn't seem to mind who knew. I guess it didn't matter since it never is a secret when you're drunk, God knows; everyone has something to say about that.

"Sometimes it seems to me," Fitz was saying, "that half of this town is drinking itself to death and the other half recovering in these A.A. groups."

And, I thought to myself, everyone probably bitches just as much if they're not drinking. It makes everyone so uneasy, me especially. But I just said, "Well, I suppose A.A. is a comfort for people who used to like bars." I never cared for bars really. I surely did not need A.A. I drank too much but I was not that kind of real alcoholic. I was, I thought, lucky to be able to stop on my own. And I had Bill. He gave me strength. But I did like parties. Bill didn't, so we rarely went. I couldn't imagine the Sedakises at bars, or parties either. The characteristic they had as a couple (and I supposed in a good marriage one would have that—a combined personality) was their apparent determination to recede, to be acute observers.

The children and I often went to the diner at dinnertime, when both Helena and George were there, and—with all the work they did, plus polite patter with customers—with their eyes they were always catching and commenting on each other's observations.

The Taylor truck was lumbering back down the road. Jennie and her friend had picked up their school books and, moving in the opposite direction from the high school, had by now sauntered down as far as the drugstore. They stood there as the truck stopped, oblivious to cars behind it. Teddy Taylor leaned out over the back of the truck, "You goin' bowling later?" he asked.

The girls, cool now, looked at each other. "Oh, I don't know," said Jennie.

"Who knows," said her friend.

"Precisely," said Fitz. "Once they have what they want, it isn't what they want anymore." I wondered, am I like that? When I feel I've failed, or lost, every negative comment applies to me: there, that's the reason!

The truck chugged off, cars moved again down Main Street and the girls, laughing, superior, trotted into the drugstore to try on makeup, skim through magazines that told them how to be sexy, famous and in love with the man with the right sign. They would read stories about stars who left towns like Medwin's Landing, found everything they wanted and lived happily ever after, for a year or two, which is about as far ahead as anyone can really imagine. And then you have to find something new to want, to long for and lust after, or you'll get bored, a fate worse than reality itself. Now: of course, I hadn't appreciated Bill enough. I should have tried harder to seem to like baseball.

Fitz was telling me that his father had once owned this whole block of two-story frame buildings, slate blue, light green and some in cream, all with white woodwork. "That used to be Packard's Drygoods," he said, pointing to the stationery store, now filled with orange and black for Halloween. I must ask the children if they'd like a party. I always wore a witch hat. And we'd ice big cookies with chocolate and orange frosting for the little trick-or-treat visitors. I made the pumpkin costume for Dylan when he was little; I stuffed it with balloons and then they popped, they burst, the sounds they made! His eyes so wide; he yelled. "Ma," he howled. He was terrified. I did not laugh. I sat right on the road and held him between my knees and rocked him and crooned to him. "I'm here," I said, "Mama's always here." Oh, and Brynn, in her black ballerina costume with the long black maribou cat's tail. Last year I asked them, "What are you going to be?" and they just stared at me. Do not ask this year, I told myself.

Over what had been Packard's, there was now a beauty parlor, under new management, calling itself The Clipper Ship —Unisex Salon. Still, however, painted cotton-candy pink. The cleaners was here on this block, the liquor store, and Sue Ellen's Fashions, with its display of lingerie, nurses' uniforms, and, always, one bridal gown.

Across the street was the hardware store, where the brides buy their pots and pans.

And here was Jennie again, alone now in front of the hardware store. She was perched on the back of a motorcycle, which was parked with its motor running. She was gazing at the bridal gown in the window of Sue Ellen's. And now Reilly ambled out of the hardware store with a package he pitched to Jennie.

It didn't seem clear to anyone whom Reilly belonged to. Or rather anyone who might have known was not saying. Surely not to newcomers. And you could be a newcomer for a long time—even longer if you asked questions. I had a hunch Reilly's father had been one of the old town drunks who had hung about the bars and died there. I heard George telling Fitz at the diner that Reilly was "the example of genetic accident that proves the rule, but I'm too worn out dealing with his problems and mistakes to remember the rule." And Helena had said, "Oh, Reilly. Honey, he is Jennie's problem, not ours."

Reilly was fond of starting businesses. He rarely got further than having cards printed, putting ads in the local paper and making contracts. He had had a small appliance repair business (once the appliances had been fixed he sold them for drugs); a moving company (in a drunken blackout he had picked up a load of furniture, forgotten where he was supposed to take it and sold it all), and a special events business which involved staging minor rock concerts and bazaars.

Reilly jumped on the seat, leaned way back, gunned the

motor. Jennie put her arms around his waist to hold on and they roared off.

We strolled on down the winding street now leveling out as it stretched to the wharves overlooking the river. On the wharf, motorcycles circled round, boys were throwing a football, others watching, beer cans in their hands, to be drained, crushed, tossed over their heads. Next to Papa Max's Bailbonds shop was another liquor store and Harry's Bait and Tackle Fishing Supply Co. Across the street was the courthouse. Kids slouched on the steps, and inside, shoulders hunched, hands dug deep into their pockets, they stood uncomfortably in small silent groups with wistful parents and resigned lawyers holding heavy briefcases. How did the parents bear it.

We climbed the broad polished wooden steps up to Judge Blanche Hutchins' sunny chambers at the very top of the courthouse. We knocked lightly on the door and walked into the large room with the dark woodwork and light green walls.

"The schools are empty. Must be," Fitz said to Blanche, and he swung his arm out in the direction of the long windows that overlooked the street. "Because they're out in droves. You'd think they were expecting a parade."

"But, my dear Fitz," said Blanche, "they are the parade."

Fitz flipped his hat onto Blanche Hutchins' hat rack, not airily, but, like all his gestures, with an implication that he was about to make a pronouncement, and he said, "It's their lurking you have to watch out for; they have something they're up to without knowing what it is and that's the worst kind."

"Well, my dear," Blanche said to me, "you're bearing up, I see. Even listening to my friend's dire premonitions." I laughed and Blanche sat down and leaned back in her father's old golden oak swivel chair with its worn black leather seat.

Her crisp rusty gray hair spun a whorl around her weathered, broad-cheeked face.

In Medwin's Landing the strangeness—the impression of lurking—came from a carefully preserved personal distance, a cloaked character of the facial expressions, all of which may have been cued by the dour quality of the light. The natural furtive atmosphere came partly from the mist over the river and partly from smoke from the factories that had been more prosperous when Blanche and Fitz were children.

The town had originally been set into a natural valley, and this cup of land, surrounded by highways, railroads and the residue of manufacturing, had created a thick lid of fog and fumes over the valley. People in Medwin's Landing had always commented with surprise on the days when the town was struck by muted sunlight. No one ever worked on those days.

"This is a pleasant day," Blanche reminded us. "And Main Street has always been like this on pleasant days." This woman did fit the proportions of the room. She commanded attention before she spoke. She always had, I was sure, even as a very young woman. I had no idea how old Blanche was. She made a point of talking as though she had been around since the beginning of time.

"It is not the same," Fitz maintained. "We never loitered."

"We did. But not where they could see us. We daydreamed. Now just what can I do for you today, my friends?" Blanche asked. "I've heard some rumors," she said to me. "Helena and Fitz are my best friends in town and it's said—by them largely—that they know everything that goes on. They do, and by indirection so do I."

Blanche was six feet tall in the woolen socks she liked to wear. Her even features came to smiles swiftly, although in repose she could appear quite stern, an asset to her position. She talked as if she were walking by you fast.

"Well, my dear," Fitz said, "it seems that two months ago—"

"Margot can tell me, Fitz, without your flourishes." Then she turned to me.

"Well." I felt as if I was in school. " 'Never,' I could hear Miss Rentsch say, 'start with "Well." ' " So. "Two months ago, one night my husband took me to see *Farewell, My Lovely*." I noticed I was wringing my hands. I put them at my sides.

Fitz interrupted, "*Farewell, My Lovely*—not a very good rendition of the book and . . ." He looked at me and I nodded.

"Fitz!" Blanche said, amusement showing in the tiny lines around her mouth. "And?" she added.

"And," Fitz said, probably not entirely unaware that he sometimes parodied himself for Blanche's pleasure, "it was Intent; I spoke with sources at the service station and was informed that Spinning did in fact check in there, and was, in fact, told, upon request, that the car would stand up to a rather long trip."

"One wonders," Blanche said, "how they'd know." She smiled slightly at me. I'd given Bill an old Buick convertible for his birthday. Perhaps I should have put a bon voyage ribbon across the hood. That's right, I told myself, embellish, distract, deny.

Fitz turned now, his thumbs up under his armpits. "A classic case of abandonment."

"Well, we haven't had one of those in years," said Blanche. During one of our interviews I had asked her if she had ever married and she looked distant, almost offended, and I thought she would dismiss the question without an answer. But she had said, "There was someone I cared for very deeply. But it was not possible. Not possible at all. I don't know what became of him." She had paused. And she paused again now and looked at me quickly. I could hear her voice click her own memories out.

"As I recall," she said, in her direct voice, her judge's voice, not the sad woman's voice I had heard that once so briefly, "it was a Spinning once before—left four small children. At least yours are older, but it's difficult enough for them at any age." She paused. "Difficult indeed." She looked at me. I wondered if anyone else knew.

"Oh, but she is devastated." Fitz looked at me, his eyebrows quivering up somewhere near his widow's peak.

"How she loved him, you know, moving here because it was his hometown."

"Nonsense," said Blanche. "You're an extremely self-sufficient woman, Margot. Fitz is hopelessly romantic and that is not helpful in these situations."

"Of course not," I said. "I have to keep myself very practical for the children." I thought that was the sort of thing Blanche would approve of. She pushed up the sleeves of her burgundy cardigan.

When I had come up here originally to interview Blanche for a program on Pioneer Women in the Law, she had taken me about and I had loved particularly, as Blanche did, the rangy old frame houses overlooking the town and the river beyond, one of which I was, indeed, living in now.

"No," Blanche said. "You keep yourself sane for your work. I liked the interview and I don't like much that I've ever seen about myself. I think I wrote you a note."

"You did. I meant to answer your note."

"It didn't need an answer." She said that in exactly the fast way you like if you don't do mail well. The astringent guilt-killer of that swift New England delivery. Don't give it a moment's thought—and she meant it.

"She really," Fitz said, "should do an interview with me. Real Estate Expert Moonlights as Private Eye." I could see Blanche was encouraged to see Fitz whipping a tail of his muffler over his shoulder. She had perfected the way to get you out of her office at the moment she wanted without saying a word. It was a subtle switch in movement. One or two gestures indicating a shift into neutral.

"Houses to persons; if it's missing he finds it. I could answer some provocative questions, don't you think?" He leaned, one hand down on her desk, glancing fast at her papers. Their eyes met as Blanche caught him. They smiled fast at each other.

"He's fond of detection," Blanche said, "because he loves to confirm his suspicions; reinforce his disapproval."

"It will help influence me, of course, if you can find my husband," I said. I laughed and Blanche smiled at me, which is what I wanted.

Blanche had told me she liked to have this time between sessions in court to herself. She enjoyed toasting muffins in her small toaster oven to eat with Keiller's ginger jam and the sweet farm butter that we could get fresh right from Murray's Dairy Farms five miles down to the south of town, near the zinnia fields where the summer people went to pick their flowers. Summer people, the way my family had once been. "So you must miss the house we used to have," my father had said when I had told him I was moving to Connecticut. "Yes, that's it," I'd said.

This year I would grow my own flowers. I stood here looking out of this courthouse window and imagined looking through my kitchen window—at my front lawn with its patches of clover, the shaggy herb garden dotted now with fallen leaves. I would be standing there with my hoe at sunset as Bill came down the road, lost and dusty, but home at last.

Stop, I told myself. Be here. In this courtroom. Today. I go off in my mind in a moment. Now I was watching the street here. The local people who did not go outside town. There were families who had never once seen New York City, although it was only two hours down to the south. I thought most people here considered the depression to be a natural condition. It was comfortable not to have any specific yearnings coincide with a thrust of positive action because you might have to change the rhythm of your days.

Now I watched Blanche preparing to say goodbye, moving her sleeves up. And I remembered the gesture and now I was back to that first time when I wished I had been filming, not just recording, when I'd sat with Blanche late in the afternoon. There was a quality of the lowering of the light that had reminded me of the color and mood in a book of photographs of old courthouses. I'd watched Blanche as she sat at her father's old rolltop desk, doing what she was doing now with her sleeves. She had told me she had always been fond of the mystery of the filtered light, finding the contrasts of sunlight too blunt. "People who aren't too trusting, who like to go about making friendships over periods of years, usually like it here, or put up with it anyway, better than the more open sort. Something about the darkness of the town has always lured the odder type of writer and artist. Maybe they hope to find a keener sense of reality in this impoverished atmosphere than they get in the city or those stylish suburban towns down to the south."

"A classic case of abandonment." Yes. No, do not go all fancy melancholy over Fitz's phrase, I told myself in the voice of Blanche Hutchins, who seemed designed to keep us all on our fundamental toes.

One could look at the invisible river beyond the fog all day and go completely awash in romantic tears over the notion of being abandoned. And, after all, Medwin's Landing had been founded by a man who had abandoned his family, by Captain Thaddeus Medwin in 1662. He'd contracted a fever on the Atlantic crossing and by the time he had pushed inland with his wife and nine children he'd gone quite mad. He thought, because of the mists which even then swirled about the valley, that he was in Chile and had discovered a legendary emerald mine.

Captain Medwin had spent his remaining days digging in the rocky hills, strands of moss and vines draped about his shoulders, convinced he was wearing ropes of precious emeralds. Nothing had been mined save limestone. Now children went into the desolate quarries pretending to be Medwin, just as Blanche and Fitz and their friends had done. They had looked for emeralds, finding mica and calling it silver and diamonds. I had walked there myself this summer, and held chips of mica, slivering it until it was translucent like the bits my father had slid between the glass disks in his kaleidoscope.

Mrs. Medwin had built the first church, and using pigments from wildflower pollens she had painted giant suns all over the interior, which convinced the other settlers that she had gone daft as well. But then they liked the nice warm feeling, and in a few years everyone started painting their porch ceilings blue to recall the summer skies.

Medwin's Landing had fallen twice to the British in the Revolutionary War, but, blanketed in fog as it was, it was hardly of strategic importance, and the soldiers had abandoned it readily the first time and taken it accidentally the second. Blanche Hutchins had told me that although little children were still taught this sort of basic history, high school here was no different than it seemed to be anywhere else. The curriculum apparently consisted of courses in Sexual Attitudes, Photography and Behavior Modification Trends in the Media. "It's no wonder that, so badly prepared, after a year or so of college most of them seem to return to Medwin's Landing." And they all worked in the diners and the service stations here, or along the highway, in the markets and the stores, selling things to each other, marking time. They felt their lives had not yet begun, but they were in no rush to deal with the challenges and responsibilities that have so clearly frustrated us, their parents. And my own were no exception, although I did not want to admit that to Blanche.

Blanche had taken issue with all the awareness our children seemed to have now. "They know all the responsibilities, all the conflicts that will come with adulthood! And far too much of the lives of each other's families. These used to be private concerns and I'm not certain this new awareness, this openness between the generations, is helpful—isn't, indeed, simply discouraging."

She had stood there looking out the window, out toward where the river had gleamed for an instant or so around noon, and where it had disappeared into the haze.

The first time I had come to Medwin's Landing to interview Blanche she had told me how she used to love to take her bike and ride on Sundays after church, far down, miles down the old black road, toward the middle lands, along the wide streams that once ran rainbows with the dyes from the yarns loomed in mills that stood empty now, rusty like so many heaps of abandoned toys.

I'd imagined Blanche Hutchins as the kind of friend I'd have had if I had lived in a book like *Girl of the Limberlost.* If I'd lived in Medwin's Landing when I was young, she'd have had her own small wooden rowboat and we'd have been up together in the soft early and late hours of dawn and dusk, when no one else was out, and we'd have walked along discovering the woods and grottoes, ponds and rivulets, on the periphery of the town. And perhaps I would have come down one morning and seen her meet a mysterious person, and I would have stopped and watched them go off in the boat together and I would have felt that pleasing wistfulness you do when a friend falls in love before you do.

So I had fallen in love with the idea of what her life had been in Medwin's Landing and did not then see that my children would not have that same life here now—and not only because the times and this town had changed, but because they were my children. Blanche would be the mother one would want for one's child—indeed for oneself, which may have been a fraction of my reason for coming here. But it was always these remarkable women who did not have children.

As we were leaving Fitz lifted his hat off the hat rack and put it on. "If you have time enough to reconsider, you may well be more grateful to me if I do not find the bounder."

"Yes," Blanche said, "selective detection: he does not retrieve what he does not consider worth having. To think upon!" And she so quickly, so lightly, so nicely, laid her hands for an instant on the tops of both my shoulders.

3

To distract myself from despondency and to fill the void left by Bill, I suggested to Helena that maybe Jennie could live with us. She had wanted to move out: "Sometimes living with another family is more like being on your own, even though it isn't, if you see what I mean." To which George responded, "I think this husband leaving has affected your head, but I would be the last to argue. Do you know what this means?"

"Reilly?" I said.

"Reilly," he said.

So Jennie moved in. She agreed to do some housework in exchange for room and board. "She's so neat!" I told her parents.

"At your house, of course."

"No, it's not just because she's somewhere else. Brynn and Dylan are messy everywhere."

And because Jennie was living here, Reilly might as well have been. He was always around, pretending to fix things. Reilly was unofficially living over a factory at the other end of town. He had sequential motorcycles which he kept wrecking when he was drunk and/or high, and he was in love with Jennie, who was now doing well in A.A. And with Jennie, and Reilly, not to mention Brynn and Dylan, there were always others around.

"There are so many people in our house," Dylan told my father when my parents were visiting in the city and the three of us went in to have supper with them, "I have to introduce myself each time I come home."

"Well, your mother never did like to be alone," my father told him; he looked at me and smiled. His smile was so like Dylan's. Or rather, I should have said, Dylan's was so like my father's.

"She might have time to answer her correspondence," my mother said. "She should dictate notes every morning after the mail is brought in." My mother had turned to me. "How is your hair?" She touched one bit, along the shoulder.

"Fine," I said. "Light brown, long, and I am washing it." I wanted to say what I think my mother half expected to hear, which was something like, "I bleached it and it has all fallen out."

My younger sister, Deborah, and I had never ceased to punish Millicent for her industry. Millicent had told everyone she had always wanted to be a mother; she'd believed that the critical eye—her own—which served her well professionally would work as well on us. Separately, but equally, we had sworn we would never criticize our children, and I prided myself on the fact that, at least, I had never (yet) said to Brynn, "What have you been doing with your hair?" I had done an interview with several women, of all ages, on Mothers and Hair, and the station got more mail, Cleo had reported, than we had had on anything, with the possible exception of abortion.

During these months I traveled, in and out of the city, doing interviews: two senators, male and female—she was the conservative; a treasure hunter whose son died finding the sunken gold; the gossip columnist who lost her curiosity and turned to teaching meditation; the movie star who'd written a novel about her housekeeper; the rock star who had become a business manager for lawyers and agents. And this one and this one and this one and I learned about each, considered and asked all the questions, and moved through it all in a kind of fearful trance. I was more comfortable in Medwin's Landing; the gloom was sheltering: it seemed to conceal feelings, although more likely it merely muted the highs as well as the lows. I could blame the prevailing lows on the weather.

I was most comfortable of all with the children. At night we arranged ourselves around each other with Spike on my big bed. We'd curve about, leaning against each other, feeling the warmth, and it was fine to be like animals but I found this lounging they would do with me had its limits. And I have never learned to do limits well. I touched Brynn's peach velvet cheek and she snarled, "Off!" Spike jumped down from the bed and Brynn said, "Not you, idiot." And Spike jumped back up. And the phone rang and we all fell upon it.

"It's for you," Brynn said, "and will you please tell your friends not to call on my phone."

"Who is it?" I asked. There were few people now I wanted to talk to. And I was still feeling guilty for touching Brynn too sweetly, and rebuffed at the same time.

"Who is it?" Brynn growled into the phone. "Oh, hi. No, she's watching TV."

"Don't tell people I watch TV," I said, whispering.

"She's not watching TV. She wanted me to tell you that," Brynn added. I pulled the phone out of her hand. "That's nice," Brynn said.

"Hi," I said, in a completely different voice.

It was Cleo, who said she would come up to help me get some of the new scripts together. Cleo was tall, serious, graceful and always almost thirty. As manager of the radio station she was innovative and noted for being completely cool under the most outrageous pressures. When she did produce my show, which was supposed to happen only when I was in some sort of crisis—which, she once said, "is always"—she chivied, cajoled, yelled and occasionally threw things. We had worked together like two little girls swinging a rope that someone else was jumping over. For years we had generated a tension and force together that it was best to enjoy, gently exploit and not discuss.

Tonight Cleo said she had an idea for a special series of interview shows, which we could edit and then syndicate to different stations around the country. "They should," she said, "be cut into a sixty-second format so they can be slotted into the news, or into music—whatever, depending upon who you're doing."

"Hardly new," I said; "a lot of people do that."

"Not like you would: we'd go for in-depth, the serial idea, and you'd talk the way you do, just about their lives and thoughts—"

"What else is there?"

"Don't be impossible—you know what I mean—you always come in with a fresh angle—and I'm not going to play up to this mood."

"It's not a mood. I'm despondent."

"Look, Margot." Cleo was always trying to move me forward. And she knew the key which would usually work: "There would be some money in it—so you could buy the house for the kids."

"I would like to get into the syndication, Cleo, but not now, it would be too much chaos, too much work," I said.

"Work," Cleo said. "Yes, and I think that's what's really holding you together."

"I'm changing the subject," I said. "What are you doing?"

"You're changing the subject because I'm right," said Cleo.

"That is true," I said.

"Addressing envelopes," she said.

"I knew by your voice you were doing something—am I getting one of them?" I could hear the sound of pillows, linens moving about. "And you're in bed, too."

"Very smart. Yes, you're getting one, even though you won't show up—yet. But you'll be back in New York life sooner or later."

"No, I won't; I'll never go anywhere again. I mean it. I'm through with all that," I said.

"You aren't interested in this syndication idea then? Ivan thought you might love it." Ivan Rappaport was my agent, and an old family friend. I thought sometimes he was the former mainly because he had been the latter. Most of his clients had been theatre people, and now he had taken to handling the best new young musicians, to the amusement and sometimes outrage of his more settled clients. My mother had said, when she heard about Ivan's latest triumph with a rock group, "He's mad." And my father had replied, "But very rich."

"Well," Cleo said, "we'll try out some other interesting people. I thought you might stand a good chance. Everyone really liked that Judge Hutchins interview, although it was not necessary of course to go so overboard as to practically move in with the person."

"You're just trying to stir me up," I said.

"Listen, being competitive doesn't mean you didn't really love him or don't feel lonely. You don't have to punish the rest of your life."

"I know," I said.

"You sort of know," Cleo said.

"You're right," I said. Cleo knew better and for longer. I had met Bill, actually, at the radio station. He'd been looking for work as a sportscaster and he'd just finished an interview with Cleo, who had not been impressed. "He will show up three to four times," she had said. "I am familiar with that expression. It is too bad he was not interested in doing the weather and I could have not hired him for that."

"No," I'd said, "them you hire because it is more satisfying to fire them." We had the fastest turnover in weather announcers in radio.

"Yes," she had said, "they are unpredictable. I enjoy mistrusting them."

"So," I'd said, "does everyone."

Cleo's father, a radio weatherman, had abandoned her mother when Cleo was twelve, and the last they had heard, some ten years ago or so, he had been in Alaska. "Easier work up there for him," Cleo had said. "He can just come on and say colder tomorrow."

"Cool," I'd said.

"Very funny," she'd said.

Fathers—it would be harder to lose a father. I thought of the children's father, the pilot—how infrequently they mentioned him. Silently they would read and set aside the cards and notes he'd sometimes send from foreign ports all about the seven seas. Perhaps they spoke of him when I wasn't around or dreamed of him at night. They had turned to my father and he had been there. To lose a father! My father is what seared across my mind.

I knew Cleo could be distracted from the hopeless task of cheering me up through specific discussions indicating I was thinking about working. "I'm not," I said, "just hiding out in Connecticut. I'm going down to New Jersey next week to interview that panty hose inventor. See, I told you I'd pull through and do it. We are going to talk about walking, how research shows your moods are revealed in little walking habits."

"That's certainly interesting," said Cleo.

"Well, you try and be inventive about panty hose," I said.

"I have. You've just never asked."

"I know. I just tease you with these fetching interviews."

"Fetching is a very good word. Be sure you work it in."

"Oh, several times."

I loved these long late night talks with Cleo. Her voice had a fresh soft edge to it like rustling leaves. I missed these talks during my marriages. Although since Bill had listened to tapes of old baseball games all night long, I had begun calling Cleo again. Actually, without Bill it wasn't a lot different really. It was the idea of Bill. The look of Bill.

After each wave of loneliness I'd buy another old convertible; one for Brynn, one for Dylan, one for me and one more because I did like the look of the car salesman. He looked a little like Bill. "Not at all," said Brynn.

"How could you remember?" said Dylan. "He was hardly here."

"He was gentle and nice to me," said Brynn. I hugged her tight. How stupid that it hadn't occurred to me that she would miss him. He never teased her. That would be enough. I would arrange for us to visit my father next week. He adored Brynn. That would help.

I had three excellent rationalizations for the cars: (1) why spend thousands of dollars on a car (which could be wrecked, leaving you without one), when for about two hundred cash each you could have four cars; (2) if one broke down you could use parts from one of the others to fix it, and (3) with all the cars out in the driveway, or along the front of the house, it would never look as if there was no one home. Although, in spite of the kids, all of them, and the dog and the cars, without Bill there I felt, lying in my bed at night, that I was all alone, which was, Cleo had said to me, "Possibly the most romantic feeling."

"You can't believe that!" I said.

"I do. It preserves the illusion," Cleo said, "that love can be completely wonderful. Somewhere. For someone."

"Oh, Cleo," I said. "It will be, you'll see." I wanted someone else to believe in it.

I knew Dylan and Brynn were relieved that even though

Bill was gone, the changes I'd made when he came along (presumably made for him) had remained, so far, intact. I still got out of bed in the mornings, and I did not yell, and most of all did not drink. After my last divorce, my briefest marriage, when the three of us had been alone together again, Brynn and Dylan would sit up with me, and we'd watch the late night TV ads: Is There an Alcoholic in Your Family?, and they'd look at me. Brynn left the phone number by my bed several times. And after I'd gotten sober, Dylan told me she had called up once and said, "I have this friend who drinks too much," and Dylan had laughed at her. "They thought it was her and she was furious. I told her every drunk calls up and says 'I have a friend who drinks.' "

"That's not true," I said. I hated the way he put Brynn down to me. But she did the same thing with him, and they both covered the criticism with such good intentions; such filial concern.

"It is true," he said, "because one afternoon when Brynn was out doing her secret eating, I called."

"Don't be mean," I interrupted. "I did secret drinking. It's a problem, not something evil."

"I know that!" He glared. "Listen to me—they treated me as if I were the drunk. 'Why don't you come in and talk to us?' the voice had said. 'Or if your friend would prefer, we'll send someone over to talk to you.' "

But as the holidays approached and Bill did not reappear, I became quieter, slept more because I no longer believed that this day, this new day, would be the one when he would come home and so getting up held less interest.

I tried to pretend I had not seen the increasing vagueness in Bill's expression, the sort of aloof boredom when he had looked at me. I did not want to ask the question that edged like the green line at the side of the mirror into my consciousness: "Did he like me better when I was drinking?"

Perhaps, I thought, but only for an instant, because it is a classical rationale of the alcoholic who wants to get drunk: I should have taken a few steps back. A drink or two, to have kept his interest. I don't like to believe we must not show our strength to men, that we pull them back from their drive to extinction by making them see they are necessary for our survival each day. What if liberation makes us more like them, more like lemmings, plunging on into the alluring tides of battle and business? Will we forget too that the rush toward victory carries the potential of defeat?

I wanted to believe in a love more powerful than the lure of extinction. But all of our favorite stories do end with someone looking off over the moors, over the edge of the cliff, bravely contemplating the memory of lost or unrequited love, the bleak and lonely days ahead. That is why men love battles, and the games that imitate war. They say they like the winners, but they love the losers more, rushing to embrace the nice guys who finish last, seeing themselves consoled. Perhaps the women who married Crusaders sat around having this kind of discussion. Without the Crusades, without the wars to go to, men go on business trips. And in the terrible tents of the motels with their canned air and nailed-down lamps they plan the battles where they will sacrifice themselves.

Love was not simply about making someone happy. I had interviewed authorities. Usually doctors—never lovers—you look at their expressions, the way they move their eyes or hands and you know these are doctors, not lovers. Perhaps love is best as inspiration for language, and, in that, worth it. True love, I was sure, is hopelessly suffused with the fear of loss, and you never have one without the other.

I told Cleo about this idea, and Cleo said, "That's exactly what everyone wants to hear, of course, because most people aren't in love and so they don't need to feel terrible about missing out."

"Well, you are in love," I said. "Are you happy?" Cleo pretended she was not involved with the French designer St. Cheri, who had been born in New Orleans and who was married to a Texas tycoon. St. Cheri's husband spent most of his time on his ranches, leaving St. Cheri in New York and Paris, where she designed her clothes and, more and more, directed the franchising of her alluring name. St. Cheri never for a moment pretended she was not involved with Cleo, and her husband seemed to understand, sending Cleo cartons of frozen steaks every month and announcements of new oil wells he had acquired for St. Cheri. None of this amused Cleo. From time to time she would take a stand and St. Cheri would announce to her husband she was leaving and then he would point out, "But, darlin', you were never here."

I made notes to ask one of the authorities on love next time about whether downward mobility in relationships may be another way of proving love doesn't work. I wrote other notes on what to do about friends who make you defensive about the people you love. Do you rationalize then that your friends are incapable of love? Or are they simply unwilling to exist in that Condition of Anxiety? Because even if the one you love *is* there, and even loves you back, even then, you sigh and know that Something Will Happen. The millennium will come, you'll be torn from each other's arms forever. Do we long for it to happen perhaps just to be freed from the fear that it will?

I went into New Year's Eve with my fists clenched. It was as if New Year's Eve should not dare exist, the year not dare turn if I am without Bill. My heart pounded with fear: the clock will strike twelve, the ball will fall down as all over the world everyone turns to kiss one's lover. Oh yes. When one quarter of the world wants to be by itself and the rest is wondering how to find food tomorrow.

Keep it simple, I told myself: New Year's Eve was not invented for your own romantic diversion. But I missed him, and beating the feelings into submission turned out to be worse.

Dylan was going to a series of grand parties at mansions and country estates with his new girlfriend, whose father was a senator. They lived in one of the great old riverside houses in Medwin's Landing and had something quite different in mind for Alison than Dylan. Such as a landed duke.

Brynn and I were spending the night with my sister, who at that time ran with her husband every weekend and belonged to several meaningful organizations. Deborah had always understood our parents better than I. They did not seem particularly magical and powerful to her. Which I had found puzzling. When we discussed them it was as though we were talking about four different people. I resented that she would refer to them in mundane terms, as she had resented the original light I cast them into. However, as I had pointed out to Deborah, "If they have no power, then why did you color your hair if not to torment Mother?" (A gesture which had in fact succeeded in enraging our mother, who could tell the color of hair by touching it.)

And Deborah had said to me, "Didn't you ever do something because *you* like it?"

"Oh, Deb," I'd said, "you can't have just liked frosting!"

"You're as mean as Mother," Deborah had said.

Deborah was taller than I was and so more resembled my father's build. But she was not like Mother, Father or me in the orderly way she had proceeded with her life, and her career. Deborah's friends had always been married, always lived on Central Park West, always went on trips together and had season tickets to serious concerts. Deborah and Mark and their friends would not have believed that I envied them; they assumed I was aloof when I said I wouldn't go with them to watch the fireworks in Central Park. Poppy and Dana, their daughters, had gone to spend the holidays with Mark's parents, who had a condominium near Disney World.

"I should have planned something like that for you," I said to Brynn, as we lay there on Poppy and Dana's two little beds.

"You always forget the part about I'm too old to plan things for. Either I wouldn't go, or if I did I'd come back in the middle saying it sucked and you'd be mad because I wasted half the money. It's not so bad just being together. My feet touch the end of this mattress, right over the edge."

"Mine, too," I said, and reached my hand out and grasped Brynn's across the narrow space between the two beds. Brynn was already taller than I was. Her eyes, like Dylan's, tapered slightly at the outer corners; their eyes to me looked like the drawings of plump birds seen in profile. Perhaps God made their eyes beautiful out of fear that otherwise I might not have paid enough attention to them. I looked at Brynn, curved now so adorably in sleep, her fist near her mouth, and I stroked her hair and even her hair gave off warmth.

We were awakened at seven-thirty in the morning by Deborah and Mark experiencing joy, which involved leaping as high as they could all over the house to the Pastoral Symphony at a volume its composer could not have conceived of.

"Isn't it wonderful that we can share now?" said Deborah.

Brynn said, "And here I was expecting a room full of winged ponies from *Fantasia*."

Deborah smiled. It didn't seem to bother her that my cynicism affected Brynn and Dylan. To Deborah, who was the new sort of psychologist, who tried always to look at everything in a positive way, it was probably a clear sign of their loyalty to me.

Brynn and I got ready to leave. "This is going to be one bitch of a day," Brynn said.

"Why? What's the matter?" I said. I smiled and put my arm around her shoulder.

"That is your phoniest, plucky smile. And you're on the verge of tears."

"I am not," I said. I swallowed, shook my head, to shake the tears down.

It was bright, gleaming cold. I drove with my teeth clenched. I should not think of Bill. I could not think of anything else.

Love is a bad blues song. Bill. You. I sit in a cube of mirrors. They reflect your face back to me. Your face. Your face is my reference point. Your face is my soft center. I exist to feel the lack of you day after day. The sound of what you did not say vibrates, runs with the beat of my pulse, the gunning of the motor, the whirring of the tires: "I don't want you, want you, want you; I don't like you, like you, like you." I arrange your face into cubes. This man frozen. Put you into a glass. Drink you down. Until you are all gone. "That's a good girl."

My eyes blurred with tears as I sped faster and faster.

"Slow down, Mom," said Brynn.

"I'm fine," I said. I went faster. We hit a shadowed part of the road. A lurking patch of ice sucked the car into a skid. It spun in slow circles, pitching us from one side to the other. I watched the rocky cliff veering closer and closer. I tried to remember what you do: slam on the brakes, no; accelerate, no; I couldn't. Turn into the skid. I panicked. Brynn threw herself across me. The cliff loomed at crazy angles. The car hit it broadside. Brynn pulled me back toward her side. The car bounced off, spun out and landed again against the cliff, head on, and stopped. We sat there. We were silent. We clutched on to each other. Brynn dug her hands into my forearms.

"Next time you try to kill yourself, don't take me with you."

I looked at the driver's side of the car. It was completely caved in. Brynn had saved my life. The police took us to a hospital to be checked. Dylan came to pick us up; his hair looked rushed back with worry, his face was pale, his eyes wide. When we got home Helena and George were waiting for us.

Helena said, "You are going with me to an A.A. meeting tomorrow."

I said, "I don't drink anymore."

"That is only the beginning," said Helena.

"Well, I can't go because I'm Jewish." I used my Jewishness then mainly to get out of doing something I did not want to do.

"Like I used to think A.A. was just for men," said Helena.

"And I thought you had to be broke," said George.

"We were," Helena reminded him.

"Actually are," he added. He placed two fingertips on his upper lip and propped his thumb under his chin after he said something clipped and direct like this. The way a pipe smoker would take out his pipe to speak and then clamp it back in at the end of a sentence.

"I will go," I said, "after I finish up editing the tapes of a couple of interviews I did, and I have to do that in the city. I have one that really moved me about this woman who teaches drama to handicapped children, and then we did one on the New Celibacy, which is clearly sweeping the country. Perhaps Bill is a founder . . . Anyway, then I have to put together a presentation, well an outline really, of some lectures I might do . . ."

"How long will that take?" asked Helena.

"About a year or two," I said.

"Look, Brynn saved your life, but you could have killed her," George said.

I might as well have been drinking. I became unbalanced

in precisely the same way. And clearly I had been thinking about it. Dylan had clung to Brynn and to me all that night when we came home, touching and hugging us.

"I'm okay," Brynn had said. "I think I like it better when you hate me." But she hugged him back.

"And Mom was convinced I'd wind up in the New Year's wreckage," Dylan said. "You got to do something, Mom. You can't stay this crazy."

So, to protect my children from myself, and to become a happier person, I began going to A.A. meetings and to understand there were worse things to live with than the loss of romantic love and that a lot of people were doing it without drinking or slamming cars into cliffs.

4

One day at a time: this, A.A. taught me, was how to approach anything, everything. That was not encouraging because I thought I truly detested each one of my days. And most of these detested days began the same way.

Dylan's alarm would be followed immediately by the loud sounds of their music. Then whichever one had turned it on first would yell, "Turn down that shit." There should be no sound before ten in the morning. Perhaps I had loved Bill mainly because he was silent then. But that was not a consideration of this day. I did not want to say to myself "Stay in the now." What was the spirit of humanity if not memory of the past and imagination about the future. I called Helena to complain. "Stay in the now," she said.

"But I hate it."

"That's because you're comparing it to yesterday and what you fear for tomorrow."

So. This morning I wandered into the kitchen, patted Spike, who yawned and stretched. I cut off a slice of cold chicken from the refrigerator and threw Spike a taste. Someone was running a shower. Someone else yelled from another bathroom, "Turn that off 'til I'm finished. I'm freezing." Be grateful, I told myself; many of them do not even wash. I put on a pot of coffee for Dylan and Jennie and me. I poured bottled water into the kettle for Brynn, who drank only Earl Grey tea.

My eyes fixed upon an unglued corner of the blue-and-white calico wallpaper Adrienne Gilpin had given me. She had ordered it for her own kitchen before *her* husband ran off with her hairdresser, whose name was Bob. Perhaps it was the Wallpaper Jinx. I tried to decide whether to glue this little corner back on again.

"Why paper a rented house?" Deborah had asked me when I moved in.

"Because the kitchen is papered in a pattern of whiskey bottle labels and that might be discouraging to people who are trying not to drink," I had said.

"I would not have thought of that," Deborah had said.

"Never would have to," I'd snapped. "You people who can handle alcohol think of us as Martians. I think of you as Martians. I wish I knew how to drink socially the way you do. All I know is I can't."

At this stage I was defensive, I was learning. Such a contrivance of a life I had invented. I had glided through, counting on everyone else's efforts, time and energy. I used my friends to define and describe who I was, could or should be. And because I had never learned diligence, consistency and forbearance I was unable to practice them. On the odd occasion when I was generous, it was to win approval, acceptance, attention.

All these characteristics were, it turned out, deeper symptoms of alcoholism, which were revealed only when the primary symptom, the drinking itself, was removed.

"These," Helena told me, "are called character defects. And you go to meetings to learn how to get rid of them."

"I always knew I was a defective person," I said.

"That," said Helena, "is another one right there. Maybe two: self-pity and self-hatred."

"What's the most you can have?" I said. "I bet I have all of them. The defects."

"You are getting closer," said Helena. "We can add ego."

"And hostility." I added that.

I rummaged through the small top kitchen drawer to the right of the sink. Who is it that does not have such a drawer in her house? Now with each move, I upend it into a box, transferring the contents into the next strategically placed drawer.

I found a little bottle of white glue, but the nozzle was clogged. I found a nail to unplug it. The nail was too large.

I felt I was sliding down a mountain of ice, a glass mountain like the one in the fairy tale where the prince had to climb up to reach the princess. Fairy tales always had impossible tasks to show children that the process of life is not easy but that if you tried hard enough, and wanted something bad enough and tried again, you might get it. I had apparently missed that, concentrating when I was a child upon the dresses, and imagining the hands and eyes of the princes. But this ice mountain I was sliding down now had me terrified—in free fall. I wanted to break. I clutched the glue, unable to move. Actually I'd get myself to the lunchtime A.A. meeting and cut out the crap.

I was standing on the round kitchen table, gluing the wallpaper back, when Brynn walked in.

"Oh, please, will you look where she is!" Brynn tossed her down vest and canvas satchel onto a chair. "That's Mom," she said to Jennie, who came dragging in behind her. "We washed her this morning and can't do a thing with her."

Jennie wrapped the dental assistant's coat she used as a robe tightly around her like an elderly woman in a shawl. Jennie was not a dental assistant; she had applied for a job and bought the uniform, but when the job came through she had been in the hospital again with a drug overdose.

Dylan came in. "Bad day already, Mom?" His fast smile was a cover, sliding up a bit on the left. He is a taller, leaner cut of person than Brynn and I. But we all have the same coloring, the curly hair, the eager, ready smile and the bitten nails. When he did not have his smile applied he appeared chilly, fierce. I loved having a son who looks like the boys I used to have crushes on in school but who never took me out.

He put down his armload of books.

"Good weights they make; build you right up," I said. He looked at me and laughed.

"As I always say, Mom, improve the muscles, not the mind, since you wind up doing wallpaper anyway."

Each day the books were brought home, thrown on the desk in his room, and not picked up again until the next morning and the return journey to school, which I thought of largely as a dating academy. Because of the moves, the transfers, and, as Dylan readily admitted, goofing off, he would only finish high school and, God willing, start college next year when he would be eighteen.

I climbed down from the kitchen table, kicking over one of the nests of mail I had all over the house. Brynn picked up the pieces.

"I can't find the envelope for the phone bill," I said. "You know, if you're going to take care of these things for me . . ." Brynn had agreed to play bookkeeper for three months. This was in return for the cost of repairs to her car, which she had loaned to a friend who had run it into a tree.

"It should be right near the bill. Mom, do you want an egg?" Brynn was wearing her white painter's overalls with a red rugby shirt. Her hair was drawn up in tufts behind her ears. She had on her gold chains, dangling medals and green sweatbands on her wrists.

"Me?" I asked.

"You are generally who I have in mind when I address the person as Mom."

"Oh, an egg, yes," I said. I looked in the bread drawer

and threw out some moldy slices. "No, probably not an egg," I said, considering the look of the bread. Brynn was also wearing purple sneakers. "But I love your outfit a lot." I looked in the refrigerator and threw out a container of coleslaw and last week's box of Kentucky Fried Chicken. "Well, maybe. One egg."

"Choose one," said Brynn. "I am about to crack some eggs. How many eggs should Brynn crack? Here are two for Brynn. Is Dylan going to eat an egg? Is their mother going to eat an egg? Or will Mother have two eggs this morning?"

"Knock it off, Ralph," said Dylan. His nickname for Brynn was Ralph-Anne. She had a gas station attendant's shirt which had the name "Ralph" on it, and I suppose it also had something to do with the way she rolled her pack of Marlboros up in her sleeve.

"Did you have your hand up?" Brynn said.

"You have the most brilliant way of doing voices, Brynn," I said, too eagerly. "You absolutely should make a tape. You could do voice-overs and make a lot of money." She did not even bother to look annoyed. I don't learn. And I hadn't even the excuse that I'd forgotten how much I hated it when my mother always overpraised me as a prelude to some suggestion for self-improvement. Such an heirloom trunk I have, filled with yards of manipulative techniques. Brynn put a chunk of butter in a skillet, turned on the burner, and cracked two eggs with one hand into the skillet.

"Brynn is making herself two fried eggs. Mother and Dylan are not having any eggs this morning. Dylan is going to be mugged at Burger King on the Interstate and come home in a takeout box."

"And then Brynn will have Dylan's car to fill up with gum wrappers, old socks and tree-dwelling friends," said Dylan. He poured out orange juice into four glasses and put them on the table.

"It is not my car that is in the shop with a fucked transmission because I was peeling out and forgot to put fluid in it." Brynn sat down and began to eat her eggs. Then she got up and put salt and pepper shakers on the table. And sat down again.

"I cannot deal with cars this morning. Brynn, did you do your homework? What are you doing with school?" I poured myself a cup of coffee.

"Driving by," said Dylan.

"Shut up." Brynn glared at him.

I was moving slowly, tying napkins for the breakfasts the children were already finishing, tying them into cute shapes. I put my blue and white creamer and sugar bowl on the table just so with a little potted fern in the center.

"I think," Dylan said, watching me but talking to Brynn, "that she is winding up to ask us a lot of questions about school."

"Yes," Brynn said, "and then we will have the lecture on how difficult it is for her because she never learned to appreciate the structure you can get from paying attention in school."

"Which mainly means," said Dylan, "that she is having trouble right now with a deadline."

I bit. I snapped right into it. "Well, Brynn, you do never seem to be doing any homework, but you always say it's fine." Brynn put more jam on her English muffin, rubbing the jam into the muffin with her knife as if she could rub out the sound of my voice. "It can't be just so fine. If you've got a problem at school, then talk about it. I don't deny I have trouble getting my work done; opening up makes it easier and then I get help, you know."

"Yeah," said Dylan. "Cleo just can't wait to rush right up here." Brynn glared at him. They were jealous of Cleo, uneasy with anyone I was close to. It was the three of us which balanced, which must only really matter, and Cleo represented the New York world, the work they had grown to know I was as attached to as much as love; an unpleasant thing for me to admit, because I thought work was what my mother had loved the most.

"I've got no problem. I'm working on a project for biology, and a paper on American history at the library." She paused.

"You're inventing a project; you'll invent anything, and Mom will believe it because she wants to believe that everything is all right and the more it isn't the more she wants to think it is."

"Oh, Dylan, stop it," I yelled.

"Yeah, stop it," he yelled back, "you're more angry at me for telling you Brynn's in trouble than you are with her for skipping school."

"That's because it's something to help with, not be angry about."

"Stop," Brynn yelled, "both of you! It's my business. Just mine!"

Jennie looked at all of us. "I didn't leave home to get into this, guys." She picked up her coffee cup and a muffin. "You all ought to cool it." She went back upstairs.

"At least I'm not a snob," Brynn said to Dylan. "I hate hanging around rich kids. You don't learn anything about reality. Of course, they can afford better drugs." Dylan glared at Brynn. She turned red. She had said that under her usual pitch anyway, her head averted. One of the things she hadn't meant to say, one of the things I pretended I had not heard.

"That's a funny thing to say in front of Mom," he said. No one in this house ever used drugs. Certainly not after the trouble I'd had. God knows, my children had learned.

"Reality isn't bowling alleys and diners either," Dylan said. "Reality is getting ahead. Wanting to learn how doesn't make me a snob. And I wouldn't know about their drugs."

I knew Brynn was uncomfortable with the kids Dylan hung around with. She could be glib with Dylan and with me but she clammed up with almost everyone else, giving the impression that she was aloof or uninterested.

"What's this paper on?" Dylan asked.

"Don't put Brynn on the spot," I said. I looked sharply at Dylan.

"Stop protecting her," Dylan said. He stared me down.

"It's a paper on the issues that led up to the Civil War, eat shit."

"And what are the issues?" Dylan persisted.

"Economical. A lot of things. I don't have to take this from you. You start in on me and wreck my day." Her face got red; tears welled up making her eyes look especially glacially blue. Brynn's eyes were clearly, strictly blue, like her father's eyes, and I had once loved those eyes. I should remember to tell them things I loved about their father. Dylan's eyes and mine were khaki. Like my father's.

"You're pushing me, Dylan, very close," Brynn said.

They had a ferocious exchange of expressions: Brynn threatening with a look to tell me something; Dylan saying, *not* I dare you, but *don't you dare* . . . Something I should know. She opened her mouth a bit. Then his look won and Brynn rushed from the table and ran upstairs. Her bedroom door slammed shut.

"You have got to leave her alone. It's not as if you were perfect." And at that moment I did not want to imagine what ways in which he was not perfect.

"Fine," he said, "I'll leave you both alone. I'll join the air force."

"And go up, up and away with your father? You already tried that once." That was not loving. "I'm sorry," I said.

For almost a year, during the breakup and bad time after my second marriage, Dylan had gone to be with his father in Texas.

"Don't be sorry," he said. "But someday I will go to be with him again. Maybe. When he calls both times a year, he says he'd like that."

"He would," I said. Don't go, I thought, missing him already.

"You know he probably feels like you did about Bill. You did leave him—and he thinks of you and us as one thing."

"We are more," I said. I sat at the table. "I left with you because he was always away." We had been in Virginia alone, the three of us, for four months, and we'd gone home to my parents' and never come back. "It wasn't fair. I agree. But I was young, Dylan, and it is done."

"I know," he said.

Some time later we had tried again. He had been doing an administrative job on the ground. But I had changed. Or he had changed. We did not know each other well enough to be sure.

I touched the ferns and looked across at Dylan's serious young face, the edges of his curly hair sunny where the soft light struck it through the windows. I touched the fern instead of touching his hair. His hair reminded me of my father's hair. I remembered touching the back of my father's hair where it reached down toward his shirt collar once. I was about Dylan's age then and my father had said, "Don't touch my hair like that again. Ever." And when I was even younger I once touched the hair of the boy sitting in front of me at school. He'd turned abruptly. "Don't do that!" he'd said, and I got the impression you never touch their hair unless you are married and most likely even then one should wait until one is invited.

"Just because the table looks fine doesn't mean anything else is. Brynn is not going to school." He paused. "Mom, I wish you'd concentrate. I know you do even when you are looking around and touching things. But I like you to look like you're paying attention." Dylan thought he could handle things; he was confident he was never going to make the mistakes I had because he was so aware.

"I know that. I am not an idiot," I said. I turned, uncomfortable. I didn't want to cry. And he was staring at me. Hating me, I supposed.

"Hey," he said.

"What?" I snapped.

"You're the only mother I know whose lashes cast shadows even without mascara."

"Oh. Dylan," I said. Such a perfect distraction.

"Mom, I'm really not trying to get on your case, but Alison's brother says Brynn hasn't been in any of the classes they're in together practically since school began." Dylan pushed his chair back, balancing it on the rear legs. Perhaps he stared at people when they talked because I never looked at anyone. I liked to assume that both of my children did almost everything in reaction to me, even though I also understood that was an arrogant assumption.

"Dylan, I don't like people who keep tabs on other people," I said. I pulled back my hair, pressing at my temples. I couldn't keep my hands still.

"You have a problem with reality too."

"That's original," I said.

"I know," he said. "I heard it on a TV show that was trying to be meaningful."

"You're always cranky and picking on everyone when you've been drinking beer the night before. I'm not saying anything, but you might want to think about it." Now I leaned forward and I looked at him. I was trying not to be Mother, but to be like I was for other young people. And it didn't work. Of course.

"Why do you hate me today?" I asked, in my most understanding voice.

"You're figuring I'll say I hate myself when I hate you. But I hate you more. You play it both ways: you want me to like you, but you're saying things I don't like and"—he leaned, eye to eye with me—"you're avoiding the real trouble." He said this quickly, angrily. "You start flinging your A.A. shit at me because you can't handle the truth about Brynn."

"I'm not saying that. I'm just saying there's another truth, about you, and you can't handle that." I was frightened for him. I saw so much of me in him and knew it was a hex to even see it, to reach inside his confidence, to touch the anxiety; to notice it was to stir it, heat it, and make him dig in deeper to defend himself. I twisted my fingers around my hair, twisting it tight. He'd hate every little gesture right now. I thought of the corners of my mother's jaw when she was trying to tell me where I'd gone wrong. The lines of her cheekbones, defined and quivering.

"I'm doing fine and you were the one who was standing on the table with that heartbroken look this morning. I don't understand why you think you can't live like a person without a man." He got up, pushed the chair hard up to the table. He was looking at me. My robe was too loose. I was always uncomfortable when my father would walk about in the monogrammed voile nightshirts my mother gave him. And my mother would watch me trying not to look at him and he'd clasp his hand on the front right down there to hold the buttoned nightshirt together and I'd stare. But not, I think, because I was interested in seeing; in fact I remember I did not want to. I didn't want to acknowledge these dangling shadows at the edge of his body. I wanted only to see my father's beautiful spirit, his power. And I wanted to possess and be owned by that. Sleeping with him was not what I had in mind. I wanted to inhabit him; I wanted to worship him; I wanted to sit next to him and have him want me there every minute of every day. I watched Dylan bristle at me.

This discomfort with a parent is so powerful, it feels like hatred one moment and the next moment we seem to want everything so much we cannot even name what we want, and only assume it is taboo and so think of the most taboo thing we know.

"It's my generation," I said, turning flippant quickly. "I define myself by the man I'm with and when they leave I don't know who to be." I got up and wrapped the robe tighter again. Why can't I tell him what I feel? Tell him I know how it is to need someone to be happy.

"Then we'll never have a woman President," he said, "because it would have to be someone of your generation, and if they're all like you, they'll be too scared. It's bullshit anyway. Your friend Judge Hutchins wouldn't spend a minute feeling like this over anyone."

I slammed open the dishwasher, put in one glass and slammed it shut and turned to Dylan. "If I were President they still wouldn't call me on a Saturday night."

"Yeah, but think of the cute secret service men." He grinned. "Mom, I just want to cheer you up. If we were still in New York I could stay home and we could go to movies all afternoon."

"You are cheering me up. And afterward you'll be wiped out." Here I was, making the excuse. He'd go, and we both knew it, with Alison and have a beer or two and watch the river from the car. All kids drink beer, I told myself, and probably have a little joint now and then, and I could not do one thing about it.

"Listen, don't bully me," I said. "Just because you've got a deep voice and a way of saying things doesn't mean you know how to handle everything. You don't understand how I need things to just be nice. I can't stand any more trouble. I just don't like it." Now the twisting of my hair moved into the picking of the scalp. Then I stopped that, revved up for drama and slammed my hands on the table. I leaned forward. I started in on my I-tried-the-best-I-could speech. "I really did. It isn't great but I'm trying still. I can't do everything. Brynn needs me." I reached out my arms now. He didn't walk easily into those arms anymore. I clasped my hands around my own arms and left the kitchen to go upstairs.

Four steps. Dylan shouted at me, "Does it ever occur to you I need you too? It isn't easy for any fucking one of us." He put on his muffler and his down vest. He banged the front door open and shut. I paused midstairs. Which way to go? Which one to reach for?

Perhaps it had been all right to keep an aura of chaos in the house. Perhaps it distracted attention from the absence of their father. Oh, the rationalizations one invents to cover the muddy tracks of the contagious drunken personality. Dylan came back in; he followed me up the stairs and shouted in the direction of Brynn's room, "If you're not going to school, at least you could hit the market, Ralph-Anne, so Mom can do some work this afternoon."

Brynn swept open her door and shouted, "Markets all over northwest Connecticut now have a policy of selling to boys. Try it."

"You have the checks, Brynn. Listen, Mom, I've got a paddle tennis game at Alison's after school—make her go. I love you—I'm sorry I started a war."

"It's all right. We're all tense. Brynn and I will hit the market together. I like going."

Brynn stormed out of her room, past me. "I am going to school and I will go to the market myself and get what I like and you can work and the prince can play his game." She shot a look at Dylan. "It would have been nice if you'd been the one who ran away!" She went into the kitchen.

"No one ever gets along with a brother," I said quickly to Dylan. "Not at her age."

Dylan shrugged. "Except why is she always waiting up when I come home?" Dylan grinned his conspirator's charming grin at me and left.

"Because he'd wake me anyway!" Brynn said, hearing everything, charging out with all her paraphernalia and shouting over her shoulder, "Just get to a lunch meeting, Mom."

I heard the cars choking, sputtering, catching and chugging off. I went into my own room and under the covers again, even as I told myself, stay out of that bed. George had tried to teach me that teenagers were just very young indigent relatives. But that was such an easy out. Look what Dylan and Brynn had been through, I always reminded myself—look at the childhood I gave them. I was really annoyed with Jennie, who was supposed to help with the marketing, but then I hated to pressure her; I also hated to tell anyone what I expected.

Brynn checked to see that I was at the lunch meeting. I heard her car, the one without the muffler, cruise through the parking lot. I glanced over my shoulder, out the window, and saw her drive off. She liked to get a Coke and a sandwich from Chickens and go down to the river. She'd load her camera and take a few pictures. She liked that boy, Freddy. He was tall and blond and quiet and probably reminded her of Bill, whom she'd known better than her father. And Bill had loved Brynn better than he'd loved any of us. Freddy had a bike he'd just bought with money he'd earned working for his dad, and he would come down to the river to meet her. They would take off with the others, roaring forward across Main Street, spread out in a pack. She probably felt tough and complete.

These guys were her friends and they would protect her. They would treat her like a nice girl. They wouldn't talk fresh the way Dylan and his friends did about girls, not in front of her. She could lean back and feel the wind in her hair and feel power and energy enough to handle anything when she was going fast like this with a motor roaring under her and someone big and rough to cling to. Sometimes when I was looking for Bill I'd watched the kids here on these roads and the one I'd see would be Brynn and we would wave, but we would not talk about it later. The bikes would swerve and dip around each other, cruising easy along roads, going by empty orchards with old apples hanging from bare gray trees.

I knew Dylan and I were inclined to be too critical and that criticism made Brynn just want to do the thing that would drive us crazy. At least A.A. made me calm down, and I knew that made Brynn's life easier.

However, I think Brynn felt Dylan and I did depend on her, and that when I talked to her about school (picked on her, as she probably saw it) it was my way of avoiding picking on Dylan, who probably got away with more because he was simply smoother. I could feel how hard Brynn tried to do the right thing, whatever that was. And I couldn't begin to tell her how much I understood that, too. She would be embarrassed, would have tears in her eyes and look away.

No, I thought, it is you who cannot say it; who runs from direct, serious conversation. And I might not even catch her eyes because I was beginning to see how hard it was to look anyone right, steadily, in the eyes.

Like Brynn, I started out every day meaning to be perfect, and then my very good intentions would slip away with the day's confusions and demands.

I was sitting in the stable behind the church, built when church estates had need of such things as stables, and gazing at a sign pinned to the wall bulletin board: "Bloom Where You Are Planted," it said.

We sat on folding metal chairs and the room filled quickly with smoke. Men leaned back on their chairs, tilting them precariously. Women, even the younger ones, like Jennie, who was here today, too, leaned forward, wrapping their arms around their elbows, holding themselves tight. Some men crossed their arms across their chests. Some sat hunkered over, some with hands clasped tightly in front. Most people had paper cups of coffee and paper plates with sandwiches made from the cold cuts put out on a long table in the front of the room.

Then the leader remembered to ask if there were any newcomers. Reilly was showing up at meetings again. George told me that Reilly liked everything about the program except the part about not drinking or using drugs. He raised his hand.

The leader said, "Oh, come on, Reilly, you're not a newcomer."

"But every time I start out again I feel I'm just beginning."

Jennie punched him in the ribs. "Take the cotton out of your ears, honey, this time, and put it in your mouth."

"Knock it off, Jennie," he said, "I'm tryin'."

The topic was Serenity, which, I said when I was called on, was not something I was familiar with.

"That's for sure," Jennie said softly, and smiled at me.

Someone was saying the clue to serenity was faith—a subject I could then not abide. I tuned out. I was thinking about how people formed most easily into groups of three and wondering whether that came from the desire to be the child with two parents, perfectly attended to on either side. Two by Two was not a good idea at all.

The Christians knew better. All of the roles in life seemed to trace to a vision of that original Trinity, the parents and the child, who wants the generating force of two to itself. The Father, the Son and the Holy Ghost was a naturally appealing invention. But which one was Mother? I had a friend, an actress, who had said, "God is the Producer who tells you the part isn't right for you; Jesus is the Agent who softens the blow, and says 'But He thinks you're great and will keep you in mind for something else.' "

I was surrounded by lapsed Catholics in A.A. I could not decide whether that was because there were more Catholic alcoholics or whether they just were more likely to get to A.A. because, even though many of them said they were—at the least—uncomfortable with their religion, that ritualized background did make them accept a program more readily. Perhaps I should ask some of these questions. But I already knew the answer. Work on myself first. Or. Hateful: "Keep it simple." I don't keep it simple.

Threes. Alone, now, I was happiest with another couple, like Helena and George, or two women friends. With my children there were always shifting formations: Brynn and I played parents to Dylan; then Dylan and Brynn became parents to me; and Dylan and me to Brynn. Perhaps Bill had felt left out. Did the ancient Hebrews have the better idea? Would the two wives have played parents to the man, giving him the undivided attention?

And when we were children Deborah and I and this boy from the next apartment used to play among our father's model sets in our big apartment on Central Park West. We used to take turns playing men, playing women, playing soldiers and prisoners, playing priest with two nuns, nun with two priests.

Nuns. I used to drift away into long considerations of religion when I was in school or supposed to be working on listening to something that might be helpful. Who could fault you if you were contemplating the notion of God, anyone's notion? A certain variation on their precious fascination with faith, and, for God's sake, trust.

Pay attention, I told myself. I asked the woman next to me

if she wanted more coffee. Her hands were still shaking. She nodded and I went up to the coffee machine and poured out two cups. I brought the woman a cookie and patted her on the shoulder.

I sipped my coffee slowly, and tried to listen.

Reilly raised his hand again, and Jennie sighed. He turned to her and said, "I'm talkin' about serenity, too. I was on the way to the slammer, with shackles on, and I see this lawyer in the hall who stood up for me one time and he goes 'How's it going?' and I go, and I mean it, 'Oh, everything's cool. I'm fine.' There I am with shackles on and I'm cool, right, serene as hell. I don't know what it is to be serene straight. I've been a basket case unless I had a drink from the time I was five. I used to take a bottle of beer and climb up the apple tree in my foster parents' backyard and drink it every day after school."

That reminded me, of course, of the apples I had bought for the pies for the children and that reminded me, as if I needed to be reminded, of Bill, and I could not sit still another minute without talking. Every consideration and limit I'd tried to apply just cracked.

I raised my hand. "I know I cannot drink, but I don't even want to, really don't. I want to die, and I'm shaking as I say it. I can't bear it, I *cannot* live with the idea that I wrecked my life. I lost everything I cared for. I didn't want to be alone again and I did it. I mean, what do you do when you've failed?"

A compact man, Scotty, raised his arm. "When I hear myself not being grateful for everything I have now, I know I'm not working the program. God gives me what I need, and I have to check out my wants from my needs. I came to these tables because my life was unmanageable. And I'm sober today. When I don't hear gratitude in my heart I know I'm not working my program. Thanks. I get what I need when I come here."

George had told me when I looked miserable (one of the times), "Keep coming; it gets better. More accurately, it doesn't get better, but what the hell else is there to do?"

Because I was being so very good, I knew Bill would surely come back. I had prayed. On my knees. I had friends make novenas, in case God was Catholic. I put magic powders under my pillow and sent powerful ESP messages.

And when Bill did call, he called at five o'clock in the morning.

"Hi. It's me," he said.

"How can you assume 'me' is you?" I said.

"I didn't think of that," he said. I did not want to be difficult. My mother would say, where is your pride? I could see my footprints, dancing on the ceiling.

"Bill! Most of all I love you. I must have been terrible to live with. I used to be so obsessive. I didn't even die without you. I'll let you feel so free now. What I'm trying to say somehow, and please don't see it as pressure, is that aren't we really practically our oldest friends? I won't play Big Wife anymore. I can be quiet. I've been practicing, really." Well, for me I have been quiet.

"Margot." I could hear him take a deep breath. But I am at least listening.

"I love just the sound of your breath," I said.

"Margot. Look. I'm kind of an eccentric. I'm a little like one of those playboys Franchot Tone used to do so well. I like to stay up late, dress with style and never be married to a middle-aged woman."

"Oh, Bill. That can't be you. Everyone says that kind of thing. It isn't at all eccentric." Now I could not breathe, at all.

"I've met someone. She's nineteen. I want to get married."

"You are. Married."

"Margot, I want a divorce."

There was a long silence. I recalled that Franchot Tone was dead. Another resemblance: neither one of them was making too much sense right now.

"Bill. I tell you what." I sat right up in bed now to say this. "This isn't like me to say this, but you're not even like you. So why should I be like me? I don't want any divorce. So if you want your divorce, you get your divorce." I hung up the phone.

I had never hung up the phone on anyone before. Immediately I picked it up again. He was gone.

I tried to be quiet. Very quiet. I opened the closet. I'd get dressed and take a walk by the river.

Then Brynn walked in. "I heard the phone. So what did he say?" She looked at the clothes in my hands. "Are you going to meet him?"

I put my slacks and boots back down. I gave her a hug. "No." I patted her hair. "No, I'm not going anywhere."

"It's okay, if you want," she said. "I'll handle things here. He may want to be alone with you before coming back to kids and everything."

"Oh, Brynn, no; that's not how it was. Don't worry. Let's not talk about it. We're fine; that's what matters. Now try to go back and sleep a little more. I'm going to work for a while. We'll do a super breakfast tomorrow."

"You're talking too fast and it already is tomorrow. I'll help you," she said. Yes. She needed to be with me. If he could go, I could go. I grasped her sturdy hand. And I wanted her with me. We got dressed and went downstairs. We sat silently for a while on the window seat mending two shirts, a couple of placemats, all of the odds and ends we always meant to get to. We bit the thread; we held up the needles, we jabbed these needles in and in and in and put this together, and this. We finished a piece, we folded a piece. We looked at each other and then picked out the next and went on until the basket was empty and the sky was pale gray and day was here to deal with.

By the time Dylan came downstairs we had grated Jack cheese, the eggs were in the bowl, the muffins split, marmalade on the table (warmed). Dylan acted as if nothing was unusual, but we all moved very quietly. Brynn put the bacon on a plate, Dylan got out the foil to go under the muffins; I put the oranges Brynn pared and sliced into wheels in a big flower shape on one of the blue plates. Dylan did not turn on the records.

"Something terrible has happened," he said, after about fifteen minutes. "When you're both this quiet it always means the worst and you're both too quiet." Dylan looked at me. "You talked to Bill. That's it."

Brynn said, "She doesn't want to talk about it."

Dylan snapped at Brynn, "Yeah, who am I to know. I'm just the son."

"Stop now," I said. "Just eat. Yes, Bill called. He isn't coming back."

"You didn't really think he would, did you, Mom?" Dylan said, his voice quiet.

Brynn kicked him under the table and he glared at her, but added to me, "I'm sorry, Mom, that's really hard for you. Do you want us to stay home with you? We could go for a ride."

Yes. That was exactly what I wanted, of course, but it wasn't right to arrange their days anymore about what was essentially my problem.

Brynn hurried Dylan along with breakfast. "Will you stop rushing me," he said.

"Mom needs to be by herself so she can call friends. She's being a good sport for us."

"Yeah," said Dylan, "well, I'm not sure we ought to leave her alone."

"I'm just fine," I said. I did not want them to worry. Brynn had a friend who had come home one day and found her mother bled out dead in the bathtub.

"You know," I told them, "it's much easier now. Because I know what I am dealing with. And I have work to do."

As Dylan and Brynn were leaving I hugged Brynn. I held her and she clasped me tight as if she'd wanted to be held all that morning and I said, "It's okay. We'll all be fine." I tried to sound brighter. "We are fine. We have each other and we're all fine."

I waited until Brynn and Dylan had gone to school and then I called Helena, who said, "It's resolved then. You should feel good about the way you handled everything."

"I feel dreadful. Bill won't even know how to get a divorce. And I am not getting a divorce."

5

Every time I do it, *I hate it.*

"This is not a tollbooth!" I sobbed. "I have watched four people, three women and one man, come up here, sit down married, answer three questions, and walk right out divorced. Love vanquished in seconds. The ritual is a triumph of demons, all your hope gone, a villainy, the commercial interruption between living love and living death. I hate being divorced."

A woman at a meeting a week before had said that you only get divorced when there is nothing there. There was still something here. Me. But that was not enough.

I looked out and caught Deborah's glance at Helena, who had left Chickens to the care of George and a new waiter to be with me. It was different this time because I understood where I was wrong. I had insufficiently sympathized with Bill; I'd been too self-involved and not tried enough to draw him out. I used to resent Deborah and friends like Helena because they managed to stay married. But now I could begin to see that the problem had been that I was inconsistent. I gave what I decided someone wanted (a car, leather slacks, a surprise party—with all my friends), rather than what was really needed. I stopped. I still was not sure, with Bill, what that might have been—exhortations to "Get out there and play ball"? I did not know. This realization about giving what someone else wants was only the beginning. A trouble with these small milestones is that one tends to take them, at the time, as the complete answer and proceeds as if one had an overwhelming resolution to all problems.

"Now, Mrs. Spinning, will you just answer your attorney's question, please?" That formality in Blanche's voice alone reduced me to more tears, and she now urged me more softly. "Miss Fox," she said. Perhaps that would remind me of my responsibility, as a professional person, to represent a mature acceptance of adversity.

I knew from our interview that Blanche Hutchins heard the divorces ("and we used to have so very few—perhaps four a year") at the beginning of the day. She had considered divorces to be the least complicated of matters. I recalled what Blanche had told me when we had tea a few days before. I had been so calm then—she must be appalled now. She had said that she was genuinely puzzled at the way most astute people seemed to lose their equilibrium over love. "Although I was distressed to hear he left you," Blanche had said, "you will do well without him, as you have before." I had not argued. But that was possibly because I, somehow, hadn't really believed this day would come. Bill would change his mind, reappear, magically full of love.

"We might," Blanche said, looking severe and distant in her robes, "address the procedures." I wiped my tears, mascara on the backs of my hands. "Yes, perhaps we do rush a bit," Blanche Hutchins said. And gave me a small, quick smile.

My lawyer, a person with the face of a biscuit, an acquaintance of Fitz's who had all of his pretentions and none of his charm, shook hands on the steps of the courthouse and said, "You probably should purchase life insurance now. I'll be pleased to help you with that."

"There's no life to insure," I said. He walked away. "Such gall!" I declared, recovering enough so I did notice that I was clearly not totally adrift in self-pity. Only nine-tenths.

"Chutzpah," said Deborah.

"No. Fee," said Helena, who saw the surprise in Deborah's face. Everyone assumed Helena was as sweet as she seemed. Just as I hoped to catch some of Helena's wry serenity, so Helena said she would like to have some of my fever. But when I tried to be like Helena, people assumed I was tired, and when Helena tried to be like me, people thought she was hostile.

After court, Deborah and I went with Helena to Chickens, and I sobbed into my rice pudding, snuffled into the Kleenex Deborah always carried and complained, "I will never find anyone. I will die alone. I'll never sleep again, because I dream of him and it is too sad."

"Nonsense," said Deborah, "this is the worst of it. You'll feel better tomorrow."

"No, worse tomorrow," I said with assurance. "I have to show up at a party tomorrow."

Cleo had sent me the invitation a month before and we'd talked about the party lightly a week ago, but lightly in the way that meant she really thought I should show up.

"Is this latest party I'm not coming to going to be good?" I'd said. "Or just an extremely expensive donation, especially since your candidates are always the interesting ones who do not win."

"This one will win. And it's deductible and mainly it's a very good party with all the people you like to see except when you're pretending none of that matters, which, even your very own agent, Ivan, pointed out to me the other day, is every time you're getting married or getting over one."

"That would appear to be always," I'd said.

"Yes, it would," Cleo had said.

"Ivan's going to be there?" I'd said, considering what I could conceivably wear. Black velvet. No, too late in the season for black velvet. But I would be virtually in mourning.

"Ivan is hoping you'll come: he may have news for you. Everyone wants," she'd said, "to see you."

"Not everyone?" But I would be too depressed to notice. And getting there. I'd be so lonely on the road. I'd obsess over Bill. And my eyes would melt down my cheeks and over my chin by the time I arrived.

"Oh, I think so," Cleo had added. I could see her lounging back in her chair, bouncing a bit, one long leg crossed over the other knee. She might be examining the heel of her latest boot, dusting a flaw no one else could see.

"I will think about it," I'd said, "but I'm a little scared of the trip. Or something."

"Of starting your actual life again," she'd said. She was crunching something.

"Probably. What are you eating?"

"Wise Ridgies potato chips," she'd said.

"Noisy eater," I'd said.

"Messy too," Cleo had said.

"You're so fastidious about everything else. And a real pig with food."

"One can only be almost perfect," she'd said, adding (knowing exactly what could get to me), "St. Cheri is having her chef do his famous dessert buffet."

"Oh," I'd said. Such a table, with cakes, with pies, with tarts and mousses, such cremes, such soufflés, "how could I eat anything, Cleo. You know the divorce is set for the day before."

"That's why you must come, if only to recover your appetite."

So: "You don't *have* to go to the party," Deborah was saying. "Maybe you want to."

I paused. "Well, I promised. I'll never make it. I can't drive. I can't think straight even. I can't get out of myself."

"That's the answer, you know," Helena said, her voice hesitant, picking over her words, nodding her head forward with each word, like a lovely bird selecting bits of grain. "And you are stronger than you think. You really are."

"I'm not," I said. "This time I'm falling apart." I noticed Deborah's coffee cup was empty. I looked up to wave to Agnes to bring some more.

"Oh, the new waiter?" I said. A young man was already on his way to our table at a nice fast clip. "Two coffees," I said.

Helena laughed and slid out of the seat. "Hi, Hedy," she said to him, and then to me, "No, this is not a waiter—he didn't show—this is my darling favorite new rock star, this is Hedy, Scotty's son. Sit for a sec, dear; I'll get the coffees." She put her hand lightly on his shoulder, "Coffee?"

"No . . . well, a drop maybe." He looked at me. "So you got back home?" he said.

I was blank. "I'm sorry. I am distracted today, and," I blurted, embarrassed at my mistake, apologizing, I supposed, by offering an intimacy, "I just got divorced so I'm very crazy."

"Oh," he said. "I'm sorry." Now he was embarrassed. "You don't remember me?"

"Meetings," I said. "I've seen you at meetings?" No. That wasn't it. He had an interesting face, rather a complicated face for one so young. Intensity. This was what was different. No. He was not one of the children's friends. He was older. Yes. Much older. Well. Perhaps not that much older.

"You gave me the best apple I ever ate." He grinned at me. Yes. Intensity, but very pretty features, actually.

"Yes," I said. I smiled wanly. "I was lost. The limousine. Yes. I did get home." I paused. "You were helpful." I nodded. "I was crazy that day."

"I was worried a bit about leavin' you there. I was sorry."

We were both quiet. We looked down. We looked back up at each other, then switched eyes away fast.

Helena returned with the coffee and sat down. "Hedy, this is Margot Fox; her sister, Deborah . . ."

"I think they've met," Deborah said; with such a glance going over to Helena.

He stirred his coffee, round and round with a spoon. Now he was looking at me again. Even when I turned away I felt the eyes and he sat next to me with kind of a jostle, as if he had a living motorcycle, not a salmon pink banquette, under him. Still without taking his eyes off me, he leaned over to ask Helena to pass the cream. And Helena and Deborah did their own glancing again. What was their problem. I glared at Deborah.

He was very young. Too young. But surely not nineteen, and Bill had left me for someone nineteen. Do not think of Bill. This is now. And you are here.

This boy was wearing a blue button-down shirt with the front open over a black turtleneck sweater and jeans tucked into red cowboy boots with stars, and his hair—a spill of black curls waved about his face.

"So how's your rock group?" said Helena.

"We're doin' real well," he said. I sat back and I dug my hands, still wearing the wedding ring I swore I would never remove, deep into the pockets of my black blazer.

He had the slightest wrinkles around his eyes, a texture to his face. Yes. He was much older than Dylan. Obviously. Perhaps even almost thirty.

He turned to me. "I heard you on the radio. That voice had to be you—talkin' your head off with some love doctor. I don't usually listen to talk. I was just flicking by. You were real good. It was all about trusting people you think you love and how we don't, and, wow, did that hit home."

"Yes," I said slowly, sadly. "Trust. How no one does. Trust each other. I certainly don't." I gave Deborah a quick look. "Hardly!" I said, softly. She was not receiving my look. She was watching the conversation. Helena was watching him, too, with the same eager glow older women get looking at enthusiastic young men. You can adore them and they bask in the appreciation. I would not play. I was enjoying grief masked by callous detachment. I had imagined people saying, months from now, "No, she has never been the same since he left, hardly speaks, but you can see it all in her eyes." And only an hour after the tragic divorce of my life here I was, asking this boy how he did get his name, actually: "Is that your real name?"

And he was saying, "When I'm asked I say Henderson, which is what most people call me now, but when I was born, up in Troy, in New York, you know, well you know now, anyway, they called me Wayne and when Dad and I moved down and I started the group they started calling me Hedy, which I like."

"So, tell me about your group," I said. "Do you have outfits?" Where, I thought, is my authentic sense of loss, grief and misery? Knock it off for a while, I told myself. There will be enough early, lonely mornings and late, chilly nights. Perhaps there had been enough.

"Outfits?" He looked at me. "We just have one group so far, if that's what you mean."

"No." I was laughing. Yes, laughing. "Oh, no—I meant clothes. What do you wear?"

"We all wear blazers with badges and Ivy League shirts and rep ties. We're called Headmaster and the Class. We kind of go a little wild when we play; take off our ties and so forth. I don't know that it would be your sort of thing, but we're getting some good reactions lately, at least in Connecticut. I'd like you to come and see us sometime." He was saying that to me, then quickly looked at Helena and Deborah. "All of you, of course."

"We will for sure," Helena said, "all of us." She looked too pointedly at me.

Could he have given himself his nickname because of his resemblance to Hedy Lamarr? He would be a person then of some awareness of the past and humor as well. He did have those light eyes, the lips shaped like a loveseat, and hair so black the highlights came up ultramarine. But I was a lot older than Hedy—would he even know who Hedy Lamarr was?—and could you have long conversations with someone who did not share such trenchant points of reference?

He knew he had that power in his looks and he smiled now in that way lovely men do: a slinky grin came up all over from the absolute pleasure of being admired; his lashes just swept shadows over his eyes, all shy and proud at the same time. There was one of those slow, still moments. Then he looked around quickly, then back at me. "Well," he said briskly, "I guess you guys have things to talk about, so . . ."

Helena stood up so he could slide out. I almost wished she hadn't. Not almost. Wished.

"Maybe," he said to me, not getting up so fast himself, "I could call you sometime. I'd appreciate talking to you about some things, and maybe there's something I could do for you . . . If you've had this divorce and all, I could help you with—well, driving places . . ." He was stumbling over himself. "Not that you won't have lots of people—but, you know what I mean." And he smiled. "I'd like to see you."

"Oh," I said, the word lingering so a moment in the air—I could see it. "Well." I wrote down my phone number. "So call when you like. That's very nice."

He got up; then, unfolding his well-made body with the series of authoritative boy-man movements Dylan did so well, said, "Helena and my dad know each other," as if to imply he was all right. He now put his arm around Helena and winked at her. I'm not crazy about winks. Or assumptions that being in A.A. is a big secret.

"I know your dad from the same place," I said, a little cool now.

"Oh, great. That is great—I didn't know that. He never,

you know, mentions who is and isn't. Well—so I'll talk to you." And he bounced in his straight-from-the-hip walk off to the counter to pick up *The New York Times*, which was presumably what he came in for to begin with.

"So he reads too," I said to Helena, who sat right back down.

"Don't be so arch," she said, "you liked him. He liked you; and you're crazy because one minute you're too scared to drive to this party you ought to go to—"

"Perfect!" Deborah said. "Exactly what I was thinking. Get up to the newsstand."

"I thought," I snapped at her, "that you were never directive."

"I have my moments," she said.

Helena was on her feet. And I went up. I pulled a quarter out of my pocket. I didn't want to look as if that was all I had on my mind.

"Hi, again," he said. He knew it wasn't about newspapers.

"Oh, hi," I said. "You just reminded me I forgot to get the *Times*."

"Yeah, right," he said, not exactly rushing right on his way. "I might get another one too. My dad sometimes reads it, but I'll wait 'til you're done."

In a pig's eye Scotty reads the *Times*.

He picked up his second paper and still stood with this one under his arm. "You were lookin' so sad when I came in. I had to do somethin', so I thought I'd say hello, but maybe you were busy, you know, I hope I didn't interrupt too much. I thought about you, standin' so mad on that road, hitchin' . . ."

"You were so young then," I said.

"I got older." He smiled. "But you didn't." He put one newspaper back down on the counter.

Helena's waitress, Agnes, behind the counter said, "You could save money. Get one paper and read it together."

"Very funny, Agnes," I said

"Cute," Hedy said. "I read so hard I wear one out."

"I could have guessed that," I said, finding a grin somewhere. So with a daring that came of desperation and bravado enhanced by having an audience of friends, I said, "Look, I have to go to a business thing in New York tomorrow night. It's a kind of commitment. You mentioned about driving and all and I would like it if—it would help if you could come with me, and it might be a neat thing for you—a lot of people will be there—there's an agent, Ivan Rappaport, he's my agent, actually really a friend, and he does a lot with young rock people and you may have even heard of him probably." I could stop now perhaps with the qualifications, the insecure chattering. "I know it's crazy," I added.

"It's not crazy," he said. "We've sort of known each other for months now. And that would be great. Sure, I've heard of Mr. Rappaport." I could see his eagerness; I knew how that expression feels from the inside. "I've been wanting to meet him, but, hey, who wouldn't." He paused. He was smart. "Mainly I'd like to go with you—you don't have to do a number." This smile glistened. He put his hand, just a touch, on my shoulder. "We'll have a good time whatever. I'll pick you up. Just tell me where you live."

How amused Ivan would be to know his role here, as bait. Amused but not surprised.

"Well," I said, after arrangements had been made, and he had walked out and I had come back to the table. "So." He was so jaunty. So agreeable. "That was a good idea," I said, "and with a father in the program, he'll understand about me not drinking. Thanks for making me do it. He is adorable. Actually."

I could arrive, I could show: look, I am not alone. And for the duration of the party even believe it. And for Hedy, would it be quite the reverse, the cover story graciously applied, possibly a little real—do not try to consider how much he meant by "mainly." And so what was the matter with any of it? Doesn't anyone have a lot of reasons for going to a party and isn't the point just to go? And I was. And he was going with me and if I got to just look at him, I decided to pretend his own reasons didn't need to matter.

"Easy Does It," I could imagine Scotty telling him.

"And you waited so long . . ." said Helena. "He's a sensitive young man, very mature for his age. When his mother died Hedy used to come in here for meals with Scotty all the time; now I think he does a lot of the cooking. But just be careful. He is very ambitious, I think, and you're very vulnerable." She was also saying, "Easy Does It."

"Don't tease me. I hate being teased," I said now to Helena and Deborah, shaking my head, twisting one of the tangles which fell along down to my shoulders. I put my hands then on the table, pleased with myself for a moment. "You never do know, I suppose, when something good will happen. I guess you have to have given up and accepted and then you're ready."

"One thing you can say for yourself that's positive," said Helena, "in case you ever should be so inclined, is you don't brood over anything for too long."

"Perhaps," I said, "that is because I have no attention span." I patted her arm. "There is always a negative way to see everything."

6

I woke up on the kind of early spring day when everything can begin, the color is coming and you hear a different sound. I jumped up and put on jeans and sneakers and Spike came clicking down the steps behind me and we walked out and up along the road. I took long steps, stopping a bit, here, there, to touch new leaves and buds.

Sun shimmered through the mist. Cardinals darted like poppies through the bare branches. The crocuses had come up and there were late valentines of snowdrops around the trees in front of Theodore's church, which is what we all called it.

I snapped off branches of forsythia to bring home and I put them in pottery jars around the house downstairs. Then I went upstairs with flowers for Brynn and for Dylan. I went from one room to the other. I hugged and kissed and tussled them awake, and they let me, as we forgot for a moment that they were not babies. I burrowed my face in their hair, damp from sleep, and covered their hands with mine, my fingers reaching to go round Dylan's big man's hands. Spike bounded from one room to the other, pouncing and licking, announcing this was, indeed, a new and good morning.

"Come," I said, "let's all go to Chickens for breakfast!"

"You got it," said Dylan.

"Terrific," said Brynn. They jumped into their jeans and sneakers, pulling on sweatshirts and down vests.

There was, to be sure, a skittish kind of merriment in our

customary hostile encounters—which were more exciting than the times when one of us was truly blue and therefore required serious sympathy.

But we liked best these rare times of celebration when we'd go out together, aware of our blooming gay appearance and jaunty presence. I looked at them. This. I had done this. No. Pride goeth before—I had not; God made these golden, buoyant people. And He let me look at them. Being the mother means I could reach over, take a chin in my hands and give a kiss whenever I pleased. I leaned across the dinner table and kissed Brynn's nose.

"Oh, I love you both," I said, beaming. To insure these times, I suppose I indulged at other times, giving and giving, because I was afraid if I didn't they wouldn't love me and, worse, they might leave. I loved them, I loved them and oh I would do anything for them, I would withhold nothing and they knew that.

We sat around exactly the table I'd been at yesterday when I saw Hedy. Agnes was on. George was cooking. "The fry cook had a bad night. Wrecked his car," he said. "Hear yesterday wound up okay," he added to me.

"Just fine," I said. I smiled. I wanted to give all my attention to Brynn and Dylan. I asked them questions, not a word about myself. "How is the history class?"; "How is your paddle tennis going?"; "Do you like that boy who called, was it Freddy?"; "What is Alison's father like?"

"What is this," Brynn said. She ordered just a cup of hot water to start—she brought her own tea bags. "Trying out for *Face the Nation*?"

"No," said Dylan, "she's practicing effective parenting." He drank his second glass of orange juice and ordered another with a wave of his hand which reminded me of Hedy's gesture. Or had Hedy's gesture reminded me of Dylan? Now he turned to Brynn. I liked when they talked to each other. I remembered when they were tiny and shared a room and I'd hear them wake up in the morning and jabber at each other like soft-voiced birds.

"It's called 'establishing open lines of communication,'" he continued.

"That," I said, "sounds like one of Deborah's lines. I hate the word parenting. You just have children and you love them. Children are people, not an issue to study."

"Relax, Mom, we're all doing fine." Brynn patted my arm.

"I know," I said. "Where is it written that a child and parent have to be hostile during adolescence?"

Everywhere it was written. How else would they engineer the force they'd need to break away, to turn to others? I didn't want to think of that.

"You ought to do an interview with some children. The New Child. The Human Being You Build Yourself," Dylan said, taking one of Brynn's cigarettes from her purse.

"Why are you kids smoking?" I asked. "And before breakfast and why don't I try to stop you?"

"That is something to think about," said Dylan. "A good parent would risk hostility by taking a stand."

I put a bunch of quarters on the table, which Dylan took and slid into the little jukebox on the wall.

"Put that cigarette back!" said Brynn to Dylan. She also swiftly punched up three songs before he could get started. "She shouldn't do any interviews with kids, actually," said Brynn, "then she'd be thinking of us as issues. And we're not an issue, we're us. And odd."

"May I please have one of your cigarettes?" Dylan said.

"When she built you," Brynn said, "she put the jokes in wrong."

"And that was supposed to be funny?"

"So, to risk hostility, then," I said, "why don't you both really think about not smoking?"

"Because we come from several broken homes and we have a lot of self-destructive impulses," Dylan said, lighting the cigarette.

"I quit," I said, and ordered pancakes and bacon.

Brynn ordered French toast and sausages and Dylan ordered a cheese omelet, ham and waffles.

George left the griddle to help Agnes bring the food to the table.

"Man waits on table," said Agnes.

"Miracle," I said.

"I tried to get one and he never showed," said George. "I really wanted to see all this food on one table."

"I don't want to look thin and divorced," I said.

"I don't think," George said, "that's going to be a problem."

We all jabbed our forks into each other's breakfasts taking tastes, licking syrup off our fingertips and tapping our feet to the music from the jukebox.

"Since we're starting out so well," Brynn said, "why don't we go down to the city today. We could go to the Museum of Natural History."

"And check out the dinosaurs for the eight hundredth time," said Dylan. "That would be cool. Then we could all catch a movie." He looked gentle, open and eager, undefended in his enthusiasm.

It sounded wonderful and seemed safer suddenly, because familiar, than what I was going to do. But would we all be feeling like this if I hadn't started the day happy precisely because of this date, this party that, at this instant, I did not prefer.

"I can't tonight. And I really want to."

"What's the matter with tonight," Dylan said. "Of course. You've met someone. That explains everything."

"What do you mean?" I said.

"Probably the cheerfulness," said Brynn.

"And I thought it was just us," said Dylan, his expression

instantly rearranged, on guard. "Do me a favor, Mom, and don't marry it until the ink on your divorce is dry."

"And I thought," Brynn said, "that you were just happy that the thing yesterday was over. Then can I use your car?"

"I know," said Dylan to Brynn, "you're taking the bowling team to a match in Bridgeport."

"Actually, no. It's down in Norwalk. See, smart ass," she said.

"Maybe Mom will need the car. You never know if they're together enough to drive." Dylan found a corner of one nail that was not bitten off and bit it off.

"He is. And he has a limousine, anyway," I said.

"Where did you meet him?" Dylan said.

"At lunch. After court." There was a silence. I sipped my coffee. Dylan drummed on the table to music. Brynn tapped her feet.

"He's a musician. It's very nice." I looked at them. I wanted their approval, their interest. I was placing demands on them that I used to place on my parents, then later (when my parents had ceased even wanting to meet them) on friends. The right person, I suspected, would be the one no one else would have to meet. Brynn and Dylan were both gazing out the windows at the stores across the way, at kids ambling by.

"Oh, he plays Muzak?" said Dylan.

"I don't know," I said. "It's just to take someone to this party. I am not getting involved again." They looked at each other again and nodded. Sarcastic. "Cut it out. I promise. No surprise marriages."

"My mother, the groupie," said Brynn.

At five-thirty precisely, Hedy's limousine pulled up in front of our house. Dylan was on the couch, watching TV; Brynn was on the floor doing a magazine quiz—What Your Favorite

Foods Reveal About Your Sexual Fantasies—out loud with a friend; Jennie was gazing through the window at Reilly (he was cleaning up the yard's winter debris, liking to be around where he could catch glimpses of Jennie).

Headmaster strode down the front path in brown suede cowboy boots, white jeans, a brown leather bomber jacket, and a white silk pilot's scarf floating around his neck. I watched him from my bedroom window. The lilting arrival of this magical cavalier was like a gift. The reward for staying sober is the freedom from feeling miserable, but I could not help believing that this was an extra reward.

"Do I look okay?" Now I was at the top of the stairs. I was wearing my best sort of shades of cream outfit; no black today.

"He is a kid," Dylan said to me as I twirled a little on the first landing of the stairs. "I've seen him around."

"Of course you have—he lives here! We're just going to a party, Dylan. Will you get the door?"

"No, I won't."

"You could be polite."

"You only talk about polite when you're having a date, so it's not just going to a party. I'll get the stupid door."

"I'll get the damn door; you both stop fighting," said Brynn. It really should be her turn for this. I should be watching her twirl; watching her go out. Don't, I told myself, start that. It will change.

"Welcome to *The Brady Bunch*," said Brynn. Jennie was watering the plants. Brynn's friend was plunked in the lotus position between the couches.

"Hi, everyone," Hedy said, and waved, leaping in. Spike, who had been in the yard, bounded in behind him and began to bark. He started to jump and Hedy backed away.

"I'll be just a minute," I said, so conditioned to not being ready exactly when men arrived, a ploy left over from the time when you weren't supposed to be eager. I puttered about in the coat closet. I grabbed my brown cloak.

"You can't wear that thing, Mom," said Dylan.

"You don't want her to be cold?" said Brynn.

"Do you want a Coke or something?" Jennie said.

"No, we're kind of pushing it for time," Headmaster said. He looked like any young man picking his girl up at her parents' house, so shy, now, shifting from the left foot to the right. No wonder: this time it is the parent he is picking up.

I pulled out my tweed overcoat and put it over my shoulders.

"Neat," said Brynn.

Hedy sneezed. He sneezed again. Spike jumped up now, leaving a long paw print on his white jeans.

"Oh, dear," I said, "I'm sorry."

"I'll get a sponge," said Jennie.

He sneezed and dusted at his pants.

"Here," I said, dabbing with the sponge Jennie brought.

"No, it's really okay," he said, sneezing.

"Mom—he already brushed it off," Dylan said, grinning at Headmaster, sort of a you-know-how-moms-are-they-forget-stuff look.

"Do you want a Kleenex?" said Brynn, bringing the box.

Hedy took one and blew his nose, and took some more and put them in the back pocket of his jeans and sneezed again. "I'm allergic to dogs," he snuffled.

"Oh no, I'm sorry," I said. "Spike, go outdoors with Dylan." Spike walked to the door obediently.

"It's not your fault. Everyone has dogs. My agent has a dog. Everyone. And I really"—he sneezed—"like dogs."

I swung my bag over my shoulder fast. "I'm ready." I paused. "Maybe I need a muffler, just in case." I pulled a beige one from a line of pegs by the front door. "I freeze. It's a sign of age."

"Fishing," said Dylan. He and Hedy grinned at each other.

"You don't look bad for a hundred and eight," said Hedy. He put his hand gently on my back.

"Thanks," I said, "and you look fine for twelve. With a red nose." I touched his nose with the tip of my finger.

I watched Dylan, standing on the stairs, looking at me, his mother standing next to this young man, much closer to his age than to mine, a young man with a manager and a limousine. This stranger's face turned, looking down at mine; my face turned up smiling at Hedy the way I smile at Dylan. I looked from one to the other fast. And Dylan saw and caught my eyes and felt in charge because of that exchange. This was a game, he seemed to decide to see it; and when it was over I'd be back home where I belonged. So Dylan said, "Listen, guys, have a good time but, by the way, Mom, don't you get back too late. You know, Mom, you've got a deadline and I don't think you got a lot done today."

"I won't be late, darling." I looked up. I smiled. He lifted his chin like a slim golden godfather and smiled too. Godfather, nonsense! Like my father, exactly. I hugged Brynn. I would feel more comfortable if the children were going. This thought surprised me. I decided I would file it and discuss it with Helena. I stood a moment longer, absorbing Brynn, who had picked up an orange from the big copper bowl on the old pine table and was tossing it up and down; Dylan the consummate concerned male; Jennie lounging on the rosy rag rug; my calico pillows, and the lacy hanging plants. I looked at all that meant home to me as if confirming my identity before plunging into another world. I was more adventurous when I was married. Now I disliked leaving home without at least one of my regular companions. "Everybody, eat something, please, and be sure to feed Spike, and—"

"We know, Mom," said Brynn, and she smiled her completely charming smile at Hedy. He returned her smile and touched her shoulder. "Have some fun and don't worry." Yes, he understands very well what it is to be the child of the erratic single parent.

Outside I took long strides to keep up with Hedy. "I love the scarf," I said.

Spike pounced up beside us. "Cool it, Spike," I said.

"It's nothing personal, pal," said Hedy, looking at the dog, then he took my hand in the friendliest way, as Dylan might.

The blond boy, the driver I'd seen before, opened the limo door for me, and I settled down into the back seat of the car. Yes. The limousine lure. You sit in a different way. I remembered how my mother would insist on renting limousines for my father when a play he'd done the sets for was opening. "Why," he'd say, "don't we wait and see if it's a hit and then we'll go in a limousine to all the parties."

"Because," she would say, "part of it is showing up as if you know it will be a hit because you have agreed to do the sets."

Hedy raised his head, looking more aloof as he came around the car.

"We got to truck it," he said, a little curtly.

A little arrogance, I supposed, was to be expected in someone successful so young. And when you're wearing a white silk scarf around your neck you need all the tough talk you can find. Hedy sat back, leaning into the corner, his long legs crossed high, the ankle resting on the other knee. I loved the lean jut of those knees—and the jeans, men's legs were really fine in jeans. Boys. This was a boy and we were just going out to be possibly helpful to each other in the most friendly new way.

"You're going," I told him, "to have a very good time, I think." I patted that knee. Was that a maternal pat or was I patronizing and did I know the difference? The backs of our hands were side by side. His joints, knuckles and veins were well defined. Even still, for this moment, they looked mobile, lively, on the verge of gesture, listening for a sound, the direction to move into a beat.

My father had always looked at the hands of the boys Deborah and I went out with. "Clean nails indicate good character," he had said.

The pilot had clean nails, which was the argument I had used when my father had protested that I was too young to marry, and knew too little about him. The publisher had elegant hands. "In his case it is more style than character," my father said. "He moves his hands as if always wearing fine tight kid gloves." "Three months," my mother said, "does not a marriage make." My father had liked Bill Spinning's hands, which rather resembled his own—and now, Dylan's.

These were different hands. Clean nails, but they looked a little used, a bit chewed up. Old hands, as if someone had switched them on him in his sleep.

I had decided, in the way that I selected what I would wear, that driving into the city we would discuss Hedy's career. I sat forward now, turned slightly toward him. "Tell me," I said, "what instrument it is that you play?"

"Lead guitar," he said.

"Oh, like Pete Seeger. I love him!"

"Well, not exactly . . ." He looked at me a bit oddly.

"And what song," I said, going right on, "or sound, if that's a better way to put it now, first drew you, lured you, so you knew: this is what I want to do?"

He looked even more amused, he shrugged almost imperceptibly, he settled deeper into the soft seat, and he began, "Well, I remember long ago my mother humming and the house feeling calm then, but the truth is for the most of us I guess it wasn't very different, I guess it was hearin' the stories, you know, about the Beatles and how they got together and so . . ."

And so he answered the questions I asked and I listened; exclaiming softly here, shaking my head there, leaning forward now, drawing time back to another point then, and in this manner we rode into the city exactly as I'd planned, and as the limousine cruised down the West Side we passed a bar on 118th Street and Eighth Avenue that had a sign, "Dope Addicts—Take Out Only. No Pushers." I pointed out the sign to Hedy and we laughed and Hedy said, "Yeah, I'll have six Seconals, a Valium shake to go with a side of Biphetamine Sixty, hold the coke."

I thought of Michael Arlen's lovely line, "Addiction is where Thanatos and Eros cross." Keep it simple, I said to myself; for you Eros is addiction.

"Everyone is here!" I knocked, Hedy rang the bell, the door flew open like the door in a ballet and we swept into the entry hall through an arbor of guests reaching arms to each other, angling by, laughing and turning heads, and whispering and watching and we sidled along, glancing at each other. "Oh, I love parties, I do love parties!" And I turned to Hedy and grabbed his arm and smiled like new.

"Yeah!" he said, and "Dynamite!" he said, and we moved into the huge living room swirling with faces I knew and almost knew and wanted to know, wonderful glee and such serene authority, such poses and chins-up hugs. Shy grins here; eyebrows lifting aloof there; icy glasses clinking—yes—"Yes, Hedy, just Perrier."

"Perrier, please," he said to the young waiter, and he looked at me. "Do you mind if I have a drink?"

"Oh, no," I said, looking for an instant at him; how cute he is here, what luck to have him here. How fast it all changes. Today is not good. Hang on, here comes tomorrow and look, just look.

"I'll have a Scotch and soda," he said.

And just look at the curving, perfect hair, the dresses and jewels, the soft expensive colors of woolens and silks, and look beyond the curving branches of blossoms set high on Lucite pedestals, through the arched windows, over Central Park to the lights of the city glittering and shining, oh, more than stars, much more than stars, and I wanted to just open my arms and say, oh, yes, I do love this, I love this too, I love this very much and how could I have ever, ever moved away?

Look at this one gliding through alone with such a long neck, haughty, how original, no one's been haughty in years, and these three men clustered so seriously with arms around each other's shoulders, hands seeming to be clasped about each other's drinks. Members of the Entrenchment, considering the next end of the world, and these two women, whispering, heads nodding, swift furious agreement. "Celibacy Without Rage," one said.

"I'll have it written in a month."

But what if she falls in love on the way. What indeed, I wondered, and looked at Hedy's nice long legs. Fresh! I said to myself, don't be fresh! And he looked at me looking. "I hope I'm not too rock-and-roll," he said.

"No, you're splendid." I smiled and I quickly said, "There's our hostess, there's Cleo!" And I waved and we moved through the crowd and I kept my eye out on the way as well looking up and over, arching my own neck some, looking for Ivan.

"Come, I want you to meet Cleo, and St. Cheri. This is her apartment. St. Cheri Solinger-Rhodes is a marvelous designer." St. Cheri was wearing several layers of soft greenish suede.

Cleo watched us move through the room with a slightly amused expression. I threw a grin right back across the room. On the way I introduced Hedy to Jack Farrell. "Jack," I said to Hedy, "is the reason for this party." Jack was a novelist turned paramedic who was running for city council.

"There's never a problem," Jack said, "coming up with an

impoverished candidate or an emerging catastrophe, interchangeably fine excuses for a party."

"Hedy's a super new rocksinger," I said. "If we're lucky maybe he'll do a benefit concert."

"Margot!" Hedy laughed.

Jack shook hands with me and kissed someone else going by at the same time, "Oh, yes," he said, "we're doing an interview next week." And he put one arm around me.

"I know. I'm delighted," I said, covering my surprise, I hoped. Here Jack had a polished tweedy look; when he visited neighborhood tag sales around Columbus Avenue he wore worn jeans, and at board of education meetings he wore a rumpled seersucker suit with a narrow tie sort of pulled to the left of the center of his shirt. "Terrific," Jack said, as he now shook hands with another person.

St. Cheri moved forward slightly and took both my hands, smiling up at Hedy. "Such a treat you are," she said to him. "You can feel his vitality. I'm embarrassing you, darling; aren't I dreadful." She turned to Cleo, who was leaning now under a painting on the wall, the russet tones matching her hair.

"Yes, you are," said Cleo.

"You picked the perfect place to stand," I said to her.

"I did that, didn't I?" she said. I kissed her twice on each fine cheekbone. "Hi," she said to Hedy.

"So I'm doing a show with Jack next week?" I said.

"I would have told you, but I know you've had enough to deal with," she said. "I think we'll arrange to do an hour interview, and keep the phone calls pretty much at bay."

"I missed the phone-ins," said Hedy. "I just had the interview part on the way here."

"Oh, right," Cleo laughed. "Margot's idea of conversation is you answer questions."

"Yeah," Hedy said, "I kept waiting for the commercial interruptions."

"You'll see," I said, "on the way home I'll talk nonstop about me."

"Hey," and he put his arm lightly around my shoulder, "that was the first time that's happened for me and I really liked it."

"I thought so," I said, a little too sweetly.

Caroline Kalish waved and beckoned from the other side of the room.

"Oh, Hedy—I'll be right back," I said.

"This," Cleo said to him, "is called working the room. I hope we get along because she will not be back for a while."

"No, come on, Cleo, I was talking to Caroline a month ago about her work and I just want to see how it's going now."

Hedy laughed. "Listen, I understand—go on."

"Well, Hedy and I will find something to talk about, since our friends are clearly occupying themselves." Cleo looked at St. Cheri, who had her long arms stretched over the shoulders of two short young people who, by their costumes and flat-footed stance, appeared to be ballet dancers fresh from a rehearsal.

"Oh, darling," said St. Cheri, quickly looking at Cleo, "come, I want you to meet the most enchanting young developers in all of Manhattan real estate."

"I'll be right there," said Cleo. "You have two minutes to sort out Kalish," she said to me. Caroline was a journalist who was always, in the years I'd known her, just about to leave New York forever.

"And here we still are," I said. "How are things going?"

"Not wonderfully. I think I hate my editor-in-chief, I know I loathe my apartment and I have no lover and no money. So I'm going to L.A. and I thought you'd be the perfect person to encourage me because you picked up and got the hell out."

"Well," I said, waving with one hand, blowing a kiss with

the other, "give up the apartment and write an article about how to manage when you don't have even a roof over your head, and we'll do a radio show on it which will bring you offers of interesting places to share."

"But what do you do without a roof over your head?"

"That's what you'll be able to tell everyone. Worse comes to worst, you'll move to Connecticut and stay with me."

A man walked by carrying two drinks.

"I'll take one of those," Caroline said, reaching out, "and then I'm going to L.A."

"These parties haven't changed," I said to Cleo and Hedy. "I used to go with my father when my mother wasn't feeling well. I remember we'd walk through and I'd watch everyone be so pleased to see him." I'd mimic his manners, his distance with this one, eagerness with another.

"The pessimism," Cleo said, "is always radiant. Hedy, do you think you could find me a Coke? I'll keep Margot here."

"Oh, I'll find her," he said, "if she gets away."

"This one you cannot take charge of," Cleo said to me.

"So, I was in such charge of Bill I wound up in Connecticut?" I said.

"Yes," said Cleo, "which was so clearly where he wanted to be."

"Perhaps he is in Alaska," I said.

"Perhaps my father and Bill have frozen together on an ice floe," she said. She touched my arm. "It's okay, at least you're having a good time. That's an improvement."

"Well." I waved at someone across the room. Cleo gave a quick nod to someone else and I shook hands with a man who put kisses off to the left and right sides of Cleo's face, blew another kiss at a woman behind us, then, pivoting suddenly, waved at another person and finally trotted off with open arms to embrace an irrepressibly cheerful TV news person.

"No, you can't have his job," said Cleo, watching me.

"Such a thing would never occur to me!" I said.

"Not on your bad days, but when you're up everything is a wonderful job for you." Cleo lifted her eyebrow now in the way I wished I knew how to do. "No one is really gone, nothing is ever over," she said; "it just slides into another arena of consideration."

"Back burner," I said.

"From food, as you know," she said, "I know nothing."

"The evidence," I said, "is overwhelming."

At the studio, around her desk, on her shelves and at her elbows were always the half-full boxes of Kentucky Fried Chicken, the milk shake containers, cheeseburger cartons, and wadded-up candy bar wrappers Cleo adored, to the amused consternation of St. Cheri, who had invested in a couple of the most celebrated new restaurants.

Cleo remembered the name of anyone who ever ran for the city council, all the members of the Supreme Court and what their opinions were on every issue, but the last movie she had seen was a Carnegie Hall cinema rerun of *All the King's Men*, which I could drag her to only because of the political theme. Cleo did not listen to music, never read fiction and somehow stayed thin, even though she ate enormous amounts of appalling fast food.

Cleo loathed shopping. Once a year she would go to her tailor and have things made. Behind the bravado that compelled and sometimes terrorized others, she was sympathetic and afraid of the horrible things always happening to other people. Some of which had happened to her. She avoided some of the fear and sadness by immersing herself in work, politics and comforting friends, even to the extent sometimes, as she had with me, of taking us out and watching us eat what she had referred to as "these expensive little flower arrangements in places that look like beauty parlors."

"How would you know," I had asked.

"Because at least I don't try to cut my own hair," she'd said.

"I'd get mine done too, but then what would my mother and I talk about," I'd said.

"We already did that show."

Hedy returned with Cleo's Coke, and a Perrier for me. "Just in case," he said.

"Whoops—oh, here you go," Cleo said, and swiftly joined St. Cheri.

Ezekial Max came walking through. "My second husband," I said to Hedy quickly, and reached out my hand to Ezekial, who published small books everyone wrote about in literary magazines. When his writers complained about distribution and advertising, Max reassured them: "Look, you don't want just anyone reading this book."

I had seen Ezekial at parties like this, and my father had been pleased. "He's terribly smart." But is he cute, I had asked myself, knowing that was the wrong question, and I had accepted his invitation to dinner at his apartment.

He had prepared elegant food. I had brought my best brownies, heavy and dark with bittersweet chocolate, and we had drunk two bottles of marvelous wine and gone on to brandy. We had each decided to be charmed, out of common sense and loneliness, but we'd conversed like people using not quite comprehensible foreign tongues. Discussing a battle of the sexes, I had said, "I do think men are a little ferocious." He had leapt from the chair, flinging his arms about me, crying, "Not so ferocious, not so ferocious at all."

"I am the last of the fifties women," I had said, indicating a reserve which was not entirely accurate. We got into bed. He came inside me. I got myself off.

"I like the way you have worked it out; it is practical and generous. I was moved," he had said, and we had gone off to Martha's Vineyard, come home engaged. We'd married, and then my children had returned from summer camp and, after a Thanksgiving dinner with my entire family, we had divorced.

"Thanksgiving," he had said, "was disastrous. Christmas, I am certain, will be terminal."

"But what is divorce," I had cried, "if not terminal?"

"At least, my dearest, it will be only terminal for one of us." He had patted my hand. "And you do have your family. It is more than enough to distract you."

"So," Ezekial said, looking at Hedy as I looked at the tall blond young woman standing now beside him. We introduced our friends and kissed each other on the cheek. "I had heard," he said, "that you married again, congratulations." He smiled at Hedy.

"No, no," I said, "Hedy is a new friend. I'm divorced, again. Just yesterday, actually. Hedy's just being a wonderful sport keeping me company here." I leaned my elbow on his shoulder as if we were boyhood pals.

"That is unusually wise behavior for you," he said. "Wounded people probably should not have nor expect more in the first year than sexual exchanges with reasonable consistency."

"I think," Hedy said fast enough and well enough and I could have, if only for that, kissed him, "Margot deserves more."

"Yes, she is a lively woman, as long as you remember she is also like a child who must be the center of the universe." He kissed me on the cheek and shook Hedy's hand.

"Wow," said Hedy, "at least you guys aren't into this we're-divorced-but-still-great-friends stuff."

"No," I said, "but he is not entirely wrong about me at all." I smiled. "He may be entirely right. Actually."

"Well," said a young man walking by to a woman wearing a quilted satin jacket painted with pansies, "since relationships don't work anyway, why not make sex politically useful?"

"I'd follow that jacket anywhere," another woman said.

I dusted cheekbones with the songwriter Amy Young and her new partner, Jamestown Philips. "Such fun on the show last week!" Amy said.

"Absolutely," said Jamestown. "Super response."

I introduced them quickly to Hedy. "He's marvelous, too," I said; "you'd love each other's work."

"I already dig yours," Hedy said.

"Mutual," Amy said, fast before it could get specific, and they were off.

"They never heard of me," Hedy said. A distinct darkening of expression.

"Well, they will," I said. "The energy it takes to start. It isn't easy, Hedy."

And constant encouragement. How much I still demanded.

"Do you have people do music on the show live?" he asked. I wondered how many shows he had actually heard.

"Not often," I said. "As you know it's mostly talk, talk, talk —sometime you'll come on." He brightened. Cleo would kill. She hated when I made promises. "Younger demographics," I would tell her.

I shook two hands, patted one back and kissed three cheeks, one with beard, two soft and creamy.

"Some of these people thrive on despair and I just won't," I said. "I remember in the fifties, or early sixties, seeing *La Dolce Vita*, the Fellini movie," I told him.

"I saw it down in New York last year," he said. "I broke up with this girl Denise, who drove me crazy. Always down on everything. Like it was hip."

"Oh, Hedy, bitterness always has been. I remember in that movie when the intellectual killed his children rather than let them face the world. And I understood. The future seemed hopeless. But look, we had the sixties, and there *was* hope."

"Until it was shot down," he said. "I'm soundin' just as bad."

"Maybe," I said, "that's why I like being home, where we aren't expected to be aware that everything in the world is falling apart."

"Oh, I wouldn't give up universal despair for my own actual problems," said Cleo, who appeared at our side. "Ivan is in the dining room, by the way, and looking for you."

"Yeah," said Hedy, "you do the despair trip the way we go to monster movies to escape from things we just can't deal with on a daily basis."

"You sound wonderful," Cleo said, "but don't use the phrase 'on a daily basis.' When you're a big star and on the *Tonight* show I want you to remember that everyday is a perfectly respectable word."

"I'll remember to use it on a daily basis," Hedy said, with a flouncy little salute and the most charming smile.

We moved on into the dining room, where several people were gathered around the buffet table, some with plates, one or two here and there, sort of leaning along the edge of it, picking up food with fingertips rather as if they were standing at a bar eating peanuts. I would never do such a thing, I told myself, as I strolled by and popped a tortellini in my mouth.

Ivan motioned us to join him at one of the three small round tables set into a bay at the end of the dining room. It was his custom, at all parties, to hold court, to find the one place, if there was only one, where he would be conspicuously inconspicuous, where he could be surrounded by people he liked, knowing that most people might be too intimidated to just settle upon him. I had known Ivan since I was a child. He had taken me on because he loved my father and my mother, and that was all right. You start somewhere and Hedy was starting with me. It's all steps . . . Ivan's grandfather had owned a chain of theatres and his father had booked *his* first clients into *his* father's theatres. Ivan, as I had thought from childhood, was elegance itself, only my father—to me—had more.

Hedy and I arrived at Ivan's small table with large white porcelain plates full of the brisk, lean-sliced vegetables, which Cleo particularly detested, the tortellini salads, chunks of the best-reviewed breads and bits of pale odd cheeses.

Hedy had forks and linen napkins sticking out of his jacket pocket. He settled me at the table and shook hands with Ivan. "I'm especially pleased to meet you," he said. And then he excused himself, "I'm going for Cokes for Margot and me; is there something I could get you, sir?"

"I'd love a glass of white wine." Then, "Wise young man," Ivan said to me.

"I don't know him very well," I said.

"You never do." Ivan smiled. "But if you'd ask me I'd tell you, this one is self-possessed enough not to, as they say, play it cool with me. He's been tracking me all evening, quite eagerly. I could do without the 'sir,' but thank heaven he's polite to you."

"Oh, Ivan." I laughed. "That's like a fortune-teller. I just really just met him!"

"Fortune-teller? I suppose that is what I do for a living. I like that." He reached out and patted my hand, then took a bit of the cheese off my plate. "A chèvre," he said. "Very nice."

"You look quite sleek tonight," I said. Ivan's three-piece black silk suit was in fact sleek, but Ivan was now quite frail. His long bones did not seem to go where he wanted to place them. If he crossed his ankles, then he would seem to have trouble with his arms, and would wrap them tightly around his body.

"Well, my dear one," Ivan said, "success in love fortunately does not affect one's success in other areas. I have two choice pieces of news for you. I was hoping you would be here tonight, though I'd heard from your father that the divorce was only yesterday." He put his fingertips together into a steeple.

"Don't drive me crazy," I said. I laughed. "Tell me, quick before he comes back." I wanted it for myself, to myself.

"Just between us, then," said Ivan, "for now, is the first news. There is a new magazine of the air being put together for a cable TV company and they want you to hostess the feature portion. It's in the very earliest planning stages. But it will happen."

I beamed. And only yesterday such despair. How could I! "And?" I said.

"This is immediate and rather lucrative. We've prepared a contract, with a more than presentable advance, for your syndication."

"Cleo didn't tell me. How wonderful. Rich!"

"Not rich. Now, Margot—comfortable, but only if you're wise."

"It all is lovely, lovely news! The children will be delighted. And my father. Some surprise!"

"He's only pleased, never surprised by your success." Ivan said, "Just do us a favor and don't marry for ten minutes, please. And let me find you someone to save your money for you."

I saw Hedy coming toward us managing to carry three glasses. I would have to speak quickly. I didn't want to talk about this in front of him. "Ivan," I said, "I was just thinking a couple of things about the TV thing; I don't mean to sound ungrateful, but I despise the word hostess and I was hoping soon I'd get to do real news; I hate always being the light weight . . . I know that's stupid."

"Margot"—Ivan dabbed around his mouth briskly with his napkin—"don't complain." He was annoyed and rightly so. I shouldn't quibble; the thing hadn't even happened and already I had problems.

"I'm sure they'll be reasonable. I don't know why you would want to do news when you do what you do so well."

"So that took forever, sorry," said Hedy.

"Now," Ivan said to me. "You always say you're going to

call me and come for a visit in the country and then you don't. You must both come soon." Zoltan Wargo, the director, walked up and greeted Ivan. He lifted my hand almost to his lips but his eyes were looking at Hedy.

"He'll put you in a dreadful movie if you're not careful," Ivan said to Hedy.

"I'm a real good musician," Hedy said. "But I sure do know I'm no actor, not even for a bad movie."

"The wisest thing," Ivan said, "may be to know what one cannot do."

I wondered if Hedy really believed that, or just knew it was a smart thing to say, which would have been almost as wise, I suppose. I was so tough on him. I'd never questioned Bill or judged him like this. I was getting too cynical, too beady-eyed. I also realized Ivan had said that for my benefit.

"I will call," I said. "We are almost neighbors." Ivan's house was in Brightriver, the town south of Medwin's Landing, where New York people had summer houses perched on cliffs looking down at the river. There was no more to the town than a post office and a general store with gas pumps in front.

"Now," Ivan said, "I'm pleased that you're not despondent over your divorce. I do not accept despondency in clients. Are the children well?"

"Wonderful. And how is Stan?" Stanford, the man Ivan lived with, was a painter. He hated parties. (Why does one person in a couple always have, at best, a sort of contempt for parties?)

"Stan is terrific. Just don't buy those children any cars. It's worth your life to drive in Connecticut these days, throngs of infants careening around."

"I wouldn't dream of it," I said.

And Ivan stood up. "Now I must be going." And I said, "And miss the famous desserts?"

"My dessert, darling, is a client who must be pampered far more than I hope you will ever need to be, but we will be speaking soon; so you must have an extra dessert for me." And he kissed me on the cheek, and took Hedy's hand in both of his. "It was a pleasure to meet you," he said.

And we stood by the table and looked, and, shimmering under a dozen ivory candles in silver candelabra, there they were, the desserts: candied pears on shadows of bittersweet chocolate; lime mousse swirled with melted silvered sugar dragoons—"More, my dearest," St. Cheri said, "to wear than to eat"—caramel squares, café espresso torte with crème fraîche, a cake of chocolate on chocolate on chocolate, the whipped cream coconut cake; cakes shaggy with cocoa shavings, twigged with toasted almonds; fresh, damp lemon-like daffodils to eat; this Russian icon's collar of a cake with currants, walnuts, and deep dark cherries, perfumed with marzipan; more chocolate with orange peel, with apricot jam, with whipped cream, with strawberries, and sugared pecans, slender tarts laid out in pairs like elbow-length gloves, gleaming with kiwis and peaches and plums and raspberries. "Oh, fresh raspberries so soon, oh, Hedy." And I grabbed his hand. "I don't know where to begin, and which to have."

"I think," he said, "we'll start in the middle because that's where we are, and we'll have all of it."

"Yes. Just look. Yes. Absolutely all of it!"

7

"I'll put the dog in Dylan's room?" I said it with a question mark.

"Okay," Hedy said. "I'll come in for a bit. Is it okay, Gary?"

"I'm cool," Gary said. He was already lounging back against the seat. He stretched his arms. Born laid back. As they say.

"Do you want some coffee?" I asked.

"Never touch it," said Gary.

I rushed Spike up to Dylan's room. He crept in with long, light paces, like a dog doing tiptoes in a cartoon, and he lay down softly by Dylan's bed. I came downstairs. Hedy sneezed once.

"Are you sure you're okay?" I said.

"Fine," he said. He pulled out a Kleenex from his pocket. Folded. Who folds Kleenex?

"Really?" I asked.

"Really," he answered again. "It's quieter in the house. I can deal with the dander and stuff easier when it's real quiet."

I showed Hedy sketches my father had done and some framed designs my mother had made long ago, and photographs taken of me during interviews with Benjamin Spock, with James Baldwin, Paul Simon, and with Joni Mitchell.

"Maybe someday there'll be one with me," he said.

"Probably," I said.

I told myself to calm down and hold on. It hadn't even

begun and already I was thinking about how it would feel when it was all over. That feeling was too familiar, too raw. "Don't go," I would be saying someday. "I won't," he'd say once, then be pulled away.

The time to stop is when one look is levitation. If I stopped now before it went on I would escape the tearing regret. But perhaps it will not go on. There will then be nothing to regret.

Hedy walked around the living room. I had never liked curtains, so from here you could see the river's night glow, as from my bedroom I could see the river of highway cars, their lights passing like slow, horizontal shooting stars. Hedy peered at pictures, more books. "Have you read all these really?" He loved the miniature stage my father had built for me. "My dad would like this. He builds houses. For other people, other contractors. Do you get along with your folks?"

"I love my father. I sort of admire my mother," I answered.

Hedy picked up some apples I'd glazed from the first bushel I'd bought. "You and apples." He put them back in the old bird's nest I kept them in. "Let's put on some music."

I thought it might wake the children. But I decided not to mention that. I did sometimes play music when I was working. He saw me hesitate.

"Are you worried about waking the kids? We don't have to."

"Oh, they're used to it." I didn't say it was almost always Aaron Copland, the Best of Beethoven and Mozart's Greatest Hits, and they would sometimes call down to me to turn it lower. I took off my jacket. If one was to be the seductive older woman one should probably not play it down.

He moved with authority through the records and tapes stacked by what I still referred to as the phonograph. "Why," Brynn always said, "do you think it's so cute to call it that? You know it's called a stereo. We don't want parents playing dumb."

"Hey, this is nice." Hedy picked up a Chuck Mangione album I really did like.

"Oh, I adore that," I said. Something in common.

Hedy sat down on the couch, leaning over the coffee table. He took a fifty-dollar bill out of his back pocket and rolled it up into a tight little cylinder. I assumed he was trying, in a very odd way, to show me he had money. "Why don't you sit down," he said, "unless you have to get to your work right away."

"No, I have hours. I always work at night."

"That's when I like to work, too," he said. "I always used to do my homework at night, waiting with my mom for Dad to get home from the bars."

"When did your mother die?" I asked.

"You're not getting into that again, are you?" he asked.

"What?" I said.

"The interviewing."

"No. It's okay," I said, "I'm not. I shouldn't have asked. It must be hard."

"It's been ten years." He smiled. "Whenever I tell a girl my mother is dead her voice changes and goes all soft."

A girl? Was he including me, or confiding about how "they" are? I hadn't been involved with a man who had a living mother since my first marriage. Maybe it was a Wendy complex: I was drawn to Lost Boys, a look in their eyes, perhaps, that says "I need you." And you will be compared only to memory—there will be no one telling you: you should take better care of me.

"It doesn't get easier," he said. "I remember things. Her hair." He looked at my hair. And I touched it fast, sweeping it up, with a fluff, to its best look. "And it goes over me stronger," he said, "not so often, but with more power. You try to clear it like a dream when you have to get up."

He placed a pocket mirror on the table. The better to see

himself? Then he took a silver box out of his inside jacket pocket and tenderly drew out two paths of white powder on the mirror. I began to follow the paths in my head, then decided, "Live and let live." I thought of the slogan on the wall of St. Matthew's stable.

"Did you used to like to do sex when you were young?" he asked. He leaned forward.

"I really don't remember," I said. No, it will not even begin. And I felt a hundred and eight. I leaned forward. I looked at his hands deftly piping up the coke into the coiled bill. A tooter. Of course. Dylan said there were even silver ones of those. I preferred not to think how he knew.

"Here," Hedy said, handing the thing to me. "You know what to do?"

"Oh, sure." I had not ever done coke. When I was young—that century ago—it was not around. Hard to believe a drug I had missed. *Some get a kick from cocaine. I'm sure that if I took even one sniff that would bore me terrifically too.* Of course. It was part of his generation's passion for recherché, recycled clothes. Nostalgia. Cocaine was for movie stars then, the older people; now it was kids' stuff. And I wanted it. I wanted not to say no. I wanted to act without thinking.

He watched me carefully. "Maybe this isn't a good idea," he said, "if you're in the program. I just remembered they're not into this stuff either."

"Well, probably not," I said. Then I laughed, uneasily, "But I won't really get into it. I'm just browsing, let's say."

"Watch me again," he said softly of course, so I would not be insulted. He put his head down. "Now, try again." He touched my hand.

He was watching me with his mouth lifting on an angle in amusement. Such an appealing expression. I tried again. And I sneezed—the powder blew right out. Probably a hundred dollars that sneeze.

"Damn," I exclaimed.

He laughed.

"I'm very clutzy." I laughed too.

"I think I'm relieved," he said suddenly.

"Yes," I said. Yes. I did not at that moment want the temptation, or even the tension of worrying about seduction. It was fine to know *that*—sex—would not be what this was about. Let me know right away, I felt, and then I can deal with it. Friends. I love friends. And I would not look at his legs again.

"I can tell you what music I really love," I said. This time I would not pretend to like what I did not like. Without sex at stake I could relax. "If you like Mangione," I said, "you'll like this—I love big band jazz—this is Don Ellis. Listen."

I went to the stereo to put on *Indian Lady*. I fooled with the array of knobs, buttons and dials. "I can't get this to work," I finally admitted. I hated being bad with machines; it seemed so cliché. A long time ago, I stopped taping my interviews after Cleo had had to sort out a garbled tape I'd made. Cleo had told me, "You have no mechanical or electrical ability. If you were a man you would be the kind of man who has no mechanical or electrical ability, so stop trying."

"Here," Hedy said, his jacket off, sleeves rolled up, showing strong muscled forearms with straight, dark hair, like lashings of copper wire. Do not look at him. Breathe deeply, and do not sigh.

"What's the matter," he said, "you lookin' for the crank to wind it up?"

I turned to him. Be direct, I told myself, and I said to him, "That was harsh."

"I'm sorry. It was." He softened. Perhaps, like me, he had been toughening up, trying not to be open. And because of that the more we each felt like reaching out the more we'd attack, to push the other one back. We might not be able to control our own reactions, but we could make each other retreat. And we'd be safe in isolation.

I felt his warmth as he fiddled so expertly with these knobs and dials. Perhaps the best part was simply knowing I could have the feeling. That kept me buoyant. Acting on it was dangerous, so the feeling must be a warning signal. The feeling will go no further this time than an exchange between myself and my journal. The phone rang.

"Rats," I said.

"Let it ring," he said. He was breathing heavily. The allergies. Thank heaven for Spike. He could not stay here much longer. It was hopeless. And therefore safe.

"I can't," I said. He was wheezing. I wanted to answer the phone because I was probably glad it rang. I did want to be enfolded, sheltered and embraced—but by an appropriate man, I told myself, not a boy.

"Hello," I snarled into the phone.

"Uh, who's this?" A dreadful beat-up voice.

"You called. Who were you calling?" I asked. I looked at Hedy and made a drinking gesture and he nodded. He understood. A drunk. As Scotty's son, he would live with these calls all the time.

"I don't remember. Fuck it."

"Well, let's try it another way. Who are you?" I thought I knew.

"This is Reilly. What the fuck do you want?"

"You called me, Reilly, and I think you're stoned again."

"Fuckin' A. Where's Jennie?" His voice was fading.

"She's not here. Where are you? Home?" Home for Reilly—I knew because Fitz had driven me by there one afternoon—was in a loft over an abandoned mill, down where the river narrowed into what had once been, Fitz had told me, a lovely glen, now filled with stripped-down cars and old heaps of broken fences and machinery.

All efficiency now, I asked Reilly, "What have you taken, Reilly?"

"Nothing much. I'm fucked. Life sucks. Have you got Betsy's new number? Jennie sometimes stays there."

Hedy sneezed. I heard him going into the kitchen. He came back with a paper towel to sneeze into.

"How many downers did you do, Reilly?" I said, trying to keep him talking. You learn the important thing is not what you say but the tone of voice. You must generate strength and calm. Do not reinforce the fear.

"A couple of Seconals. Twelve. Fourteen. Twenty. Does anyone really give a shit?"

"Reilly. Just hang on. You want to. Or you would not have called." We had all been told never to try to work with our own families. It was far easier to maintain steadiness and detached support when it was not your own child.

I thought of calling Helena and George, but remembered it was Helena's night off, and she'd looked so tired lately. Let her be. And Jennie was having enough trouble.

"You just home?" I asked, trying to make it sound casual.

"I'm going to lay it down, now," Reilly said.

Lay it down, truck it, book it, screw it, junk it, cram it, shove it, jam it, fuck it and if you can't drive it, do it tomorrow. *It* is a drag, a hype, a wipe-out, a gig or a real bummer. *It* is everything that lasts for more than a minute and has no speakers, no motor and requires patience. Sometimes I thought I had no patience for these aging kids. But that was possibly my fear of making a commitment and failing. I always tried now, when I didn't want to do something, to figure out what I was afraid of—the impatience or laziness was usually a cover. His voice was droning off dangerously. And he was somebody's son. God knows whose.

I hung up the phone and Hedy immediately said, before I asked, "We'll go in the limo."

"He may like that too much," I said. "And this is the thing I'm involved with. You probably have enough of this."

"Let's just go." Hedy stopped me. "I know you never say no to anyone."

We got into the car and started out. "Your dad's been in the program a long time," I said.

"Yeah," he said, a little harshly, I thought, but perhaps I was defensive. Very.

"I've been around one drunk all my life. And he seems busier with not-drinking than he was with drinking."

I wondered if my children felt that about me. I was bouncing back and forth too much right now between seeing Hedy the way I wanted to and identifying with his father. And worrying about Reilly.

"You're an odd lady—you have a fierce kind of attention and it's either all turned on or all turned away. Other chicks only half focus all the time. I mean you're already there with that kid. You're not here."

"I suppose that's easier to deal with because you know what to expect, the way other women are, is that what you mean?"

"I guess," he said. "You don't like the word chicks?"

"It's cute for the children of hens. Oh, Hedy, I don't mind." I turned and tried to give him the attention I thought he meant. I looked right at him for an instant. "I'm not used to people being so direct."

"You mean men. With you."

"Yes."

"Then get used to it." He looked startled, as if he hadn't meant to imply what came out.

"I'll think about it," I said, lightly.

The grimy windows flickered with candlelight. An old dog, probably belonging to a former roommate, stood with his paws on the door and growled.

"Hell," said Hedy. "Dogs. Well, let's just get in and get him out."

"Oh, I'm sorry," I said. "I'll go get him together and bring him out myself. You wait."

"Don't be crazy," Hedy said. He sneezed.

"There you are, puppy," I said to the snarling dog, with its teeth flashing.

"Nice boy, shut up, rat bastard," I continued in my softest voice, stroking the dog.

Reilly slunk up behind the dog and pulled him down by the collar. "Down, fuckhead."

"Open the door, you asshole, before I break it down," Hedy yelled, and grinned quickly at me. I shivered, and said, "Oh, my God," under my breath.

"I'm passing out," Reilly said. "Leave me alone."

Hedy slammed his shoulder hard against the flimsy door, which gave instantly, and the dog backed up by the bed and bared its teeth. The inside of this room looked like the pits around the riverbed where everyone tosses junk.

And here I was, with Hedy, his eyes red, watering, sneezing and wheezing, sniffling and puffing, staring down at this now unconscious boy, lying on one dirty sheet, wax from a candle dripping on his pillow, dirty jeans, fly open. I closed it.

"Hey, man," Reilly muttered now, half-conscious, white caking the corners of his mouth. "Do I go with fifteen percent or tell them to fuck themselves?"

"Don't pass out, now," Hedy ordered him. "Keep talkin'." Hedy knew exactly what to do. We pulled Reilly up from the bed.

"I was in the middle of a big business deal," Reilly babbled. There were pill bottles and a half-gallon, almost empty, of Popov vodka on a shelf balanced badly against the wall. The red candle on the second shelf had toppled and fallen onto the floor, congealed into a scarlet pool.

We tried to get Reilly to stand up, but his skinny legs kept collapsing. We balanced Reilly between us, his arms lank over our shoulders.

"Blow out the candles. And don't tell Jennie," Reilly erupted in a rough voice.

Hedy laughed. He put his arm around Reilly and straightened his head up with his hand. "I understand you, man."

"Bullshit," Reilly said.

"I had friends like you." He kept talking, which may have been to ease his own discomfort, but it was also the right thing to do, trying to keep Reilly alert. "Yeah," Hedy said, "I grew up watching rich kids who lived in fancy houses my dad repaired. 'First figure out how to feed yourself,' my dad always warned me. I'm going to show him, too, I'll make more money than he ever did. You're an ambitious guy; you got to keep it together to make it like you want." He patted Reilly's face to keep him conscious. Sort of conscious.

"I'm not going to make it," Reilly said, between us in the back seat as we sped down the road. I remembered these sudden moments of lucidity, pieces of awareness, then the lights going out.

"But you want to go out in style, man," Hedy pointed out. "Wait 'til it's your own limo."

"You'll be fine," I said, patting Reilly on his bony shoulder.

Hedy watched me carefully. "You know something about him without knowing why, as you know something about me. I saw it at the party. You know about keeping a little hungry, looking out for someone else, just to keep from fading out altogether. Never get everything, that's the thing."

He turned, leaning around Reilly to look at me, his hands tight down on his knees, elbows locked out straight. "Even if I'm imagining a crowd in my own room, I got to feel that when I'm playing I'm on, and when I'm hot, I can feel me getting a tough look on my face. You know, sometimes I listen to my tapes and feel the rhythm pounding: I feel big and bad and dirty with fame."

I could feel his feeling right in the back of this car.

"I get a glow coming through and my head gets light. And yeah," he went on, putting one arm around a wiped-out Reilly, "I understand guys who want to be bad and big, who come up with sharp ways to cover up what they really are, which is scared, you know."

"I think that's very wise," I said, but I felt wary, and I wasn't sure why, of the cocky attitude he must have learned as a kid, and it was like Reilly although he was much tougher than Reilly in the ways that matter.

We arrived at the hospital and got Reilly out of Hedy's limousine and into the emergency room. His skin seemed loose. We all slumped against the counter: Hedy was sneezing and coughing; I was looking haggard and nondescript in the bright light, and Reilly was falling down between us.

The alert girl behind the counter tapped with her fingernail, cracked her gum and asked: "Which one is the patient?"

After forms had been filled out, Reilly was taken away. A young resident came out and said we could go now. I explained that George and Helena, who worked there, were close friends, and asked if I could say goodbye to the boy. I always overexplained everything. "If you want," the resident told me.

I saw Reilly lying unconscious on a wheeled bed. The stomach pump was churning. Through the plastic tube I could see pills moving up. "You crazy son of a bitch," I said. "Please make it." I meant it. It could be Dylan. Inconceivable. I thought of the times I'd been out of it. And I thought of earlier in the evening. I could have started it all again with a little coke to be sexy. The need to mask everything—the delight in anesthesia, the pitch, tumble, chaos and broken spaces in my days—nights I could not recollect. So young. It never hit me this young. It was one thing to tease, to see them at meetings, quite another to see him like this.

I walked out of the emergency room quickly, the heels of my shoes clacking on the pale yellow floor, the fluorescent lights, I thought, utter disaster. And then reminded myself there is disaster and disaster.

Hedy was waiting, sniffling into a handful of Kleenex, his urgency coming through the initial easy charm, you could feel it like heat. It had seeded within him, taken root and twisted him as vines take over a young tree. I recognized it entirely too well. It was as much a part of his allure as his eyes, his legs, his lips, and as unsettling as seeing your own expression on someone else's face.

The children were in my room the next morning with coffee on a tray. "Well," they said.

"Well," I said, "Spike, don't jump." He crept onto the bed carefully. "Reilly's back in the hospital."

"Figured he was about due," said Dylan.

"He'll be okay," I said.

"So," said Brynn. "Grandfather called. Right after you left. The limo had just gone down the hill."

I sipped my coffee. My parents were at their house in Florida. My father's best sets had three-level rooms, which always featured a library with leather books and a spiral staircase, and their house in Sarasota had just such a library. In that room, my father told me, he could pretend he was in England or New York while he played chess and exchanged dialogues in the language of the theatre with visiting actors and playwrights. They would turn up the air conditioning and light a fire in the fireplace.

"It's beautiful here," my father had announced to Dylan on the phone, hoping, I'm sure, that the children would visit for the holidays. A desire that I was not certain my mother shared. Then my father had asked how I was.

"He did not," Dylan said, "mention the divorce." "She's fine," Dylan had told them. "She's out. At a dinner party." He turned to me and said, "I thought they'd like that. They'd imagine something quiet and elegant."

Dylan was convinced his grandparents separated their impression of my life into two parts. They were pleased with my professional life. But they also still thought of me as a young girl, an eligible case for a young Harvard graduate who would want a "lovely wife and a family to cherish and protect forever." In this regard, Dylan had suggested, they thought of Brynn and him as poised forever somewhere in early childhood.

"Grandmother," Dylan continued, "was, of course, on the extension. So she said"—and he did my mother's authoritative voice very well—"how nice, someone who works for a living?"

"And then," said Brynn, interrupting, "I told him to tell them you were out with a lawyer or something."

"If I can get a word in," he said, "then I told them he was a real nice *doctor*."

"Jewish, I told him," Brynn whispered, laughing, and we were all beginning to laugh.

"Yeah, a Dr. *Rach*singer—German-Jewish, or something," said Dylan. "And I said, 'He has a limousine, Grandfather.' I did not tell him that it was a sixty-three."

"Or," said Brynn, "that the chauffeur has some other connections in Medwin's Landing."

Then Dylan shot such a look at Brynn.

"What's that," I said.

"What?" said Dylan, giving her a grip around the wrist with his strong golden hand.

"That look," I said.

"He happens," Brynn said, "to be a dealer."

"That," said Dylan, "means everyone who buys a joint is a dealer."

"Don't argue," I said. "No one here is buying anyway."

My children were not going to be involved with drugs. I thought of Reilly. I must tell Jennie, and call the hospital to see if he was okay. I touched Dylan's shoulder. "And so," I said, changing that uncomfortable subject very fast, "what did Grandfather say?"

"Oh," said Dylan. "He said he hoped he'd be nice to you; it's time you met someone right. And then Grandmother said, 'An appropriate man.' "

And we all thought it was wonderful. Like so many moments you look at later and you think, What was wrong with that picture?: three people sitting on a bed, laughing. What could be wrong? The charm there is in proliferating family illusions.

8

It would have been nice, I thought, if Hedy had called, if only to thank me for the party. Perhaps he didn't do that sort of thing. Perhaps he hadn't really enjoyed the party. And perhaps he thought I should have called to thank him for taking Reilly to the hospital. My life was too complicated anyway for him. Brynn watched me holding my coffee cup with both hands, grim at the breakfast table. "Get that look off your face," she said. "How do you know he didn't try to call? You've been on the phone all weekend with everyone else in the world."

"I wasn't thinking about that," I said. "Much."

"We ought to get two phone lines anyway," she said.

"Yeah," said Dylan, "one for you and one for Mom."

"That would be good, since you have your own connections," she said.

"The pony express works just fine for me." Dylan glared at her.

"Stop it!" I said. "Stop chewing at each other!"

I wondered if Hedy had asked his father if he had seen me at A.A. meetings. But Scotty wouldn't have told him. "This is an anonymous program. And I go for me," he would have said.

Well, that was Friday, and this was Monday. You'd think a month had gone by, I told myself, and remembered I was always let down after a party. Get out of yourself. I called

Helena, who said Reilly was out of the hospital "Again for today"—"and I'm going in again—for a biopsy." Helena had had a mastectomy two years before, which she had told me about one day as I was sitting just having a cup of coffee at the counter, at a most ordinary time, in a most ordinary tone of voice. Yes. Yes. Stay out of yourself.

I filled in forms for the college in Boston that had accepted Dylan and I called the Rhinelander Florist to send lilacs to St. Cheri. Then Cleo's secretary called to say that I had to come to the city to interview the new Secretary of the Interior, who was supposed to be on someone else's show, but his plans had been rearranged and they'd decided to put him on my show live.

"But I haven't any background on him at all. And this sort of thing you cannot just wing!"

"Cleo says we'll go to the phone-in format. She'll be there and you're not to worry. Every antinuclear group will call in. You could go for weeks and never have to say a word."

"Okay," I said, "now I'm on my way."

As I was leaving, Ivan's office called me with the name of a lawyer who would handle the radio syndication contract, and the name of an accountant. I called the accountant, who said I should consider buying my own house.

"It's a good investment, Margot."

"I know; but I hate to tie up cash," I answered.

"Well, you won't have any to tie up unless you put it where you can't get your hands on it."

"I'll call Fitzgerald Packard and check on it. Promise."

I called Fitz, who fortunately was not in. And then the phone rang again. Brynn's English teacher was calling to discuss her absences. And I said we'd come in the next day to talk to the principal.

"Good luck," the teacher said. "He asked me why I was bothered that Brynn was missing so much school."

"I'll be there with Brynn tomorrow," I said. And I left for the city.

When I arrived at the station I went into Cleo's office. "Well, you won't be pleased," she said. "He's refused to do a call-in show so the whole thing is cancelled. We'll do the taped program we planned. Or you can wing something."

"I'm in no mood." I said.

I stood there. It was all falling apart. The kids. The work. The idiotic illusion that I could survive without Bill. I leaned forward with my hands gripping Cleo's desk. "Nothing ever works out. I'm exhausted and depressed."

"I really haven't got time to deal with this, Margot," Cleo said, picking up one of two ringing phone lines.

My eyes filled with tears. "Well, excuse me," I said. I glared at Cleo. I turned. I slung my bag over my shoulder. I'm going to have to get out, get out of my life. Just for one day. Just out.

And I could smell it. I could see it. I could taste it. I wanted it. I wanted it going down through me. I could not stop it. I loved the taste of it. I loved the look of it. I loved the smell of it. I would sink my teeth into solid rock to get at it right now.

I wanted to sit in a warm dark bar. Sit right up there with loud music drowning it out. Just sit up there numb and hidden. I ran to the elevator. I got in. I heard Cleo coming after me. The doors closed in time. I didn't want to think. Didn't want to be stopped. When the doors opened again Cleo was there. She'd run down five flights. Her hands flew to my shoulders.

"What the hell's the matter with you?"

"Take your hands away. I am going to go and I am going to

get drunk. Just for today. Blind, smashed, potted, out of it. And don't stop me."

"Knock it off." She would not let go. "Look. I know that when a drunk announces she wants to get drunk it means she wants to be stopped. So cut out the crap—you're wallowing in it."

I pulled at her hands. "Don't fight me," I yelled, crying, "that's fine for St. Cheri. Not for me!"

"Listen to me." She shook me. "Let's go have lunch. After we talk, if you still want a drink, I'll leave you to get it."

"You will buy me one," I half queried, taunting, through the tears.

"Never. But give yourself one half hour. You owe me that."

"Why? I don't owe anyone anything." I sobbed. We walked. She trotted to keep up with my angry strides.

"Do you really want Brynn and Dylan waiting at home, like you waiting for Bill? You really want them wondering who the hell to call, where the devil to go looking for you. You want to put them through that?" Cleo tried to put her arm around my shoulder, to walk together, to link elbows. I jerked away, again, again, fixing my hands stubbornly out of reach. "I hated you drunk. I know you're supposed to stay sober for yourself or something—but you have the self-esteem of a cooked goose, so knock it off, Margot. Those kids have been through enough shit." I could feel it going, the gnawing compulsion. And I knew she felt it in the easing of my shoulders.

I sat at the table in the luncheonette she took me to. "Very clever. No booze here," I said.

"You bet your ass," she said, and she went to make a phone call.

In fifteen minutes we were joined by an extremely unruffled St. Cheri. "I might have known." I glared at Cleo. "So go do me something."

"There's nothing so bad, Margot, that a drunk won't make worse."

"I know. Don't preach at me."

"It's okay." St. Cheri grabbed my hands. And I did not pull them back.

"I almost blew it."

"The point is you didn't."

"But it's always there," I said, shaking with fear, "always right there. Suddenly you want it. And everything can go to hell—it's *always* right there."

"No. Not always. Time, Margot. Time."

The next morning I got up. Terror at first. Then relief. No, I did not drink. I called Cleo and thanked her. And I called St. Cheri. First things first. I went with Brynn to school.

The principal said he believed it caused undue stress upon "youth" to have more than two consecutive classes, which he called "learning periods," in a day.

"He makes it sound like you sit there and bleed," Brynn said to me, after this odd conference, where it had been the parent saying the school should be tougher, should make these kids stay in class, while the principal had been giving the reasons why the students shouldn't.

Brynn had explained, "I hate hangin' around school without a class; it's easier to split, even though then it's harder to go back."

"This is a problem with that option; I can identify with that." The principal had nodded.

Brynn started to explode. She was usually flippant, but quiet. But then her fury would bring up just a bit too much and, at last, she'd get angry.

"Look," she had said to me and to the principal, "I like jobs, waitress jobs, clerk jobs, gas jockey jobs, vet assistant jobs, anything, because in school there's nothin' to do. You can look at the other kids and watch them look around at someone else, you can doodle, exchange notes—"

"Maybe," the principal said with such understanding, "you have a problem with teachers, a conflict with authority?"

Who doesn't, I thought, but someone has to be in charge. I did not sound like myself. I have always hated authority.

Brynn stared out the window, biting her lip. She turned her head more away from us. "No, you don't get it. I don't mind teachers; some of them are interesting. I don't mind doing the reading when they ask you, which isn't often, but it stops being interesting when I have to prove I understand or know what I've been reading. You can know something without knowing why. And I'm like that and maybe school is just not for me."

Brynn went to class then. Grim. Then I went to a phone booth and I called Blanche Hutchins to make an appointment to talk about the principal; and, since I was looking under H, I looked up Hedy's name: Wayne Henderson. Then I called Helena and arranged to join her at a lunch meeting.

It was freezing in the Theodore's stable. The bologna sandwiches were already gone and spring was in retreat. Helena rubbed her arms. Scotty was leading the meeting: the topic, his favorite, was self-pity. As usual, he only called on the men. A woman practically had to pour a drink to get his attention. Helena raised her hand twice and then said the topic was good for her because she was going back into the hospital and was beginning to feel sorry for herself until she realized how much love these friends gave her, how lucky she was to live in a time when there was so much help available.

"That's the program working. Attitude insurance," said Scotty. "I'm going to meetings, and not drinking; there's no situation I can't handle."

I thought Helena ought to scream and yell, sometime, just

once, to let go. I believed in the myth that if you were a son of a bitch you wouldn't get cancer. After the meeting Scotty told Helena he was taking Reilly up to a drying-out farm in Massachusetts that night.

"I just have to turn him over," said Helena.

"Tough love," said Scotty, patting Helena on the back as he did with the guys he liked.

"Wonderful," said Helena. We went back to Chickens for hamburgers and coffee. We talked about her prognosis so far—about George's fear, how that fear frightened Helena more than her own. Then she asked, "What have you been up to?"

"You don't need this," I said.

"You're worried about Brynn."

"Oh, Helena. Yes, but you have enough."

"Listen, your situation is my distraction." She clasped my hands between both of hers. "Brynn was okay yesterday. I saw her with Teddy. Or Freddy. I never get those guys straight."

Yes. Freddy. Maybe it was as simple as that. I surely ought to know.

After I left Helena I drove by and saw Brynn's car at the Main Street station. I decided to pull in, gas up and not mention a word about school. As I pulled up to the pump, Brynn came out, cheeks all bright, trailing behind Vince.

"Caterpillars." I grimaced at Brynn, pointing out the mascara marks under her eyes.

"Fatal flaw," quipped Brynn. "Do you want your oil checked, lady?"

"Sure, Mac," I came right back at her. "So I suppose they closed school because of the storm."

"Yep. I went over there and pounded my fists on the doors just trying to get in and they were all shut up, locked up tight."

"Broke your heart," I said.

Brynn got the squeegee out of the pail and worked it

across my windshield. "Must be like you'd feel when your typewriter goes out. I guess there's a power outage on the hill or you'd be up there right now working."

"You oughta get your mom one of them new battery typewriters I heard of," Vinnie said, winking at Brynn.

"That's going to be her birthday present for sure. Okay, lady. That'll be twelve-fifty. And five bucks for the service."

"Highway robbery," I protested. "What service? Oh, I'm buying you a present, I guess."

"Heavy weather. We all get a little something." When Brynn was funny, I could not resist her. And I could tell Brynn had to be funny today. She did not want comfort, advice or sympathy, and if she started thinking about it again she'd get upset and she did not want to be upset.

A man in a pink nylon parka, plaid pants and striped suspenders sat on an oil drum, licking a lollipop, and stared at us through yellow sunglasses.

"I'd really like to talk to you," I said to Brynn. "Can we go for tea, or something?" I got out of the car and leaned against it, my hair blowing in the wind. "I think you should try to tell me what's going on. You're having trouble. Is there somewhere you'd rather be? Another school? Are you unhappy here?"

Brynn whispered, "Stop asking me, stop criticizing, stop moving me around. Just stop." She stalked over to a car that had just pulled up and began filling it with gas. She did not look in my direction. I stood there, my hands lifted where I'd started to raise them, to reach out, to hold Brynn.

The man in the yellow sunglasses with the billowing pink parka said to me, "You have to let go of these kids. They have to find their own way. No one could do it for any of us." Of course the insane have the right answers and this is why they are insane, because they know that the right answers do not work. I stood and looked at Brynn.

She rubbed her hands on her jeans, stamped her feet, blew on her hands and stomped back, ignoring me, to the car she'd been working on. Vince looked at me with the very slightest understanding shrug. Then he flicked his fist at Brynn's forearm in a friendly way. "You doin' okay, kid?"

"Yeah—let's find an engine to take apart."

"You got a name on that engine?" Vince laughed.

"I'm thinkin' of one," Brynn said. "I'm thinkin' of two, maybe. And yes, Mom," she called to me, "I'm dropping my g's. Fuck it." She blinked her eyes and sat down, just for a minute, on a pile of old tires. "That liar. That liar. Don't anyone say a thing to me all day," she said. "I do not want to talk." I sat next to her. She let me put my arm around her shoulders.

"So," I said, "what happened?"

Brynn had driven down to the river to Freddy's favorite place. She had smoked a cigarette and waited. I could imagine her in her car, all in tones of a black and white movie, the tones of this afternoon now as we sat here with the sky darkening and a big storm coming. The wind would have been churning up the river, the water darkening to match the sky.

"I'd parked behind the stand of spruce trees," she said, "and behind the wind, I heard a car and saw the red nose of his Valiant edge out to the border of the parking lot, framed in the trees, and I got out of the car, you know, to surprise him. And I stopped and he was leaning over, his arm around the back of the seat, like when he is with me." She shrugged away now, huddling deeper into herself. I would have done the same. "But he was with this other girl who's in my class. He said he'd been working nights. He lied like I thought he lied." Brynn turned to me, eyes all red, so furious. "But I didn't want to know it, to see it. I stood there, feeling so crazy and angry and hurt and so slow. The girl caught sight of me as he turned to kiss her, I just waved to her, you know, and turned away. I was so sure I was goin' to slip on the mud. I mean you know how it felt, Mom. I know how that car smells, how his face smells, exactly how she felt to be there. I shouldn't be saying that but you know what I mean."

"Oh, Brynn. Oh, yes." Don't go on and on, I told myself.

"I got in my car and I told it to start very quietly, and I even clicked out the tape. Listening to music would have been very dumb and so I just drove real carefully up here and I fetched meatball sandwiches and Cokes for Zack and Vince and I told them I was pissed off, and they kind of talked me out of it and got me working on something to get my mind off it. For a while."

"I know, darling. I know." That is all you ever really want to hear. And she let me hold her hand real tight.

The storm settled in with the darkness, the wind scrolled around the house and through the window frames. I huddled in bed, working on the lineup of shows for next month; to keep a balance of topics. Two political interviews a week, one local, one national; one on a new Broadway show; one live show with someone in town to promote a new movie. One serious writer or artist each week, and then fashion people and, always, always the shows that seemed to get the most response: the ones on love, on how to live a life, and the inevitable ones on the new diet or exercise program to take off what you gain at the new restaurant or using this terrific new cookbook. And then there was always something seasonal. Planning Your Spring Garden Now. And always every year, How to Decrease Your Fuel Bills. Yes. How, please.

There are only two seasons, I decided. Winter and summer. Spring was winter's tease. It seemed colder inside than outside because it was unusual, unexpected. And actually it was colder inside, it dawned slowly on me, because the furnace was not working. Upstairs it was shocking. I thought of a shopping bag lady I'd seen last winter in New York, sitting, only her head showing, inside a large arrangement of packing cardboard cartons, like someone inside an old steam cabinet, her bags piled up against the cartons. She had looked straight ahead, a fringe of gray hair, red cheeks and nose. Fierce little eyes not seeing here, looking far inside. I imagined that being that crazy you did not feel cold.

Once in midwinter when I was walking along the beach in Montauk with Bill, I had put all my attention on the shape of his winey gray shadow moving ahead and across mine as we walked, and I had not felt the cold at all. Yes. You probably had to be in love for positive thinking to work as a hedge against cold.

In my bedroom it was perhaps twelve degrees. There was a pile of laundry on the floor, wrecking the look of the room, laundry I could not do because the machine was broken. I put on long underwear. I put on a sweater. I put on two pairs of long socks. I shook. I slid jeans on over my long underwear and went downstairs.

A tent of blankets had been erected around the fireplace, vaulting the blankets and quilts on the backs of chairs. Alison. "Where on earth did you come from?" I asked. Dylan's girlfriend was in the Good Boarding School. "I'm always delighted to see you, but aren't you in school?" No wonder it had been so quiet. Like a startled fawn Alison pulled up from Dylan's shoulder. Her reflex was surely as much manners as fear. Alison would have been taught that you stand up when an adult comes in the room.

"Does it look like she's in school?" Dylan said.

"Well," Alison said, "we had a recess and I said I was going home. Which I am in a way. My parents are in Bermuda, so I'm here."

The only perfectly brought-up person of her generation in

Medwin's Landing, Alison owned short white gloves and wore an add-a-pearl necklace, and had long silver-blond hair and flawless skin.

Alison and Dylan had met that first summer we had come to Medwin's Landing. Dylan got a job working as a busboy at the country club. Alison was exactly the sort of girl a mother hopes her son will go out with. But Dylan had cut his hair that summer, just enough so that by July he had eased out of his job and into the club as Alison's beau, playing tennis and eating club sandwiches. Brynn had said to him, "Do they know over there that you know us?"

"Get off my case," said Dylan.

By that August Alison had been wearing Dylan's t-shirts and jeans, cut off to show her long, tan legs, cruising around by the river, and eating pizza and cheeseburgers. Senator Jones and his wife, Louise, were only too pleased when it came time for Alison to go back to school. Dylan said they were polite when he showed up at their Labor Day picnic; I suspect they became a bit displeased when he arrived for dessert at their Thanksgiving dinner; they must have been relieved when Alison agreed to spend her Christmas holiday with them in Switzerland; and I knew only too well from Mrs. Jones's letter how apprehensive they were when they got the three-hundred-dollar phone bill featuring calls from Gstaad to Dylan in Medwin's Landing; and according to another note, this time from the senator himself, they were simply grim when Alison's school reported that she stayed on the phone an hour every night talking to Dylan. But if I really believed in love, in its power and magic, how could I deny theirs its own course?

"You aren't going to suffocate in there?" I asked.

"No, they're just going to get stoned," said Brynn, walking in from the kitchen with mugs of hot chocolate for Dylan and Alison.

"Lighten up, Brynn," said Dylan.

"Want a marshmallow, Mom?" Brynn asked. They had molded wire hangers into sticks of a sort and were toasting marshmallows. I took one and burned my tongue.

"Delicious," I said. I decided not to notice Brynn's remark.

"You can't sleep all night in there, can you?" I asked. It seemed the considerate thing to ask. "I'll call someone and get this blasted heat working."

"Blasted is the adjective she saves for when you're around, Alison," said Brynn. "I thought you'd never notice the heat was off, Mom. I already called and they can't do anything."

"I'll call," I said. "You were probably nice to them."

"It generally helps not to scream at people when you need them to do something for you," said Brynn.

"Yes," I said. "But you'll freeze tonight. It's terrible up there."

"That's okay," said Brynn. "I'm staying at Kimmie's. Maybe you could stay with Helena." Gentle Brynn always looking out for herself, but also always looking out for me.

I went upstairs and called Tollan's Heating Service. "All lines are busy," a voice said, pretending, I thought, to be a recording so as not to have to deal with irate customers. "Due to unseasonably cold weather, our servicemen are all out on call now, but we'll place your name on the list and as soon as someone can get to your area—"

"Let me talk to Andy," I said.

"Is this a personal call?"

"You bet."

"Okay." The voice lost its recorded tone and shrieked across the office. I knew, from hearing Andy at A.A. meetings, exactly how the system worked.

"I am sitting here freezing, with my two children turning blue, and you are hanging out with five bags of sugar in your goddamn cup of coffee." I sounded exactly like Cleo when she was trying to get something done, and, of course, it always worked, which Cleo had figured out years ago.

"You got it," Andy said. "I can't do anything, honey, until we get you another motor. I got one comin' out from Hartford first thing tomorrow."

"We'll be dead by then."

"Think of what people did before heaters. Put on another sweater. Where's your gratitude?"

"On ice." I put on another sweater. Maybe I should call Helena. The phone rang. It would be for the children. I let it ring. It was too cold to move.

"Mom. Will you pick up the fucking phone," Dylan shrieked from downstairs.

"Will you watch your fucking language!" I screamed back. Oh, my God. I forgot Alison was here. Rats. Brynn was right. She intimidated me. But girls like Alison always had. I'm as bad as her parents. Categorizing and classifying.

"Hello," I snapped into the phone.

"That's a real swell hello. Should I call back and we'll start again."

"Yes." I hung up the phone.

It rang again.

"Well, hello," I said sweetly. "Hedy, is that you?"

"What's going on?" He did not drop his g's. He only does it for effect, I'll bet. The Rocksinger persona.

"I am freezing. The furnace quit and they can't get parts until tomorrow. I am thinking of flying to Florida but I'm too cold to move."

"I have heat here. Why don't you come over?" he said, and I could tell by sounds that he was cleaning up, phone to his ear as we talked. Because of doing so much radio, I guess, I hear things very precisely. Everything except music, that is, which I hear, but not with training. I love guessing at sounds: this would be a cup and saucer he is washing so I can have coffee. And he is now throwing out beer cans so I won't see that he can drink.

"My dad isn't going to be home."

"I'm too cold." But I took my boots out of the closet. Perhaps I decided to hear so well because my mother has this eye thing. Nonsense, I had my hearing before she did that. Will I capitalize by pretending to be deaf when I decide I don't want to work anymore? Do genes really hold our life plots? No. No. Please no.

"Bundle up," Hedy said. "I'm putting on some tea. I'll pick you up in five minutes. Do you like Constant Comment? Or do you always drink coffee?"

"That's a bother."

"It's a bother but I don't mind bothering."

"Every time I see you there is something complicated going on with my life." All both times.

"I was wonderin' what I missed."

"Oh, a couple of broken cars, some busted machines, screwed-up deadlines, nothing unusual."

I put on my jeans over my long underwear, a muffler, and I pulled on a crimson woolen hat. I went downstairs again, a large canvas bag over my shoulder. I put on huge rubber boots and fastened all the clasps so I would not change my mind.

"I'm going over to Hedy's to get warm."

"Now that's a bright idea," said Brynn, who was bundled up in her muffler, hat and down jacket.

"We're going to stay right here by the fire," said Dylan.

"Not that you could move if you tried," Brynn said.

"Now, Mrs. Spinning," Alison said, "we're just fine."

"Mallowed out, is it?" I commented, taking another marshmallow.

"Bad joke, Ma," said Dylan.

Hedy was announced by Spike. Brynn grabbed his collar. "Down. He is not crazy about you."

The wind around him as I opened the door made it look as though he had been blown all the way over. His cheeks were slapped red, his hair all blown forward. He was carrying an electric heater.

"I thought you guys could use this."

"Hey, man, that's really neat," said Dylan.

"Hedy—that's thoughtful," I said. He was completely unlike his father. Genes do not determine life plots. Don't be crazy.

"They won't freeze their little toesies," said Brynn, taking the heater from Hedy, smiling at him, wanting to please. I liked Hedy's swift look at her which seemed to say, we're the competent ones here.

And then Dylan said quickly, "We'll put the heater in the kitchen while you make us chili. Would you and Mom like to stay—Brynn makes great chili." He laughed and he stood up, which, for Dylan, was a gesture of considerable graciousness.

Hedy sneezed. The dog! "I think we'd better go," I said. I preferred the idea of staying, everyone together cooking, getting warm. "But since Brynn is going out, why don't you guys make your own chili?"

"Because mine is better," said Brynn. She preferred to stay too. Or was I now making assumptions, getting her genes into line.

"I'm sure it is," said Hedy. He winked at Brynn. She sparkled. Hedy sneezed again. If we stayed one minute longer I would be asking Hedy if he minded if we stayed a while.

"You guys better go," said Brynn, considerately, handing Hedy a Kleenex.

"Have a real good time, Mrs. Spinning," said Alison.

"She certainly will die trying," said Dylan, laughing again.

"Mom, call if you stay over, okay?" Brynn said.

"Oh, I won't even be late," I said. I blushed. I did not look at Hedy.

"Tsk," from Dylan.

"Don't be fresh to your mother," said Alison, slapping him on the arm. He rumpled her hair.

Brynn followed us to the door. "Thanks again for the heater," she said to Hedy.

"No problem," he said. He patted her shoulder. "Stay warm."

I looked at Hedy. He had the distant, switched-off expression he got when I even mentioned the kids. He could put on friendliness for a few minutes, I could see that, but the irritation welled up fast. I wanted to tell him: they are extensions of me; when we tangle together you can not find where I begin and they leave off. And it is as well we will not do that. To make sure, I had removed my flannel nightgown and perfume from the canvas bag and put them away again.

9

Hedy was driving the limousine himself tonight. "This is your real car?" I asked.

"Some people own a bunch of weird Chevies. Others have one excellent limo. Are you cold over there? I left the motor on so you'd get warm."

"I'm cold now." I watched, all alert, as he drove, wanting to see exactly how to get back fast just in case. Branches raged and prayed. Here and there Hedy swerved to avoid fallen trees and broken limbs. All color was swept into the action of the wind.

The house Hedy and Scotty lived in was a small frame river house which had been carefully winterized, on a street well in from the river. It was furnished with heavy, upholstered brown furniture, an aqua rug and a maple dining room set.

"It is so tidy," I said. Maybe you do have to trade love to achieve serenity.

"That's about the best thing you can say for it," Hedy said.

"No, it's very warm." Perhaps he was not into sex, perhaps sex was too messy.

"I like the touches you put on a house," Hedy said. He took my mittens, my muffler, hat and jacket and put them in a closet. "My mom used to do a little of that."

"You do, too," I said. I noticed he had put fruit, still

beaded with moisture from the refrigerator, in a glass bowl in the center of the table.

He poured tea in two mugs and put sticks of cinnamon in them, and heated up an Entenmann's pecan coffee cake. "That's what we have at meetings," I said, pulling off a piece of the cake.

"I thought it would help you feel more at home," he said. He was sitting across from me now, leaning back on the two rear legs of his chair, tilting it back and forth.

There was a silence.

"Maybe you might want to stay over, I thought," he said. Which I knew he would say, but I was still not sure if he was sure what he had in mind. I looked at him and decided he meant exactly what he said.

"Well, if you have a spare room. I could call the children and tell them I won't be home until tomorrow. I think, frankly, they expected I might stay here." Of course—I looked around—what if he doesn't have a spare room. I would surely not want to sleep in Scotty's room. "If it wouldn't bother you, since you offered, it certainly won't bother me to share, or I could sleep right here. I'm so tired—you get tired from the cold, you really do, you know. The wind rattling through your head."

"What do you think I'm talking about?" he said. He sat forward now and leaned toward me with his hands on the table.

We stared at each other for a moment. Then I looked down at my hands as if I'd never seen them before. "Well," I said, not looking up, "it's hard to discuss it like this, with you just sitting over there." I laughed, very uneasily.

"I could get closer maybe, but," he said, "I didn't want to make a move until you let me know it might be all right."

"It might be," I said. "Is," I added.

"Well," he said shyly, "I'm going to take a shower. Would

you like to come in and lie down?" He avoided referring directly to the bedroom. "It's funny that this is so difficult for us." He touched my hands quickly. I held on to his.

"Yes," I said, and I followed him into the bedroom and sat on the edge of the bed. He clicked on a tape and went into the shower. This room was obviously where he lived. It was pristine; no heaps of socks, books, sweaters, underwear, papers and so forth like Dylan's. The bed was even made, with a chenille spread and a small round cushion between the pillows. In each corner, however, rather like peculiar corner cabinets, were massed speakers; and all the machinery for music was set about on shelves on the walls: tapes and albums, instrument cases and sheet music, all carefully placed, clearly valued and well maintained. I had left my house with a new friend and was sitting here waiting for a stranger, but perhaps men always became strangers when you first made love to them. I could not actually remember. Perhaps because I had always begun with a drink I'd never really had the chance to notice how it was.

He came out of the shower, smelling fresh, slightly tropical, a coconut perhaps. He was wearing a towel, like a loincloth. I avoided looking directly at him, but I had an impression of shoulders, drops of water at the ends of dark curls about his neck, knees, the beautiful modeling of his back. I had taken off my boots and jeans and sat wrapped, in my long underwear, in a blanket which had been folded on the foot of the bed. "I—uh." How to begin? How to just say I wanted to go into the bathroom. "I'll be right out" was as close as I could get.

"You're taking the blanket?" he asked.

When I came out, my clothes were off and carefully folded under my arm, which I had done for his benefit. I was wearing the blanket. He was sitting on the bed brushing his hair with a silver hairbrush.

I sat next to him. "Can I brush your hair?" I asked.

"Sure." I felt warmer, easier now. His hair was like heavy satin.

"That was my mom's brush." He paused. "Your hair is really pretty." He turned off all the lights and left the bathroom door ajar.

I put myself on the bed in my best naked position, the light chenille spread draped over my stomach. I hoped it was dark enough so he could not see the dappled details of my body. Young people weren't, however, as critical perhaps as we think. I remembered when I had stayed with Cleo at the beach once, I'd taken off my bathing suit to run into the shower fast and she had said, "Your body's okay. From the way you complain I thought you'd be in pieces."

Rita Coolidge was singing, *Your love is making me higher* . . . I was full of hope that my feelings were going to come back.

Your love is lifting me higher . . .

He turned toward me, the soft light from the bathroom glowing around his body, so lean, so pretty, look at those legs. I reached my arms up to his. With a man, even this tender young one, I realized, I tried to match strength, to use ferocity. I touched Brynn and held her differently from the way I touched and held Dylan. Is that how we perpetuate the denial of vulnerability in boys, the acceptance of it in girls. It was automatic. The attempt to be gentle would not be unerotic, but simply a different sort of eroticism. I felt Hedy's breathing tighten and quicken; it could get hotter, and we would grasp and pounce and tangle and get hot and wild and fierce, and I didn't want that to happen yet.

"Listen, just relax," he said, softly, gently.

"I am relaxed," I said.

"You're fine, just fine," he said. He approached me tentatively. I wanted to stay with this stroking, kissing, patting, this childlike idea of sex, as elegantly dangerous as the seductive exchanges I had with my children, exchanges that one note darker, one look longer, would shatter forever the melancholy power of completely unconsummated love. On this plateau, from which, I could tell, we were both about to fall, this tentative embracing, I could pretend there was a sort of graceful, aesthetic sex I might like better.

He moved his hands now the way one might play a hot guitar. His fingers were fast. Perhaps a little too fast. I wanted to concentrate, to think of the images I thought of by myself. "It always takes me a while. Never works the first few times." I should not have said that. How many times are the first few.

"Hey, don't just smile at me, get into it," he whispered. He urged, "I want to get you really wild, really going. No posing now, you're fine."

I was posing, yes, lying so my flesh would be taut around me. He must have thought an older woman would be all easy and passionate, that I'd teach him things he never even dreamed of. He moved over on me, lifting above me, bending, kissing my breasts, his hair sweeping over my shoulders, as he stayed with it, kissing and kissing, tightening into nibbling, tense, drawing, sucking kisses.

Oh, this he understands, I thought, falling a bit into feeling, twisting and moving and wrapping my legs around his body. "You like this," he said, "you like it." He swept back his hair and looked up at my face, looking so intently that I threw my arm over my eyes. Then I turned and moved up and over him and he turned on his back, and I came up on top of him, and he pulled me down with his hands nipping and nibbling, making a harmonica out of my breasts, and I was moving, now really feeling.

"You can, you can," he whispered. My hair streamed with sweat, and I grabbed him with one hand, settling down over him. Oh, don't think of it like that, don't, I told myself, as I saw myself settling over him like a billowing white parachute. I laughed and I shivered and I pulled away from the feeling.

"Don't get out of it," he said, "stay with it," and he pulled me over down on him and stroked my hair as my face lay next to his now. "Poor little lady," he said. "You won't let yourself get it."

"Oh, Hedy, what a sweet thing to say." I was not sure I liked it at all. But he meant well and he touched, oh, how well he touched.

"I never get off right away," I said, so quietly, close to his chest. "But I want you to come now, but on top of me, come now." I locked my legs around his back and clasped his head to mine, whispering in his ear. "Higher, come in deeper. Do it now, come now, come," softly I whispered in my deepest voice, and he did and then he turned on his side, and I turned and held him in my arms as he plunged instantly into sleep.

I napped for perhaps an hour. I woke up and watched him for a while, lean and still, in his beauty sleep, dreaming perhaps of himself. I sat on the floor in the living room glancing at the few books there, which included our A.A. Big Book. I remembered Jennie telling me about a man, her first "older man," who had only the latest feminist best sellers on his bookshelves. He wanted to get along with women now that he was sober, he told her. But he hated his mother. "He would never touch breasts," Jennie had said.

Even though the heat was good, I should have brought the flannel nightie. I put on Hedy's short gold shaving kimono. This was the sort of man's robe made for tall women with long legs.

The wind was dying down. Outside the sky was cobalt, dawn coming soon. I tried to bury a flurry of sneezes in Kleenex. I heard him getting up, coming in, in bare feet.

"Oh, there's my robe," he said. He was naked. I looked at

him for an instant in the early soft blue light. "I heard you sneezin'. Are you allergic to me?" he asked. He kneeled down behind me and kissed my neck. "Listen, sex isn't such a big deal. We can take it or leave it if that's what's bothering you."

Sniffing into a crumbling Kleenex, I said, "I liked sex a lot better when I used to fake coming."

He picked up the old Kleenexes and put them into the wastebasket, then brought the basket over near me. "Why? That must have been awful."

"No," I said, "at least one person would have a good time, thinking what a lovely time I was having."

"The one person was you," Hedy said, "doing a number. I would have known. We're not idiots. I can always tell when chicks fake."

"Do they still—young girls?"

"Sure." He rubbed my shoulder. "Do you want a few vitamins?"

"Well," I said, "I was very good at it."

"You don't know that. Maybe they let you think you were; maybe they acted as if they believed you. I think that whole bit, 'good in bed,' means that everyone is doing a good act. So they come off with Grammys, big deal. I'm sorry you didn't have a good time last night." He looked so rueful, like kids when they give you something they have made, and they suddenly see, as you unwrap it, that it isn't very attractive.

"I had a good time. It was very earnest, like friends trying to be helpful." I wanted him to take me in his arms and kiss me, to try again without trying so hard.

"Why don't I make you some coffee. I know you guys can't think without it."

"What guys?" I laughed. "Adults?"

"No—that's crazy—A.A.'s, I mean." He went into the kitchen and got out a can of coffee and put water into a pot.

"I think your dad and I are not crazy about each other." I laughed again, pulled the robe tighter.

"Well, we won't tell him anything," said Hedy, sounding very young.

I would not say he resembles Scotty. At that age you don't want to be at all like your parents. "Maybe that's a feeling I was catching—something about being in his house." I wondered if Alison was uncomfortable in my house.

"It wasn't a great place to begin," Hedy said. He handed me a cup of coffee. Strong and black. He understood that. "I have a plan in mind if you're free for the weekend." He stood near the counter, one ankle crossed over the other, his body hair like carefully placed foliage.

"Yes," I said. To whatever it was.

10

"Get dressed," he said. So brightly. "We're going to the Big Apple. I got tickets to the Springsteen concert. And we're staying at the Plaza Hotel." It was Hedy. It was March. It was Saturday morning. And it was ten o'clock.

"You're on!!" The Plaza! I flew about, getting fluffy and fresh as I could, packing up my most seductive things in my suitcase. Hedy might think this weekend was about the concert and the fancy hotel: I decided it was going to be about making love. "I'm going to the city, to see Bruce Springsteen," I announced to the children, who were arranged around the TV.

"My mother, the groupie," said Brynn, in her nightgown.

"My mother, the chicken hawk, is more like it," said Dylan.

"Mom, I'm kind of out of cash. Can you leave me a little?" Brynn asked. "I want to pick up some food. Freddy is coming over later." She looked so happy and allowed me to hug her.

"Excitement for all," said Dylan.

"Cool it," Brynn snapped.

"I'll give you twenty dollars, Brynn," I said; "that should be okay. You'll make something wonderful. Dylan, are you all right?"

"I'm fine."

"He's just cranky," Brynn said, "because Alison's gone back to school."

I was pleased that he always seemed to have enough

money left from his after-school jobs. He had new friends, too. Deep male voices called now on Fridays, asking for him, voices I didn't recognize. I imagined these school friends clothed in preppie outfits, boys perhaps from Westchester County whose parents had tennis courts Dylan would play on in summers to come. The kind of boys I wanted Dylan to be like; the kind of boys I would like Brynn to go out with; the kind of boys Alison's parents would surely have in mind. Was it detestable snobbism? Or did I just want the order and safety I liked to believe these lives represented?

"So, navy blue weather's beginning," Hedy said to me. We both had put on navy blue blazers with our jeans. He wore a navy blue turtleneck; mine was indigo—almost purple.

"Such a coincidence," I said. I had seen him coming down the path and changed my pink shirt and tweed jacket quickly.

"Aren't we cute," said Hedy.

"You look like a dynamic duo for the Mafia," said Dylan.

"I brought you guys a couple of the new Rocky Rhodes albums. We're dropping over there today and it reminded me I had a couple of freebies."

"Hey, thanks a lot, really," said Dylan.

Since I had not heard this part of the plan, I decided right away I might not care for it. I had heard of Rocky Rhodes, but wasn't sure who he was.

"You know them?" asked Brynn. "Freddy thinks they're really good."

As we pulled up in front of the glossy apartment building in Hedy's limousine, I asked, "Is this where he lives?"

"It's not a he," Hedy said, grabbing my bag and swinging it over his shoulder with his own. He was brusque now; in his professional mode. "It's a them. God. What have you got in here?"

"Oh. Things." I smiled up at him. "Later," I said.

Hedy explained that Rocky Rhodes was not a group, but two brothers who had come out of country and western into rock. "One of them won't be here, but my manager, Wally, has the tickets for tonight's concert, and I want him to have my new tapes. He'll be up there helping Al get his act together for a concert. Louis, the other brother, is drying out somewhere."

Hedy rang the bell. We waited. "I heard somewhere everyone can be described as bird, muffin or horse. Watching you now, you are all bird."

"I like that," I said.

The door was opened before I could tell Hedy that I thought he was horse with cheeks of muffin.

They must have just moved in, I thought. When I was very young, I had visited friends who were already married, girls newly out of their parents' "gracious family homes," as the real estate ads called them. I had regrouped my own life too many times to bear the reminder of how it all felt and looked. A silver Lichtenstein poster hung on the wall over the purple velvet couch. Two very thin, very young women, blushed with henna on hair and sepia tones on cheekbones, sat looking at *Vogue*, one blow-drying the other's hair. A large black satin ottoman faced a TV set tuned to *The Best Years of Our Lives*.

It was only one o'clock in the afternoon, but you could not tell whether they were beginning or ending their day. The person who opened the door was Wally. He had a hearing aid—which was surely understandable. Amazing that any of them kept their hearing intact.

"My, what a lovely large window you have," I said, in the direction of the girls on the couch, one of whom must surely be the lady of the house and the other, smirking at Hedy, clearly the girl he had told me he was not seeing anymore.

"Hi, everyone," said one of the girls, loudly, over the hum of the dryer, plunging forward while the other continued blowing under the hair at the nape of her neck.

"That's Sheila, Wally's wife," Hedy said, "and Denise. Hello, Denise. This is Margot Fox, who does a great radio show." Maybe Hedy had hoped Denise would think I was doing research on an article about him. Denise looked cross, her eyes narrowed within their circles of kohl.

I quickly said, "I'm hoping I might do an interview about the group."

"I can tell you anything you want," said Denise. "I can hardly hear over this thing, Sheila. You done?" She shut off the dryer.

"And don't believe any of it," Sheila said, sweeping a mouthful of hair away.

Denise was exactly what I would have expected, tiny, slender, with sexy, reddish, permed hair. Her eyes were wide and blue under the kohl.

"You talk mostly about sex and relationships, don't you?" Sheila said. "I've heard your show. Almost called in a couple of times."

"Yes—but we talk about other things," I said. "Politics, work, social issues, although it's important to talk about sex." I smiled. "It isn't the easiest subject for anyone."

I watched Hedy, who had been half listening while he was talking to Wally, who apparently had his hearing aid off because Sheila shouted, "Turn on your fucking aid, man."

"Wally only likes to listen to music, not people talking," Sheila explained to me. Sheila had a certain weary competence, like a lot of performers' wives, like the theatrical wives I watched backstage when I used to visit my father to see his sets being put together.

"Do you guys want some beer or a Coke or something? I think we got a couple of joints around. Or bread and peanut butter?" Sheila went into the kitchen off the living room. Where did I get the idea all rock people lived like royalty? Most of them probably lived like all of us when we were young, with friends, poaching and perching, sending out for food. Rather like I still lived, actually.

"Sheila eats it by the spoonful," Wally drawled. "Stands in front of the icebox eatin' jam right out of the jar with a spoon. When she's stoned she can eat a whole jar of Super Chunk. I guess I have to hear a piece of that tape you got," Wally said. Then he muttered to me, "She's goin' to look like a hog time she gets thirty."

"Fuck off," said Sheila, peering out of the kitchen.

"We're goin' to a—" Hedy stopped himself. Denise was smiling at him, her high-heeled black patent leather boots twitching. "Something Margot has to cover."

"I know where you're going," said Denise. "Hedy goes to more concerts than anybody. I got so I couldn't tell who I was listening to."

"Wally," Hedy asked, "have you got those tickets?"

"What?" Wally yelled.

I was amused by the discomfort in the room. I wanted to tell Hedy that this was the value of going out with an older woman. We understood everything. Hedy must have received more encouragement about his tapes than Wally was showing today or he would have given up by now. Hedy looked so urgent, eager, and yet when he talked to Wally, Wally only nodded his head coolly. Hearing aid or not, it was too familiar to me, too much like conversations I had had with program directors at radio stations.

Hedy could have had the tickets sent, of course, and mailed the tapes. But he had clearly wanted to deliver them personally. He had such hope for enthusiasm, the positive and instant response you always long for.

There was a shout from the back of the apartment. "Denise, Sheila, one of you get me out of this thing."

"What are you doin', Al?" Denise shouted back, not moving from the couch. She looked at Hedy, a look implying everything and anything to make him jealous. "Al is so funny," she said.

"You got your space suit on?" Sheila yelled.

"Come on out and show off that thing," Hedy called. "Wait 'til you see this, Margot."

"He's making a big deal out of nothing," said Wally, looking at one half of the Rocky Rhodes, who was wearing a silver lamé jump suit with a curious array of wire on it. "He is not wearing that shit. He's too goddamn old, for one thing. You look like a burn out, baby."

This was not the right person to be handling Hedy, I decided. Even if they're crazy, you don't talk like this to your people.

"I'm bustin' right out of this," Al said.

He had long red hair, was lean as a snake, with freckles and mean little black eyes, so unattractive. He must be very, very good. And to think he had a brother in such bad shape they had him cooling off somewhere.

"You're getting as wild as Steve Tyler," Wally added.

"Steve Tyler's with Aerosmith," Denise said to me.

"I know, dear," I said. How happily I remembered something from *Rolling Stone*. "He told me a marvelous story," I said, determined to make it sound as if I had interviewed him myself, "about coming back from this exhausting tour. He had gone home and slept that first night in his own bed, and when he woke up he dialed room service—'on my own damn phone,' he said. I feel like that after going around the country doing interviews, so we really understood each other."

"Oh yeah, I read that story, too," said Denise. She walked, with a kind of a drawl in her hips, over to Al, who could barely move. "Turn around. Look at that terrific ass."

I could tell Hedy was embarrassed for her, and angry. Even when something is over you don't want to see your former person coming on to someone new. Not in front of you.

"Dan Hartman had one like that with a guitar built right into it," Hedy said.

"Yeah, see, Wally." Al struck a pose. "Under lights it's gonna be dynamite."

"On him it sucks," Wally said, opening a beer. "Like I said, Hartman's young, you're over it, baby."

"And I think we ought to go," I said. I knew when I talked like this there was never any question. I looked at Hedy. He took the tickets.

"Sorry about that," he apologized in the elevator.

"I am going to talk to Ivan," I said. This was impossible. "You are, in my professional opinion, beyond that kind of scene. Let's go drop off our things at the Plaza and take a walk," I said.

"I wouldn't want you to get the idea," Hedy said, "that rock people are all like that."

"Oh, I know they're not," I said. "They're just like you and me. They get jealous, hostile, and when they're strung out, loony and combative. But you need someone totally unlike that to manage your career. And not deaf, for openers."

With me rooting for him it could be a real beginning. I snapped, "And stop droppin'—I mean dropping your g's!"

"What?" he said.

"Nothing. I'm sorry. I forgot myself."

I walked alongside him now to the car, my boots clomping on the sidewalk. "Sounds," Hedy said, "like those boots are goin' to cut footprints right down to bedrock."

We checked into the Plaza, and hand in hand, arms swinging between us, we strolled down Fifth Avenue to Bendel's on Fifty-seventh, where I bought both of us sunglasses with candy-apple red frames.

"But I haven't got you a present yet," said Hedy.

"You have," I said. "You." I touched his nose with my forefinger. We looked in the mirror at our faces together, grinned and stared, wide-eyed, making faces at each other. People watched us happily. Everyone, I guess, loves to look at a happy couple in early spring. Such hope it brings out. And the two of us knew, as lovers do, that we were being watched and, in this early expansiveness, we shared their high good spirits.

We took the Fifth Avenue bus down to the Village and bought raisin buns and fresh-squeezed orange juice. Hedy bought a helium-filled silver balloon shaped like a heart. He tied it on my wrist. I imagined Cleo walking by; she would say, "Oh, that's very cute. The new romantic Hindenburg look."

Hedy said, "Your present."

We walked down to Soho, stopping in galleries. I explained some of the pictures, talked about some of the artists, and then I listened as Hedy took me into a music shop and showed me lyrics on a Springsteen album. "You'll like it better, I think, if you've seen the words. You're more into words than music."

"Oh, I'm sure I'll like the sound," I promised him. I tried on a cherry red forties jacket in a little store with two pale young women wearing Love That Red lipstick who were not amused.

"They think if they're really aloof," Hedy said, "it shows the clothes are so good they're doing you a favor to let you buy them."

"They confuse hostility with status," I said.

"Exactly what I was trying to say," he said.

He bought me a bunch of violets from a kid on a corner. We walked into the Broome Street Restaurant to have supper before the concert.

I looked around the restaurant. When Cleo and I were not being fancy we would sometimes go to the rough, "in" hamburger places, where they would put ketchup on the table, where you'd see big famous newsmen at the bar, drinking, talking about contracts and going home despondent, which was the condition in which they believed they were most effective. Here there were more of the very young who still believed success would make their troubles go away; they flocked to this place like the young cyclists pedaling happily into the garden of the Finzi-Continis, eating their blithe food and drinking wine and discussing the new idea that would change their lives.

"I'll have to bring Brynn here. She should spend more time in the city. I don't want her to become provincial." I looked everywhere now except at him.

"I've always liked getting into the city," he said quickly. I did not hear that he was trying gently not to talk about my kids; I went right on, talking about them.

"They were both raised here, you know. It gives them more curiosity, I think." I stopped. Finally. He wants to talk about himself.

"Someday," he said, "I'm going to have my own apartment in the city, just to stay over, and a big place in the country that's mine. That's my real dream." I started to say, "My parents did that . . ." but that was like talking about the kids. However, I looked away from Hedy for an instant, just one second really, and spotted Piero Frasconi. I waved. "He does these murals on the buildings down here," I said. I could have stopped there. I didn't. "He did an incredible backdrop for one of my father's last sets. It was an Off Broadway thing—I never thought he'd do Off Broadway, but the play had unusually rich images . . ." I paused. "You know, I can hear my father's words, hear his voice. I used to sit like this at coffee shops on Forty-fourth or Forty-fifth. I'd meet him after school and he'd talk about his work. No work can ever be as engrossing as he could make his sound. His enthusiasm—"

"You're not talking to me," Hedy said.

I watched Hedy carefully cut his cheeseburger down the middle. Riveted I would be. To him.

"We like each other," I said. "And I do want to keep it that way. I have not been attentive." I lined up my snow peas in rows, then, dipped them in the sauce from the fish, and began to eat them with my fingers.

"You shouldn't worry," he said, his manner edgy. "You could use me as a kind of social experiment." He watched me eating. "A case history—younger man, older woman—and move on when it's over. People like you and me are people eaters."

"Really? We're that tough?" I said. "I thought I was just into snow peas right now. Perhaps I am biting too sharply?" His smile was quick and cold.

Maybe with each twist, each love gone wrong, I had grown tougher, without knowing, hardened into emotional silence, which was why my heart did not pound with Hedy as it had with Bill. Maybe I had stopped believing in love and the stopping had calcified me. Maybe I'd accepted that I'd never again feel that burning kind of love. This would be a light sort of thing; I would make it easy to tease, easy to hold back, so it would be easy to part. I would control it. Of course.

"Yes, maybe we are, that tough," I continued, "and when you're a big star, when you make it, you'll get yourself that blonde in the Rolls I saw you eyeing."

"You miss nothing," he blurted out. "And with one of those ladies I'll make all the decisions about everything." I felt the sweetness of the day leaving; I was not surprised.

"Or she'll let you think you do. You made all the decisions about today, or didn't you notice that?" I would control it? Why is the conversation so uncomfortable, then. Why do I feel like this? Change the subject fast, I thought, and added, "At least you are not into the New Vulnerability. I've heard so many young guys in A.A. say, 'I'm too vulnerable to work.' You're luckily still steeped in the Work Ethic."

"Well, I come from working-class people, so it figures," he said with a little deep hostility. I control nothing.

"I don't know what that means," I said. "I know I have to make it. I'm not inheriting anything, you know."

"Sure, like your kids," he said, "who will have nothing to worry about."

"Hedy, I shouldn't even pick up on that—there's so much resentment; it's such an incorrect assumption. We're in the same field, essentially; you know how it comes and goes. You were raised by a drunk; so were my kids—now we're all just trying to do the best we can." Now I was closer to Scotty. What would he say?

"Let's stay in the now, Hedy," I said.

He glared at me. "I heard that before—I don't choose to be bitter," Hedy said. "It's there sometimes—that's why I'm best when I'm working out songs or arrangements. I have to lose myself in the music. I can only lose it in the music."

"Hedy, that's how all the best musicians must be."

Angling, grasping for success, in his rough road coming up, Hedy must have jutted this way and that, the dark and light forces within him constantly at war and of course they would explode sometimes into this anger. I was sure his drive, his huge ambition might collide with his recognition of what was authentic. How to be good but fast enough please, because I could see the right brands were important, the right symbols, including the right agent. I should reassure him.

"Hedy, you know it's going to happen for you. I know Ivan will represent you and that's just the beginning."

He brightened. We were talking about him.

"I know my attitude is not so hot right now," he said, "and if I do make it it will be a combination of attitude and being worth it. I want to be genuine and appreciative, though I know that can get into compromises that will be at odds with what I want, which is, I guess—I don't fool you—money and fame. And if you compromise you get bugged about it later. I cannot get it straight." He looked so perplexed. He could not arrive at a point of safety or conviction in either mode and so tripped himself up constantly.

"Hedy, you have a real conflict—we all have something like it. There's this materialistic nature snapping at the tail of the talented guy whose longing for appreciation is whipped by impatience." I opened my hands wide and shrugged lightly. Then I touched his chin. "It's okay."

"That simple." He laughed. "I like when you explain things like that, when you talk like you do in some of the interviews; half of it goes right by—but I like it."

"Don't patronize yourself. It does not go right by for a second."

He looked at me. "I did make all the decisions today, I guess. And it's been okay with you? I like to do that. Does it drive you crazy?"

"No," I said. "I like it. Today. But you can't count on me. I'll want to make all the decisions, probably tomorrow."

He smiled at me. And, having finished his cheeseburger, he dipped the tip of his napkin ever so quickly into his water glass and neatly wiped his fingertips.

At least his manager understood the first thing to learn about being an agent: get your clients good seats to everything.

Suddenly here they came fast onto the stage; it was alive and they started. People were pounding thighs on all sides and Hedy became one of them; his hair bounced to the driving sound. Pounding in this old theatre cannot be good. But even when my friends had screamed "Go, go, go" at Krupa and Kenton, I had not known how to go with the beat and had expected to be trampled to death on the dance floor. I froze in disorientation. The only person here of my generation was the large black saxophone player. I looked as if through a telescope, peering right down the cylinder of light from my eyes to his double-breasted, white linen suit.

He shifted from leg to leg, just blowing such a dirty sound. The place turned into a hot, young animal. Get the heat, the sound and the frenzy, be here with it, don't fight it, feel it, I told myself, and I went into it and when they all applauded, I stood up and cheered, fists raised, and when they moved and yelped and called out for more and more, I called out for more and more. And then they lit matches and lighters all over the theatre.

"They're setting it on fire!" I shouted into Hedy's ear. I grabbed his arm. He patted me. He laughed. "They're showing they want more. It's okay. Happens all the time." He stroked my shoulder. "It's really okay."

I did not want to see it, to see such feeling. I fear the animal crowd because the animal is me. To look at it was catching.

"The saxophone," I said to Hedy as we were leaving, "that's sex. Never mind the rest of it. You must, whatever you do, have a saxophone involved. But that one, my God!"

Hedy moved me protectively through the crowd. "Your eyes are shining! You liked it. I knew you would. You'll like a lot of things now. Lady, I'm going to show you a whole new world, and that's just the beginning. Now we're going to this new disco down on Third Street. Just see what's going on." He put his arm around my shoulder. "Unless you're tired?"

"No. I stay up all night. But I'm a lousy dancer."

He said, "You don't have to worry about it. No one notices. Just do your thing."

We waited in a basement entrance filled with young people, mostly guys in t-shirts and jackets with sleeves pushed up, some with crew cuts, all with eyes looking above each other, around, but never at other eyes. Courtiers, centuries ago, sniffing snuff must have had such a look. Vagueness, detachment standing in where style is insecure.

Finally we went upstairs through the cellar door. One floor was filled with milling people, like a store opening where they had forgotten to put out the goods, except the goods were the people, glazed, eyes not seeing each other. A black girl in white bobby sox and high heels, with an outfit entirely of white balloons, wafted through, like someone in a kids' pageant representing Clouds. And there were boys in black harnesses over t-shirts, like doped cart horses.

Up more stairs, in a room flickering with strobe lights, every dancer was practicing its own strut, asses out like so many apples to bite.

The music was of such a loudness that you could not hear it, and we moved in and Hedy just started prancing, swinging, jogging in place; he did a twirl and took off his jacket and tied the sleeves around his waist and I watched and did it too; he hiked his shoulders, he tossed his head, jutted his arms and knees like a figure on an Egyptian frieze and everything Hedy did I did on the next beat, at a different angle, and every time I moved he grinned and did a newer and odder sort of step; a move, a pose, a lurch, a lunge, a whirl or thrust. The strobe lights flashed and he became a figure in a silent movie, in the instants between light flashes he split out of sight, reappearing somewhere else in another pose. Hedy here one second, left arm raised, another second, chin raised, mouth open, both arms over his head, now his eyes closed, then his arms waved, then he pinned them to his sides, he turned his head side to side, with his jaws squared, his hair flying, images of ecstasy, and I reached out my arms for him and his back was turned; he was trotting, swaying, and I put my arms down, and twirled to face two guys who were waving kerchiefs which were doused in amyl nitrite, which I remembered quickly I was not supposed to sniff and never mind because if I laughed enough and moved enough sooner or later I would hit a beat and ignite to a pitch of energy that would bring me right through to dawn in high gear.

We came into our room at the Plaza. I walked over to the window, drew back the drapes and looked out on the city. Hedy was standing behind me.

"What?" I asked.

"What do you mean 'what,' just like that?" he asked. He put both his hands on my shoulders, very firmly, and slipped the shoulder strap of my purse off and pitched it onto a chair. "I want to have you really with me. I want it to be different. I'm tired of playing this stupid game."

"What game?"

"That you don't want this a lot. That I don't. Because I do. And we both wanted it the first minute we looked at each other." He put his arms around me, not tightly in an earlier friendly hug, but gently, and he placed one hand under my chin, tilting my face up to his, and kissed me on the mouth. His lips were soft now and opening; I felt the tip of his tongue just lightly going from side to side, very lightly against my closed mouth, moving ever so much deeper until I could not help but open my mouth. This is what a mouth that looks like his is made for. This is the kiss I had in mind.

We came out of the kiss slowly, hands pulling each other back into it for minutes and then for another minute more, and just this. Yes. And then we took turns getting undressed in the bathroom, me first, then Hedy. While he was there I put gardenia-scented candles on the night tables, a bottle of coconut hand lotion by the bed, and my treasured black Sanchez batiste nightgown on me.

"Dynamite," he said. He looked me up and down. I stretched and posed a bit, at my best angles.

"Lie down," I said. I was thinking of Catwoman or Dragon Lady. Put on translucent black and suddenly there is authority in every move. I suspect the lingerie is more for how we are with them than how they are with us. The question of the black nightgown perhaps is like the chicken and egg situation. "I want to rub your back," I said.

He came up to me and pushed me to the edge of the bed, sitting me down, turning my face up to his, and I loved the sure feeling of his hands framing my jaw. "Seniority doesn't count. You are not giving orders in bed." He pushed me back against the pillows, raised my black nightgown and kissed and kissed. "And if I wanted a rough, tough massage chick I'd know where to get one."

"Oh, you're very tough," I said. "I just thought it would feel good."

"I feel good. I am turned on and I'm wanting you." He was on top of me now, and he was inside me, fevered, quivering. "I know. Do the kisses." I turned my mouth to his. One move and he'd be off. "Come—there's more—we have all night—all day."

"We do. And I am." He lifted up his arms. I could see right down his body, see him moving against me, his throat above my face now. I reached up and touched his throat, all along the shadows and columns of muscle and vein, and I moved down and forward against him. And then he dug himself down and in all along me, his head into my shoulder.

I heard him come. His sound was a fast little coo. If they did not make the sounds, would you know when it happened? Could other women tell without the sounds? I put my hands to either side of his head and lifted his face from my shoulder and kissed him on his plush lips. This sound, his sound reminded me of the babies' drinking sound, the little satisfied noise as their hands would grab on to my breast, and they'd coo like that when they got their first gulp. My deepest physical feelings went back to nursing, never to sex, although this coo was a little like Bill's soft whimper, and that sound had made me tender, not raw and rough with sex. Hedy reached his hand down. I turned on my side, my legs closed, and pulled his hand up to my lips and licked his fingertips.

"What do you want?" he asked, softly speaking close to my ear, his breath warm and quickening.

"Nothing now," I said. "I'm cool." I pushed myself against him, twisting him easily onto his stomach, loose and slender and light next to me. I swept his long hair up from his shoulders, up around my hands like black satin reins. And I licked the back of his neck, so like a child's neck, the place that never grows up, the scruff where I could get him, damp and all mine, in my jaws and carry him anywhere. I blew and nibbled at his neck until he giggled and snuggled and burrowed like a baby.

His trim buttocks made a soft saddle and I posted forward, keeping one hand on his hair. "I'm going to ride you," I whispered, leaning forward, and with the other hand I reached under his belly, feeling him. "Getting there, getting there," I whispered with more of a lick to the words than a sound, and I pulled my hand back and lightly lifting my hips, poised now on my knees, I drew my fingertips back and forth, circling now, feeling him pumping.

"What are you doin'?" he said softly, but his breath was eager.

A memory of dancers, images of expressions and gestures grabbed in infrared light, sober selection capitulated, and I saw myself, riding him now unblushing, fierce. I wanted to get Hedy, to own him, to ride him and I had him now, his hair damp against his forehead, his one hand escaped now and tucked under his belly, the elbow going. And I reached up, like a rodeo rider going at full gallop, sweeping my arms high over my head, bearing down, twisting down, riding hard and forward on his back.

"Get it, baby."

"You got it," I said, and put my hands straight down in front of me like a pommel, going against my thumbs, sliding deeper along his lightly furred cleavage. "I'm doing you, doing you, now get it, get it." I leaned close down on his back, breasts softening my toughness, and grabbed his neck in my jaws and took one hand and thrust it around under him, then he cried out, no coo now, and went rigid, then collapsed.

"Oh, wow," he said, his profile smiling. His eyes closed. "Ride 'em, cowboy." Then I lay beside him stroking his face, kissing his eyes, laughing softly.

"We could be great lovers," he said.

If only he didn't sound so wistful, didn't have this soft and urgent look in his eyes. Hedy could reach me where I did not want to be reached.

"Don't look at me sweetly," I said. "I like my lovers mean and rough." I giggled as I said it, and he laughed and jumped astride me, tickling me. I reached to push him back, my arms and legs flailing like a child's, and he leaned his head down close to me and bit at my ears. "Mean and rough, is it, mean and rough."

"No, no, not tickling"—I kept laughing—"no, stop!" And his hair swept across my face, the nipping at my ears and neck and shoulders turned me on, and his tickling slowed down and the nibbling deepened into sucking and I purred and hummed and twisted up against him. "What lovers," he whispered, "how many others?"

"Tens of thousands," I said.

"No more, not now, no time." He was stroking me now, just like I liked. He had remembered from watching me, which no one ever had. Yes, a musician would understand. Stay in this moment, I told myself. And the minute I did, of course, I could not. I was at a meeting, hearing someone say, "Stay in the now." I was on the air, being told, "Go, you're on." Then I was on a stage (and this always worked when I was alone) in a music hall, a stripper, being done by two other strippers, being watched by a dark, smoky audience of faceless men with hats in their laps. And now I felt lush and plummy with feelings, and he got me to the edge and I pulled back, but he kept the beat and brought his mouth all open down on mine, breathing his own breath and I became part of the crowd, one giant hot animal. Now I was on that stage with ten thousand lights glittering around me obscuring everything except heat and breath and brass, all down and closing in to one point of heat, and it caught, it ticked off, and spun out, right through; I rocked from side to side. I grabbed Hedy and pulled him on top of me, in me, and kissed at his neck and his ears and his eyes and remembered only not to say, I love you. All the rest he could have. It was a day and a night. Tomorrow we will hate each other. Something will happen to keep this in its place. Perhaps the children will call at dawn.

We did not hate each other, and I had not told the children where I was. It was worse, I sighed to myself, because it was even better. The sun beamed through the window. No fog; no mist; just fresh New York sun. We hugged each other.

"I'm glad to see you here, to wake up with you," he said.

"A very bad sign," I said. Maybe, I hoped, it was the sound of traffic that made me feel so alive this morning. He touched his lips with his fingertips and then touched mine.

He ordered coffee for me. We showered quickly, and alone, dressed, then walked out to Central Park. He bought me daffodils. I snapped off one flower and put it in his buttonhole and kissed him on the nose.

We walked down Sixtieth Street and stood in line to see a movie. We sat, with our shoulders touching, eating popcorn. I licked the butter off my fingers. He took a paper napkin out of his pocket and wiped my mouth and fingertips too. We looked at each other and agreed we wanted to leave the theatre. We walked back up to the park.

He hired a horse and buggy for a ride through the park. I whispered, "I think it's very expensive," and he said, "Never mind," and put his arm around my shoulder. "Next month, when Ivan Rappaport has made me famous, like you said, I'll be able to buy us a horse and buggy."

I got the reminder to call Ivan, although I decided not to say what he wanted to hear right now: Oh, yes, I'll call Ivan.

We looked at the tips of the tulips and daffodils coming up along the paths in the park and we looked at each other. He put his hand on mine. I looked off to the West Side. He tightened his clasp on my hand. And he looked off to the East Side. Then quickly looked back to see if I was looking at him again. I took a long time to turn my head again and put my eyes back into his.

11

Stanford Draper, who lived with Ivan Rappaport, invited me to come over with Hedy for a late lunch. I had called to invite them to lunch at my house, but Stan explained that Ivan really preferred to be home on weekends. "We'll make it a Saturday," Stan said, "because I like to see he gets his rest Sunday evening before he goes in to the office. We may have a couple of other people, but since Ivan really wants to talk with you and your friend, we think we'll keep it family, if that's all right with you."

"Of course," I said. "How marvelous. We'd adore it."

"A stone wall and a long curving driveway," I said. "That's a real home." A real home, because it reminds me of my memory of my childhood house, which was not quite so grand. I have never wanted to go back to know for sure.

"That's a real fortune," said Hedy. "I used to do gigs at kids' parties in houses like this when I first started and I was no older than the kids having the parties."

"Yes, I remember when my parents would have parties for me and for Deborah in our house, a house like this. My mother and father would dance once or twice to the bands of young boys who would play for us, and then my mother would go back to her studio to work, and my father would dance with us." I trailed off. Too much of that now. Stop. I remembered, too, how later my father would capture everyone's attention with his magical stories about the theatre.

Hedy had brought some brand-new tapes, and Ivan took them from him at the front door. "A treat," Ivan said, "which I shall enjoy later." Stan thanked me for the terra-cotta pot I'd planted with solid budding tulips and the loaf of country bread I'd brought from Farm Days. "I love this bread," he said, and I felt right. He wiped his hands on his checked apron and took the tulips and the bread and gave me a kiss. I loved the way Ivan looked in the country, his hair a bit on end, an old cardigan on, with khaki pants just a bit too short. Stan reached up and folded down the collar on Ivan's shirt. "Sartorial splendor," Stan said. And Ivan laughed and I missed that way you are when you live with someone.

"You've never seen our family?" Stan said to me. "Of course you've never even been here. I forget. I listen to you all the time and think how deliciously you must shock Millicent, although I know your father's pleased to have a performer in the family; of course, we always felt Sylvan should be an actor. Speaking of which, Sylvan called, Ivan, while you were in the shower—they'll be a bit late."

"I didn't know they were coming," I said. I remembered "keep it family." He did say it. Sort of. "Oh, Hedy, my parents!"

"That's going to be interesting," he said. I could see disappointment. And so did Ivan, who said, "Just as well Sylvan will be making a late entrance. You and I, my boy, will go to the terrace and have a little talk."

"First," Stan said, "you must have the Cartbridge tour and meet the rest of the family."

"Oh, yes," I said; family?

Cartbridge was one of the oldest houses in Brightriver. They had added wings, and a pool, but every pewter plate, fireplace tool, carved decoy, harvest table and quilt was authentic, and priceless, according to Fitz, who knew every object in every house in mid-Connecticut. It didn't look priceless, just warm, gleaming and smelling of rosemary and lime oil. I must learn how to be neat, I decided. On almost every wall was one of Stan's marvelous primitive paintings.

"Man, are these good," said Hedy. "You're a terrific painter."

"Oh, yes, Stan," I said, "when are you going to have a new show?" I remembered one he'd had in New York years ago which had sold out. Looks went like crossfire between Ivan and Stan, and Ivan quickly said, "I've been insisting for years. You know how brilliant he is, and there is no better agent in the world for anything! I've told him anytime he wants the best gallery, the biggest turnout anywhere on Madison Avenue, he can have it. You talk to him, Margot; I get nowhere."

"Well, it's not that easy," Stan said. He ran his hands through his clipped silver gray hair.

"Nothing's easy, but you have to believe in yourself; that's the beginning," said Ivan.

"I do," said Stan firmly, staring at Ivan. "Enough. I want to introduce you to my dear ones."

We walked down through one hall lined with Stan's paintings, about which it now seemed best to be quiet, and off to another small wing. Hedy had begun to sneeze. Stan knocked and the door was opened by a lovely young blond man in white, followed by three very large dogs, all of whom were living in this wing which opened into sunny kennels and dog runs.

"This is our marvelous Mr. Miles, and Binky, Sundance and Madge."

Hedy had his Kleenex out. "He's allergic to dogs," I said, "but they are marvelous."

"Can I get you anything?" said Stan. "I can't imagine; Mr. Miles keeps them immaculate, of course."

"It isn't"—Hedy sneezed—"that; it's dander or something.

I'll have to go outside for a sec, I'm sorry, really." Sneezing, he bolted from the dogs.

It must irritate him to have to explain all the time—the apologetic feeling I sometimes had when people would say, "But surely you can have just a little wine; it's a very fine light wine."

"The English," Stan said confidently to me, as we walked into the kitchen, "are born knowing how to raise anything. Mr. Miles has worked miracles. No one would take Sundance because he needed corrective surgery—you might have noticed he limps a trifle; Binky was considered an incorrigible and wouldn't begin to leave the kennel unless we took Madge, too. It was a horror at first."

Through the window I could see Hedy as he stood on the terrace, the lawns sloping down to the river, the swimming pool, the guesthouse and the tennis court. He had his hands in the pockets of his cream-colored jeans, his pink button-down shirt open, a maroon sweater tied around his neck.

"To the manner born," I said to Stan.

"Yes," Stan said, "he has the confidence of a potential star. The hunger, the right quality of yearning. Anyone can be wistful—and drown confidence in self-pity; and unalloyed confidence makes a performer impossible to teach. This boy, if the talent is there, and Ivan says it is, has the right character, the looks, the personality and"—he paused and looked at me—"the sense to attach himself to someone who can be helpful."

"Yes. I try. But I'm scared to get really involved again—you know." Enough always, always about me. Switch it, I told myself. "You must feel a little like that about having another exhibit. I felt you really don't want that." Stan was heating a kettle for asparagus. He handed me a knife and I cut off the pale ends.

"I do and I don't. It's not quite how Ivan says it is. He wants, or likes, the idea of my working, success, all that—but he doesn't quite like it when it happens, and he hates himself, despises himself, for resenting it. Competition, my divided attention, whatever it is he feels." Stan shrugged; he opened a lid on a pot and tasted the liquid with a spoon. "This is sensational."

I could see Ivan sitting with Hedy around a glass table under the big willow tree at the far end of the pool. Hedy was sitting straight, Ivan arranging and rearranging his positions. As Ivan talked, Hedy relaxed, then I could see Ivan talk less.

"So," I said, "you sort of pretend you don't want it and he can enjoy the role of encouraging you?"

"Something like that," Stan said, "but it's not just pretense at all. I can't convince you, I'm sure. I love this life. I love him." He handed me five eggs, an egg whip and a bowl. "Will you separate them and do the yellows for my hollandaise?" Then he went on, "When we get along that's the best. The painting simply means less."

"I can understand that—I used to feel that way. It's funny . . ." I cracked two eggs. I paused. I cracked the others and separated them.

"What?" he said.

"Most people would assume—if you said the situation—that it was male/female, you know. That's what's so crazy. It's people. Always the issue of balance. How do you have that success, whatever it is you want, and love, too?" I beat the yolks and whipped and whipped them around with a wide oval tunnel opening and angling, precarious as a race car track, and I could see myself speeding inside, beating around that golden track, winning. "And what do you do with your whites?"

"This time I'll probably do a meringue for fresh cherry pie. We should have the cherries soon. About having all of it, I don't know. In my case it just seemed to be a matter of 'choose one.' "

I watched Hedy now beginning to move around, standing, then gesturing, eager and earnest.

"They get along fine," said Stan. He put a linen towel in a basket and put in the country bread and a loaf he had actually made himself. Choose one. I wondered if I would get some time with Ivan, too. I remembered the party. I wanted it all. I remembered old dinner parties in my first marriage when I'd be in the kitchen. At least Ezekial was an elegant cook. Bill would stay in the kitchen and talk. Or not talk, but he would be there sometimes. And it seemed important to remember good things, too.

"I'm all set," Stan said, "but if you could get the butter from the refrigerator. I always forget to do the simple, obvious things that usually matter more than all the elaborate nonsense. Now where the hell are your parents?"

"Probably waiting until we are crazed with worry so we'll fuss over them wildly and give them all the attention the rest of the day. Oh, I love a big kitchen like this," I said, getting the butter, which had been molded into an antique crock. I also would have loved to be the one getting all this attention from Ivan. But that wasn't the point this time. Next time, my turn. I wondered where I got this enticing characteristic. Probably it was all my own. Deborah was my parents' child and she was the least demanding person I knew, the most giving, the least self-involved.

"Well, after Ivan makes Hedy a star, perhaps you'll find a big house together."

"Oh, Stan, it isn't that sort of thing, I don't think. Not really." I paused. Only a hint, a corner of a fantasy, and I'd be off and running with it, making a life out of the most casual comment.

"It is a good investment, though, isn't it?" I said.

"The best," Stan said. "Oh, there's the car. They're here."

We went into the entry hall. I looked quickly in the mirror, lifted the puffs on the shoulders of my new navy blue sweater and fluffed my bangs.

Even with my father tall and silvery guiding her, his face

composed in his easy, country smile, my mother presented herself in the flagstone entrance hall with the drama she'd always had on the runway when she'd show off some of the fashions made from her own fabrics. She was wearing a flaring, lavender tweed coat and dress, designed during the fifties, the matching scarf sweeping off behind her shoulders like wings. Her gray blond hair as always in its classic French twist, and the dark glasses, today, had burgundy lenses.

"Oh, to look at everything as if through wine; I love the glasses," I said.

"You would think of that," she said. But she smiled. "God forbid you'll ever need such glasses, but you could borrow them if you do. How, by the way, speaking of that, is your doctor?"

It took me a moment. "Oh. Dr. Rachsinger. Yes. Fine. He's fine. Yes."

"Margot," my father said, "you look very nice, very trim, an early nautical spring."

"Yes," I said. I was so fast to be sensitive, too sensitive, to them. But was it perhaps, in their formal seasonal world, too early for white gabardine? My father was all in soft gray tweeds.

"As always, the duke and duchess look perfect together," Stan said.

"That's all Sylvan," my mother said. "He selects. I just put it on and keep my fingers crossed."

I am mean-spirited about my mother's vision. It was a condition which came and went, and, although she was always extremely, uncomfortably sensitive to light, she could, on a good day—and this was one—catch expressions and see almost normally. And she saw precisely the way I looked at my father.

"There's your girl," she said to him. And I looked up at his smiling face as he stood poised next to her, his chin lifted, that slightly aloof hesitation before I could hug him which said to me: look how you love me. I do, I do, I thought, without a reservation, and I kissed my mother but off at the edge of the cheekbone because she quickly turned her face to my father and said, "She's got a new perfume," a critical tone, designed, I decided, to turn him to me faster, get him to come closer; her perverse gift to me, her odd way of getting him to move from her to me, and to give to me some piece of himself if only for an instant, and she would watch, pleased with her subtlety, from behind her wine-dark glasses, as he said, "It's an interesting fragrance." Then he kissed me on either cheek and I hugged him, laying my head down against his chest, feeling the combination of cashmere soft tweed, silk and fine cotton, all the fabrics, the scents of laundry, lemon verbena and soap, which meant man to me more than the scent of skin and hair. I stroked his arm and my mother took an uncertain step forward and my father quickly pulled back and guided her onto the terrace, as Stan said he would get Ivan, "who's listening to some music brought by this nice young man Margot's been kind enough to introduce to Ivan." Wise of Stan to put it that way. They would surely not see Hedy as an "appropriate man."

"Has Stan been painting?" my mother asked. "He's so good."

"No," I said. "He explained it makes Ivan uncomfortable, even though Ivan insisted he wishes Stan would."

"Stan's crazy," my mother said. "You never give up something because it makes someone else uncomfortable." But I remembered how many more projects my father had taken on after my mother stopped designing and sold the business he had helped run for her. Of course, her eyes—her eyes had been the problem.

Mr. Miles came strolling across the terrace as we waited, with the dogs prancing single file behind him. As they paraded by, they'd each pause, to receive a pat, and then move on politely. "We're going on for our lunch now ourselves," Mr. Miles said. My father laughed, and my mother said, "We spoke to Deborah; her children are doing wonderfully at school. How are Brynn and Dylan?"

"Well, you can't have everything; mine are driving really well."

"Margot," my father warned quickly. "Don't be mean. Don't bait her. Don't worry her." I didn't start. I switched to something else fast. "I had three new designers on my show, Mother, and we talked a bit about your influences, the way you mixed reds and pinks, and blues and greens, long before the Scandinavian imports."

"Oh, Margot, your father was designing rooms with those colors when we met at the Art Students League."

"That's simply not true, Millie darling. Margot is right."

"Oh," said my mother, "I hear Ivan coming. It's marvelous what not being able to see can do for your hearing: everything is so acute—that's why I can barely listen to radio, I suppose, Margot; the sounds are so jarring now."

My father gave me the cautionary look as he turned to greet Ivan. I did not say that it didn't seem to keep her from being hooked on her TV band radio, which I'd noticed my father had set down in the entry hall even today.

My father embraced Ivan and shook hands with Hedy. Then he looked out over the lawns, sniffing the air, breathing in the sun. "I miss this. I miss it very much."

"Margot looks more like you, Sylvan, than ever," Ivan said.

"That," said my mother, "is because she is getting older."

We all laughed. Hedy and I grimaced quickly at each other. I loved when people said I was more like my father than my mother, but within the positive lives the negative and perish the thought I should have his life; that marriage—although (one could say) at least theirs lasted, but at what cost. And then at what cost had I persisted in failures of another kind. In trying to be different had I only proved they were right: that theirs was the one perfect marriage?

We all sat down to a glorious lunch, hot potato salad with a touch of mustard and fresh spring peas, cold asparagus with hollandaise and a veal stew with white sausage sliced into it. My father cut a piece of the bread I'd brought from Farm Days and dunked it into the gravy. "Margot, this is lovely bread," he said. I beamed at him as if I'd made it myself, but I said quickly, "I didn't bake it." Wanting, wishing I had.

"Margot is a real cook," my mother said. "Hedy, you must have been to some of the parties she throws for the children, they've always had the best birthday parties."

"No, I haven't," he said. He passed the butter for Ivan, and turned down the bottle of white wine Ivan passed along to him. Then he smiled at me and poured me some more Perrier from the other bottle Stan had thoughtfully placed on the table.

"Millie, I think he's a bit older than Dylan," my father said.

And Hedy smiled. "A bit. Like a lot of years."

"My husband thinks Dylan might be very talented in art," my mother said.

"Really?" said Stan.

"Yes," said my father. "He has a better line to his drawing than I did when I was his age . . ."

"He hasn't been doing much with his work though," I said.

"I'll have to talk to him," my father said, "get him down to Florida after the summer. I've told him I'll put him through the Art Students League anytime he wants to begin, to make the commitment."

"I know, Dad. I could put him through a private school, too. But he doesn't want to yet. I guess." Did I say that too quickly, defensively: I can raise my own.

"Actually, I'm thinking of buying a house now, if I'm able to find something," I said, trying to invent assurance.

"There's the best broker in Medwin's Landing—I'm sure you've found him," said Stan.

"Of course; Fitz," I said. "He found me the house I've been renting."

"I don't think you should rush into that," my mother said. "You'll meet someone and then where will you be?"

"Home," I said.

"Ruling the roost will not be attractive," my mother said; "you'll think you're right all the time and then there you are again."

I finished off a glass of Perrier and my father reached over and poured me another one.

"Where?" I said. "Divorced?" Why do I harass her?

My mother ignored me and went on, "We're very lucky. Sylvan and I simply never disagree about a thing."

"Ivan and I rarely do either," Stan said.

"Yes," said Sylvan, "but Millicent and I never argue because I always agree with her. It's a subtle difference." He smiled at my mother.

"He always says things like that to please Margot," my mother said.

There was an uncomfortable silence. Into which Hedy sneezed. And again.

"Bless you," my father said. "I suppose you play this new sound now, but you must have started with the classics. Do you miss that ever?"

I could tell Hedy was uneasy with the way my father watched him as he talked. It was different from the way he had been with Ivan. "No," he said to my father, "there has never been a time when I wasn't going to be a musician. And it was classics. That was what my mother raised me to do, and I was always good."

"Hedy is an amusing name," my mother said. "There was a

little actress in California, I think, with that name. One of the motion picture people. She wore one of my dresses in a photograph. Could not begin to carry it."

"Wayne Henderson is his real name," Ivan said. "He may go back to it."

"I like real names," my father said, "but perhaps that is not distinctive enough. My grandson has a good name."

"Yes," Hedy said, "we talked about that." He looked shyly at Ivan.

Ivan laughed and said, "Hedy had a teacher who would say"—and Ivan made his voice sound precisely like that sort of teacher—" 'Wayne Henderson, have you been practicing these scales?' Actually, the name will not matter—his songs are original; he has style and the motor. You worry about names when there's nothing else."

"That's true," my father said. "A great set will not save a play."

"It should," my mother said.

"Millicent!" my father said. "So," he said to Hedy, "you compose your own songs. And are they good, or is that an unfair question?"

"They're never bad," Hedy said, with his own best aloof lift of the chin, the airiest of grins, his hair fluttering, like a slightly dismissive wave of a hand. "I don't want to seem too full of myself, but it's easy to put together decent enough songs. The really great song will happen for me. I feel it. If I make a lot of money, I want to really handle it well. I don't want to wind up broke like a lot of big stars do. Maybe that sounds cocky, but I'm willing to work hard, and work well with a band—you have a great time then when you all appreciate each other." He grabbed another Kleenex, which I had pulled out of my purse. The last one. He was possibly more allergic to my parents than to dogs.

"That's a nice attempt to be modest," my mother said, "but Sylvan has always said one must not be too modest; as you get older there will be plenty of people to tell you you are not as good as you must believe you are."

"Millicent, I have never said that. It's good to be teachable. You'll probably do very well." And Hedy, who had been sniffling and talking in and around his Kleenexes, sneezed again.

"When you can," my mother said, "you should probably move to the city; you have to be very healthy to live in the country."

"I am very healthy," Hedy said, "actually." And sneezed and excused himself as Stan explained there was more Kleenex in the guest bathroom.

"You must," Stan said, "buy him dozens of good handkerchiefs."

"Margot was always so fond of young people," my mother said; "she always enjoyed her children's friends." My mother looked at Mr. Miles, who could be seen out beyond the pool putting the dogs through some engaging tricks.

"A successful woman," Stan said, "can make an excellent companion for an ambitious young man."

Ivan smiled and shook his head. "Not a good topic."

"Of course not," said Stan, "but why work so hard avoiding it?"

"I give Margot in that role about five months," my father said.

"Mother started out your marriage like that," I said, too fast, "supportive, when you were in art school."

"That was different," my mother said. "Sylvan was an extremely competent man and he managed my business, ran my career, diverted his talents in my direction."

"I wasn't that generous, Millie," my father said. "Ivan and Stan know you earned the big money. We had very compatible talents."

It had been perfect once. For them. How long would I

need to go on trying to believe it wasn't so I could insist myself into the middle, to see only her craziness. He liked the oddness.

"I see no potential for such gracious deference in this young man," Ivan said. "But you will have a fine time while it lasts."

"You're ambitious too, and what you don't need is another child, Margot," my father said.

"He's not a child," I said.

"I don't," said Stan, "see that as terrible; her children will be leaving home, in what, a year or two. We need what we need."

"Oh," I said, so quickly. "Not really. I mean they'll go to college, but the house I'm going to buy"—look how I was already practically doing the wallpaper, which I did so well—"is going to have wings and guest cottages so it will be a country house for them forever with families and everything."

"I had that dream," my father said. "When I was designing sets for some Restoration comedies, I came across these marvelous arcades, you know the English used to design inspiration walks in their gardens in those days . . ." My father looked at Hedy as he returned to the table. "I'm talking about the country house we had," he explained, and then my father's eyes drifted out again with his dreamy storytelling expression, and his voice got softer and slower, and he'd move his hands in these intricate, delicate gestures and I knew he'd be drawing what he was telling in his head. Sometimes, not lately, more often when he was little, Dylan would do that; he'd gaze at my father when he talked, as I supposed I'd do, and then later I'd watch Dylan talking to Brynn or one of his friends in the same bewitching fashion. ". . . and," my father said, "so when we bought our place I spent days walking and studying the land. And now, I can sit here, Ivan, and contemplate your lawn and see at the same moment my own and walk through the willows with their ribbons of yellow green into my arcade all shadowed in periwinkle blue and I am home again. I do miss Connecticut."

"Oh, Daddy," I said, bursting out (I had not called him that for years), "you'll have one of the cottages, for you and mother. That's the point. It will be wonderful."

After my parents left, Hedy insisted on clearing the table with Stan. I stood up to help. "Sit still, Margot," Hedy said, "maybe Ivan wants to talk to you. Anyway, you get to do this stuff all the time." He smiled, neatly balancing plates.

"Sweet young man," Ivan said, as we sat now alone on the terrace.

"Too young, you're saying. God, my parents!"

"They try to understand, Margot. They are unusual people, but not unique; no one is. They're concerned about you and the kids." He paused.

"What?" I said.

He put his fingertips together in the way he does. "A question you might ask yourself, if you haven't, and it occurs to me you may not have: why have you never tried to find a father for those children?"

"I did," I said. I laughed. "Over and over. And they did have one of their very own, actually."

"That's not precisely what I mean. I think it's one of those questions to think about."

"I suppose it is."

"Yes, we all do live unusual lives; we invent lives that seem to work, but the important thing, I suspect, is to know why, to understand the reasons for the choices."

"Oh, Ivan, I'm not sure about that yet. I think I just want to look back one day and be surprised. If I knew and understood everything, I think I'd be frightened to death to make the choices, do the things I have." I paused. "Well. Yes. Maybe I should have been more scared; then I wouldn't have done some of it and life would have been simpler for the kids. You are right. Yes. Oh, please God, I hope I don't do it wrong anymore, for them."

"It's all right, Margot." He patted my hand with both of his. "It's not that urgent, dear no."

As we drove down the driveway, Mr. Miles was strolling up with the dogs all walking briskly along beside him. The light was soft and mauve. He could be a shepherd returning home with his flock. Mr. Miles saluted us graciously, and I waved. Hedy sneezed. I handed him a Kleenex from the box Stan gave me as we were leaving. "He's a piece of work," Hedy said.

"This must be how the English country looks at twilight," I said.

"Maybe we'll go there someday," Hedy said. "Ivan thinks after a while he could get me a concert there . . . things are really goin' to happen now."

How romantic, I thought. And I saw Hedy being entertained in an English country garden and me beside him, both of us strolling and smiling and nodding sweetly in our charming matching tweeds.

12

Inspirations for romantic domesticity could come from a situation some people might think was impossible. Some people might also think there could not be a worse idea than that of Hedy and me and Brynn and Dylan all living together.

Now we were sitting in my kitchen, having coffee. Dylan was out, and Brynn had gone to the movies with two girlfriends from the city, Sandy and Carla, who had come up for a weekend in the country. It was warm enough for Spike to stay outside, so Hedy had agreed to come in. "I figure you can only sneeze so much on one day anyway."

"Well, so that's my parents," I said.

"They're interesting people. It's not just them, you know. The three of you together—it's like you do an improvisation to see how miserable and uptight you can get each other. It's some act. You do set each other up."

"I guess you're right. In time maybe I'll see it," I said. I poured some more coffee for me. "It's just random tension. I guess that triggers the sneezing too."

"Probably," he said, "the predisposition is there. I hate the edges of scenes like that even worse than big blowups."

"I know," I said, "me too." We sat quietly. We could hear the crickets, the birds. I loved the late afternoon light indoors in a kitchen, so soft and homey.

"I think I would trade in your parents, though, for Ivan

and Stan. They're neat." He paused. "I guess," he said, "that is what might be considered an alternative life style."

"Except," I added, "*that* style is pleasanter than almost everyone's, and what is everything, actually, if not an alternative to something else."

"That one will take me a while," he said, laughing. He stopped laughing. "I want it. I want to live like that. Ivan says he's going to take me on. He may have something real good coming up for me. I should feel like celebrating, but I feel restless, or something."

"I know," I said. "And so letdown. It's all comparative. No one feels arrived. You goad and whip yourself, and then you have to plummet to build more steam to move on again. I believe great things are going to happen. For both of us, actually."

This was, indeed, an alarming feeling. Such closeness in his conversation: "Both of us." I changed the subject.

"Where was Gary today?" I had thought he was going to drive us.

"Gary got busted in a coke deal. I wasn't sure I'd tell you because I didn't want you upset."

"Why would I be upset? I mean it's too bad, but it's a risk he took. They always think the other guy will be caught."

"Okay, now I figure you know how to handle this stuff as well as anyone, with your A.A. training and all."

"Hedy, what on earth are you talking about?"

"Margot. I'm really sorry I have to tell you this if you don't know, or especially if you don't suspect at all, but well, Gary says Dylan is one of his best contacts."

"Really, Hedy! Dylan doesn't have money for coke. Don't be silly. It's Gary's rap—they all try to lay it off on guys they know when they're afraid of getting caught."

"Dylan's got money, Margot. Listen." Hedy made me look at him and put his hands on mine on top of the table. "He gets money by selling, dealing."

"Hedy. I'm hardly about to believe that." Was he *this* jealous of Dylan? "Dylan may do a bit of pot and coke now and then—but he's not like that. Gary is just making trouble. He's probably jealous of you and trying to create a problem between us, because I am not having this discussion."

"We don't have to if you don't want to. It's probably best for me to stay out of it. I remember my dad saying you can tell a woman whose husband has a shot liver and is blacked out on the floor that he's an alcoholic and she will look at you and say, 'Why, Harry hardly ever drinks at all!' "

"Hedy, I know all about that, and I'd be the first one to spot a problem with denial. I'll ask Dylan. And then we'll know."

"And Dylan will really tell you. Come on, Margot. If you want I'll talk to him."

"No, I'll handle my own son."

"I'm sorry. I thought he might talk to a guy easier."

Only a couple of weeks ago I had planned a lovely party for Helena's birthday. I wanted it to be perfect because Helena hadn't been feeling well. I made a bittersweet chocolate cake, roast lamb, all Helena's favorites. Their friends, the crazy owners of a drying-out place, came down and fought all the way, of course. Alison had been there, down from school on an unscheduled vacation; and she'd stayed over. Her parents, who were away, had found out and arrived at my door. The senator's wife had shouted at me right in front of everyone. Matters had been made worse when Dylan and Alison took off the next day. When they had returned, at Dylan's, not Alison's insistence, she had been whisked off to school. I had wanted to think it was all one more outrageous installment. But installments do link, do build and gather weight, and Dylan, at first full of bravado, had changed. I hadn't quite understood how. And didn't want to now.

"Hedy, let's not talk about the kids." I thought that would please him. "Not tonight." I handed him a piece of peach crumb cake I'd made.

"I thought I might be able to help—that's all." He looked rejected.

"Oh, Hedy." I stopped. "I'm grateful. I guess you feel damned if you do, damned if you don't. I'm so used to handling things, I just don't know to react—how he'd react. Maybe that would be good—if there is a problem." I touched his hair. "Thank you."

I got up on the chair; he looked at me. I banged down a piece of the wallpaper. "Loose again. This house! See, I do have to buy a house soon." I got down. I ground some coffee beans. "I was thinking I could buy a huge old farm sort of place somewhere, perhaps with guesthouses." I made coffee, sprinkling in fresh cinnamon. "I know we hardly know each other, but I've always had the idea that I'd buy a big place with a carriage house or so and lease it, or them, to a friend or two. And maybe you'd want to be one of the friends. You will need your own place, won't you? I mean, it's just an idea."

"It's a crazy idea," he said. He got up and poured himself some coffee.

"I know," I agreed instantly. "I was probably having fantasies about Ivan's." I turned away, rinsing a baking dish in the sink.

"I know that," he said. He stood at the counter, leaning on his elbow, so he could see my face. "Just 'cause it's a crazy idea doesn't mean we can't think about it. I've always planned to get my own place soon as I can. And when I get more money, I could invest in the house, sort of like a business. But mostly," he said, "I could help you keep a place together better, keep things running right and working. It's not a crazy idea. And it's a hell of a lot better than going back and forth around town."

"Well," I said, "if we stop going out—we'd have to think about it—that could be awkward."

He paused. "We'd be adult or I'd move."

He might have said it would be somewhat more than awkward if we broke up. Like sad. Neat trap I set there for myself.

"Well," I said. "I doubt if I could afford anything that would give us the kind of space we'd need anyway. It would have to be very big." I smiled. "But it was a nice idea."

"We'd need the Plaza, at least," said Hedy, "especially if you have to have your dog. The best idea would be to find some place where the kids could have a cottage of their own—a barn, something like that. They could have their friends and come and go on their own. Or we could each have our own place on the same piece of property—you would have someone nearby—and I could put up the band when we were into doin' an album. We'd keep the privacy thing we like."

"It's all fun to fantasize about," I said. Privacy we like? I hate privacy. "Spike could be in my house. With the kids. It would have to be very separate." Dylan would be going to college in the fall and only be home on weekends. And Brynn was warming now toward Hedy.

"Well," he said. "It wouldn't mean we were getting more involved. There would be nothing involved about it. In that way."

"Nothing," I agreed. We looked at each other. "Whatever we mean by that." We laughed. We moved into the living room. I looked at the old school clock on the wall. I knew Brynn and her friends probably had gone over to Chickens after the movie.

Hedy sat on the rocking chair—"It doesn't have any dog hair on it; I can't even look at the couch." I was lying down, feeling deflated. It was so simple, and he had agreed. What else did I want? Not to think, not to imagine anything that would get in the way of things being so simple. Not to wonder about those voices on the telephone to Dylan.

"Everyone would think we were living together. It would get people crazy," Hedy said.

"Oh, people are more adult than that." I paused. "Would they get crazy because I'm older? You mean your friends, does it bother them that we're going out?"

"No more than your friends probably say dumb stuff like you're robbing the cradle," he said. "My dad knows."

"Oh, God!" I exclaimed.

"He wanted to be sure I wasn't using you, like taking you out because of everyone you know and all that. But he said it's better than other girls I was going around with." Hedy rocked a bit in the chair. "What he exactly said is funny if you take it right. He said the others were like those lightweight foreign-made bikes. They're good for short rides, he said, but for the long haul you need a Harley Davidson."

"That's nice," I said. Exactly the sort of compliment you hate because it's true.

"You could probably get one of the magazines to fix an old place up as part of some deal. Don't they do that?" Hedy asked.

"I suppose that might be possible." I was feeling wistful. "Don't you think it would be nice, too? Not just economics, I mean."

"Well, it would be sort of like living together." Was he just trying not to sound too eager? Playing it cool?

"I've never been crazy about living alone," I said. "If it is the right place you could have friends come in and work on an album, say, and there would be room."

"And if you get in a bind you could always lease out space. You could have some people there, if you were working on shows. We could eventually set up a little recording studio to share." He was imagining it, I was sure, without Jennie, or

Reilly, and, of course, without Dylan and even Brynn. He would have to understand that the children would always have rooms anywhere I lived.

"Maybe there's an old school, or an inn, or something." It would have to be worked out so there's a very separate place for his music. Not that I don't almost love it now, but I would have to be able to work.

"Something like that," he said, "an inn or old farm, but not too big. We wouldn't want to rattle around. I like the idea of coming off a tour and finding you there, working in your room."

I thought, it would be such a relief to have him near me at night. I stopped. My room, he said. Working room, of course, he must have meant that. He doesn't really know I do a lot of work in bed. Most.

"I think we're saying we're almost going to think about living together." He laughed. "Stop beating around the bush."

To celebrate the idea of living together, I asked Hedy to stay with me for the night.

"Well," he agreed, "I thought I might just try that. If my allergies act up I'll just go." He sneezed. "See, I had to think about it."

"I have a nice bathtub, in my very own bathroom. And there is not a child anywhere in it." I walked over to the rocking chair and pulled it back, leaning forward and reaching down over his upturned face to kiss him. "It's fun," I said, "to make up ideas. What we've been doing is the best part, believe me."

We went up to my room. The bed was covered with pens and papers. I brushed them off. "I work in bed once in a while," I said.

"You go get ready, or whatever it is you do, and I'll make the bed. I can't get into a bed with the sheets all falling around like this. You really need someone to take care of you."

"A nanny?"

"Yeah, but I'm not wearing any white slacks, kiddo." He opened a bag he had brought from the car. "I have a present for you. I wanted to give you something special for what you're doing for me."

"Hedy. Your silver hairbrush!" I touched his hands. I kissed his cheeks. "That's beautiful, oh, Hedy." I sat in front of the mirror and drew it through my hair.

"It was my mom's," he said. He stood behind me, took the brush from my hand and gently, gently brushed my hair.

"I used to brush her hair like this," he said. I put my hand over his and looked at him in the mirror.

"Hedy. This is the most splendid present I've ever had. If anything happens I promise I'll give it back, you understand?"

"No. Don't think about that. That's not the point. If it stopped now, it would still be yours."

"Well, it isn't going to. Today," I said.

I went into the bathroom and filled a lemon-scented bubble bath. I arranged little candles around the edges of the tub.

He undressed and got into the tub. "Bubbles, cute," he said. "Do you wash backs?" The candlelight flickered on his smooth young skin. "Love to." I knelt by the tub and leaned over. I thought of Dylan's back, which I could never wash again. How fortunate to know how it feels to be Alison. I had it all now—the mother and the lover. You could do both.

"Hey," he yelled, as he grabbed my head and plunged me underwater.

"You're drowning me," I screamed. I smelled the burning hair and the water sizzled and smoked.

He threw a towel around my head. He got out of the tub and put his arms around me. "It wouldn't be simple. I knew that. I never had a girl set her hair on fire for me before."

"There's always a first." Perhaps I should not have thought of Dylan. Surely this was punishment for that taboo consideration. No, you surely do not dare be both.

I looked in the mirror. "Oh, Hedy. I really burned it badly." Strands and chunks of hair, frizzled and charred to white and orange, hung about my face.

"Maybe your mother's spirit was enraged that you gave me her brush," I said.

"I knew you would think of that sort of thing," he said, "but I think you just got carried away by my body and put your head into a candle."

"There'll be nothing left for that beautiful brush." I picked up the shears I used for editing interviews.

"What the hell are you doing?" he yelled. "Don't."

"Hedy. I have to do something. It's all out of shape now. You go away. Don't watch. Please. It will be okay."

I clipped my hair off into a long mop, actually just like Dylan's. "That was willful," he said. "You didn't have to chop it all off."

"Don't be sad. You'll just have to use shorter strokes when you brush my hair." I kissed Hedy's eyes, which looked red. Allergies or sadness? I held him in my arms in a rocking way, and he seemed to go right to sleep. Tender, tender boy, I thought.

A car drove up. Laughter in the driveway.

He stirred, opened his eyes.

"Oh, the girls," I said, bouncing up. I went down to greet them and gave them cake and milk, and there were twenty minutes or so of chattering and then I came back to bed, kissing him. He was sniffling. I went looking for Kleenex and then the phone rang, Reilly calling for Jennie. "But he's sober," I said to Hedy. "Isn't that wonderful. He's doing so well this time."

"That's fine, but I really can't sleep," Hedy whispered,

breathing heavily, wheezing and sniffling. "I think they must have let in the dog," he said.

"I know. I'm sorry," I said. I turned and stretched down against his body, holding him by the waist.

Then another car. "Dylan," I said, letting go of Hedy too quickly. We heard the door slam, heavy feet on steps, more laughing with girls, then more doors.

"Forget it," Hedy said. He pulled on his jeans. The zipper closed. Then the snap. He was leaving.

I put on a robe. I walked him downstairs. "Don't your kids ever turn out the lights?" he said. Then, "I'm sorry." And he looked at me, cocking his head; my hands went to my head, covering the hair. "Maybe it's going to be okay. You look about fourteen years old. Little Harley. I shouldn't say stuff about the kids." He noticed a pizza box on the floor by the couch and picked it up and then put it down, with irritation.

"You will," I said. He would always say stuff about the kids. Just by the way he would pick up a pizza box like this.

He rumpled my hair. "You did a good job on this hair. Hey, thanks for today. It meant a lot." He kissed my forehead.

I just looked at him. "This is too abrupt," I said.

"I know," he said. "This is also a whole hell of a lot to absorb. I mean a lot to think about."

"I know from absorb."

"So. Just try to sleep." He kissed my nose this time. He looked at my hair—"That hair!"—and he left.

I turned off the lights and the stereo, sniffed for traces of pot in the air and was relieved to catch only the whiff of old pizza. I would have to find a place where the kids would have their own territory. Would it happen at all? How do you move in with someone when you cannot even say you love each other? I ate a bite of a piece of the pizza left in the box. Because people do that all the time now. Do not have illusions.

Brynn's door was closed. Do not disturb her with plans in

the middle of the night. Brynn will think it is crazy and she will be right. The guest room door was open. I thought about being at Ivan's; there was too much to think about. My parents. We hadn't even really begun to deal with that. I closed the door quietly and walked past Dylan's room, practicing restraint. I heard laughter. Brynn and her friends were in with Dylan. They were capable of amusing themselves without a little offer of more cake and milk. Dylan was being sweet to Brynn's friends, Carla and Sandy. Hedy was probably crazy. Perhaps still a bit jealous. Gary surely made it up about Dylan and drugs.

I got back into bed with a sense that nothing was quite right. It wasn't just that Hedy was gone, or that I felt odd that I did miss him, almost as if I'd had a foreshortened period of living with him in this swift night and now was seeing how I would feel when it ended.

Something else bothered me; it was less about the absence of Hedy and more about a presence here. Houses give hints of disorder in their night sounds, unbalanced breathing, too much silence here, a stealthy hush there.

In the gray morning light I was awakened by that feeling and opened my eyes to see Brynn standing by my bed, hands on hips.

"This is really it!" Brynn was saying. "Sandy and Carla are both in his room. Disgusting. And in his bed."

I pulled myself up on one elbow and patted the bed. "Come sit down; it's okay. They probably were watching TV, or got stoned a little and flaked out." The things, I thought, that one says. I did not think TV was okay, and I detested pot. I sounded to myself like one of those people at meetings who says, "I'm broke, mad at my wife and I hate my kids, but that's where I am today and it's okay." I thought of Helena telling me, "The cancer has spread, but I'm sitting here with you drinking coffee right now and it's okay."

Some things have got not to be okay. You have to start somewhere, in some way, to say: "This is not okay." In the mists and fog of this town certain realities had become obscured. There had to be a middle ground between going crazy over things you couldn't change and simply saying they were okay. There had to be a moment of clarity before you pitched into an acceptance where you could rant and rave and despise what was happening. Whatever had happened in Dylan's room last night was not appalling on the level of Helena's cancer; but specifics seemed beside the point today. Things must stop happening. No more people leaving, no more accidents, no more people not going to school, getting stoned, dealing with drugs, no more irate parents, no more changes, even the positive urges, the quickening of my drives, my various drives, yes, and his young eagerness. I wanted it to be simple, to go back to what I came here for: the predictable manageable everyday.

We had allowed strangeness to get a foot in the door, and it had moved in like the worst tenants.

Brynn sat dejected on the bed, staring through the window, down over the pale hazy hillside, the backs of the houses below, the river out in the distance.

"Friends," I said, "change. And it's hard when you haven't seen them for a while and you're going along thinking it's the same, and then, after a couple of hours, there's nothing more to talk about." I was talking too much.

"That isn't it," Brynn said. "I am in no mood to agree with you. I don't want to tell you everything, and I don't want you to tell me what I should understand when I'm not even sure myself what I'm feeling."

"What is it then?" I stroked Brynn's shoulders. When I couldn't help any other way, I felt I was doing the right thing just to touch. I wanted to pull Brynn down next to me and snuggle the way I would have when Brynn was small.

"I told you what it is." Brynn moved away from me. "I feel smothered now. I'm going out."

"It's so early."

"I like it early, being out early, before everyone."

"I know what you mean," I said. "It's good to be up and thinking before everyone else's thinking and moving around muddles up the day."

"No. Don't complicate it. I just like getting out early."

I stopped myself. Let her be angry and edgy; don't make her feel she has to apologize for real feelings. It was very difficult for me to believe truly that I did not have to be sad or angry along with them.

"Well, have a nice time or whatever."

"I am not going to have a nice time." Brynn wrenched herself off my bed, as though part of her did still want to curl up there and go back to sleep.

"Okay," I said.

"And stop saying 'okay.' Everything is not okay, you know, it just isn't." She stopped. She looked at me. "Especially your hair! I certainly hope that wasn't his idea."

"It wasn't. Believe me. Listen, I'll see you later." That seemed safe.

Brynn went back into her room and dressed noisily, drawers pulled out and slammed back, shoes thrown about. I was pleased to have someone else on my side. Almost nothing, I felt, was okay.

Around nine-thirty I heard footsteps, tentative; then whispers, and the door to the guest room closed. The girls had left Dylan.

By ten o'clock I was dressed. I came out of my room just as Jennie was coming out of hers. She looked at me with almost the same expression as Brynn had. "I knew Hedy'd have a hang-up—they're all into somethin', so what'd he cut the hair with, a Harley Davidson?"

"Funny you should mention that," I said. "And I did it."

"Lucky you don't get on TV this week," she said. She walked downstairs before me.

"Yes, isn't it fortunate how well things always work out."

We made coffee. I drank down two cups. I marched myself back upstairs.

I stood by Dylan's bed with my hands on my hips. "I hate what you did last night." Startled, he moved his hands around his head as though trying to drive off gnats.

"What did I do?"

"The girls. They were in here. With you."

He sat up, holding sheets around him. "It was everyone's idea, and nothing went on."

"But you are the one who is old enough to say that someone else's idea might not be so good."

"Mom"—his voice was cold and cruel and hard—"I have had it up to fucking here with being the example: it doesn't work; it got me nothing and nowhere. Do you hear me? I want to get up. You're in my way." He stuck his feet onto the floor.

"You don't always get what you want. No one does."

"Give me more news."

"You want news, buddy, you got it." I hated him when he talked like this, his voice with a razor edge whining with hostility. "I know Gary was busted, and he's saying you were dealing too."

"I can't imagine where you got that bullshit."

"That's irrelevant."

"It is fucking not. He's trying to clean everyone else out of your life so he can take over and screw his way to stardom. You're being used, Ma, and this is a fucking frame."

"Dylan! That's creepy, drug paranoia. I love you." The phone rang.

"I gotta get up, Mom."

"Jennie," I yelled downstairs, "will you pick up the phone.

Damn it, Dylan, nobody's coming down on you for anything. I love you to have a real life. But if you live with me it cannot include taking advantage of people."

"Well, you'll just have to put up with who I am until I go to college and we'll be out of each other's lives, okay?"

Jennie called up from the bottom of the stairs, "It's your father, Margot."

"Oh, God," I said.

"Say hello for me," said Dylan. "Tell him he's missing a really great Sunday morning at home with whoever the hell we are."

"Hello, darling," my father said. "How are the children?"

"They're fine," I said. "Brynn is out for a drive and Dylan is having a quiet morning upstairs."

"That was a sweet boy we met at Ivan's yesterday," my father said. "Very talented. It was nice of you to bring him along—an opportunity I hope he appreciated." He was saying, of course, that he hoped I was not going to take this seriously.

"I'm sure he did," I said, telling him that I would not tell him. And not telling him possibly felt like rejection, so I added, "It's a sort of a light pleasant thing. Nothing serious."

"He's a cute kid," my father added, making Hedy younger and less appropriate by the minute.

"Is that nice doctor still seeing you, or did he stop?" my mother asked. And before I could answer, she continued, "Your independence is the problem. You must marry. You've never been alone too long."

I bit my tongue to remember my determination to appreciate my mother. "How long is too long?" was one question that came to mind. I would keep the call appealing. "Actually, everything *is* wonderful: Brynn has two adorable friends here for the weekend and Dylan has been entertaining everyone." I decided to embroider, just a bit. "And the doctor and I have been thinking of looking at houses. We talked of it only last night."

"Oh," my father said, maybe wise to it or maybe not because he didn't want to be, "a late date?"

"Yes," I said.

"It would be nice," my mother said, "for you to have a real house for you and the children."

"Yes," I said. "This quonset hut is so chilly in winter."

"Margot!" my father said, protective. "Don't be fresh to your mother." The watchwords of Deborah's and my childhoods.

"Well, I know what you mean, Mother." Why keep at her —who will it change? Who will it help? "I'd love something like the Rappaports," I said.

"Yes," said my mother, "such a gracious home, such well-behaved animals; you ought to have someone English with the children. They have such excellent manners."

"I'll think about it, Mom," I said.

"They're a little old, Millicent, for a nannie," my father said softly, so as not to hit her over the head with reality. Although she knew it anyway and played dumb to torture all of us; especially, in some way, herself.

"Well, a houseman," I said, "may not be a bad idea."

"See," said my mother, "she knows I'm right—but he shouldn't be too attractive like that nice Mr. Miles. You wouldn't want to make your husband uncomfortable. You have to show a doctor some respect."

"Oh, absolutely, Mother." I said.

Sandy and Carla came downstairs and I handed shears to Sandy and a basket to Carla. "Would you pick daisies? There's a rash of them by the front door." I put the red calico tablecloth on the kitchen table, took out a white pitcher for the daisies, and folded navy blue bandannas for napkins. I put one of the bandannas around Spike's neck. "Now everything matches," I said, "which means everything cannot help but be wonderful."

Then Dylan came downstairs, all neat and scrubbed. "Hey, you cut your hair. I like it," he said. "Looks like mine."

"I know," I said. I put sour cream in the light blue pottery bowl Brynn had made in her fifth-grade pottery class at the Village Community School. We never should have moved.

"There's coffee if you want some."

"Hey, Mom." Dylan put his hand on my shoulder. "I'm sorry I acted that way, talked that way. You know I do drugs a little sometimes, but you've also got to know that the guy who gets busted always fingers someone else. I am not into any scene like that. You'd know if I was. You've been around enough just to feel it." He kissed my forehead. "Please don't worry about me. And I think you know how it is, and it's natural we're going to overreact to each other. Come, you sit down. We'll finish the breakfast thing."

Brynn returned. "Oh, the party's over?" She was cheerful now.

Youth is to be envied. It can be despair now and hilarity a moment from now. No consequences, and no lingering remorse. It all seemed so simple. A brother, a sister, two friends and a Harley Davidson—a neat little family sitting around the table, having brunch, with flowers, what could be a problem?

13

Ivan called on a summer Saturday morning and asked if he could speak to Hedy. "He's at his house," I said, pleased at the implied respectability. "Nine o'clock! Ivan?" I did not think Ivan even got up until noon, when it was late enough to call California.

"Something very good for him may have just come through. There's been a problem with plane schedules, and we'll need a warm-up group for The Grateful Dead. I'm sure," Ivan said, "this is all perfectly clear to you."

"Oh, perfectly." I laughed. "But it sounds like Hedy will be happy."

"He is," Ivan said, "very talented. You should know that."

"Oh yes, he is wonderful," I said. I gave Ivan Hedy's phone number. Would I have introduced Hedy to Ivan if he wasn't good? Of course. Love's judgment has my mother's selective vision. Do I love Hedy? Probably. And is he wonderful? I'd watched Hedy rehearsing with his group, so serious and intense. I'd gone to the recording studio with him and watched him, totally immersed, listening to his tapes being mixed: judging and selecting; frowning and impatient when the sound wasn't right; leaping up and happy, hugging the engineer, the producer, the drummer and even me when it was. Love. He must love me too. It was one thing to let them assume you are sleeping with someone, quite another to hug her in front of your friends.

"This is everything I've waited for: The Dead! They never have warm-ups and now this once they have to, and it's us! This afternoon!" Hedy crowed over the phone to me. "This never happens. We'll have to really jam it. Nothing this good." He paused. "Something will fuck it up."

"That's a terrible attitude," I said, wondering just what would happen, because I also believed that manifest destiny means probable disaster.

Hedy drove, playing on the floor shift of my Chevy as though it was not an automatic. The group—drums, guitars, fender, banjo, trumpet and sax—had all gone on ahead, trucking the equipment down to a meadow near Danbury in their parade of vans. Hedy had planned to take his limo, but it was the most perfectly gleaming day—the ideal sort of day to go with the top down and we must go, I told him, down the old east road, right down from Medwin's Landing.

"The Interstate is dreadful, Hedy," I had said, "and why ride over west when we are going more east and will have more than enough time. I just have to wait for these peach tarts to finish baking so they can cool."

"A fucking flat—right now, today!" Hedy spoke with forced calm. He was trying not to blame me. So easy when it was all my fault. He took his red sunglasses, which had slipped down his nose when the car had shuddered and thudded and wobbled to a dead stop. Now Hedy pitched his sunglasses over into the trees by the roadside.

"A fucking flat." He would need to say it eight times I supposed. "We should've taken the limo. Here we are with a fucking flat while the band, even my roadies, are cruising to the gig in nice, cool, superfitted vans."

"We could have been killed. Keep it simple." I was shaking. I'd have been much angrier if I had to be somewhere and someone else controlled it and it hadn't worked.

"Cool the slogans, Margot." He took off his white silk scarf and laid it neatly over the back of the seat. "You got a spare in this thing? Look who I'm asking. I'll check it out. Don't go anywhere."

Hedy looked in the trunk. "Of course," he snapped, slamming down the lid. I knew instantly: Dylan had the spare tire in the car he'd loaned to his friend to take up to the Cape. Hedy leaned over and ruffled my hair, looking up the road, squinting at the sun. He was jiggling on high idle. I had actually never seen him still. Cleo also moved about all the time; it probably had to do with being under thirty and wanting to get on with it; that sense of urgency. It wasn't until this moment that I realized I did not have it in quite the same way. But then this was not the moment to judge. This was not my event. And the least I could do now, it seemed, was to be calm and supportive and avoid making further suggestions. Oh, I'd hate myself if I wrecked this for him. I far preferred it when I only sabotaged myself.

"We're hitching a ride," he said.

"And leave the car?" I stroked the dashboard gently.

"Yeah, all by itself. Let's truck it."

Hush, I told myself. And said, eagerly, "Well, I haven't hitched in years. And rarely to a rock concert."

"Yeah. Like *never*," he said. And he put his arm around my shoulder. We had walked about a mile when we came to a shrine.

"Shepherd's Haven," I said, reading from the sign. "It's enchanting. It's wonderful. Oh, look! Look!" I was panting, searching for an excuse to rest.

White plaster statues of Jesus, Mary, Saint Francis and Mary Magdalene had been set in niches cut into the hillside. Saint Francis stood under a roof of bright yellow ripple plastic, with birds. The others had sturdier shake roofs. One small saint was sheltered in a white arch, half of an old bathtub, stamped Eljer, upended and set firmly into the hillside.

Hedy stood with his thumb out. We might never make it now. He was trying not to let me see he was angry.

"Ass-fuck," he snarled at a car that slowed, then whizzed by.

"Your language sucks when you're mad," I shouted at him over my shoulder. And I was angry because I felt guilty, of course. How wonderful to be a Christian and never have guilt. Except, I suppose, Christians have despair. No one wins. A saint was buried alive in a coffin, and, when the coffin was opened later, it was determined he had pulled his hair out in despair. Because of this lack of acceptance his sainthood, if that is the proper word, was revoked. A Jew would have been honored for feeling despair, for believing in God's essential irony. That saint, his patchy, raw scalp and all, would have been given a very lovely testimonial dinner at a distinguished hotel.

I thought of the old Yiddish curse: in which you wished your enemy had twenty nations, with forty states, each having eighty glistening cities with one hundred and sixty marble hotels holding three hundred and twenty canopied golden beds, and in each bed the enemy should be lying with a toothache with every dentist in every city in every state in every nation out of town at a convention and their answering machines all broken.

I saw myself now in twenty convertibles, rushing Hedy to forty rock concerts, and standing trying to hitch a ride outside eighty shrines in one hundred and sixty steaming-hot Connecticut valleys with three hundred and twenty furious young lovers who, even when things were going well, did not know the virtue of patience, the value of serenity, and the wisdom of staying in the moment, as only thirty-eight years of chaotic experience and a few months in A.A. had taught me. All of which I now demonstrated by stamping my feet in front of the shrine and bursting into tears.

What am I doing here and how could I have done this to him and why do I expect the answers to come from this plaster person standing in half a bathtub?

I prayed for a car to come, to stop. Then, espadrilles dragging along the dusty road, I walked off, ahead of him, not looking behind. I would walk the entire way to Danbury if it would help. His boots clomped behind me. He grabbed me by the waist and turned me toward him. "You aren't crying, for Christ's sake?"

"I don't like you to do religious swearing. I've just been praying to your God to get us to your concert."

"Hey, it's cool. If we don't, so we won't, so it's fucked. No big deal. Foxy lady." He laughed, tracing the silver glitter writing across the red t-shirt I had borrowed from Brynn. "You hate rock concerts anyway."

"Don't be crazy, Hedy. I know what this means for you. I should have hired a real limousine for you the minute we heard about it." I looked at the shadows of the trees along the road dappling his lovely face with sunshine. I could not bear this disappointment for him.

"It wasn't your responsibility. And anyway it's my deal. I'm not one of your kids. You don't have to put on the moneybags thing for me, babe."

I decided to let that go. For now. I will never try to control anyone's day again. I will only, only, I promised myself, do their plans.

Too fast a response for any modern system of communication save prayer, or possibly, as all good things only come when one has gone beyond giving up hope to the next stage where the will is suspended in a kind of white noise, a van pulled up at the moment we had decided that at the first phone we came to we would call and hire some sort of transportation. And, as Hedy's fortune would have it (it was his day after all), the van people were on their way to the concert. A half-dozen young people offering joints, "ludies," beer and red wine from a communal jug. They did not help Hedy's increasing anxiety; cars, they were sure, were already being turned back from the concert as far as ten miles away.

Fearful premonitions were clearly part of the ritual. If you expect total disaster, the reality of the scene will seem better by comparison.

Hedy took a drag on a joint, which was then offered to me.

"No, she doesn't want that," he cut in quickly.

I should, perhaps, have objected to his speaking for me, but it made me feel good and protected, which is supposed to be a contradiction in terms.

As the van bumped over the road, I sat on a hot, grimy mattress reminding myself I was having a good time. I looked out at people walking who had parked miles away. Kids in jeans and opened shirts, girls in elastic strapless tops and t-shirts, the abundance of hair, lots of patched things, thermos bottles, and jugs of wine and six packs of beer and Coke. A crowd milling in the general direction of the concert meadow. Child parents with little kids straddling their shoulders, straw hats, top hats, derbies, a wreath of plastic nasturtiums, gold metallic knee socks.

"I just hope our group got here," Hedy said. "We're doin' the warm-up."

"Oh yeah?" said one of the kids in the van. "The Dead don't ever have no warm-up."

"I know," Hedy came back. "There's always a first. They got stuck."

"Man, you better be good! That crowd's gonna tear you apart," said a kid from under a straw cowboy hat covered with Grateful Dead buttons.

A sleeping girl in the van awakened. "Hey, anybody got a joint?" she said, asking before her eyes were open.

I remembered that feeling. At this moment I didn't miss it.

Hedy leaned forward, knee jiggling, fingers moving.

A cop stopped the van. "You'll have to park out there."

Hedy leaned out fast. "But I got to get to the stage, man. I've got to go on."

"You figure it out, buddy. Shoulda used your helicopter," said the cop, not believing.

"Even stars walk, I guess," said the one in the van with the hat.

"Get off my case," snapped Hedy.

"Be cool, guys," said the girl under the blanket. "It's a hundred fucking ten in here."

"Have a drag, knock it off. We'll be out of here as fast as we can," said the smoker.

Hedy dragged on the joint. My eyes riveted on it.

"I'm sorry I got uptight. I sounded like a spoiled asshole," he said. "How you doin', Fox?"

"I'm cool," I said. "I'm always more mellow when you are a little high," I said. I hated being around pot. But I could not, had better not start in on him.

"That's funny, isn't it. We seem to catch moods from each other."

"It could be," I muttered, as the truck bounced to a stop, "that I just *seem* more mellow because you are." Fortunately, he did not hear that. It is not his problem that it is my problem. I might have preferred a little rage to show he cared. But then, and I had to remind myself of this, I would say I would not be intimidated by his childish anger.

"This is as far as she goes," the driver said.

Hedy was already out, looking for a way in. The enormous field had been circled with railroad cars, like the wagons set around an encampment, which prevented no one from getting in.

The very agile stood on each other's shoulders and climbed up, vaulting themselves on the tops of the cars, standing and squatting, looking down, hopping about joyously. Precariously near the edge some stopped, hands on hips, surveying.

Young mothers with babies on their chests in slings were lifted up. Such a place to bring a baby! But then I had nursed Dylan in a mob, outside an arena the name of which I thought I would never forget and now had, trying to stack a hall with antiwar protestors. At times I hated sobriety for unveiling my fear, teaching caution and a disdain for the recklessness I once cherished. It was not, I acknowledged, the special domain of sobriety. It was, of course, the lofty, unpalatable vantage point of maturity.

Ladders here and there materialized, and kids scrambled up, reaching down to help each other. I had always been fond of this charitable aspect of mob scenes, always maintained, against overwhelming evidence to the contrary, that emergency brought out the most positive aspects of human nature. Urgency pumps adrenaline, and I adored the feeling, the frisson of terror.

A grizzly of a boy in yellow laced-up shoes and Levi's shorts, shy eyes and features buried in hair—the kind of boy who has a ham radio, runs the tape machine at the rally and collects prefifties *National Geographics*—was holding a ladder.

Hedy came running back, eyes spinning like pinwheels. "I can't get near the fucking stage. It's a total jam. We'll have to get in, up and over, and I'll go right up, come in from the front, up. Oh God! If I was just famous enough so it showed." Someday, I thought, if he gets what he wants he'll wish it didn't show.

Hedy tossed his hair, hitched his cowboy belt. "We're goin' up and over, Fox. Can you do it?"

I looked up at the ratchety ladder pitched against the train car. "Is that a good angle?" I asked. And answered myself, "Is there any good angle?"

"Want me to go first? I'll pull you up."

"Oh, yes," I said.

He scrambled up the ladder, hands reached for him and he leapt up. He looked down. Someday he'd stand up in a place like this, and they would all know him. They would all turn. They would all look up. They would all go out of their minds just to see him and now, today, he was reaching down for me.

I looked at the ladder. Me looking up a very different matter than me looking at Hedy looking down. DAUGHTER OF DESIGNER, REPORTER, MOTHER OF TWO, TOPPLES TO DEATH AT ROCK CONCERT; or would it simply read, WOMAN MISSES RUNG ON LADDER, KILLED.? I would prefer it not to happen until it would say, MARGOT FOX KILLED IN TRAGIC FALL. God hates those fantasies, I reminded myself. "God help me accept whatever happens on the next rung."

"Come on, Fox. You prayin'?"

"Yes! Exactly!" I started up the ladder. Stoned people holding it, Hedy reaching down. "One rung at a time," I reminded myself, and did not look down.

On top, now, I bounced around, "Wow! Look at it!" A laid-out mob as far as I could see, covering the field. "They'll all be watching you!" I said to him.

On the tiny stage, way out there, figures moved, surrounded by the masses of equipment which almost made the musicians' instruments incidental. More people clambered up, and then they pulled up the ladder and put it down the other side. Others climbed down. Then Hedy.

"Hurry, Margot. Come on, jump to me."

"I'll knock you down."

"I'll catch you!" he yelled, and I beamed and leapt from a high rung right into his arms. He rocked back, laughing. "See, nothin' to it but to do it, right?"

"Right!" I love you, I almost said it. "Whew!" is what I said. I would never say "I love you" again. But at this moment, tight in his arms, amid a sea of jumping, swaying, sweating, blissed-out kids, it was a little like love. Yes, it was. He nuzzled my hair; I pulled at his. "We got here."

"Wherever," he said. We picked our way toward the stage over and around thousands of bodies.

I collected images for a dozen sex fantasies as we went. Kids are so truly sexy, so captured by sex. I remembered when sex was the only thing on my mind—or not sex, but such yearning for the idea of it. I never wanted to stop that yearning. Never wanted to get old, stiff, straight, and dull. These firm bottoms like fruit to bite, this chunky girl straddling a short, tough guy with big heavy legs; these sleek tan hands clapping, such smooth skin. I gave a quick hug to Hedy as I walked beside him. He turned his head, giving me the profile grin, the lifted eyebrow, the violet eyes navy blue in this light, his best flashy look. "I'm going to get you later, get you on the way home," I said.

"Not if I get you first," he said.

The local advance guys guarding the stage recognized Hedy, to his delight. It's going to be all right now. "You made it, man," they said. We moved up the stairs, up, through the wings, to the backstage, where Dallas and Joey and Paul waited, sharing a joint. And the terrible Denise, who was, it seemed, now hanging out with Bobbie, Hedy's new sax player. Now that Hedy was going to be a star, I decided I should be generous to Denise.

"We ain't ever going to get out of here," Hedy said to everyone in general.

At the back of the stage were tables with Cokes, urns of coffee and platters of sandwiches, cold cuts, fruits and Danish. And there were always girls: tough, large-eyed, slender girls with tottering heels, boots and tiny real gold chains, discussing reviews in the *Rolling Stone*, gossip from other concerts, where to get designer things at discount, like real wives of real theatre people. "What about Deco?" and "Did you see the entire black velvet room at Bloomie's?"

"Margot," said Denise, "I heard you on the radio. It was a scream." And now that Hedy was to be a star Denise would also be nice to me. I had heard from Hedy that Denise had decided to be a New York hairstylist. She had her hair arranged in three chignons and one pompadour today, speared with ebony chopsticks that dangled small bells.

Hedy was eating with both hands. "I'm crazy to eat now."

"So you'd be crazy anyway," said Bobbie, eating corned beef with one hand and a cheese Danish with the other. Hedy's manner changed as he watched Joey strapping on his leg mike. Hedy quieted down. I could see him drawing in, tightening his energy around him like a cloak he'd fling wide open when he took the stage.

"A real bummer," Paul said. "They're not going to like it when we come on and they're expecting The Dead."

"They know, Paul, they've already been told The Dead got hung up." Everything, to Paul, was a real bummer, except booze and broads. "You're goin' on," Denise said.

Hedy said, "You hang out, watch me for luck. I'm goin' out there and rock their socks." He was all electric authority now. I knew he could not stop now to touch, to lock eyes. He was gone. If he paused an instant he'd lose the momentum, the fever and the will that overwhelms every question, fear or logical consideration. Can I do it? Will I be good? Will I be better than ever? It's all gone, gone in the coils of hot sparked wire, gone into the veins.

I watched him prance and glow and rock his guitar and the machine it became, more than music, a driving thing, an extension of cock and pelvic force. And whoever thought it was less than sex was kidding.

The crowd was on guard. Show us. Kids bustled a bit, ignoring the band at first. Then the "rip-off" mutters subsided; some still wondered would The Dead even get there. But I heard "They're pretty good, these guys"; a bit here and there, in small bunches they began to listen, and they liked it. This was a blazing army of sound you could not help but surrender to, giving, knees buckling, shouting. And the feeling began to catch; the group, reassured, went wilder and faster. They hopped and bounded and sweated right away, shaking showers off their hair, whirling wet wreaths like circular sprinklers.

They adored it when Paul on second guitar and Hedy pranced toward each other, getting down, then backing up, raising, lowering their machines, laughing, then frowning as they got into it, then mock-scolding with eyes and shaking heads battering at their machines, showing them off to each other; all "I'll show you, you show me" amped to the Connecticut skies.

Oh, I stood there, clapping and then crying out where he could never hear, "I love you, I love you, I love you." I could get it all out because I was hardly able to hear myself. I stood there, bouncing, out of time; someone went by, and put his hands on my hips, showing me the rhythm, standing behind me, moving right, and I looked around to see and it was one of Hedy's roadies. I laughed, and he went on, and I did it wrong again, just loving it anyhow, loving moving with him, with his group, and with his long hair and his twitching thighs and his loins and fast fingers, and his eyebrows lifting and sweat like diamonds flying, he became everything I meant by sex. He is sex with his footmen, the safe-swell danger of the gang-bang by expression and sound, no touching, the distant lady's dream come true. Put this fantasy on the cassette, these faces, hands, this hair, these hipless hips, and click them on when you climb up on me and oh, do me then and then with this and this.

Out there, down there, I moved through the crowd as though having him meant I owned it like he did right now. I watched guys taking off t-shirts, hanging them like loincloths from their belts. I wanted to take off all my clothes and just leap. Just leap high above the rest so I'd be flying level with his eyes, but would he see? Who sees when he is coming except in flashes? He'd see me as a face between this drum, that mike; he'd see me but it wasn't me he was coming over. It's this getting him off.

"Tell me," I told myself. "Don't you know what that's all about? You get yours and time enough he gets to have his." I watched them listening and they loved him. They cheered, they applauded, they yelled for more, and he was flushed and moved and in his world.

And as The Grateful Dead arrived, I pushed through the crowds backstage, pushed through everyone clustered around Hedy. "Oh, isn't he super?" Denise crowed. "Hey, hey." Joey hugged me. "We'll never be that good again," said Paul. You could tell by the faces of the engineers, the light people, the roadies, the packs of kids with press cards and cameras; you could tell by the sound of the voices, the glow on the faces, that this was a real beginning.

And here he is. I felt like I was pushing through the troops to greet my lover. I found him. I reached for him grinning, jumping through a dozen people to him.

"Was I good? Did you like it? Did you hear them? It's going to happen!" He threw his arms around me with such urgency, hugging all that sound, all those faces, all this future to him.

"Yes, yes, yes," I said to everything.

He was looking everywhere wanting it all from everyone, and I wanted him to have it all.

"I want to go down there," he said, "and watch The Dead. Will you come with me?"

"You'll be mobbed."

"Don't be crazy." He grabbed me around the waist; the crowds roared when they saw The Dead, and Hedy led me carefully out to hear. "They're like my idols," he said, "that's what's so wild."

"Hedy. It's all going to happen for you too now." And I kissed him.

It would all happen for Hedy. But The Dead was another world. And I was not sure I would want that to happen to someone I love. I love. Yes. I loved him, I told myself. In this minute.

The soft glow of late afternoon faded; the heat eased; and the night was shot with cyclamen beams of light, like search-lights casting about for camp airplanes, an imitation of war. Kids were sharing food from bags, baskets, and knapsacks, pulling off bites of rolls, chomping potato chips, swigging from jugs and bottles, but all standing doing these things, just staring, numb now. Boys stood like statues (without roofs), with their eyes closed, praying to the sound. A boy on crutches, foot amputated, bounced.

I walked out, far out, losing all sense of time, all around the perimeters. I looked across in every direction; I looked high above the speakers, making this sound work, controlling the mob, a town's worth of energy, deflected, numbed and all predicted. I thought of Brynn and Dylan: they did not see this; they go for sound; they go to catch another kind of fever than the one we had wanted to catch from crowds; they did not go to catch the fever to change the world, but only to catch the longing of the road songs; the new young pragmatists, here for the sound of trucker music; roadwork, traveling-through-life-music, with a beat that says you just go on, and you don't look too far forward or too far back; no songs of strawberry fields; songs now of how it is at home and what you take to get around how it is. *Trouble with you is the trouble with me!*

I looked up at these icons: these giant black speakers piled up like safes, blocks, totems of our time, verging on toppling, unevenly piled, fifty feet high; who knows; who can count anymore; they soared up, pounding a rhythm down to follow. *Trouble ahead, trouble behind.* I looked up and up again at towers of scaffolding studded with blazing lights, watch-towers; I thought of madmen on towers, in warehouses, in shadows, with guns. They even have a song about a man watching people with his gun. Banners here, saying "The Dead," billowed in the breeze. And here cops perched up on the railroad cars like dark birds on phone lines. Young couples, refugees of the Love Generation, coolers between them, mutating into the middle class, t-shirts claiming allegiance to Led Zeppelin, Rolling Stones, Beatles. "That's where I came in!" I said to myself, tightly holding on to Hedy's hand.

This time, this sound, and it was another sound that caught me, whirled me out of safety, out of the suburban delusion, the complacent early marriage. I remembered a dancing woman, her thighs moving under her cheerful print Capri pants, red and pink harlequin, moving just so. That flesh under those pants made my face hot, missing something, longing so, that image made my decision. That plain woman I never knew wearing pants I would never wear, that woman I never saw again moved in a way that had changed my life forever. Made me start to want. To want so badly it became a torrent of need and I drank to give me the courage and then I drank to cover the fear of what the courage made me do and then I drank because I could not stop.

I clung tight to Hedy's hand and considered the thought that this young hand, now switched and firmly covering mine, was safety.

Today.

And I looked up at the Frisbees sailing across the crowds like tiny flying saucers, pennants unfurled, and I moved safely among the crowd with Hedy, who did seem for now like home. A couple were lying on top of each other; a very young man skulked by with a kid. "Do that in your own goddamn bedroom."

The muddy hope of Woodstock, the charming con of the flower people, the impact of the Revolution, dwindled here, totally wiped now of any illusion of meaning, idealism or focus beyond that of Rock Personality. The Grateful Dead were the musical version of Kerouac, of Nelson Algren, the latter-day hitchhikers; these road people wearing glow-in-the-dark lime Popsicle halos. "Get me one," someone called. A halo flew through the air. The flower children grew, I thought, to consume, electronic children, space age flappers.

Circus Maximus. They won't be able to think. Let them snort. *Drivin' that train high on cocaine.* My mind flashed to Dylan. I stood for a moment next to a tall boy, tall as Dylan, who resembled a bleached blond mummy in pose, features and expressiveness, with scarlet eyes.

There was, too, a time before the flower children; another time I remembered, before the marriage, in my black trench-coat; all cool jazz and shades, handmade sandals and blank verse and a time before that. How many times had I had? How many lives? How many would Brynn and Dylan have and claim, "This is my time." And would this time be their first and the last for everyone? Nothing left but the Dead. Do not think the unthinkable. Do not think. This was my time. It is the condition of dreaming that is bearable. We dreamed of being movie stars; they dream of being rock stars. Will this darkened cinder spin on out into the void leaving the refuse of the dreams, a cloud, a ghost of a yearning old clown where a planet used to do its orbit?

The blond boy suddenly, slowly, toppled over on his back.

Trouble ahead; Lady in Red.

The moon got lost amid the lights, muted by fireworks shooting up from the crowd, still swaying, hooting and thrilled as they went on playing, driving sound, louder, going longer than any group in the whole world, heroes of fifty thousand white middle-class kids who lurched and cheered as the banks of light beamed on the giant skull, now turned evil green against electric blue. It takes only a hundred million amps to turn them on. And coke, of course. Would there be dealers here? Would I run right up against Dylan with a paper hat and a tray: "Get your red hot tooters here."

Trouble ahead. Am I the lady in red? Do not think.

Against the stage, bright red now, with the skull gone ultraviolet, flew a helicopter. Dwarfed, real, flying right over the group. "Hey, we got our own air force! We got everything! Just about everything," Hedy shouted.

The Dead stood right up; a pantheon with mikes like Bible staffs. So close they got, shouting on and on their songs; they were blowing these mikes. Staring out then at each other, they'd take a beat; they went again and when it could not get faster or deeper, it lashed on and went faster and deeper.

A girl in a green scarf top stood with her guy; she held his hips close to her back as she moved; she looked down at her own breasts bobbing, gum chewing; they both clapped, and she seemed to have four arms. The girl turned and whispered in her guy's ear. I wanted Hedy now. Would he hear me if I said it? His eyes so mesmerized. He would not hear. This boy did not hear. The Dead were the generals of this road-weary army. Girls here were camp-following.

A guy walked by. "I want it to go on forever."

"We need water over here," called a boy with a hand bandaged in someone's jockey shorts.

"What have you got in that thermos?"

"Ritalin and nitrous oxide."

Casey Jones, you better watch your speed.

"I am so sad because it just isn't going to go forever." A girl with tufts of hair in different colors was crying, clapping her hands, her face was drenched. "Well, next year we'll get here earlier. Oh God," she sighed, "I can't wait 'til next year. Next year it'll be even greater."

"There will be one million people."

God forbid there should not be the qualifications. Heaven forfend there should be nothing left out. One would have no reason in the world to move one more step, take one more breath.

We would go back with his band, Hedy said.

"Hey," I said, "could we get some of those halo things?"

"You got it," he said.

"Come on."

He took me out toward the perimeter of the crowd, and we found a booth selling t-shirts and halos. As Hedy walked through the crowd more kids recognized and touched him now that the sound was over, seeing again; a few girls kissed him. Do you short-circuit finally if you see and hear too much at once? I clung to Hedy. "There's going to be a time soon where you just won't be able to do this, to walk through a crowd," I said. "Do you know that?"

He grinned. "Maybe in a year or three or four. I dig it. If you put this thing in the freezer right away the glow will keep for a week." He spun the halo around and around, whirling on his fingertips.

"Far outlasting its slight enchantment, its mild fascination," I said. "Sort of like a short love affair." I startled myself and quickly bought four more halos, "so I won't run out of enchantment when you're off being a star."

"You'll just have to go with me then."

I slipped one halo around my neck. "Or you can keep me in the freezer." I laughed.

Would this happy cynicism also outlast its novelty? More important, how did it begin, so if I should ever get anxious again, I will know how to stop it right away, before the loving gets me down. I flipped another halo in the air, caught and spun it about on my wrist. "A year ago I could never have done that," I said, laughing, and tried it again.

Yes. *All you need is love, love, love.* Please!

The halo fell on a kid I was stepping over. "Hello there," I said, "I have made you an angel."

A year before, I expected to feel sad underneath for the rest of my life. And less time ago than that I had never again expected to know how it was to just feel this. Just right now. This. Put the glow in the freezer. Do not think.

14

Brynn and I were going over the month's mail, doing bills. Brynn wrote the checks, and I signed them.

The *House & Garden* had come and I was looking at it, all the pictures of perfect houses, tables laden with platters of lovely summertime food. Tonight I would make a tomato salad for the children with fresh basil, slices of cold chicken with tarragon sauce. I wished Hedy were here. He had gone to Hartford to do a concert. It was becoming terrific for him. And I could not help wondering if that would mean it would not be also wonderful for us.

"Hedy's going to move out of his dad's house," I said. "I'm thinking I might buy a place with a guesthouse he could lease."

"Monkey see, monkey do," said Brynn.

"What do you mean?" I asked.

"You know what I mean. You don't even want to stay here after we're in college; you always said you'd go back to the city. And you said you'd never move for a man again."

"Well, I'm not. Moving for a man. It's a good investment. Some property."

"So when you're old we won't be able to put you in a home." Brynn put the bills that my accountant would pay directly into an envelope.

"I hadn't thought of that. You're right. I'll huddle in one

room barricaded behind a hundred years of *Vogue* and *House & Garden* magazines."

"Eating cat food," Brynn said. "I'm not too worried. He'd hate the houses you like and you'd hate the ones he liked."

"You're right. But it would be fun looking."

"Probably," said Brynn. "Here, these have to be answered." She handed three letters to me.

"Who knows, we might even see something we like tomorrow."

"I'm glad you're not rushing into anything," Brynn snapped. She took the receipts to the filing cabinet.

"Look, Brynn, if I found the right place we could even put in a little recording studio; Hedy could use it; perhaps it would all be completely deductible, and I could do some of my work right here."

"And leave Cleo? Tsk." Probably the only person who could talk me out of this insanity was Cleo. I considered calling her if it got to that.

I got up and put my arm around Brynn. "I'll always do my shows in New York; we could do demos here. You could even do some of your voices. You're so good—and it would be easy to do at home."

"I'm going out," Brynn said suddenly. Whenever I brought up the subject of her future, Brynn snapped on the TV or went out.

"Where are you going?"

"Do I ask you?"

"You could. I'm giving a little teatime talk for the Brightriver College Women in Communications Club. They'd love to have you there."

"You would love to have me there; let's get it right. And they can enroll me before I escape into another truck stop or bowling alley. Sorry, I'm just cross. I think I'll go to Helena's; see who's there."

"Will you be home for dinner?"

"You know I'd say I will even if I won't."

"I know. I'm supposed to ask. It's programmed in when you're born, like 'Have you done your homework?' and 'Is he a good driver?' "

"Deprogram it." Brynn hurled her bag over her shoulder and marched out.

Never would I have admitted it. I hated the weeks that went by without speaking to my sister or my parents, the months when I did not see them. I loved, or perhaps needed more than loved, the exchanges. There was an earnest desire to please and forgive which underscored these talks where we'd bounce white lies back and forth. I don't think Deborah and I knew, going into adulthood, that there were totally honest conversations, which might have been why we both used the interview form in our different professions: we will ask and you will please show us how real people talk. What I went for were the material facts that had been always so obscured, and Deborah went further down.

I flung myself on my stomach on the couch and picked up the phone and called Deborah.

"Is it easier to be the second child?"

"Are you asking about me today because you want to know what's happening in my life or is something going on about Brynn?" she said.

"Something's going on with Brynn, I think, but also with you. And you're figuring if I'm having a problem you'll be the adult and wait to discuss yours."

"That is true," she said. "Also that will give me the long end of the conversation. Second child. Yes. It would be very hard to be the second child to Dylan."

"Yes," I said, "go on."

"Now you sound like me, with the solemn encouragements. First children get too much of the bad and the good attention. But they really aren't children now and the best thing you can do is show you know how to live a life—and tell me when you find out." She laughed.

"That's a harsh laugh for you," I said.

"Well," Deborah said, evading, "just be a good listener is mainly the thing Brynn needs."

"That's like suggesting carrots to Dracula," I said, "but I'm listening to you, so tell me. What's happening?"

"My needs are changing," she said. Guarded.

"Oh," I said, "you're telling me you're getting a divorce. It is the end of the Upper West Side Establishment."

"No, cheese and wine, discussions of single parenting, a word even I hate, and Sunday in the park with Daddy—that's the establishment now. And it's only separation, Margot, for now."

"Deborah—I didn't mean it—oh, Debbie, that's hard for you."

"I watched. You survived it, and we just want to experience ourselves for a while. The base feelings are still there, they just are lit differently."

I flinched a bit when Deborah reminded me she also had the same theatrical references, the same background—that I did not own (as she would put it) the connection to our father.

"Listen," I said, "I'm here. You must come up with the kids—or not. I do love you."

"It's not so bad, I'll tell you when you can throw chicken soup down my throat. And over it isn't yet."

I loved when Deborah would sound like our grandmother. "Well, that's good," I said. I had now twisted the phone cord up my leg like a snake.

"I'm not so sure," she said. "Now just let Brynn discover herself."

I made my teatime visit as fast as possible, and then in the lazy Medwin's Landing twilight I stepped through my garden, going around the crouching herbs, snipping off tufts and twigs. Then I trimmed small platters of food with dandelions and nasturtiums.

"Looks good enough to wear," said Dylan.

"If," Brynn said, "you happen to be a hat." I looked at her so happily. Tease me; hate me, but do not go.

I was chattering pointedly (too pointedly) about how "for sanity, if nothing else, we have to stop focusing on men and women and relationships."

"I thought you hated that word," Brynn said.

"I do," I said, "but the others seem to have gone out of contemporary usage."

"I wouldn't even know what they were if I heard them," said Brynn.

"What's the matter?" I asked. I remembered what Deborah said: just listen.

"Oh, boys are such idiots. Sometimes."

"Very nice," said Dylan.

"Be still," said Brynn.

"Improvement on 'shut up,' " he said.

I gave him a look. The look my father gives me when I'm fresh with my mother. Catch these games, scurrying out.

"As I was trying to tell you," Brynn said, "Freddy has this class in Applying for Scholarships and Grants, and so I asked him, 'You and Teddy make so much in your work, what do you need that for?' and he goes, 'Because I get college credit for it, and I like to invest my money in equipment. Somethin' that will pay off,' and then he goes to me, 'You know, honey, you ought to get yourself a real job—chicks can do a lot of things—not just pumpin' gas.' "

"My," I said.

"I mean really," said Brynn.

"Well, you've come a long way, guys," Dylan said, "even some of the women on TV soaps now have jobs. As Brynn should know. So what's bugging you, Brynn? Freddy probably said he was busy, so now you have to invent a reason to go out later so Mom won't just think you're cruising around."

"The reason," Brynn said, "that you know what he's up to probably is you do the same bullshit to Alison and every other person who thinks she likes you."

"You're so rude to each other," I said. I thought we'd eat at the round table in the corner of the room. And that's where I was sitting. Dylan had left the table and was lying down on the couch with his plate on the coffee table.

"Dinner is a terribly important symbol of family life," I said. "The entire trouble with houses, today, is the lack of dining rooms."

"Yeah," said Dylan, "and this house did have a dining room, but you turned it into an office."

"Well"—and I looked around the living room, considering alternatives—"we could change things around again. But"—and I paused, testing—"it might be simpler to move." I looked at Brynn. She was all wrapped up around herself, like a Henry Moore statue. "What's the matter, darling?" And before she could answer, I added, "It's hard, I know—the waiting."

"That is not the trouble, Mom," she said, voice of stone. "I am just quiet. Why do you have to assume I am depressed, or that it is because I am not going out. Can't a person just be quiet?"

"Oh," he said, "no one would ever think you were on edge or anything."

"Maybe it is you, Dylan," I said. "Every time you're having a problem you are very quick to pin it on us."

"That isn't true," he said. "You don't see it either when you are, but it comes through. I can tell by your face and you always think we're upset and you have to fix it or understand it."

The phone rang. We pretended we were not watching

each other, pretending none of us cared who was calling, arguing over which one was going to *get* the phone, and then we all three bolted for it.

"It's for you," Dylan got it. "Prince Valiant."

"Shut up," said Brynn, already brightening into direct hostility toward Dylan. He called Freddy "Prince Valiant" because of Freddy's Valiant car. "So what is the matter with a Valiant?" Brynn had demanded when Dylan had made fun of the car the first time. "It's a dumb, stupid ugly car, a car like someone's mother would drive," said Dylan.

"I resent that," I said, but better to drive a two-hundred-dollar convertible with problems than a new regular car.

This was not the time to say anything to Brynn about how much better she seemed because Freddy had called, but when she went into the kitchen balancing plates happily on her arms, Dylan said, "You're a fraud when you pretend it shouldn't matter if a boy calls or not, when you tell her there are more important things. You should see the look of relief on your face when it was Freddy. You don't care what makes Brynn happy, as long as she is."

"Actually," I said, "that is true. I have expectations but I'm trying to learn hers won't be mine; mine were hardly what my parents wanted." I remember my father's cordial, icy manner when he met Hedy at Ivan's. And I was pleased with Alison, but I wondered readily about how warm she might be; would she be supportive of Dylan.

"I suppose," Dylan said, "that when any one of us is in the reasonably pleasant initial phase of an affair, there is a symbiotic response. Conversely . . ."

I was still startled when Dylan used formal adult words. I had to stop myself from congratulating him for his language, as I once remembered, when he found a yo-yo a while ago, saying, "You know how to work a yo-yo?" And he had stared at me. "I studied it last semester," he said, "and passed."

He continued, "When one of us is having an overtly rotten time, like when Bill left, we band together and there's a kind of festivity over the crises, more dinners out, less of you pretending to pull a family-on-TV act, which always ends in tension like this."

"That's very smart," I said, "very wise." Enough. Also, when one of us was embarked on such a happy romance, the other two joined, pairing off, amused, watching, playing parents to the couple. This would last a very short time, of course, because then the criticism would creep in, a disguise, I supposed, for the jealousy. No different at all from the pattern I remembered from my earliest dating. My parents both, both of them, absolutely both of them, would remark with light teasing on my expressions, or Deborah's, when we were first attracted to someone, and then, slowly, subtly, as the allure went on—the distraction from our attention to them as beacons of glamour—the criticism would begin. And so now I asked Brynn, "Is Freddy coming over?" I inquired with hope, anything was better than Brynn's sulking.

"Has Hedy called?" Brynn shot right back. Then she cooled it. "Actually I may go over there. Or we may be going out later. Or not."

Dylan and I looked at each other with a kind of zap . . . a look so fast as to be subliminal.

"Stop being parents," Brynn snapped. And huffed up to her room. Her momentary brightening over the phone call had fallen, already; her small plump face had darkened again. So he had been evasive.

"I could kill him," I said now.

"He's a creep," Dylan said. "But," Dylan added, "she learned that from you. You do the same thing."

"I don't," I said.

"You try not to, but then the phone rings and it's that baby rocker."

"Don't talk to me that way. Oh, never mind," I corrected myself immediately, remembering how my mother used to draw herself up and say, "Don't talk to me that way."

It must never be like that with Dylan and Brynn. No matter what. I did not want them to feel that anger, to leave me, to hate me, to think I did not for even a minute understand everything.

15

"Let me see," said Fitz, in his element now as he whirred through the pages in his spiral notebook, rattling off listings, with descriptive phrases thrown in here and there.

"Here's what we have: rustic ranch, painting been done, roofed last year; won't do, no guesthouse." He looked up at us. He did not, I was sure, believe for a minute that Hedy would be living in the guesthouse. "Here's a sprawling colonial, twelve, room to add. Antique reproduction fixer-upper; ash: paneled family room with built-in TV. They fixed it up so you wouldn't want to look at it. Interesting Tudor, in-floor goldfish pond in breakfast area."

"Possible," I said.

"Spike could drink from the pond," Hedy said. "And eat the fish."

"Drown," I said, "is what you really have in mind." We smirked at each other.

"Distinctive regency; it does have room," said Fitz. "Ruined romantic; basic new-baby cottage."

"Yuck," said Hedy, sounding exactly like Brynn.

"Upwardly mobile Darien redo; barbecue in the master—that's real different. Maybe too different," said Fitz.

We looked at a former restaurant, which had been painted lavender and was now a rooming house. People designed by George Price were sitting in old, overstuffed armchairs with their ankles bare.

Hedy looked at the single light bulb hanging in the living room of the guesthouse. "There aren't any outlets there. I couldn't work."

"Out," said Fitz, herding us along like a small, furry sheepdog.

"But I love the color," I protested.

"You'll get some paint," said Fitz.

We came up to a pristine colonial, and I said, "Fitz, this isn't interesting." The dining room was Tahitian.

"Wait," said Fitz.

In the basement were a giant sauna and bath all tiled in black with black plumbing fixtures I thought were rather intriguing. "You could do a lot with it," said Fitz.

"You start by razing it," Hedy said.

And in the back was a barn with lofts in a skylit wing, done wall-to-wall in tartan carpeting. "With six or seven singles living here, it would pay for itself."

"This is interesting," I said.

"Margot," said Hedy, "you couldn't ask Ivan and Stan to come to a creepy place like this."

"I could ask anyone, anywhere," I said, with my most aloof expression.

"You have to learn with houses, young man," said Fitz, "that you do not look at what you see."

"That's it exactly," I declared.

"This," said Fitz, "should be primarily an adventure for all of us." And he showed us what must have been his most peculiar listings: the old private hospital; a convalescent home with recessed banks of neon lighting and built-in aquariums around the dayroom walls.

"This is too depressing," I said. I had visited Helena a week ago, and Fitz had come in. He sat there so formally, looking at her. How hard it must be for older people to see younger ones so terribly ill.

"There is nothing so lovely as a good hospital," he had said, in a desolate tone of voice, trying hard to say something cheerful. "Food, flowers, phone calls and friends. Lovely," he had added, sitting bolt upright on the chair.

Near the end of the day I said, "Fitz, have we seen the ruined romantic?"

"Hopeless," Fitz said. "You'll adore it. I warn you."

"I identify with it already," I said.

The long driveway was more like a path designed for carriages, shadowed with evergreens, ending in an old stone arch, rather like an ancient ruin, and set into the side of the arch was an old bronze plaque that said 1802.

The trouble with Upshot began on this day we saw it and neglected to tell each other what we thought we saw.

Fitz watched us carefully and I'm sure he knew we both saw what it could become, not what it was today. We saw a grand and sunny estate with a white frame main house, a two-story guesthouse, a carriage house, a gleaming pond, with cream and dove gray stables and gardens. We did not see the peeling paint, rotted timbers, the brambles choking every plant and vine, the collapsing structure, the seepage through all the plumbing, the smashed and dusty windows, the water marks throughout the ceilings; we did not smell the sewage.

I looked, beyond the shadowed path, beyond the stone archway, out to the other side of the trees where the meadows extended up to the distant misty hillside; and I saw picnics of merry children living in the lovely stable dormitory, young people who could get sober working on gardens of vegetables and flowers; and I saw Hedy, as the merry major domo, dancing in the sunlight, inviting everyone to join in our good fortune, including Brynn and Dylan and their mates and ponies and romping dogs, and a lot of tumbling little baby grandchildren and my mother in a studio, somewhere there, and my father swinging in a hammock between those two big trees while I sat on the grass and listened to his grand old stories of the theatre.

And what I watched Hedy imagining was a fastidiously maintained estate, with rolling lawns and perfect promenades for famous people to promenade; music laced through the trees; I would preside, in glittering chic gowns like St. Cheri's, over sumptuous buffets by the pool that we would surely put in. He would see himself as the charming young performer, entertaining the most important people in the world with his glowing, mature and utterly competent mistress. And it did not seem impossible to combine these two fantasies.

"I have to have it," I said. Hedy was strolling around the pond, pulling out dead vines. "It will be perfect." He would take wonderful care of everything.

"Before you do anything," Fitz said, "you must collect detailed estimates of the renovating expenses, Margot." He put his hand on my arm, and looked at Hedy. "You must consider your resources carefully, and your priorities."

"Oh, Fitz," I said, "I am. I promise." Hedy came over and handed me a bouquet of honeysuckle he had picked from the vines overgrowing the stable. "Smell this," he said. "Isn't it wonderful?"

If I knew nothing about reality, what a light operetta of a life I could envision from a summer day's house hunting.

We were silent on the long late afternoon drive back home from the house on Upshot Way. Silent with our own possibly very separate ideas; our spiraling delight.

"You'll come and stay with me tonight?" Hedy asked.

"I want to," I said. Give more. "I want you," I added, "but I can't. I have to get some work done. I'm really getting a little distracted—I don't want to get too crazy, Hedy." I looped my forefinger all around the outline of his lips.

"We could stay somewhere else, so we could be all alone."

"Like where? We are in Medwin's Landing. I am not swinging down to some motel along the Berlin Turnpike."

"We could go up to Salisbury—or out to Litchfield to an inn. It would be romantic. We could even camp out on the screened porch over at the house on Upshot. That would be *really* romantic." He laughed, to lighten his eagerness.

We were sitting on our knees on the grass in front of my house, facing each other, palms down on our thighs. "We must look about four years old," I said. I picked three dandelions and stuck them in his hair. I kissed him; I threw my arms around his neck; I licked at his ear, I nuzzled him; I said, "You're the most romantic man I've ever known. But I really have to do these things—and I have to pick up Blanche tomorrow and take her to the hospital to see Helena."

He had given me the chance to be with him. And I'm sure he thought I didn't want to, and I wasn't sure why, but I didn't. I would try to pretend to myself it was because he didn't really love me. I could not admit it might be the other way around, not because I couldn't love him, but because I feared I might. "I really don't know why we should fight about this."

"You're the one who's fighting," he said. "You always say we have to be together and now when I can, you come up with a deadline on something you should have been working on anyway. You get started at the last minute and then drive yourself crazy."

"That's not true. I have been working. Why do I have to bother to explain it to you, anyway," I said.

"You don't. It's as crazy as if I started getting songs for an album together the night before a session. You can't bear it because I understand how you work. You come up with a deadline just to get me to back off. To turn me down."

"I didn't just come up with a deadline. Don't start telling

me how to do my work." I stood up. I started walking toward my house.

"You conveniently forget that you have that dog. If I was one of your kids you wouldn't forget."

"Well, you're not." I stopped. "I'm sorry, that was mean. I think we just are both scared, Hedy. We made kind of a plan today or, at least, started thinking about it, and got scared by our own enthusiasm. That happens."

"You're the one who's scared, then, not me. I want to be with you and celebrate." He kissed me. I knew he expected the kiss to be convincing. I loved the kiss, but I could not be convinced.

"We'll celebrate tomorrow. I promise." But then tomorrow night I had to lead a meeting. I would see him afterward.

"Well, I can't tomorrow," he said. "I'm going to be recording." I suspected he had just made that up. Tit for tat.

"Okay, then, the day after."

He drove off fast, too fast.

A plan. I thought, every love affair needs a plan. Was every lover as frightened to consider that plan as I was?

16

And I sent flowers to Hedy the next morning. Flowers being, of course, easier than conversation. "More to come," I said on the card.

I called everyone to tell them about Upshot. I had not mentioned it to Brynn and Dylan. I would on the next weekend; make a picnic and just take them over there. I called my parents, and my father laughed. "I remember how you said you would never live in Connecticut."

"That was different."

"Well," he added gently, "I hope no one is influencing you; you are a very kind, vulnerable young lady."

Not so young, but why remind him. "No," I said, "I have some money from my new deal. It's not an expensive place and"—here I was saying what I did not think I would say—"you will love it, both of you—and you'll have so many ideas for it." I could see my father in his sheepskin coat walking about appraising the light, selecting colors with me. And I did not see Hedy in that picture. My father, as always, moving with just the ignition of his soft voice into all my dreams.

My mother's voice came right through now; she asked what the children thought and said, "I don't think you can just take people their size somewhere. The older the child the more it detests moving." It had not occurred to me that my mother had ever noticed. And when, I wondered, will I permit my own mother her motherhood. When, I suppose, I give myself my own house, as I thought I had done. But change is probably always two steps forward, one step back.

"And what," said Cleo, "will happen when you and that person stop speaking to each other?"

"It is not," I dissembled, "just for Hedy. We're being very careful."

"Oh, I know that old place, you're crazy," said Jennie. "But if you're going to do it you should get Reilly over there to take a look; he knows all the best guys to work on houses."

"Hedy would adore that," I said.

"But you're buyin' the house," said Jennie.

Ivan called me to say he had an interview coming up for me with a producer who was putting together a new night-time talk show. "Wonderful!" I said. Oh, Ivan would be thrilled about Upshot. Ivan clearly understood estates. So I traveled right on to a babble about the house.

"I don't know why on earth either of you would want that kind of responsibility at this point in your careers. And the burden of it would fall on you, my dearest. I hope it will go well with the cable deal, but we see such upheavals with them every day, Margot—it's too soon, darling. I've got the coast on another line—don't sign anything; regards to your boy. He's very good, dear, as a performer. Put away your pots and pans, this is not the one; not the time."

I hated it especially when people I respected implied that it was not a perfect idea. Maybe I hadn't explained it right.

I had actually been pleased Blanche had called me to suggest we visit Helena together the next time. I had wanted to talk to her about whether I should put Brynn for her senior year in a private school which Brynn said she would not go to.

"Why pay for me to not go to a private school when I can not go to this school for free?"

A very good point. Blanche would have something wise to say. Helena and I had talked about it when I'd visited her at the hospital the last time. She had said, "You have to do what I did with Jennie—you have to let her go her own way until she sees there must be a better way."

When I'd dropped by Chickens, George had told me Jennie hadn't visited her mother—Helena. "She's angry. It's one of the stages the family goes through. They tell me. Which is supposed to make it just swell."

"Do you want me to talk to her?" I'd asked.

"Just let it go. Helena wants to be alone most of the time now—to deal with herself. She'll call you when she's ready. I just let her run it right now."

"Are you okay?" I held on to his hand tight.

"No. I don't drink and try not to think about it and then I don't drink and send her more flowers and then I don't drink and go to a meeting. It's like alcoholism, cancer is, it goes in stages but only the people who have it understand the stages. The big difference is we get well."

"George, a lot of people get over cancer—live for years. Don't do that. I had a doctor on who said that's the worst thing you can do, that's the phobia, the terrible myth. Don't!"

"Margot, I know. But this is it, Margot. We got the word. It will not be long, Margot."

"George." We just looked at each other. Eyes filled. Look away. Clasp hands.

It was exactly that way when I visited Helena; we just sat. Her hand on my arm. My arm around her shoulder. Then she had insisted on talking about Brynn. I would turn the subject back, asking questions. But she moved it away from herself. "Don't treat me different, don't push me out, don't make the conversation so careful, not now, need me, remind me I am alive in this day by being yourself. By needing me." I had tried to remember. But my face would fall. I'd go still suddenly. She'd nod and ask another question.

"I come to visit and you spend the time making me feel at ease," I had said quickly, looking away.

"I know," Helena had said. "Look, about Brynn. It's no different. You have to let her hit her own bottom, whatever it is."

"Brynn is not a drunk," I had said. "I'm sorry, that's really mean."

"No," said Helena, "it's true. But she was raised by one."

"Which is why she hates drinking. So thank God," I'd said.

"However," said Helena, "it is also why she has all the characteristics we have, including the ability to be doing something for everyone else while letting everything that really matters for her go to rack and ruin."

"Oh, Helena, there has to be another answer." And we had sat there looking at each other in that long way. Helena'd then shook her head and turned away. "Go," she'd said.

I picked Blanche up at her perfect small Federal house with the small polished door knocker: B. Hutchins. Such a competent way of living. The small hallway had a brown-on-ecru figured wallpaper, and a pine table with stamped mail to be posted on one corner and a brass oil lamp in the center. Blanche shook hands with me firmly and picked up some letters, and a pastry box.

"I like that sweater," I said. Blanche was wearing a classic linen sports dress with a tennis cardigan yellowed the way very old good wool yellows.

"It was my father's. I'm fond of it myself," said Blanche.

"Yes. My father has a great tennis sweater like that." I hadn't seen him in it for years. "I used to love to watch my father play tennis."

"I did, too," said Blanche. And we were quiet together.

When we arrived at the hospital, Helena was standing in the corridor, holding on to her chrome IV staff.

"You look rather like a frail Saint Christopher," said Blanche, taking Helena's other elbow. Blanche looked stricken. Her eyes locked in with Helena's.

I kissed Helena's cheek.

We walked back to Helena's room. She got into bed. Her legs and feet were white and dry. But then I had never seen her legs and feet. I was watching her differently, laying on signs. Were her cheeks more fallen? These little broken capillaries—is the disease making notes on her face? Stop watching. She sees me looking for it. Do we imbue the terminally ill friend with magical powers in desperation, to replace the mundane strengths we are helpless to restore?

"Well," said Helena, now uneasy, being cheerful. "So, Margot, how is your favorite project?"

"Oh," I said, "I just got three new sponsors."

"I'm not that sick"—Helena laughed—"I can still see what you're up to."

"I don't mean A.A. sponsors," I said; "I mean commercials."

"Terrific," said Helena, "we're making ourselves very clear today. I meant Hedy."

And I laughed. And Helena smiled. And Blanche smiled, an embarrassed smile. Everyone smiling in ways we normally didn't.

"Well," said Helena, trying to make us comfortable, "let's have some of Mr. Gold's glorious lemon cake."

Blanche opened the cake box. "Julius Gold is a splendid man," she said. We had a brief distracted discussion of Mr. Gold, as I helped Blanche cut the cake and put it on plates from Chickens. I knew George brought food to Helena every night, trying to invent something irresistible. Then we talked about Mrs. Gold's effectiveness in the Westport school system, as superintendent. We were clearly trying, guided tenaciously by Helena, not to talk about her, not to ask the questions.

"Maybe," I said, "I should send Brynn and Dylan to Westport."

"Oh, perfect. Pull Dylan right out of college," Helena said. "Maybe you should realize the time is past where you can do anything much about them.

"Your children are adults," said Blanche.

"I know. They're fine," I said. "Let's talk about anything else."

"Blanche," Helena said, "how is Fitz?"

"He does hate to visit, doesn't he?" Blanche said.

"But he has," Helena laughed. "And when he does he's terrified, I'm sure, because he cares so much—doesn't want to see it, imagines all sorts of ways I might be looking the next time, you know. He's also terrified that it might be contagious." She looked at Blanche, then she said to me, "Enough. Listen, maybe you know where the staff kitchen is, maybe Blanche would like some tea, and you can get some coffee."

"I'll be right back," I said.

Yes. Now she did want to talk about it. And Blanche would be the right person. I would take my time.

After Blanche and I left Helena we talked about how astonishing she was. "I'd scream and yell and cry," I said.

"She has," Blanche said. "She told me she did that last night. She fears the total acceptance because that will be the end."

"Oh, Blanche."

"But we didn't just talk about that. I'd like to talk to you, Margot," Blanche said. We were passing the coffee shop on the ground floor of the hospital.

"I was going to suggest that myself," I said. We picked up our coffee at the counter and sat down at a small table.

"Margot," Blanche said, looking directly at me, "I will

come directly to the point. Dylan is heading toward some difficulty. This difficulty, I'm sad to say to you, involves trafficking in cocaine."

I sat, my hands clutched tightly around my cup of coffee. This was not what I thought we would be talking about. This was never something I thought I would be talking about.

I could not believe I was sitting here on a summer day, hearing from the woman I respected most of all in the world, perhaps, that my son was a drug dealer. But then Helena, at some point, must have sat in her doctor's office while he told her the cancer had returned.

"This is one of those unbearable things," I said. "I don't want to believe it. I'm not doubting you, Blanche."

"Margot, he should be spoken to as directly, firmly and strictly as you can. I would suggest immediacy. One would not want even the slightest suspicion overlooked at this time; one would wish for one's own son a life uncomplicated by certain connections. My own hunch, and I say this as a friend to you, Margot, as someone who has had experience . . ."—she paused, and shifted her tone, not saying possibly what she had started out to say—"is that he is a sometime participant. I suspect most of them are but, now, even if it could be determined he only purchases the substance for private use, his young life could be seriously shadowed."

"He'll be furious, Blanche. What's he going to do? Say, 'Okay, Mom.' What if he isn't? I mean they all rat on each other."

"Margot, you're afraid and I understand the sense of failure—the responsibility. I've made horrible decisions." I do not want to hear anymore things I do not want to know. "There was a man, a man I liked sober—a terrible drunk—who I jailed—he killed himself." She stopped. She looked directly in my eyes. "He hung himself in that cell. We live with things we cannot bear. So I understand more than you know. Reilly is that man's son. I can tell I understand your," she hesitated, "yes, unutterable dismay." She stopped again. She held on to her cup with both hands. "I've had to invent a persona to do my work. And that is what you'll have to do. My invention is more circumscribed. But we have different jobs.

"I wanted," she continued, "to tell you something difficult about myself—and to tell you that no matter the risk, which I take every time that Reilly shows up in court, I tell you, you cannot protect Dylan by pretending you are not aware of his problem. You do not help him by protecting yourself from your fear of his anger. He may indeed have to be angry. It is uniquely difficult to feel that anger. To let go, as they say now. And to do what you must."

Let go. The last time I heard that suggestion was from a madman in a gas station. And all my body wanted was to run to Dylan, to grab him in my arms; to get Brynn, throw all our things into the car and run as fast and as far as we could go. Not let go. Cling and protect, stand at the mouth of my house with my teeth bared and keep everyone else away. Not let go at all. "Detach with love," we were told at meetings, and I never understood it for a minute. A contradiction in terms, it seemed to me.

Dylan was sitting on the front porch of the house when I came home. He said he was waiting for Brynn so she could follow him down to the service station in his car, which had blown its muffler.

"God knows," I said, "you wouldn't want to attract attention when you're driving around."

"What do you mean by that?" he said.

"I'll let you know. Soon." I couldn't yet.

Brynn was mad as hell when she came home in her '70 white Chevy with the green door and learned she'd have to go out again.

"Don't ask me," she said, "to remember where you left the Buick. Don't ask me to get you back there to pick your car up."

"Anything else?" Dylan said.

"Yeah," she said, "and don't ask me if you can use my car."

"Mom's found a house," Dylan said, looking at me, quickly, "with Hedy, and I hope it's got no room for you."

"That's very sweet," Brynn snapped. She turned to me, and went right into a lie, right in front of me, as if she did know. "It is a very big house," she said, "and they're letting me have your room as a study because you're going to be away anyhow. So."

"Stop it," I said, finally. I had heard enough of family secrets to last a lifetime. "Yes, there's a house, room for everyone, and I don't even know if I'm getting it. So stop!"

"I don't care how big it is," Dylan said, "because it's time Brynn went out into the real world and went to college like everyone else."

"I have another year of high school," she said. "They generally like you to do that before you go to college, which is hardly anyone's idea of the real world."

"The way you do high school, it doesn't matter."

"You brought it up, zitfinger, and you probably got it all wrong, anyway."

"I brought it up because it's about time we realized Hedy's not going to want kids hanging around, and we had both better begin making plans. And you don't need to pretend you knew about the house because Mom hadn't even told you yet. I picked up your messages today, Mom, that's how I put it together myself. Nice to learn from the service that we're moving."

"Don't anymore; let's all go to pick up the car. We can eat at the diner—we aren't moving yet—we can talk all about it—we can always, I promise, talk about anything."

"Yes, we can. When you decide how you're going to present what you want to tell us," Brynn said, "but I'm having dinner and sleeping over with Kimmie tonight, so I'll have to miss the explanations, and maybe, Dylan, you can rope Mom into taking you to pick up your car."

"I was going to make it a surprise. I thought you'd both be pleased," I said.

"Yeah, like a surprise car wreck." He looked hurt. Perhaps he was just scared there would be no place for him, or for Brynn.

"You'll see it this weekend. It's a huge estate with room for everyone. You'll love it. We'll have horses, swimming, wonderful parties."

"A neat cover story, Mom. A real love nest, with live rock concerts anytime you want."

This was clearly not the moment for us to have this conversation I knew we had to have. He was already upset. We would talk calmly later and I would explain that unless he stopped whatever it was I would have to let go. I hoped I would be clearer about what it all meant when we did talk. I carefully pretended to myself that I did not understand.

He got out at the gas station. "I'll skip dinner, too," he said. "I've got to meet someone."

"Dylan, don't be angry—we'll talk later—I have to lead a meeting, but, mainly, don't worry."

Yes. Dylan was jealous. It wasn't the same situation as Reilly or Jennie or anyone else. It wasn't as simple as drugs. I would have to reassure him. I would explain that love was expansive, that loving one person stretched your spirit, made it possible to love everyone more. I had told him that before, however—when?—before some marriage, and he had not been convinced even then. Not everything is a simple drug problem. I had enough trouble and I could see it very clearly —I thought I saw it very clearly, more than I used to and that was enough, accepting that my own father was married to my mother and not about to leave her so I could be hostess at his parties. I could understand Dylan, or was I trying too hard. Give him your own troubles, Margot, and that way you can understand. Too easy.

Let him invent his own psyche. That right there would surely be the beginning of what they mean by letting go.

And stop rationalizing, I told myself.

"The topic tonight," I announced to the twenty or so people sitting around at the stable, "is Detaching with Love. What it means to you, how you do it." I paused. "How you let go of someone you love; or how someone lets go of you; how it affected your early sobriety; how you feel about that person now." I did not mention Dylan. A woman said that her friend's son had already been arrested on charges of rape. "I asked my friend how she could bear it. She said she had looked at him and said, 'That is not my son.' Can you imagine?"

"In that case," I said, "violence is unforgivable. But if it's just drugs or drinking it would be so hard to be tough on someone." Wouldn't it, I pleaded silently, wouldn't it? But wasn't Blanche, every day, at some point, seeing that man Reilly's father. Seeing him there—

A man said his wife had handed him two suitcases full of his clothes as he started to come in the door of his own house one night, and she had said, "You are not my husband until you come in this door sober, and if you try I'm calling the police." He said, "I hated her guts but it worked. I'm here."

Another woman, Ann, said, "I was thinking of what you were sayin' about how you can be mean to someone if it's just drinkin' or drugs they're doin'. You never know when it isn't a just this or that. My son got drunk a lot. And nothing ever happened, and I didn't like to make a scene, but two weeks ago he got drunk on a Sunday morning and drove through the school playground and killed this little boy."

"Yes, but sometimes we overreact, you know," said a man with gray hair and a rather unusually well-cut navy blue blazer. "We lay our own trips on our kids. We get a little melodramatic. There's got to be a balance between denial and paranoia; there isn't much I can do about my kids except to see myself as clearly as I can and to live with that."

That was better. I heard what I wanted to hear. You can imagine things; you can listen and hear the worst and turn a lovely summer day all dark with fear. You detach when you have to.

I went right home after the meeting. I would talk to Dylan. Or work on the application blanks Cleo had this lecture agency send me, which looked harder than writing any lectures. I also needed to listen to the album Ivan had sent me. One of his clients was coming in to do an interview this week. Soon it would be only fair to have Hedy on the show; although technically we only had music people on to introduce a strong new record, and usually, if Cleo had her way, only if they were appearing in New York. There was also a new book to read, *Failing Up*, a guide to failure in the face of unlimited opportunities. The authors had been scheduled over a month ago originally, but had failed to show up. Perhaps I could fulfill their expectations and fail to read their book.

I called the answering service. I wondered why Hedy had not called. No one stayed mad with flowers.

The house was quiet, so quiet I could hear crickets. "Brynn?" I called. But Brynn's car was not there.

"Dylan?" Silence.

"Dylan?" He was there. I had seen his car.

"Up here. What is it?" he called down.

"I'm home," I called up the stairs.

"So am I," he said, "what a coincidence."

I wanted to say, "I want to talk to you"; I wanted to have a calm conversation about character. The responsibility one has if one has it. "Mom, I guess this brings me to my senses," he would say. "I'm never going to go near any of that again, I promise. Mom, I'm sorry if you were scared." He'd hug me tight. "I love you, Mom," he'd say. And we'd talk about the new house and I'd make him understand it would belong to him, to Brynn and to me. Only to us. Really. I would try to make that very clear.

Dylan called down again, "I thought you were going out."

"I was out; I'm home now. Stop having this conversation from your room and come talk to me."

"I'm doing something. Hedy said he was meeting you at Chickens after your meeting."

"Did he call?"

"No, I heard it on *Newscenter Four*."

"Why didn't you tell me?"

"I'm telling you."

I called Chickens and asked George to tell Hedy, when he arrived, that I would be there soon. I was just hanging up the phone when the door opened.

"Who is it?" I said, without turning my head. "Jennie." I turned. Two young men, smooth continental-cut suits and briefcases stood in the living room, staring at me with cold expressions. They were both wearing the sort of sunglasses one calls shades. "Is Dylan here?" one of them asked.

"Dylan?" I wanted to absorb them, stall them. My body felt translucent, shimmering with fear. "You're here to see Dylan?"

"This where he lives?" one of them said, a little edge to the voice. Thank God, Brynn is not here.

"Yes. He's upstairs." Why did I say that.

"Thank you, ma'am. We'll just go up. We're sorry to bother you." He nodded to the other one.

I froze. I heard their hard-soled shoes going up the

wooden stairs. Kids just walking into a house was one thing. People with briefcases and suits were no longer in that category. I should call the police. No. You don't call the police because you don't know your child's friends. I was behaving like Alison's parents. Too many stories all day.

I went up the stairs slowly. I knocked on Dylan's door. "I'm busy, Mom." I turned, automatically, to go. Don't be silly, I told myself. I opened the door. There was a scale on Dylan's desk, which was by the door. A gun, a blue-black metal gun was lying by that scale, and there was white powder. Dylan looked pale. The two men stood near him. I did not understand how I was saying what I was saying but there I was, saying it. "All right: you have three minutes to get out of this house. Three minutes before I'm calling the police."

"Cut it out, Mom. They're just leaving." He tried to cover the gun.

"Not they, Dylan. All of you."

"Close the door, Mom." He looked at me as coldly as they did. I understood a new kind of limitation of feelings, a frigid detachment, the kind of distance from which a woman could say, "That is not my son."

I did not close the door. "Three minutes," I repeated. I went downstairs and stood by the phone. The men came downstairs first. One of them paused. "Do not call the police, ma'am." His shades reflected light, moving flashes, as he spoke, like robot eyes. They made the kind of departure which usually involves curt tipping of hats, except they were not wearing any. I heard Dylan. He had a sweatshirt over his shoulders and his duffel bag under his arm. "I'm taking my car," he said.

"Pull your life together. You got just one," I said, my muscles all hard; all movement stuck to keep from reaching out.

"Tough talk, buddy." He stood by the door, furious.

"Tough love," I said. I could not soften. I kept one hand clutched on to the phone.

"A.A.'s really fucked your head around." And he left.

I love you, I love you, I can't stand it, I wanted to call out after him, and I could not; I would not. I could not begin, or I could not go on with this, and it had to be. Everything I knew, everything I'd ever heard. No halfway measures. Not just tough talk. I wanted to call the police to get those guys. But they would get Dylan. He had to go through whatever it was. Just as I had. Detach with love. If you try to interfere, I knew, it just takes longer. It takes—I had been told a hundred times—what it takes.

It takes, I thought, the life out of you. That is what it takes.

17

"We'll lie in the sun; you and me. We'll forget everything." Hedy had a concert to do in San Diego and he was trying to persuade me to come with him. "What you need," he said, "is a real vacation." We were eating pizza by the river. "And when we come back," he said, "things will have all worked out. They'll have all the estimates in on the house so you'll know what to expect. And I'll even bet Dylan surfaces. There's no way you can make a difference staying here, and if you come with me you get a chance to relax—even play a bit." He kissed my neck, he tousled my hair. "I like it like this now," he said.

"Smelling like pizza," I laughed, and rubbed his hair. "Hedy. I can't. I have a tryout to do for this news program." I rubbed my forearms with my hands. The main thing, of course, was that Dylan had been gone for two weeks, and I had not heard a word.

"What kind of tryout? You didn't tell me about it." Hedy sounded exactly as I did when I was asking the children where they were going. Used to ask.

"I know. I guess I'm telling you now." I had gulped down Coke from a can and wiped my mouth on the back of my arm. As Dylan would when he was pretending to be rough.

"I don't know why you need to do something like that. Is it the money?" he said.

"Yes. It could mean more—and it's a commitment." I

didn't really even want to go down to the city to do that. I hated being away from the phone. If Dylan called I wanted to be there. Which was not, of course, letting go. It was enough I had not tried to find him; that was hard enough. Not knowing.

"I just think you use yourself up. You talk in these A.A. meetings; you talk on the phone all day and night."

"Well," I said, "when we move to Upshot you'll just be able to walk across the garden and get me off the phone." I said it right out and was sorry I had brought it up.

"If we actually get around to buying it," he said. He looked out at the sailboats floating along down the river in the warm breeze. "We could be sitting on a real beach in Coronado, watching the ocean. They say it's a neat place."

"You know I don't like to leave Brynn alone."

"She's not a baby. There is always a complication with you. And it's always them. Why can't you simply say, 'Yes, that's fine'?"

"Hedy, let's not fight. I'm not going because I don't want to, and you're not going to understand this, but it's important, trying to stay straight, that I honor my commitments." I picked up a crust of pizza he had left and chewed off the crisp parts.

"Being straight is also getting honest enough to know when you're overdoing, but you'll never admit that to me because you can't ever say I'm right about anything. I mean that just isn't in the cards, is it?" He brushed crumbs off his jeans.

"Not true. You're right, and I like the fact you worry about me. But you don't have to."

"I know I don't have to. I do it because I care about you, even if you're a messy eater." He picked up the remains of the pizza and pitched the box into a trash can.

"I'm grateful, Hedy, really, but how would you like it if I told you what gigs to play?" I should not have said that. Right away I knew the answer.

"I'd figure you were caring about what I was doing. After you're finished caring about your kids, your friends, your cars, your houses, your work and your dad."

"Hedy. I do care. But I have enough confidence in your ability to decide what's right for you to do and that list is just crazy. I care a lot because you I don't have to worry about. Can't you see that?"

"Very swift," he said.

Ten days later, around midnight, Alison called.

"What is it?" I was on the alert.

"I figured you'd be really worried about Dylan, and I thought about it and thought about it and decided he doesn't have to know I called, so please don't tell him, but he's okay. He's staying with friends of mine in Boston, real nice people. They go to Boston University. And he's working at a parking lot."

"Alison, dear, you've saved my life almost; I was so worried."

"I thought so. I've been telling him to call you; he won't. But he is okay. He makes me furious."

Alison promised to keep in touch, and I said to call for sure if she needed to talk. The dimension of my relief showed me exactly how frightened I had been. Just knowing Dylan was somewhere, near someone who cared, made it seem clear and possible to go with Hedy. Jennie would stay with Brynn, and Cleo even agreed I should postpone the tryout and go. But I don't think Hedy believed it until the plane left the ground.

We stayed in the Hotel Del Coronado in one of the huge old rooms. I wore a white lawn dress with Victorian sleeves and high neck for dinner the first night in the vast wooden dining room, where violins played behind ferns, and then we whirled into our empty ballroom and swooped over a moonlit floor.

"You can waltz!" I murmured to Hedy.

"I can do a lot of things." He danced with his head high, his back so straight. We spun and floated. A veritable prince, I thought, and I felt like a feather in his arms.

Our room had whitewashed dressers with old-fashioned legs and bronze drawer pulls of old summer houses, walls washed in pale pink, and twin beds which Hedy pushed together. He undressed me in the moonlight. The windows were open, and we could hear the surf, the call of an occasional seabird. There was a white chenille bedspread on each bed, lying with its special soft weight. The pure intent of this immaculate room made sex unthinkable and therefore especially interesting. I felt as if we were lovers from another century, and the moonlight crossed our bodies with shadows.

"This was a brilliant idea, Hedy," I whispered.

"I knew it'd be good." He leaned on his elbow at my side and softly he said, "Tell me this time exactly how to be, how to love you; tell me what you want me to say, tell me what you want me to do." He spoke close to my face, his eyes staring right into mine.

"Not aloud," I whispered. "Just don't say. Just touch me. Let's just kiss for a while, you know, like beginners. Until we can't hold the feelings. Just kissing for ages as if we don't even know there is anything else to do."

We kissed, our lips soft and dry as velvet, drifting over each other's face, we kissed each other's eyes and cheeks, temples and neck. We kissed; our lips open, our lips still; breathing into each other. He lay lightly over me, both our hands clasped out on either side, like dancers lying down.

"Where are you, gettin' there?" Hedy asked. He was joined to me now, and I moved up to him, catching his rhythm.

"Oh, it's cool, beautiful. Come, come on, go with me," I lied, swearing as always I would not lie the next time.

"You're lying," he said. He kissed my breasts. One, then the other. "Talk about it."

Here he was saying what I'd always wanted to hear. Someone who knew when I was lying.

"Talk to me, tell me."

"I'm fine. No talking."

"Okay, but no thinking. I know when you start thinking." He moved to my side again, and we lay with our faces almost touching; he talked so quietly. "You need to just be with me like this. I want you to think just about what we're doing, just you and me, and sex and no old tapes, you know what I mean." He touched now lightly along my neck, up and down, so slightly.

"I know," I said; I stroked his neck as he touched mine. "I try not to think much about what I'm doing when I do it." I smiled. Could it be I liked this part of sex best, lying together and talking?

His voice was soft and low. "You only think about how what you're doing reminds you of something else; you worry about how it's going to go and then you don't feel it. I'm smarter than you think." He kissed me. And kissed me again. "And you think about houses, about kids, and," he said almost whispering now, "about how to handle it if it gets serious or if it doesn't, instead of just feeling good and having fun, which is how we hoped it would stay."

How, I thought, do you have this sort of conversation without mentioning love? You don't.

"Hedy," I said, "it has to stay like that."

"Yeah," he said, quickly, "I guess we shouldn't even talk about what would happen if we fell in love, really fell in love!"

"Hedy, don't. If I loved you I would have to worry about

losing you and then we'd have to face the fury when the love goes awry, at the time we'd given it—the waste of our focus. Hedy, love is such a trap for the spirit." I looked at his face, such a serious expression; I thought of the feeling of him next to me, such carnal confusion. "Hedy, if we really give in to each other, we might lose ourselves."

"Why couldn't it be," he said, "that we'd each have more, part of each other?"

So here we were talking about why we couldn't talk about what we were talking about.

"Hedy"—I held his face in both my hands—"I'm a distant sort of person in love and it shows in sex; you see that, I know you do. I've been so private with it. And the closer I get to you, the more I know you, the more I do this—holding back." I kissed his forehead.

"It's safer with sex. I do understand that. We want it from an audience where it's fast and clean—over and out. I get off strongest when it's not even you I'm thinkin' of. I'm doin' it in my mind for a whole crowd out there. I know you're telling me you're scared. We aren't much different. I let go most of all when I'm doing it to myself, and I can control it. It's not so strange, you know, for people like us who like a lot of attention. Across a stage. Touch me, watch me, but stand back, I know you, baby; that's why we're probably here, and why we could even really love each other." He placed my hand on my own body. "We could be alone with each other. I want to see you get it. This is your trip now."

I know me, too, I thought, and at this time in my life the things like work, like houses, like success and one's family would not, would not be overwhelmed. I tucked my face in under his chin.

We lay there like children, stroking ourselves. I laughed. "I'll tell you something I never have told. I used to lie in bed when I was a young child and give my fingers names and personalities. The thumbs were like stocky engineers on a little boy's toy train, the index fingers were sulky, the middle fingers were tall like princes, or grenadiers." I looked at him and giggled. "But unbending. I thought they might get hurt, standing up so straight. The ring fingers had long faces and the certain slender quality of pretty girls, and the little fingers were babies about to be abandoned." I paused. "I feel like the Story Lady."

He laughed. He kissed my hand. His own hand moved on himself. He played himself rough and knowing and faster than he ever was on me.

My voice slowed down as my fingers speeded up. "The ring fingers were named Annabelle and Amelia and wore bride outfits. I knew later there was something about the middle fingers, and that came to be true and so when I make love to myself . . ." I went silent and saw myself as him in the middle of a meadow jammed with boys on a stage; I sighed and threw myself on him. "Yes!"

And he, on his own stage, yelled, "I got it." No little coo—this time he soared and flowed and fell onto me. Our audiences faded. He went to sleep. He breathed his fresh breath like a child's on my shoulder, his hipbones sharp against my hips. His hair tickled my nose. And as I fell asleep I rubbed my nose and smiled.

The concert was sold out. "You can sell out anything in San Diego," said Paul; but all the other guys in the band were excited; seemed to work together. They looked at each other with more confidence. The fun onstage seemed less contrived. Or maybe, I thought, I'm just learning how to watch.

After the concert the band went back together on the ferry from San Diego to Coronado, and I felt it was a little like going to a graduation party at someone else's school. There was a midnight picnic on the beach, everyone wrapped up in sweaters. And they had a lot of beer and pot and I told myself my discomfort had nothing to do with that; I was surely beyond that. I watched the moonlight turn the beds of shells to silver. I walked along through the shells, like walking through the fragments of an old party where everyone had thrown their glasses against the wall. The shells clicked and clattered against each other, shushing forward and back as the ocean swept them to and fro like a big broom.

"Hedy"—I crouched behind him—"I'm really tired. Would you mind if I hit the sack?"

"You'll be all right?" he said.

"Fine," I said.

Much, much later, I felt him climb into bed. I turned on my side and he lay tightly behind me. I liked feeling how the lively cock and so forth, even in sleep, moved on their own, even at rest; they breathed and shifted as if they had absolutely no connection to the rest of his body.

I awakened early. I sat up in bed, looking at Hedy's lean, neat body. I wanted to reach over, to touch him, but something about the way he had arranged himself in his sleep said, "Don't touch me." His mouth was sweet and small and private in sleep. It was nothing like the angry, full mouth crying out sounds on the stage, wailing and whooping and open, birthing out shouts and howls. I looked out the window toward the wide gray ocean, and I missed the view from my own house, the contained, gentle view of the river.

The phone rang. He twisted sharply in his sleep; reached for it; knocked it on the floor. I picked it up. "I'll get it," I whispered. I touched his back softly. He turned and went back to sleep.

"Hello," I said, almost a whisper.

"Hi, Mom." Brynn's voice. Was I beginning to get defensive when my children called? I would not.

"Brynn!" How wonderful. Immediate cheer.

"How y' doin'?"

"Fine. The concert was terrific. We're going to spend a couple more days in the sun and then perhaps go to L.A." I told Brynn the story.

"A couple of more days," said Brynn. There was a pause.

"How are you, Brynn, really."

"Fine. Just fine." Another pause. She was perhaps not fine. I looked at myself in the dresser mirror. I looked concerned. I pulled my hair back from my forehead, as if that might help me hear more clearly.

"Mom?"

"Brynn?"

"Freddy slept over last night."

"Slept over. With you?"

"Of course. With me. What do you think I meant?"

I decided to be reassuring, to be modern. I must, I told myself, be calm. "So. Well." I made my voice warm and soft and understanding. Be approving, open. Be ready to hear her, I told myself. "Was it comfortable? Was he sweet and tender? Did you enjoy yourself? It's nice, isn't it?" The questions rolled right out.

"Yeah, it's fine." There was hesitation in Brynn's voice. Had I not been comforting enough. Had he been terrible. Were the questions making Brynn sad because it had not been like that at all; not what every mother hopes it will be like for her daughter the first time; not the perfect lover, gentle and tender, a lover like no mother ever had her first time out.

"So," I said, trying to sound even more cozy, ready to listen to any confidence Brynn might want to give me.

"It was okay. I'm fine. I just wanted to call you. How are you?" Brynn repeated.

Suddenly someone with whom I was not entirely familiar welled up, like a dybbuk in my throat, a voice emerged, and it was not my voice at all, it was a mother's voice, a father's voice, but surely not mine. "Freddy?" I heard myself say. "That boy who hurt you so, over and over? What's his last name?" As if I did not know. The questions just ticked out of me, like a print-out from the fifties. Questions invented perhaps by Alison's parents: "What sort of family life does he have? Does he know you aren't the kind of girl you just sleep with like that? What did he say to you? What kind of boy is this?"

"Mom, hold it. I said I'm fine." Brynn sounded shaky.

"I'm sorry." I stopped. I had most of all not wanted to shake Brynn's fragile confidence in herself. And I had. I could hear it. I hated myself. I always started out right and ended up wrong. "I just wanted to be sure it was good for you." Now I sounded like a bad lover. There was no hope. I would always come on too strong and back off too late. Best to be honest.

"I know I reacted like a mother. I'm sorry. I guess I was trying too hard. You know how parents always overreact, and I try to be different, but I'm not." I mercifully left out the part about you're-still-my-baby. "I love you. I'm grateful you called me. That was terrific."

"Mom," said Brynn patiently. Always having to be the patient one. "Don't overtalk it. I just wanted to check in with you."

"I know, darling, I love you. Is he still there?"

"Of course. He's nice. He's still asleep."

I looked over at Hedy. "They always do seem to sleep better than we do," I said.

"I know," said Brynn. And now she did know. And I wished it were different already. I erased the image of this young man sleeping in Brynn's little bed with the stuffed animals, the baseball hats (some of them Bill's) hanging on the walls. I was glad Brynn had called. Grateful I was there for her to talk to, but sad, somehow, that Brynn was not lost in her lover's rapt attentions, too swept away by his sweetness and embraces to have the time to call.

"It was really kind of neat," said Brynn.

"I'm glad," I said. "I can't wait to see you. I'll be home very soon."

"No rush," said Brynn. "Love you," she said, and hung up the phone. And I sat by my young man.

Hedy reached for me in his sleep and made love to me. I could not stop the images of Brynn; nonspecific traces of feelings on me liked spilled perfume you cannot wash off.

I remembered borrowing one of my mother's nightgowns. I wondered if Brynn had slept in my bed and if that had made things more comforting or more difficult, more complex, perhaps; and then I decided, I hoped, that sex was not as troublesome to them. As long, of course, as Brynn did not go out of her way to make it so. Primarily, of course, I reminded myself: it is completely and totally none of my business.

Hedy continued to sleep. Perhaps he had made love to me only in his dream, on a stage watched by everyone he's ever wanted to impress, sitting in the audience with hats in their laps. I had surely not been there, although I had liked the feeling. I liked being occupied, attended to and always, always held. Why, I thought, is that not enough to be called successful sex? Why has even sex now got to come (exactly!) with its rating system and its charts and goals? How rather marvelous it was before you knew about that. How alarmed I had been when I discovered I was not getting what I was supposed to at all and that if I had thought I was satisfied I was wrong, terribly wrong and possibly inadequate.

I wondered if Brynn worried about all that. I wished it would have been someone wildly in love with her; oh, someone wise and kind and well educated. Stop it, I told myself. More detachment-with-love to come.

I remembered how I had snapped at Deborah when she had called, oh weeks ago, to tell me she was "in love."

"You're just having an affair," I had said.

"Do you have some perverse idea you have a priority on sexual expression? With you it's experience, with everyone else it's creating trouble?"

As Deborah would customarily say, I had better take a look at that.

By the time Hedy did wake up I was thoroughly depressed. And I could not precisely—or imprecisely even—tell him why. He was too quickly—much too quickly—pleased about Brynn's news. I knew he had the idea that once they got old enough I could just stop and turn only, totally, to him. Oh, for a person who had children of his own; but then his children might hate me. Perhaps if he had known them when they were little. Why can't he comprehend we are all one; people can try, but families cannot outgrow the need for each other. I remembered when an old man in A.A. said at a meeting when his uncle died, "Now there is no one who remembers me when I was small." Perhaps I should take up with Hedy's father.

I sat on the bed Indian-style with my chin propped on my fists, my satin robe wrapped tightly around my body. He tried to be fatherly: he ordered hot chocolate and pancakes and strawberries with powdered sugar from room service. He greeted the room service waiter with a towel around his hips.

"Everything fattening in the world," I said, lifting up all the gleaming, silvery, dome-shaped lids.

"Sugar will pick you up a bit." He would know, from Scotty, that alcoholics eat a lot of sugar.

"I know," I said, "but then it lets me down further." Just like booze, I thought, but did not say. I did not like to remind him all the time that I was a drunk. I had once heard someone refer to an actor as an "A.A. retread."

Hedy tried to be funny and charming. I remembered trips with my parents when Deborah and I were small and my father would order from room service at fine hotels. The waiter would leave and my father would serve us with such flourishes of all these platters and dishes. And now when the waiter left, Hedy swept off the towel and put it like a napkin over his arm. "Shall I serve you, madam?" He took the carnation from the vase on the table in his teeth and did a loose-hipped sort of stamping of the feet, waving the towel like a matador. Then he handed me the flower and bowed. "May I have this dance?"

I faked a smile. I got off the bed—why not try—and moved into his arms. We danced around the room, whirling through the sunbeams coming through the windows. He hummed. I laughed and felt his chin nuzzling my hair. I softened into his arms. I turned my head and watched us glide past the mirror above the dresser like statues. His body was lithe and graceful. I thought of Dylan. If Dylan called while I was away, would Brynn tell Dylan, and would Dylan blame me for leaving Brynn alone and why was I setting Dylan up as an authority figure. He was having enough trouble dealing with his own young life. Dealing, yes. Precisely.

Someday, I thought, noticing the sun catching burgundy glints in Hedy's hair, I'm going to remember this moment as one of the romantic highlights of my entire life and I will long to be back here in his shapely arms. I will remember it as perfection. I will not remember that I was thinking only of my children.

He waltzed me over to the bed and settled me down on it, smoothing my hair back, slicking his fingertip along one eyebrow, then over the other. "You have neat eyebrows." He kissed one, then the other. I looked over, fleetingly, at the phone and for a moment I wanted him to be Brynn's father, so I could put my arms around him and tell him, and so we could worry together and feel something, not precisely celebration, but something about the movement and circles of time, the process of a child's life, which is touching in this way only to the parents. And to the child itself, who also somehow knows that beyond herself it has monumental significance only for her parents—not, most likely, for the person sleeping beside her.

I was lying beside Hedy on the beach. I stood up. I sat down again. Brynn had been touched, gone into. I was turning now, this way and that, too, with this feeling. Why hadn't it occurred to me that it might have been good for Brynn? A taboo consideration. Get out of their beds.

I could not, would not, of course, look at my own. Hedy had reached me this morning. I felt all plump and touched and buffeted. I had been the center of a party, a balloon bobbing about in a swinging chandelier, a balloon kept in the air with all his leaps and looks and touches. I did not think love and fear were exactly the same. But they both isolate, and today I had both.

Hedy was wrong, wrong, wrong for me. Too young. Too needful. Too nervous. Too eager. I loved him. And in spite of one hundred alarms, a full-fledged rush hour Sig Alert screaming "stop," howling "don't," I was rushing toward it, into it again, and he could not take care of me any more than Bill, any more than I could take care of my own children.

I got up and began to run. I pounded along on the hard sand, splashing through the palms of surf spreading up on the shore. I wanted to plunge into the ocean; to run from the fear of falling in love, the fear of losing again, the terror that he could not sustain me; and I had only begun to sustain myself and was losing that again. I ran farther in and danced back.

I remembered when my mother took me into the ocean one day, and we were carried by an undertow against the rocks, and finally washed up violently onshore, apart. But alive. I had screamed, and my mother held me and shook me and said, "I have you. You are all right."

I'd run far down this beach here now. And he was not following. Of course he was asleep, tanning himself like a stick in the sun. I ran and ran more, and I fell finally on my knees, sobbing, sobbing in stark terror. And then I was suddenly two people, and I clasped my own hands around my arms and shook this screaming infant, and I sat this fearful creature down firmly on the sand. And I sat there on the sand way down the beach from him, trying to hold on to myself, shuddering and shaking and knowing I would be all right if I could grasp this terrified child in the center and never let it go.

Hedy could never hold me, never begin to hold me as he held himself, or celebrate me as he did himself. I had watched him play, watched him plunge forward, pitching his spirit into the sound. I had watched his music rocket him out on his own fear. Power, I could not give him that power. I would have to keep my fires banked so as not to burn him, smother him or lose myself.

He wasn't like Bill, who didn't have it to give, but what he had he wouldn't be able to give to me. He would need it for himself. Now. And I felt myself beginning to want more. When would I take the risk of saying: this is not enough for me; risk just being there for myself, being enough for myself, which was already more. There was perhaps a solitude, the kind Blanche Hutchins had, decided to have, which filled you more than a love affair whose character was partly defined by what it lacked. And this was a new, a terrifying thought.

I would run it right out of my system, and I kept on running, watching my shadow running right along. I was never going to run—I was never going to do a lot of things. Running was the least of it.

I went back. I sat down on the sand next to Hedy. "I have to talk," I said. He turned on his stomach, his elbows in the sand, face in his hands, looking at me. I told him I had to go back, that I would not go on to L.A.

"I cannot relax anymore. I wanted to be here—and it was exactly what I needed. You have work to do in L.A." Ivan had set up meetings for him with record producers, a drummer Ivan thought might be an improvement, a songwriter who had a song Ivan thought might make a hit single for Hedy.

"Brynn needs me," I said.

"I can't believe you. Months ago when we were sittin' in that restaurant in Soho you were telling me you didn't want Brynn to get too provincial, as if what you want has to be what she wants, and now she acts on her own and you run right back to put her life back your way. You've got to let her try, let her get it wrong on her own so she'll learn how to put it right on her own." He sat up and picked through the sand pebbles and then threw them.

"Hedy, don't, just don't tell me how to handle my kids." Especially since it sounded so right. He sounded like Helena. He was saying "let go." My instinct was always to clutch, to cling.

"I don't even think that's what's goin' on," he said. "It's one thing if I go watch you do your thing." Not, I thought, that I have really been doing anything. "It's another if it's all my way. Don't you see, it's goin' to be good for both of us?"

"Yes," I said, "but sometimes it has to be each of us, and we have to do our separate things."

"I'm hearing exactly what you just said. I hope you're hearing that too. And I'm telling you if there's going to be an us, Margot, there can't be them. You know they have to get out on their own, if I was here or not; you use them. It's your cover story, babe." He did not drop his g's. But he used the one conceivably unattractive gesture he owned: the arrogant lift of the chin. "Cover story." Exactly what Dylan had said about the house being the cover story for wanting to have Hedy. I saw them standing in front of me. "Choose one." You do not choose family. You are chosen.

"I *heard* what I said. I am not threatened."

So I sat on the plane with my fist clenched in my mouth, beating back tears until I remembered I was doing what I had wanted to do. So. I picked up a magazine and read a piece about being on your own. And then I started talking to a young woman next to me who was having trouble getting over this guy who . . . and I sailed into it with the voice of the Woman of Experience, with . . . and then I stopped. "I don't really ever do too well with that myself."

Brynn was waiting for me when I got to the airport. She had on high-heeled boots, her good jeans and my white turtleneck sweater. Her cheeks were rosy, her features looked crisp and defined. If Brynn blushed or looked abashed or uncomfortable, it was only for such a brief moment that I could well have just imagined it.

"Stop staring at me," Brynn said; "it doesn't leave marks."

"Not at least," I said, "for the first thirty years."

We stood waiting for the luggage to come around. Hedy ticked with impatience waiting for things like this, which made me frantic. Brynn just did what I was doing, just stood there, not talking, watching people.

"I hope you didn't just come back so fast because of me," Brynn said, once we were in the car, on the highway going north.

"No, I wouldn't do that," I said, turning the volume down on the car radio.

"Certainly not," said Brynn. She turned the volume up, but not as loud as before. It was some sort of rock music.

"Could we not have any music?" I asked.

"You listen to this all the time with him," Brynn said, turning it back down a bit.

"I know. Which is why when I am not with him I really don't want to hear it."

"How can you go out with someone when you hate his music?"

"I don't hate it. All the time. Just not now." I turned off the radio. We rode quietly. In just these couple of days, I noticed, the angle of light had changed, the summer colors had softened. It had been almost two seasons since I had driven this highway into the city with Hedy. I wondered if two seasons from now I would be actually living with Hedy at Upshot. Would it not happen because I found it so difficult to imagine? I had not of course imagined, ever, not living with Bill. And that had happened.

"So," I said, "how are things going?"

"You mean with Freddy?" Brynn reached into her pocket for change for the tollbooth. I found some in my purse and started to hand it to Brynn. "I got it," Brynn said. "Thank you," I said.

"For what?" Brynn asked, handing the toll to the attendant, giving him a sporty salute.

"The money. It was thoughtful." I was probably overreacting again. I loved the way little wisps of Brynn's hair ducked out over the back of the turtleneck like wings. I hoped Freddy had noticed the way Brynn's lashes went out off the sides of her eyes. I wanted Brynn to be extravagantly appreciated. I had a sharp understanding, like a stitch in my side, of how my parents must have reacted to the boys, then men, that I had gone out with. It might be an excellent gesture to let them know I finally understood. When will I give them the gift of my identification?

"We're just friends, Mom," Brynn said. "He has this regular girlfriend at college. We decided we didn't want to get that involved. He really was there to keep me company because Jennie was over at Reilly's, and it just happened."

"That's very grown-up," I said. Certainly more grown-up than I would have been. How much hurt this cool statement must be covering. It is not the mother's role to carve away the shell, to dig out and reveal feelings. That should be, I supposed, the job of friends—and retrospect. I peered at Brynn's face, and put my arm around Brynn's shoulder. Brynn shrugged.

"Don't take it more seriously than I do, please," said Brynn.

"I'm not. God knows, I understand these things," I said. "Which does not mean they are wonderful or easy."

"Well, just don't look like that."

"Like what? You haven't looked at me. You're driving."

"I know," said Brynn. The ruddy fall light of late afternoon cast rose madder shadows along her profile; tears stood in her eyes. She swallowed. "But I can hear the look you have in your voice."

A couple, young, sped by in an open C-J Jeep. I wondered if Brynn saw them, if their closeness made her feel the way I have felt seeing couples when I was sad . . . I wondered if I had felt as sad then or if the experience of love not working so many times just added a kind of weight, if maybe I felt more now than I had then.

"It isn't easy," I said aloud, "anytime. Love. It's always yours and, no matter when, it just hurts."

"Please stop trying to understand. It's really nice. He's a very nice person. And we were very honest about the whole thing. I have something more important to tell you."

I froze. "Dylan!"

"No. Not a word." Brynn paused. "I'm sorry. No, what I was going to tell you is that Sandy and Carla are going to England and I'm going." She sat perfectly relaxed. "Sandy's mom has it all worked out. I told Cleo when she called, and she thought it sounded neat."

"My. You have been busy. As Deborah would say, do we want to talk about this trip."

"Not unless we talk about where I'm getting to go and what I'll need to take with me."

I liked Brynn's attitude. She could just sleep with this person. And then move right on to another continent. I decided I would not mention school and my conflict in that direction that this excursion might present. Better to be not going to school in England than not going to school at the Medwin's Landing Main Street Auto Service Center. "But"—and I heard my own wrongheadedness and rushed right in—"I've just come home to be with you."

"I said I think that you didn't have to."

I wanted everything to be impossibly easy for Brynn. Especially the things that were tough for me. And now they seemed to be easy, and I was astonished, uncomfortable. There was no place for me to make it better. She had made it better on her own, as Deborah had told me she would. And I thought of Hedy on the beach. What he said—and how he looked. I could be there. But I had to rush right back and fix it. And there was nothing to fix.

Find a possibility, somewhere to jump in: "So Dylan didn't call at all while I was away?" Somehow, asking again I thought might have changed the answer.

"You weren't gone that long," Brynn said. "He'll call when he needs money."

"That's cynical," I said.

"That's kids. I do the same thing," she said.

"Not quite. Well, we'll have arrangements to make for the trip abroad," I said, pleased to be driving past the towns, the road signs I recognized now as milestones leading to my home. I had become attached. I was looking forward to being back in Medwin's Landing. To the soft misty acceptance I felt there. I was looking forward to my regular meetings, to my house.

"You're not going to move or anything while I'm away?" Brynn asked, in the tone of voice of a statement.

"I doubt it," I said, seeing Medwin's Landing now in the distance, the tops of the factory chimneys barely peering over the hills, brown behind the russet and rose, the graying greens of the trees.

"I know how you feel," I continued. "Even when I knew I wouldn't maybe be living with my parents much longer, I never liked the idea of them moving. But I wouldn't move without you there, you know that."

"You guys had a fight out there," Brynn said, hanging her arm out of the window now that we were off the highway, looking cool.

"No, we didn't," I said. "Actually that would make it easier. Why did you think so?"

"If it was going well you'd be moving anyway. You wouldn't be thinking about waiting for me." She was matter-of-fact in her manner.

"That's not true," I said. Could I catch a little wistfulness in her voice. Did I really need to have that there so badly.

"Yes, it is. I've developed a very philosophical attitude about that. When things aren't going well we turn to each other; it's natural." She was becoming a friend, a contemporary. I just stared at her. For "philosophical," I thought "brave." I didn't want Brynn to go to England. Perhaps I had wanted Brynn to be a little undone—because I needed Brynn. And here was Brynn being—seeming—very all done.

"I think that place is the pits anyway. And I don't like to think of you off in the woods there all alone."

"Well," I said, "I wouldn't be all alone." I bit my tongue to keep from saying, "You won't be gone long. You'll be back soon with me." Brynn had to be on her own—and she was learning to try it, to talk about it, faster than I could. Too fast. For me.

18

This day had the look, the feel of the first day I had seen Hedy, in his limousine. I had given him that apple.

Fall, the fastest season, was rushing through then, as it was now. Flocks of small brown birds whirled up from the meadows and hedges of tangled vines, flurrying up into trees, considering winter plans, twirling through the sky like soft brown stars. The vines were covered with the fall berries birds love; bittersweet bursting from its ocher pearls; the last of the wildflowers, drying on bushes; black-eyed Susans; lavender blue cornflowers paling now; Queen Anne's lace, tilting on slender stalks. A softening golden note had appeared on the green moss; gardenfuls of basil had been gathered and made into pesto; last roses flounced like tipsy old can-can dancers on fences; pumpkins and squash hid under their vines; Canadian geese had already come this far south to float amid the cattails in the shallows of the river, and chain stores, in the shopping center by the highway, were filled with Halloween party things.

Now, driving from my house to the train station to pick up Cleo, who was coming for the weekend, I watched a sudden storm coming over from the northeast from Boston. Would it bring Dylan? "Don't," I told myself. As the wind roared down, with big hearty drops of rain, leaves came down, wafting, scurrying, jumping off early.

In town, school supplies were on the shelves, in the shop windows; students in droves had charged records and books to their parents before going back to college. I wondered how many really stayed. And I wondered when Dylan would call, and when I would stop aching for Brynn's face and voice. There had been two postcards in the mailbox. And more invitations again, openings, shows. Producers, directors and stars had been coming in for interviews; such eager anticipation of the hits the fresh season had seemed to promise. Artists and dealers were bustling along Madison Avenue; designers wrapped in tweeds; glowing with the success of irresistible trends; restaurants had filled with people glancing about, casing each other for news, what to read now, to see now, to wear now, to serve at little dinners with the fresh fall gossip. I wondered if rock had a season. It had, I feared, a year-round season, rather like Bill's variety of baseball.

New Yorkers had come back to the city, and I had more stories, more work to do, more places I could pretend I needed to go.

"What are you going to do in this relic all by yourself?" Cleo stood in front of the stable door at Upshot, scowling, her hands in the back pockets of her jeans.

Hedy was still in L.A. and I had invited Cleo up to show her the house, and also to show her that I was really working.

"You also hate being without your kids. That's what it's really about. This house, and this weekend, too, actually, as you would say." Cleo gave me a pat on the shoulder.

I turned fast. I could not talk about that, think about it. I had night-lights on, little odd sound boxes, alarms turned toward them every moment like the old-fashioned remote control radio things we used to put in the babies' rooms when we were in other rooms. They never worked, either. I turned and turned my heart to the children and I could not catch a sense of them.

"I won't be alone. For one thing, these stables are going to be converted to little rooms, and I'll have my kids and their friends and other young people staying here, while they're pulling themselves together. They'll help take care of animals and gardens and everything. As some move on there will always be new ones. And even when I'm older I'll never be alone. When the kids grow up and get married, they'll be here summers or weekends and over the holidays with their kids."

"Exactly the way you just ride over in the sleigh with your kids to your parents' house every chance you get."

"That's different. And few sleighs hit Florida," I snapped.

Right now I felt already older because Cleo reminded me so sharply of Brynn. "Don't you think it's beautiful, though?" I put one foot on the stone wall. I put my hands in the pockets of my tweed jacket.

"Is that your landowner pose?" said Cleo.

"You bet," I said. It was right here I had seen the snake last week. Yellow and black, going through the grass. "I hope," I had said to it, "you are a snake in the grass and not a symbol."

I looked at the wooden outbuildings, and the large, graceful old house. Reilly had brought almost everyone over this morning. They were measuring, scraping off bits of paint, leaning ladders up against the walls, writing down figures. The roofer was up on the roof of the cottage; he pulled off a slab of rotted asphalt, and shook his head. Andy was down in the basement inspecting the furnace.

"Should they be taking the place apart before you buy it?" Cleo asked. "Or, actually, before it falls apart by itself, which I give it a week and a half to do."

"Well, it's important," I said, "to know exactly what it's going to cost. Maybe I just can't afford to fix it up, then that's another question." I watched another piece of roof come gliding down onto the lilac bushes, fading, drying now, lashed with vines of huge yellow leaves.

"Hey," I shouted up to the men on the roof, "I don't own it yet."

I turned to Cleo, trying to be wildly enthusiastic, flagging at Cleo's expression. "The electrician is waiting until Hedy gets back. He's going to use the cottage as a sound studio, and then give me part of the income from that. It's really all worked out."

"Enterprising," Cleo said. "The rising star will have a gracious, accomplished hostess with a stylish estate she nearly kills herself to put together. You'll make vats of pasta in a big white apron for swarms of music business people."

"You've never liked the idea, but that's because you just don't understand the relationship." I hoped Cleo would not ask me to explain it this morning.

With everyone running around, workmen arriving, it reminded me of a rehearsal for a big old-fashioned musical; I felt the way my father must have when they were pulling a set together. It was action; and in the middle of this I did not feel alone.

The huge golden oak in front of the house glistened in the sun and I looked up at the balcony where Hedy and I had imagined we would sleep under stars on warm summer nights, where I'd been too scared to be. In case it wouldn't work.

"You have to try to believe in something to get it to work out, Cleo. If you don't believe in it, nothing works."

It could be one of those projects that keeps people together.

"I think I'll do a show on it," I said, to reassure Cleo that I was not going to be distracted from work, heaven knows. "I'll call some other people who have restored houses, although the subject may be so familiar and successful it almost isn't a new idea anymore."

We walked across the long grass to the back porch.

"Yes," Cleo said, "but those people who restore houses together actually have some other things in common. And enough money." I heard the first step creak badly as Cleo put her foot on it. "And no termites," she said.

The house was conspiring, being its worst.

"That's not true," I said, "they're always writing about how just before it was finished they were broke, discouraged, and then, somehow, it worked out."

"In the article, Margot, it has to end happily."

"But look at the rooms—they have the most incredible proportions," I said. "I'm going to build benches all around the screened porch. Think of weekend gatherings with the kids and their friends; the summers will be wonderful for them when they're all home from school . . ." I saw tables with little candles on them, calico mats along the benches so everyone could stay over. I'd wake up to the sounds of swimming early in the morning, all of them laughing.

Reilly and a plaster man were checking out the dining room walls.

"Why are those people peeling off the wallpaper?" Cleo stepped over a heap of torn faded floral paper.

"We're checkin' for rot under here, see how much of these walls we got to replace," Reilly said.

"You'll have to get that septic situation cleared up, ma'am, before I can get you an estimate on the front of the house. I'll get asphyxiation. I'm dyin' now," said the plasterer.

I had avoided taking Cleo through the front door where the seepage from the guest bath was particularly "gross," as Brynn had said when I had taken her to see the house before she'd left. And when Brynn had been there I had thought, "This is just what Cleo would say."

"I'm glad he was the one to mention it," said Cleo.

"It will be fixed," I said, uneasy now. "I told you everything, absolutely everything, is falling apart and has to be fixed. Who can buy a perfect house? Once it's in shape it will be a glorious estate."

"This whole wall's gonna have to go, lady," said the plaster man. He sounded like a filling station person. I knew when they called you "lady" like that they thought you were an idiot. They also called you that when they were telling you it was going to be extremely expensive.

Cleo said, "I'm going upstairs to look at the palatial bedroom suites."

"Remember," I said, "the paint will be all new, windows widened. I'll be right up."

"Reilly, what do you think?" I asked, inspecting the powdery patches of damp gray wall where the paper had been peeled away. I thought of the people who ate plaster in tenements. Was Dylan living in a tenement? No. Surely not.

Dylan would be good at anything he did. He would be a successful dealer, riding around Boston in one of those cars with smoked glass windows, air-brushed swirls, and heavy leather roof. Silly. Alison would not permit it. I rubbed my forefinger on the wall and licked it. You could get into it. Despairing enough, you could get into anything. I remembered tossing a cigarette butt out of the remains of a Scotch and soda after I had drunk up all the rest of the booze in the house one night. Three years ago. They had told me it would take a year to get the physical self back, the second year I'd get my thinking together, the third year I could begin to accept myself, to live an entirely sane life. Or perhaps now I was just sober enough to see how crazy I continued to be.

"I don't know, Margot, you got a lot of heavy stuff to deal with here." Reilly leaned against the wall, and plaster rattled to the floor around him. He brushed it off his shoulders, kicked pieces into the corner. Andy came up from the cellar. "You got a problem down there, baby." He wiped off his hands on his jeans.

"Don't be burned, Margot," Reilly said, "the foundation's solid as a rock. In the main house, anyway."

"It is rock," said Andy.

"I know," I said. "Fitz said it might be the best cellar in the northeast."

Fitz was going to be furious about the wallpaper. I'd glue it back Monday. If the wall was still standing.

Cleo came back downstairs. Too fast. But how could she not have been impressed with the divine cedar closets, the little built-in glove drawers.

Reilly and Andy were still discussing the rock out of which the prerevolutionary cellar was made. I would have to ask Blanche if perhaps Mrs. Medwin had lived here. She would have seen to the construction of such a cellar.

"It's goin' to play hell with getting a proper size furnace in there," Andy was saying.

"Probably have to blast," said Reilly, "or you could set up a big new system right outside."

"That would take care of the flooding problem," Andy agreed. "It would cost a bit more."

"Flooding I understand, and hate already," I said. "That's been the trouble with my house I've been renting." As Andy knew all too well.

Cleo was pacing. "I'm waiting outside," she said.

"I don't know," Andy said, "how they keep that thing rented without doing some work on it."

"Charm," I said, "just charm."

"Well, you sure can pick 'em, honey," Andy said.

Cleo and I were in the car now, driving back to the house overlooking the river. "All I'm saying," Cleo said again, "is you can't afford not to work, and you can't put the time and energy into this kind of project and get your work done. I know what you think you see, and I understand; but I question what you're getting out of this."

"An investment they've been wanting me to make, for one; and for two, fun; and for three, it's not something I can explain because you don't trust men anyway."

"Neither," she said, "do you. Trust them—or anyone." She winced as I swerved to avoid a speeding car full of teenagers.

"Kids," I said.

"Yes. Kids," said Cleo. "And what I do not understand is why you are doing this instead of going up to Boston to chase after Dylan and get him back here and shaped up."

I froze. I pulled the car over to the side of the road. I grabbed the steering wheel with both hands to keep from punching Cleo, only because I wanted to punch myself. Only because Cleo asked the question I kept asking myself, knowing the answer even as I would try to explain it to Cleo now. "I am trying, and you cannot understand that, to create any goddamn distraction I can. He is there because you cannot just shape a person up. You cannot believe how I want to be there. How I see him on those streets. I follow him in my heart with every breath. But I have talked to every authority, every expert, I have remembered me when I was him, and I know with every sore piece of feeling, Cleo, I know I have to wait. And I thank God I have this house to obsess over or I would tear every nail out."

"I'm sorry. That was stupid. Of course—I guess I'd go crazy." Cleo put her hand in my arm.

"I know," I said. "It has nothing to do with following instinct. Or sense. That's what's so hard."

For dinner I made cheeseburgers for us out of chopped steak.

"The cheeseburger needs more grease," said Cleo, "and I don't think you used the right kind of cheese, but otherwise it's perfect."

Now we were sitting on my bed. The reading lamps were on and we were both wearing flannel nightgowns. Cleo had one of Bill's old sweaters over her shoulders. I usually wore it when I was editing the notes and schedules for the interviews, some of which Cleo was now scratching out bits of while I was scrawling additions and changing the schedule of others.

"Whatever close is, I haven't sat on a bed like this with anyone except when I used to do my homework with my grandmother; that was maybe the last time."

"What is this, please, Literary Hula-Hoops?" Cleo said, looking at my list.

"Oh, there's a guy who wrote and said he did his dissertation on the unforgettable fad books of the last fifty years. I thought it would be fun."

"Certainly timely. The Golden Oldies syndrome. Let's wait on that."

"Okay. We can do it near New Year's, when everyone does lists on something."

"I was thinking of waiting longer. Like five years."

"All right. See how I'm cooperating."

"Probably because you're going to try to convince me we need to do this interview with your friend who restores merry-go-rounds."

"I wouldn't dream of bringing that up again," I said. And we laughed.

"I want you to do this one on the widowers group. You're good at that. It's what your listeners like to hear you do," Cleo said. She wrote it in for next month.

"I really am not comfortable with that," I said.

"Which is why you'll do such a good job with it."

Sometimes with Cleo, with Helena now, with Blanche, I could feel a closeness that made me want to run, to be Bill, to invent a new life without a past, a future, without reason. Because I could not bear to look at the reason, or meaning, of this one. I could understand: all he wanted to look at were things that just would go by—cars out on the highway, lights, fast boats on the river, out that window. I could imagine how he might just want to stand there all his nights and watch the mornings come, and when it was foggy look at nothing, and when it wasn't, which it usually was, to see the river, too.

"I really would like to turn completely around and write about something else, be Jane Gross and cover baseball games, traveling and watching and talking only to baseball players."

"That's harder than she makes it look and you travel very well—not to mention how good you are at drawing out baseball players."

"Well, he did marry me for longer than anyone else."

"That proposition really makes a lot of sense after you said in the car that you don't trust men. That's such an ordinary thing to say. I wish you'd save your pop ideas for grilling your guests." She scratched out another show. "We already did three fashion pieces, two on shoes! Just buy yourself some new shoes and get it out of your system."

"Okay," I said, then returned to the subject of men. "But I don't actually trust them," I said. "I don't think they trust us. I really think it's very serious. The only one I ever trusted was Bill."

Cleo put down her pen and reached out to the night table for a sip of coffee.

"Pass me a cigarette," I said. "Please."

"I hate people who smoke in bed. And you said you only smoke when you are writing your lectures, which you're certainly not doing much now."

"Well, I'm focusing on the syndicated stuff. And there's been a lot of mail," I said. "Okay, I won't smoke."

"You never trusted Bill." Cleo drew a huge X through a whole paragraph. "You just like to think so."

I looked at the sweater on Cleo's shoulders. "Well, I liked him, anyway. I think most women expect them to take care of us, like we were conditioned to believe; like our fathers took care of our mothers."

"What fathers? Mine didn't." She paused. "And your father

doesn't really take care of your mother. She just acts the villain, from what I've heard, so he can feel perfect."

"That's not true," I said. "She does say the sharper things he may sometimes feel. But he gives her the safety net. She can say or do anything because she knows he is there. When people have been together that long, Cleo, it's impossible to separate the games—to see how it started. Or why."

"I forgot," Cleo said. "We do not go near the reality of that one."

"No, we probably don't. Anyway," I went on very quickly, "it's the cultural idea that we learn from and get disappointed by—the expectation that they'd be the strong, perfect ones and handle everything, and then we get mad when they're just like us, just as uneasy, just as scared of that idea, just as troubled about living up to it, which is why they run away and stuff."

"Stuff. That's very good." Cleo stretched out on her side, working with one pen, her fist stuffed with three others.

"You know I get incoherent when I'm trying to make a point you're just not going to agree with."

We looked at each other, beginning to laugh. "It's easier to pretend that out there the myth continues if you stay away and learn to take total care of yourself."

"Do me a favor and stop trying to analyze me based on what you think about you," Cleo said, firmly. "If you could generalize, and you can't, I'd say that most men expect women to take care of them. And everyone has enough trouble taking care of oneself. The only problem I have with men is the way most women spend so much time discussing them as if they're another kind of creature."

"I was brought up to believe they were," I said. "When I think I can't trust them myself, it's probably because they don't live up to expectations which weren't human to begin with."

"It's much easier for me. I don't actually like many people, of any variety." Spike appeared in the doorway, cased the bedroom and jumped on the foot of the bed. "Or dogs," said Cleo.

"Off, Spike," I said. He looked at me, then at Cleo, then back at me. "I can't help it," I said to the dog, "she doesn't like you."

"Not at all," said Cleo, looking at Spike, who had stretched out in the shape of the Sphinx on the floor. She held up a script to me. "We already did one on Holidays and Drinking."

"That was last year. I'm doing one every year. And this one is mostly about kids."

"I know, but you've already got a story we recorded about kids and violence. Oh, it's okay. It's actually good."

"She says grudgingly."

"She said smugly," Cleo said.

"This would be really a different tone," I said. "I thought I'd ask St. Cheri to talk to some city kids in the program, ask them if they'd like to come on the show and talk about what they do when their families are drinking, when there are parties, how kids who don't drink or do drugs do the holidays."

"I can really see her doing that," Cleo said.

"I'll bet the young ones really like her—she proves you can be sober and still original and crazy, you know what I mean?"

"She sure does. I just don't want to deal with the idea of holidays—she's going to be with him." Cleo looked miserable.

"Her husband?"

"Yes."

"Well, you can be with us. It does make sense," I said. "Hedy never understands how I can love him and still need to be with the kids."

"Margot, it's hardly the same thing! And he's just childish about that. It's completely different."

"I suppose you're right."

She lifted her eyebrows.

"You're absolutely right," I said.

The phone rang. "Want me to get it?" Cleo said.

"Probably not." I looked at the clock.

"That is true. Who else would understand that I am your grandmother." She handed the phone to me.

"How are you?" said Hedy. He had his cheerful, sexy tone of voice.

"In bed, in the flannel nightie with the little red houses on it."

"Smoking?"

"I never smoke in bed," I said. Cleo socked my arm.

"Not when I'm around," he said.

"Or anything else."

"Anyone else better not be there." He laughed.

"God knows," I said. I remembered sitting on this bed with Bill talking to Cleo on the phone, and later sitting in this bed with Hedy, talking to Cleo, and then, out there with Hedy, talking to Brynn—and always feeling divided. But also, always, arranging and creating and feeding the divisions, and that way you were never too close, and never in danger of total loss.

"How's the house, what's going on? Did you get a contractor up there today?" There was now the rasp of business in Hedy's voice. I had decided for now that I would not tell Hedy I had asked Reilly to contract the estimates. It might turn out cheaper but now I held my breath, hoping Scotty wouldn't have heard about it and told Hedy.

"The house is wonderful," I said. I turned and grinned at Cleo. "The contractor was there. A few problems. A little dry rot and so forth. Nothing we don't already know. I think it's going to be expensive."

"We'll work it out," Hedy said. "I got a good feelin' about this demo. I was thinkin' I can probably put more money into the deal than you think. I was also thinkin' we're arguing because we need each other and that you ought to come back out next weekend, if I'm not back. My treat."

"I can't do that, Hedy."

"I should have figured that," he said. "You'll never make it simple. Never just say 'yes.' "

I didn't want it to start again. Why can't he just let go a little. "I don't think I can, Hedy, unless I get more work done." I thought of a song that played when we were making love one night—sort of, I like you, dig you, but I'm not in love.

"Maybe then?" he said.

"Possible," I said. Why wouldn't he say "I love you"? Why wouldn't I? And why did we start having urgent reasons not to see each other the minute we saw the house?

"Have you called the bank about the mortgage?"

"I did," I lied. The banker I wanted to talk to hadn't been in, and I had not called back. "He wasn't in Friday. And never on Saturday. If it's supposed to be all right it will."

"That doesn't sound very positive, Margot." I sensed irritation, knew I was creating it, and knew that I was, more and more, wanting to. And that bothered me. But not quite enough to stop. He had been furious earlier in the week when Scotty had told him I was going to have a kind of drying-out place up there. Of course, that was A.A. gossip. His dad had said, "If you're going to have drunks around, what about sober old ones like me?" Which really made Hedy mad because he was "doing this so I won't have to live with him anymore."

"I thought there were other reasons," I'd said.

"There are, and you know that," Hedy had said. I felt the taste of trouble in the back of my mouth like salt, me causing the trouble. "I do know," I had said, "but I hate when you call and just grill me about all this. I'm not good at these things."

"Margot, I'm not doing this for me. I can't be there, and

you are good at those things; you just like to pretend you're not."

Cleo was watching me, embarrassed. She got up and walked to the window and just stood there looking out. She knew I hated anyone to be gentle with me when I was on the verge of tears. Cleo knew because she also hated that.

"But you make it feel so businesslike," I kept on. He was sounding like the wife who is at a stylish spa, or the wife who is a star, saying, "Are you taking care of business, baby?"

"You know I'm not into heavy phone calls, Margot. And I never say what you think you want to hear."

"And I certainly don't say what you want either." We did not know how to say goodbye. Neither one of us at this point would give an inch, say the gentler thing; the hint that we missed each other. Games! In this one we were surely even: 0–0. When I used to go out and come home from a date with stars in my eyes, my father would be cool, his fingers rubbing together with impatience, a tiny almost silent gesture, and my mother would ask, "But did he say 'I love you,' because if he didn't, he doesn't, and you're going to cheapen yourself again."

Again. Cheapen. It was like good and bad. A condition.

But there must be shades and levels. I wanted to believe that. I was sometimes a good person. Sometimes a good mother. Sometimes a good lover.

Or was it like being sober: you either were or were not. People would talk at meetings about "I'm trying to get sober."

"If you're drinking you are not trying," they would be told.

If you are thinking of trying to be in love, you are not in love, and I did not know why, with Hedy on the other end of the phone, in a hotel room in L.A., I was mainly thinking of all this and reminding myself that I was trying to really hear what he was saying. If I loved him wouldn't I want to hear everything; wouldn't I hang upon his every word; and not be wanting him to say more or wondering why we did not tell each other that we loved each other. Could I sit here with a friend and be comfortable, or spend my anxious moments thinking only of the children, if I was totally in love? I had been totally in love with Bill, and also needed to see my father, to be with the children, to talk to friends.

"That big golden oak in front of the house looked so splendid today," I told Hedy. That was trying. I supposed. "And a roofer looked at your studio today. It's going to have to be replaced, but it won't be a terrible job."

"That sounds better."

"For sure," I said, using one of his favorite phrases.

"I'm sitting in on a session down in Venice tomorrow, so I'll give you a ring Monday. You goin' to a meeting?"

"Yes. Probably," I said.

"Okay, if you think you need to do that, and hey, Margot." His voice got lower, sexier. He would say something wonderful.

"Yes?"

"Don't forget to give the banker a ring. You got to keep after people. I'll call you." In this way we rattled our way into hanging up the phones simultaneously, neither one of us wanting to be the one to hang up first.

"For sure," I repeated.

The phone rang again. "Now what," I said. I leaned over Cleo and picked it up. "Yes?" I said. Curt.

"It will be good to be back home for a while," he said.

"That's better," I said. And I hung up the phone softly. For a while. For a while was not enough.

"This is a wonderful situation," said Cleo.

"It's probably hopeless."

"Maybe. The most hopeful part of love is before you ever meet the person, and you can still imagine it will be perfect the next time."

"That's very cynical."

"It's only how I feel today," Cleo said. "Can we go to sleep now?"

She climbed off the bed to go into the other room. I followed her to the door and she patted my shoulder, and we squeezed hands.

"Whatever happens with everyone, even the kids," I said, "the house will be wonderful to have, I think. Parts of things do work out, you know."

"Yes," said Cleo. "But you will not readily settle for just parts."

"Yes, I will," I said, "provided they're the ones that matter."

19

When Dylan was stabbed in Boston I was standing at this kitchen counter in Connecticut with a knife in one hand and an apple in the other. I sliced into that apple as I said to Cleo, "I am worried about Dylan this morning." And only seconds later the phone rang. Cleo picked it up. "It's a Captain Belmont," she said, "of the Boston police." She handed me the phone. She stood next to me. Watching.

"Are you Margot Spinning?"

"Yes." I nodded. "Margot Fox. But also Spinning. Actually. Why?" I dithered with names. I held back terror. I could not bear to listen. Let it be he has eight hundred traffic tickets. Do they call the mother for tickets?

"Mrs. Spinning, we need permission to do surgery on your son, Dylan Tanner." My pulse stopped. I saw Dylan's walk. Dylan's angled smile. Dylan's eyes.

"Mrs. Spinning, are you there? He is in the emergency room and . . ."

Cleo put her arm around my shoulder.

"Yes." Be realistic. Be sensible. "Yes." They are tied to my breath, these children. The words came from my throat. "What happened?"

"He's been stabbed, ma'am." I could hear him hate to tell me. These flat tones we had to exchange . . . words with the voices of machines. I saw Dylan running. Don't see more, I told myself. Stay straight here.

"Is he hurt?" My mind was stuck. I hurled out every rope of existence. I clasped the back rung of a chair and it was Dylan's hand. Of course he was hurt. That was what they were telling me. I could not ask, "Will he . . . ?" Don't ask. Just go.

"Mrs. Spinning, are you there? We just need the parents' permission immediately."

"Oh, God. Yes," I said, "of course you have it . . . the permission. I am the parents." How much do I ask? What are you supposed to say? How do you hold on to your mind? The words now flew out: "Yes. Anything. Get the best people. You tell them to tell him, you tell them I love him, I'm coming, I'll be right there. Please. Just tell them do anything. Will you give me the name of the hospital? Thank you. Yes. I have written it down. Yes. And do this for me: tell him I love him. Tell him to be all right. Tell him hold on. Tell him I'm on my way now."

I must rein myself in. Keep every heartbeat steady. My heart must beat and beat for him. And I must be there.

I ran outside. Reilly was fixing the gutters on the roof. "Reilly," I said, "Dylan's been stabbed. I need you to drive me to Boston."

He looked at me. "Jesus!" He scrambled down the ladder. "We're on our way," he said.

Then I ran up to my bedroom and pulled out a canvas satchel. Cleo followed me. She sat on the bed and watched as I put on my gray slacks and tweed jacket and packed a skirt, a sweater, two pairs of underpants, a bra, and two fresh panty hose and a flannel nightgown into the satchel. I did not say a word. I went into the bathroom and filled a smaller kit with Ten-O-Six lotion, a bottle of shampoo, mascara, baby powder, blusher, eyeliner, brown shadow, vitamins C, B-11, Super B, and Geritol pills, and Sinutabs. I took some cold cream and cotton pads, Midol and Tampax, because you never know. I put in my brush and my hair dryer. Then, in the bedroom again, I added warm socks, waterproof boots and a slicker to the large satchel.

Cleo handed me my A.A. Twenty-Four Hour book from the night table. "Right," I said, "very smart." I stopped. "My God. I've got the French ambassador on tomorrow—live. Cleo!"

"We'll do a tape—leave it to me."

"If I'm up there a while, I can tape some interviews around Boston—Harvard people, writers."

"Margot. Just go."

I quickly put on a gold pin with a heart on it which Dylan had given me for my last birthday and the tiny gold chain bracelet from Brynn. "Brynn, my God. I'll have to find Brynn!" I could feel panic coming now.

"Just get there. I'll help—if you want me to I'll find her." Cleo grasped my forearm. I looked at my pocket watch. "*Pace.*" Indeed.

"Seven minutes," I said to Cleo.

I slung the satchel over one shoulder and my shoulder bag over the other and I went downstairs.

I hugged Cleo tight and climbed into the car. And these seven minutes, quick as they were, seemed still too long. Cleo and Jennie watched as Reilly drove me down the hill; turning then, heading for the highway, belts of asphalt covering old onion fields, split-levels over gravel pits. I thought of Mrs. Medwin being called from grinding corn—"It's the sheriff, ma'am. Your son's got an arrow in him."

I should get Brynn home. I had written her, the white lies, and told her that he had gone to Boston to be with Alison. When does protection become denial? Later. I must believe all the way that he will be all right. Please let Alison be with him.

Massachusetts: how flat and empty; I never think of it that

way. I tie states in with images, with symbols from school-days. Symbols: snake, do not be a symbol. Houses: *when life looks like easy street there is danger at your door.*

I fixed on the spelling of every name of every exit on the road. Highways; thruways; I thought of driving south with Hedy; I will not call him yet. The concert: *Trouble ahead, trouble behind.* The Grateful Dead. Don't think. I swallowed. I took very deep breaths.

"Are you okay?" Reilly asked. We had not talked on the entire ride. "Maybe it's not serious. They make things sound bad. It could be a cut. You could get a cut from a knife and they could call it a stab."

"Sure," I said. I decided it was a deep cut on Dylan's arm, perhaps the left arm, or maybe the right if he had reached out. What they meant by surgery was really a little stitching up.

Dylan had played drums once with these cut-crystal candlesticks and bowl, a present from our wedding. Our wedding. I must find his father. Dylan had smashed all the crystal and sat there, bleeding, grinning among the pieces, and I had whipped him right off to the emergency room at the base. The cut had been a small one, crescent shaped. I had noticed this summer that the cut still showed, a pale quarter moon, against Dylan's tanned arm.

Perhaps I should have reserved a hotel room in Boston. Probably that would not be necessary. Surely not. We would be coming back tonight with Dylan, and this would be it for him and Boston.

"Reilly, we may have to wait a few hours. Will that be all right? I'll drive back and you can get some rest."

"Let's not worry about any of it, Margot. It's cool. I got everything worked out on the job, and I can always hit a meetin' up there. No problem." Blanche should know how he has responded. Blanche will know. I should stay out of it.

Meetings: I remembered Ann, sober fifteen years, speaking

at a meeting about how, when you need it, the investment in meetings pays off. She had itemized the three moments of surrender which told her she was getting well: "when I called someone for help; when I decided not to buy a bottle; and when I arrived at my ex-husband's house to visit my children and felt no anger." Ann told of her gratitude and then quietly said, with no change in her voice, "And I was able to have a reconciliation with my daughter before she was killed in an accident." Then she had moved on to the rest of her story.

Coming into the city of Boston, I tensed forward on my seat, my hands tightened on the edge of the dashboard. Fear is faith turned inside out; faith in retreat.

Alison met us at the hospital. "He's still in the operating room. I'm so frightened. I broke up with him, he was getting so crazy. I said I wouldn't see him." How young she was to know how to do what you have to do.

"You don't know how I feel." Her face was silver with tears.

The police were there, and the owners of the parking lot where Dylan had been working. "We're going to take that kid apart."

"What kid?" I was confused, not asking questions, not wanting to know anything yet, except will he be all right.

"It was a kid we think—the kid that did it."

I remembered feeling panic, for a moment, on the way up, but I did not feel it now. For a fleeting moment, I thought—so fast: I want my mother. My mother! Not my father. My mother; to want infancy, the innocence, the last absolute safety of infancy. But I was the mother; I was the one their eyes were turning to. I was the one who must calm and soothe and set the example.

A young doctor came out of the operating room. He seemed no older than Dylan. When did doctors get to be younger than I am?

I put my hands in my pants pockets, to stand as a father would, not to rush to him and look like a mother who would need to be coddled, who might become irrational.

"Just tell me exactly," I said.

"His condition is serious, Mrs. Spinning. But stable. We had to do an exploratory. The initial cut was a quarter inch below the heart. If it had been closer—" The doctors snapped his fingers. "But he'll make it. All the vital signs are good."

"I see," I said. "When can he come home?" I was the picture of the model parent.

"I can't predict now. Why don't we just go a day at a time. He'll be in the Intensive Care Unit for a few days. Just a precaution. You should be able to go up and see him in a while. He'll be out of it, though."

"I know. I just want to see him." I noticed he was watching me. I wanted to keep those tears at bay. Damn. I did not want the doctor saying to the others, "You've got to keep the mother from upsetting him." I wanted to be the good influence. To be allowed to stand next to his bed and look at him. And touch him. To be given, perhaps, little helpful things to do so I would not have to leave him for a minute.

"That's all right. He's a strong kid."

"Thank you," I said automatically. Needing a semblance of approval I grabbed the notion that I had fed him right once, helped him to be strong.

He was pale and laced with tubes, gleaming with sweat; his hair was pulled back, his eyes swollen and shut. I took one hand and Alison the other. I clasped his hand. He returned the clasp and went limp. "Mom." He opened his eyes and looked terrified, then closed his eyes. "You'll be all right," I said. "I love you. Just rest."

I cried. Silently: "I love you, God. Be all right." And I said, "You're going to be fine."

"Ma, you're here."

"Yes. Don't talk."

Alison picked up his hand and put it on her cheek.

"Allie," he said.

I looked at her and knew how that felt, knew that was what she had waited for. I remembered a time when the man I loved was all that mattered. How odd, now, to know that something had changed in me; something powerful and different had happened; it was the children that mattered that way. And I felt my tears come with this awareness, this sense of a new stage arrived at, the wistfulness at the memory of the other stage, and with relief that he would be all right.

I thanked Reilly and told him I would have to stay in Boston. I called a hotel for a reservation, explaining senselessly that my son had been stabbed. I picked up the phone again to call my parents. To call my father. I put the phone down. Don't. He went through so much with you. Isn't that enough. I decided not to call Hedy either, which, I supposed, was my way of thinking of calling Hedy, of thinking of needing him.

The next morning I paced the halls of the hospital like a hunter. Was that kid here somewhere, watching, waiting? Was he here, disguised as a patient? Was this pregnant woman in the heavy black wig with sunglasses really a fevered, crazed boy? Or the little old man in the narrow-brimmed straw hat? Was that him? People who stab people are surely crazy enough to think of such details. Children who stab other people's children are precisely that crazy, and not children. Hadn't it occurred to him to wonder how his own mother would feel if someone stabbed him? But then crazy people think only of themselves. As I was only thinking of myself, and that my son had been stabbed.

When I went back to look at Dylan, he was dozing amid

the sick old men. I paced again. I called Alison. "Do you need anything?" I asked, and "He misses you." Yes, Alison needed to hear that. I started to call Hedy now, but it was too early.

It was also too early for visitors when I returned to Dylan's room, but a dark man with a moustache and shades was already there at bedside.

"Who are you?" My voice caught. "What are you doing here?"

Dylan just stared at me, then laughed, his voice low and scrambled with tubes still in his nose. "Oh, Mom, God! That's Dad! I got them to call him yesterday."

It had been, what, twelve years? Of course his hair was gray, face fuller. No uniform.

"I'm sorry. How nice of you to come." I turned away quickly, eyes on the floor, a quickening impulse to be held, to cry.

Walt Tanner reached out now and embraced me, familiar, fraternal. I had once fallen so eagerly into these arms, thinking his stability was the answer to my still disconnected emotions. After the divorce I had had to erase who he was. What had gone wrong with him, had gone wrong with each of us: I wanted to remember at this instant that I had gone to great lengths to invent a life for myself this time, and what was going wrong with Hedy, of course—I realized as I stood within the circle of my first husband's arms—was that Hedy would need to rearrange this life of mine his way. You have, I decided, to have the life and have it coincide with the other person's by sheer accident. Accident. How do you think of love now?

We stood by Dylan's bed and Dylan told us, clearing his throat, halting here and there, but wanting to tell us, what had happened.

"I've been managing the restaurant parking lot. I had on my red jacket. And I had parked a Riviera for a couple of ladies. I was walking toward the booth. And this skinny kid who'd been watching me from across the street was still there and I thought that was weird. I hadn't wanted to hire him last week. He had something odd about his pale eyes. I just didn't like him, you know, without knowing why. I just didn't. Then the kid suddenly was standing next to me.

" 'I said I got no work,' I told him.

" 'I don't want work,' he said, with this really weird grin.

" 'So go screw,' I told him, and he said, 'I want what you got.'

" 'I haven't got anything,' I told him, and I moved forward and he said, 'I think you got some coke. And I know you got bread.' And I turned, which I shouldn't have done, and I said, 'You're out of your head, man.' And I started walking toward my booth. I didn't want any hassle with anyone. I mean Alison and I just split, you know. I just didn't want a scene and so I didn't see him take out the knife, but then I felt his hand on my arm and I saw the knife. 'You can't do that,' I shouted at him, and I got a little high last night, which you'd have figured, Mom, and so my timing was off and I grabbed the kid's arms, but he was faster and the knife was in my chest. I felt it go in. The kid pulled it out and ran and I almost thought of yelling and maybe I did, 'You can't kill me.' That was so crazy, what you think about. But I didn't want to die either; I wanted only to get into the restaurant and I don't remember getting there, not that part, but I remember I did . . . The doors, swinging, were foggy. I had to tell someone, 'I'm going to die.' I felt I was holding in my blood, feeling it around my hands.

"And everyone looked up and I heard someone saying, 'Is that boy crazy?'

" 'I've been fucking stabbed! I've been stabbed,' I screamed and screamed. And Ethel, she's the hatcheck girl at the door, told me, 'Stop foolin' around,' and then she said

'Jesus mother of God!' and I fell on to the floor, my hands opened and I felt the blood spread and flow as if I had been holding it in a bowl . . ."

And Dylan's father reached out and we clutched each other's hands, and I blinked and blinked back the tears and he looked away and out the window, swallowing hard.

The next morning I went to find croissants for Dylan. I wandered through Faneuil Hall. I tried on a pair of red shoes: *Trouble ahead; Lady in Red.* I looked at myself in the mirror: I am the mother of a son who has been stabbed in Boston, and he is in the hospital, and I am here trying on shoes.

When I came to, people were standing over me, and a girl was kneeling, slapping my wrist, and another was offering me water.

I did not tell them my son had been stabbed because they would not understand why then I would be trying on red shoes. "I guess," I explained, "I should have had some breakfast."

I asked if I could use the phone. I called collect; he answered.

"Daddy," I said, "how are you?" I paused. "Daddy, I need you."

It was night and dark and still in the I.C.U. and I was sitting next to Dylan's bed, watching him. He was breathing easier. His eyes open.

"So your dad went back?"

"Yes," he said. "Up, up and away. We had a pretty good talk. He told me to knock it off. And give him a call if I wanted to talk."

"That's helpful," I said.

"What the hell would you expect him to say?" Dylan said.

The old man in the next bed, Lewin, was complaining to his wife. She touched his sock, just with a fingertip, and they looked at each other. "Hattie? You're not going?"

"I can't stay here all night."

"When you come tomorrow, Hattie, bring some money for the barber coming."

"Sometimes," Dylan said, "they make no sense. Or I'm not hearing right."

"Probably a little of both," I said.

A couple were visiting Dr. Manganero who was lying so still now in the bed across the way.

"They look like people you would have known when we lived in the Village," Dylan said.

She was wiping tears.

"I guess she's his daughter," I said.

"Last night," Dylan said to me quietly, "another old man was talking to the nurse, and she didn't really hear. 'I never eat,' he said. 'My wife died so how do I eat?' I wanted to say I understood; to ask the man about his wife, but I couldn't talk then; from the stuff they had me on. It's enough to put you off drugs." I laughed. Dylan clutched his stomach.

"It hurts," I said. "Don't try to fight it. Or talk too much."

"I try to breathe around the pain, or just into it, catch the waves like when I was surfing out in Montauk, like catching a high. I'll be okay, Mom. You know I had this dream sometime today. I dreamed of being on a white, long, empty road and, although I felt I was alone, there wasn't any danger."

My father arrived the next morning. I rushed into his arms, thick and warm and enveloping in his fleece-lined suede coat. "I didn't want to tell you."

"Don't be crazy," he said. His eyes were so sad, so exhausted; I could almost seem to see light through his skin. He looked at Dylan lying there looking back at him. His grandson with a tube up his nose, more stuck into his arms with needles, his chest and stomach bulging with bandages, the fear and anger in his face changed now to such a curious mixture of relief and embarrassment as his grandfather walked into the room. And how much do parents read into our children's faces? Was I anticipating what his feelings might be because I remembered my father's reaction when he came to see me in the infirmary during my one month's attempt at college, after I'd wrecked a car, remembered his reaction when he'd found a bottle hidden behind my bookshelves in my room?

The generations of expectations, of dashed hopes, and the simpler reactions of gratitude the child is alive. And I remembered my own gratitude that my father always was there mixed with the remorse, the sense of release: he loves me anyway, no matter what I do. And the conflict I felt as an adult, the release that my father was here to help combined with the sense, the wish that I would perhaps have been better advised to handle this on my own. I saw him falter and pale as he looked at his grandson. How very alike they were.

Since he had been a little boy, Dylan had loved maps. He had collected maps and drawn maps. The previous night, before I had left, he had asked me for a pen and some paper, and he had made a map of the hospital room, with a road through high mountains leading to the bed of the dying Italian doctor who Dylan said talked all night to angels.

Dylan watched my father now standing by his bed, studying the map.

"Don't look at it. I was just fooling around."

"You draw well. I have always told you that. How do you feel?" My father leaned his elbows on the guard rails of the bed. His eyes were wet.

"Don't be scared. I'm going to be all right."

"What do you mean, don't be scared—you scared the hell out of me."

"I'm glad you got up here. I'm glad to see you." Dylan looked away.

My father leaned down now and kissed Dylan and patted back his hair, touching his forehead, like a blessing. He sat down, so elegant in a tweed jacket, a burgundy silk muffler, his tan twill slacks falling gracefully over his knees.

"You really look sharp, Grandfather."

My father clasped his hand around the railing of the bed. Dylan touched his hand, and my father swallowed and turned away.

"I was hoping," Dylan said, "you wouldn't have to find out about what happened. I've also been hoping I'd open my eyes and see you here. Like this."

"Sometimes it amuses me when you and your mother invent things you think I want to hear. But I would have felt overprotected if your mother hadn't called."

"Yeah," Dylan said, "her generation is always saying, don't tell the children, or don't tell the parents, as if they're the only ones who can handle stuff."

The next day my father brought Dylan a box of colored pencils, Mongols, with shiny gold tips.

"I remember," Dylan said, "you brought me and Brynn a box of these when we were kids. We fought over the colors and how to arrange them in the box, and we'd break the points in the pencil sharpener and then we'd have to pull it out from the wall, and the sawdust and bits of lead would fall on the floor. I'd swear the colors had different smells when I'd pick them up. I got real mad at Brynn one day; I sat on her and striped her chubby little arms with all the colors. And she went screaming to Mom."

My father had also brought a black leatherette sketchbook. "See if you can fill that before you come visit me."

"I'd like that, visiting."

"It's not just a vacation. When you're strong I want to talk with you; there are things I'm working on that you could help me with."

"That's what I meant—just to spend time with you. I'm not just saying that to make you feel better; Grandfather, I'm scared. I feel lousy about my whole life."

My father sat back in the chair and took one of the pencils from the box. Then he took a pocket pencil sharpener from the pocket of his jacket. My father sharpened two pencils, Venetian Red and then a Burnt Sienna. Dylan said, "I remember all the colors. It's neat that you carry around a pencil sharpener, just in case, like a doctor would carry a stethoscope."

"You can have this one. I'll make you a present of it." He finished sharpening the pencils, blew the dust away and placed the sharpener on the table near Dylan's bed.

"Could I really have it?" Dylan asked.

My father handed it to him, and he held it in his hand.

"You mustn't spend time, Dylan, thinking about what you've wasted. But you must think carefully, and this will remind you, of how precious life is. Now we'll begin to plan a better way to spend your time. We never realize how much we have when we are young." He cleared his throat.

"I don't want to be didactic or to preach. I told myself on the flight up from Florida that that was what you'd expect and it would harden you against me. But when I was young"—and he smiled a little—"I was a lot like you. I thought nothing of time; I wanted only to rush through it to get to the next thing. I couldn't enjoy my work and spent a lot of time being angry because it wasn't getting me where I wanted to be fast enough." He had opened the sketchbook he gave Dylan and laid it against a copy of *Time* that I had brought Dylan, and he was sketching, looking up and squinting at Dylan for an instant, then looking down again. "When I was enjoying what

I was doing I didn't get the feeling that I should be somewhere else. But I didn't learn any of that until I was a bit older, in my forties." He smiled. "And that, my boy, sounds pretty old to you."

"No, it all sounds hard to get to, any age. Next week sounds old." Dylan paused. "I've got to change everything, and I guess that's scaring me, too."

"Why does change always have to be negative, fearful, Dylan? My life, from year to year, has always brought changes; I've lost projects I really wanted to do, and a month later, something even better has come up. You practice having hope."

My father showed Dylan the picture he was drawing.

"That's good. I didn't know you could do people too."

"When I studied art you had to learn to draw everything. It wasn't a matter of choice. I don't think it's changed much."

"I'm not going to art school, Grandfather. I don't know what I'm going to do, but I really hate school." He shifted uncomfortably. I could tell everything still hurt. "Man, my life feels fucked up."

"Dylan!" I said, looking at my father.

"I've heard that word, Margot. Listen, Dylan," my father said, "where did you get the idea you'd be feeling well? You've had a terrible, terrible thing happen. If you felt fine, you would have misunderstood your situation in a pretty serious way. I know that very well. We learned that from trying to raise your mother. You know how many times it would look as though this time she was pulling through, and then it would happen again. Another disaster. Your grandmother and I used to be scared out of our wits every time the phone rang. But she has managed to raise you and Brynn; she has changed from being a frightened little girl into a head of a household." He paused and smiled at me. And Dylan looked at both of us.

Would Dylan ever really trust that I had changed? Would he and Brynn always be on guard wondering when there would be another disaster they'd have to pull me out of? How long would it take them to feel secure enough to live their own lives? The only person who ever really trusts a recovering alcoholic is another alcoholic who understands the process of recovering one's sanity. My God, how we wear down the ones who love us most, the ones we love the most.

My father took off his glasses and rubbed his eyes. Then he put the glasses back on and looked at the sketch he had done. He smudged some shadows in with the side of a pencil and held the picture up again. Dylan. Exactly. Perhaps a sweeter smile; perhaps more Dylan fourteen than Dylan now.

"I've lived a long time, Dylan," my father said, "and I still believe the best of life is ahead of me, the best work yet to come."

A long time, I thought, but please, God, not long enough. My father looked tired, thinner, his skin looked translucent.

"Oh, optimism," said Dylan. "It's been off the charts for years."

"Well, this is a new arrangement," my father said.

Music. I thought of Hedy. Perhaps I would call him. In a day or so.

20

I had been in Boston three days. Early this morning I had called Jennie. She read me postcards from Brynn in Scotland. "And," she said, "Hedy is on his way."

Long ago, I would have thought only of having someone I loved near me. I had fought to get over that and now I was not sure how to have Hedy here with me in Boston.

In these few days, I had settled into the rhythm of visiting Dylan. Through Cleo I arranged to borrow space in an affiliated local station and I taped some interviews: there was one with Jane Davison, who had written a book about women and their houses, and Upshot seemed a distant consideration; another with the chief of police on the rising incidence of unsolved crimes. "It's a frustrating problem for the police," he said.

"Not to mention the victims," I said.

"To be sure," he said, "when you realize one of your own is one of our statistics."

The night before I had had dinner with my father, and then had seen him to his room and had calmly gone on to my own. My purpose right now was to be here for Dylan, to present order, calm and clarity. My father and I had bought him a giant silver foil kite to build, but he had been too sore, too restless.

Now the phone rang. "A gentleman is here to see you, madam." A gentleman, madam. They spoke to me as if I were a person from another play. "It's a Wayne Henderson, madam." A Wayne Henderson. *The* Wayne Henderson was what he was becoming.

"Send him up." I dried my hair fast. I put on blusher and mascara. I kept on my terry cloth robe, although I considered briefly that I could get dressed. This is just what I wanted: come chase me; how much do you care? Enough to come find me. And now that he has, is that what I want?

He knocked in some sort of signal. I opened the door.

"Neat game," he said, "making me crazy and worried, making me have to track down Jennie to find you. You don't have enough action going on?"

"Don't yell at me, Hedy. I didn't want you to have to fly back here. Things are happening out there for you."

"I thought you might have expected me to be here, you know." He had sounded angry, but he looked stricken. It took me beats longer to let him touch me than it should have. He put his hands on my shoulders. I reached my hands up and placed them over his.

He sat on one of the pristine high twin beds beside me. He nuzzled his face in my neck. I lifted my shoulder and bent my head down against his. He pulled the white robe off my shoulder and down, opening it around me.

"I am glad to see you," he said, sitting back, his hands reaching out, touching my waist, coming up, cupping my breasts like goblets. I sat there, naked, feeling shy. The only way I could be distracted would be if he took over. I wanted him to direct me. I wanted him to turn me on, to show it was still there, for now. And I knew we both understood that.

"Just lie down," he said. And I did. I started to watch him undress. Then I turned away. I could not look at this young male body without seeing images I could not yet control.

He held my hand. "Is it okay?"

"It's okay," I said, "come on." He lay next to me; we turned toward each other and kissed softly, eye to eye, eyes open staring at each other. I put my leg up over his hips. We connected. I closed my eyes.

"Open your eyes," he whispered.

"Not now," I said. I kissed him. I moved in even closer.

"Please, Margot." He kissed around my hairline. "I hate you to be sad."

"Just be here," I said.

He turned and moved me over on my back and swung into me, and I felt surrounded, wanted, protected, even as I arranged my body for my own release.

"Where are you starting?" he asked. He knew how I worked it now. And it turned him on to hear me talk, to hear the glimpses of scenes I used.

"You on a chair, watching me," I whispered. "Me on a floodlit bed. Stage sort of thing. You watching. You directing."

"What am I saying?" His breath ruffled about my ear.

"Things." I was quiet now. "Can't get it and talk."

"I know. Tell me when." He kissed me and kissed me, holding his breath, waiting on his own edge.

"Okay, now go. Closer." And, for this moment, we were together. We hugged and kissed for a few moments. My movements were angular, swift. He always knew when I was done and ready to move on. And I knew where he was.

I sat up straight and pulled my robe back tight around my body. I crossed my legs and put my elbows on my knees and jammed my fists up against my chin.

"You don't feel bad we did that?" he said. He looked so concerned. Please, I thought, do not look that way.

"No, I wanted to touch you. A couple of times I did think, I'm going to call him." I paused. "I almost did—call and say come here now." And I'd stop, knowing what I really wanted was him to need me like that—to come to me even when I didn't want it. And now he had.

"You should have called. I almost did." He stopped abruptly. "Have you had some coffee?"

I would not start it. Would not ask, why didn't you. "No, I thought I'd go downstairs. I usually do that." I only discovered that I was used to my new routine by seeing it would not be followed.

"Can I order some food from room service?" He walked across to the phone and sat down on the bed opposite me. He put his hand on my knee while he called.

I ordered coffee, grapefruit juice, a poached egg; changed it to orange juice, egg over easy, English muffin and bacon to match Hedy's order after I heard it. "That sounds better."

"You never know what you want," he said.

"Not when it doesn't matter." I paused. "Sometimes when it does matter." Often, actually. "Not all the time. I never know right away. That's a difference, but not a problem. I only know that I can't assume that what I want is the same thing as doing what will make someone else happy or what I *think* will make someone else happy, because sometimes I'm wrong. I jump the gun, carry on and confuse everyone."

"I think you're trying to tell me something, and it is not about breakfast."

The fear, the tightness in my stomach, the drawing feeling in my throat that I felt when I was getting to something true came now. I wanted to stop it before I said it. I could not look at him.

"How'd it go with the mortgage?" he said. He looked at my face. That was it. Of course.

"Can we talk about that later?" I pulled on panties and hitched up my bra.

"No," he said. "Let's talk about it now."

I started to pull on a sweater. "Okay." I took a deep breath. "I can't get a mortgage."

"I don't believe you." He stood up and turned me about to face him. My sweater caught wrapped around my arms.

"Two banks turned me down. But what you're thinking is right. I don't want the responsibility. I don't want the house. It won't, just won't work." I was breathless. My sentences ran on in panic. "I didn't want to tell you. Time's running out, Hedy, and I want to just focus on these kids now. I can't go following you around and be part of another person's life. I have to help my own son put his life together. I can't handle anything else."

"You never wanted to. You were never really goin' to do it. We had a plan and you killed it." His eyes were pale with anger.

"No, Hedy. Someone almost killed my son. I'm overwhelmed. You can't understand it and why should you. We have completely different priorities." I pulled the sweater on and slid on my slacks and zipped them up. "For example, you didn't even ask how Dylan is," I said. I was picking at straws. Jennie, of course, had told me he had been frantic.

"Don't start a whole thing that I don't care. I wouldn't be here if I didn't. I called the hospital, and they said he's okay."

"They didn't tell me you called."

"That's their problem. I didn't tell them to."

This advance into battle was arrested by the sound of the room service cart. There was a careful silence as he paid the bill in cash. We started to eat.

"Does Brynn know yet?" he asked. He buttered an English muffin and put jam on it and handed it to me.

"I can't reach her," I said. "She's touring right now in Scotland."

"So Brynn is not so provincial," he said. A little smile. Of course.

"Don't rub it in," I said. "And it was all her idea. I'm really impressed." Just when you think you've defined a child, she changes. Such arrogance anyway. The only definition of any human is its potential for change.

"I'll call her when she comes back to London. But I'm not sure I should tell her on the phone," I said.

"I really think you ought to let her know," Hedy said.

I had almost snapped at Hedy, it's none of your business. If he hadn't thought of Brynn I would have accused him of being thoughtless. He could not win.

"You know, for someone who doesn't want age to be a thing, you really don't give much credit to anyone younger than you. I'd be mad as hell if my brother was cut up, and my mom didn't tell me. I'd want to make my own decision about comin' back to see him if I wanted to. You got to let these kids grow up."

So you can be the kid. A mean thought. But I hated hearing one more word about it. "Look, Hedy, I let go of Dylan. I did exactly what I had to do. And I didn't like that. And I don't like this, either. Telling you. I didn't mean to, even now."

"Here it comes," he said; "you're only doing it for me. Watch out when someone says they're doin' it for you—this hurts me more than it's going to hurt you—comes the cop-out."

"No. It is not a cop-out. Hedy, things are going to happen to you; you can't even imagine how you're going to feel, what you're going to need." I poured coffee for him, more for myself.

"You're just frightened; you're the one who always says you never run from takin' a risk. And don't gulp your coffee."

"That's not a risk; that's panicking from the unknown. Sometimes risk is not doing anything, just waiting and seeing what's coming. We're neither of us ready to homestead."

"I don't think you'd have bought the house even if this hadn't happened. You think you live in the now—big talk! You expected it to get fucked up because things always have for you, so you sabotaged it up first."

"Hedy, calm down." I got up from the table. I went around

to his chair. I felt exhausted. I had not meant to feel anything. I meant only to be here for Dylan, to function. I put my hands on his shoulders.

"Margot." He reached his hands up to mine. "You just think it's wrong because I'm too young." He stood up, and moved away from the table, from my hands, but I followed him and threw my arms around him tight so he couldn't back away.

"Listen to me, listen," I pleaded, trying to make it better with my voice and my touch. "Hedy, we run into things like this." I would not say "love." He never could. "When all we're ready for sometimes is the idea of something." I paused. "Maybe I have sabotaged it. But when you're pushing too hard, it often means it's not supposed to happen yet." I sat now next to him on the other bed, the one we had not lain in. "Hedy, I've learned a place doesn't make something work or not work." He pushed my arms away.

"You know I'm going to be more successful. You won't be able to handle it."

"I want you to be. It's happening. I don't compare success like that, anymore."

"Come on, Margot," he snapped at me so hard. "You're going all soft on me. Don't pull the age crap."

"And don't you pull the tough kid crap; I can't be your easy-riding mistress, there anytime, the way you want, and do my work and be the mother. Something has to go, and for too long it has been the mother who has not been there."

"You probably think Dylan's bein' stabbed is God punishing you for getting what you want, and so you better give up part of it fast." He looked at me shrewdly, one eyebrow lifted, turning into Cleo.

"No! Give me credit. Dylan was stabbed because he was messing around with coke. Alison tortures herself like that: if she hadn't broken up with him it wouldn't have happened.

Hedy, don't pin this on Dylan—you know the house thing was a game. How do you know where you'll want to be? You may be in L.A. a lot. You're fighting me because you've asked yourself all the same questions."

Perhaps his expression indicated a kind of hesitation.

"You may want kids of your own, and who knows what I'll be when the kids are ready to leave? I may live out of suitcases." I got up and poured myself some more coffee.

"Listen, you like that house. You practically got all your trees named."

"They are not my trees. Hedy, we disagree about everything almost except we both someday may want that kind of big, wild house. We started fighting almost the minute we saw it."

He didn't look up. He stared at his hands, loose between his knees. His face bent down like this seemed all plump young cheeks. I sat down next to him again. "When it's meant to work, Hedy, I think you jump through the fear differently; you don't make a commitment to a house and then later on hope you'll be able to make the commitment to each other."

He turned away from me. "Hasn't it ever occurred to you that I tried to help you, and over and over to talk to you about Dylan, to be involved. You've pushed me away—"

"No," I said, "not because of you, really; it was me, Hedy. Denial—I didn't want to know what he was doing."

"Margot, I'm coming with you to see Dylan. Because that was why I came here. And then I'm going back home."

"Okay," I said. I swung my purse over my shoulder. I put on my jacket. I started to help Hedy with his. He shrugged away.

"It's too bad, Margot. I think I wanted to go the whole route with you." He said it idly, testing, like someone saying he might have liked to go to a different movie.

"Oh, really, to marry me?" I put my room key in my pocket. We were jockeying lightly, sounding like people I didn't even know.

"Yeah, marry me. How about it, Margot, would you have married me?" His voice was cold.

I locked the door to the room. "Hedy, you don't want to, and any answer I'd have would be wrong for now." I rang for the elevator. You reach, I knew, for everything when it is almost over. You begin then to imagine it was ideal. That was stage one. Knowing that did not make it easier. Maybe Bill was smarter. Going before it could begin to end.

"What about this—if Dylan hadn't gotten stabbed, if the house hadn't frightened you, if Brynn hadn't called, if we'd danced and walked on the beach in Coronado and I'd said it right then—it'd be different. We'd have said the things, got swept up and married right there." He held the elevator door for me.

"It's possible," I said. I got into the elevator. "But—it wasn't different."

"Look at me and say it was possible." He reached his hand out and put it under my chin.

I looked at him. "Possible," I said. And I wanted to kiss his mouth. But I stepped back, and we both stood, looking up, watching the lit numbers descend. He waited for me to leave the elevator first.

"I'm sorry about some of it, but I'm not sorry for all of this morning," I said. I took his hand lightly. For a moment.

He did not look at me. He asked the doorman to get a cab.

When we got to the hospital Dylan was up on his feet for the first time, shuffling in paper slippers, pushing his IV on its metal staff. I thought of Helena, standing in the hospital with her IV, the difference in the feelings when it's this you're here for, and you're young, and you'll get out.

"Hey, man," said Hedy. "We'll have to get you a gig with that thing."

"Yeah," said Dylan, "I'm about ready for the road."

They chatted uneasily. Dylan kept looking from Hedy to me. "A little fight?" he said finally.

"Nothing that can't be negotiated," I said. Brightly.

"By the World Court?" said Dylan.

"We've got our regular bowling date a month from Thursday though, so it's not all over," said Hedy.

"That's Thanksgiving," I said.

"And you wouldn't want to miss Thanksgiving, smoothest event of the year. One hundred eighty people, at least, who never laid eyes on each other or hate each other from last Thanksgiving, and four hundred pounds of food." Dylan laughed. Then clutched his stomach.

"Serves you right for teasing me." I grinned, too eagerly, at Hedy. "We'd maybe better get Dylan back to bed now."

"Yeah, come on, sport," Hedy said, and we helped Dylan back into bed; Hedy so gentle with him, like a brother. Stop.

"I have a concert in Worcester that weekend," Hedy said now.

I could not tell if he was teasing. Or lying. Or telling the truth.

"Worcester, Massachusetts?" Dylan asked.

"No. England," Hedy said. So proud. So arrived. "If it was Massachusetts I'd try to hit dinner and drive up later."

"Would you really?" I asked.

"Possible. But then it isn't Massachusetts," he said.

"That is true," I said. "It isn't." I looked at Hedy, then at Dylan watching us.

"We'll sure miss you," said Dylan.

"There will be enough going on; your family will probably show up," Hedy said. He looked at me. My parents, he meant. How relieved I was my father had not called from his hotel room this morning; was not here yet. That would have been one more thing. I wanted it clear and simple. I had turned into Bill. No confrontations. "Maybe you can save me a drumstick. If you're feelin' okay, I've got a concert comin' up in New York that next week. I'd like you to come."

"That would be fine," Dylan said. He looked older than Hedy.

They talked a bit about the concert coming up in England, Hedy's new sound, and Dylan told the story of what had happened. It changed a little every time; this time he added, "I was mad at Alison; I don't think somewhere inside I minded. I thought it would make everyone see I was in trouble."

"I guess it did," said Hedy. "Mainly you could see you were. All that matters finally is what you see yourself."

"Yeah," said Dylan.

And then my father did walk in. And Hedy looked at me. The one more thing. My father leaned over Dylan and kissed him, and ruffled his hair. "You're coming right along."

He curved his arm all around my shoulders and shook hands with Hedy briefly. He smiled his most courteous smile. And Hedy smiled at him. "I didn't know you were here." He nodded. "That's good, because I've got to be shoving off now. Nice to see you, sir."

"Hedy?" I said. I tried to sound as if I was surprised he was going, as if I didn't know he needed to go. "I'll see you to the elevator." I followed him along.

"I want to get back," he said. "We're mixing tonight, and I want to be there." He had his back to me. His movements were quick, jagged.

"Hedy. Don't leave angrily. We don't need that."

"I forgot who you need, who you'd call. Margot, it took a long time for us both to reach out. I never thought I'd leave you, too, and yet I can see now it isn't going to come back to me or anyone, maybe, from you."

"Hedy, this isn't the time. Don't tear into me now."

"I'm not tearing into you. I'm tearin' away."

"Hedy, don't; there are different moments, different priorities."

"No, or maybe yes, but for me I've got to be the priority. Margot, you don't need an old man; you've got an old man." I did not want to hear what he was saying.

I reached out my hands. I pulled them a bit back. Where to go. To start. To stop.

For an instant he took both of my hands in both of his hands. And then he dropped them. "Keep in touch."

"Hedy, don't be angry."

"Why would I be?" he said. "It's very clear. You got what you want."

"Hedy." I just kept repeating his name. "Hedy?"

"Look at it sometime." He gave me a kiss. Very fast.

"I'll see you?" I asked. He just looked at me. Tears. I watched him walk away, shoulders swinging, legs so long and thin and dancy in their pace.

"So. Another down," said Dylan. "Poor little Mom."

"Not poor Mom. Not little. Cut it out." I sat on the ledge near his bed, my feet up on the side railing. "How'd you know?"

"Where do you think I've been?" He grinned.

"I don't think we really want to know," my father said, and he rubbed my back. "I ran into Ivan, who says I'll be seeing you on TV next spring. So cheer up, my darling. Hold the good thoughts."

"Well, yes," I said. "Who knows. Mainly, look, Dylan was up already. That's the really good part."

"Her new show," said Dylan, "*Margot Looks at the Bright Side*. Optimism begins at home."

"Knock it off," I said. I began putting together the silver foil kite. So simple, it had looked in the box.

"Occupational therapy," he said to my father, "for the anxious."

"Here, let me have another look at it today," my father said, which perked up Dylan's interest again.

And I chattered, telling them how to do this part and that, telling Dylan about the exhibits and things to see in New York when he got better, chattering, chattering while they worked on the kite.

"Mom, I am not going to stop breathing, and Grandfather is not going to fade away, if you stop talking. You just be; I'll just be. It's okay." He gave me his most amused, heart-stopping smile. The pool Narcissus drowned in was the smile of her own child, full-grown.

When they finished the kite my father and I sailed it high on a rack over Dylan's bed. We looked at Dylan and saw all of our faces reflected in all of those silver triangles, like bits of mirror shifting and shimmering at the end of a kaleidoscope, and I saw myself twenty-one years before lying in my childhood bed in that summer house my parents had, the house I always and only called "my father's house," and I remembered the summer afternoon in early July when I was visiting with my first husband and we had gone to take our nap in that small bed. We lay there naked under the crisp white sheets. And the casement windows were thrown open at the end of the room, out over the apple tree I used to climb and sit in to watch my father's tennis game, and I heard my father playing tennis while I was in that bed with my young husband, and as he leaned over me, I heard my father call out "Serve" to his opponent and I heard that ball hit the racket and I heard it pounding from one racket to the other as my husband put this child, this child who is lying here right now, inside of me.

21

I once bought a small painting done in the old-fashioned academic style with figures just like the classic drawings I used to look at in my father's old art books when I had wanted to see nudes. From a distance it looked like a pastoral allegory, but as one moved closer to the picture one saw that the central nymph was standing in a shopping cart: the landscape was subtly made up of rows of soup cans, soap boxes and jam jars, and the nymph was holding in her arms a brown grocery bag. She had that dreamy look of a ballerina pirouetting downstage.

On this day before Thanksgiving, I floated behind my shopping cart in the supermarket, as celebrated as the nymph in the painting surrounded by the figures of the joyous dancer, the faun playing his violin, the embracing lovers. At this moment of embarkation on a shopping spree I might have been sailing out on Swan Lake.

I wafted down every aisle, bending, reaching, opening my arms to the latest and best delights, my acquisitive gestures growing in momentum, my smiles increasing with every pause for deliberation, the pleasure of accomplishment, of doing something I had practiced for years. This was something I did well. The hallowed act of consuming; I became the cornucopia, the deliverer of bounty. Who could fault the purity of motives? Who would not fail to greet me with delight as I arrived home, arms filled with the harvest of everyone's favorite boxes, crunchy yellow, red and pink bags, bright burgeoning fruits, rosy sausages, bouquets of leaves and roots, alabaster turkey. Everything clean and fresh and glistening in packages designed as carefully (perhaps more carefully?) as the Barbizon frame around the little painting.

I came in the doorway, balancing two of the bags in one arm as I opened the door with the other hand. I am certain I expected Brynn and Dylan to run at me, merry little cherubs, reaching out in pleasure. But I am not certain where this expectation came from after all these years. I'd lost ten years in the hour and a half since I'd left the house, marketed and walked back in the door. They did not move. They did not reach to welcome me. They lay on the couch, watching television, sunk back amid the bright Marimekko pillows, eating vestiges of last week's bounty.

Something snapped in my head. I did not think. I put down the bags of groceries. I picked up a large copper bowl from the table by the front door and I hurled it right into the TV set. The set sunk in upon itself, ate itself alive in shock and spat itself right out again in terrible sounds and sprays of glass and sparks.

The children grabbed their heads, dashed back. "Jesus, Mom," said Dylan, holding his stomach.

"Are you crazy? Are you really crazy?" shouted Brynn. She looked at Dylan. Careful of him; fearful for him, watchful always now.

"No," I said. I picked up the grocery bags and walked toward the kitchen. "I think I am just coming out of it. Get the rest of the groceries from the car and come into the kitchen. Now."

Of course. The three of us were equally aware of how fond we are of this sort of flamboyance. However, they swiftly did as they were told.

"Put the bags down, now," I said, when they returned. "And sit down." I moved all jagged, like a puppet.

"A speech," said Dylan. But he sat down. And actually pulled out a chair for Brynn.

"Diatribe," said Brynn, starting to light a cigarette.

"You bet," I said. "Put out that cigarette. Just because I didn't do it right for almost twenty years does not mean I can't start now. You're grown-ups, you really are, and this is not the time to start raising you. And I'm not going to try, exactly, to do that. But I'm going to try to tell you what you're going to need to know. And I'm not going to be scared you'll hate me or leave, because you'll have to do one for a while to do the other." I couldn't breathe, but I could keep going—no matter what they heard or didn't hear I had to start to say it. For me. So I'd hear, so I'd understand.

"It's called a crash course. You'll be good at it. So will I. I have paid my dues, and indulging you because of guilt or fear isn't going to get rid of that guilt or fear anymore. You're going to have to live in a real world. I drank myself into oblivion to avoid recognizing reality. But I have news."

They gave each other a sort of what's-this-all-about? look.

I wanted to sit down, take one of Brynn's cigarettes, and say, "Oh fuck it, I guess I overreacted," but that was what I'd always done. "Like me, please," I had always asked, always implied.

Because I hated doing what I was told, I'd sworn, like every child, "I'll never tell my children to do that." And I hadn't. And someone had to do that job. I hoped it was not too late. Brynn picked up the Bloomingdale's catalogue from the table and began to read it.

"And don't read when I'm talking to you," I said.

"You always do," said Brynn.

"Well, I'll stop. Look, reality comes up every day, and you're going to have to practice doing it and it generally involves doing something we don't want to do. It is not wonderful. You practice by working on courtesy. And for now, while you are here, when I come into the house, you look at me, you get up and ask if I want some help. Okay, you dealt with my drinking; you dealt with a lot of fathers. Sorry about that. But that's yesterday. We are all going to stop feeling sorry for or about ourselves. The world does not owe you anything because I screwed up. I owe you discipline and some notion of adult behavior. I can do that now. And I'm going to."

"Like pitching stuff through the TV," said Dylan. "You want some coffee, Mom?"

"Well, everything starts with a bang," I said, trying very hard not to smile now. "Yes, I'd love some coffee, thank you."

Brynn stood up.

"Where are you going?" I said.

"I am going to clean up the mess in the living room." She started for the broom closet.

"That's my mess," I said, "and I will clean it up. You guys put away the marketing." I got the broom and the dustpan from the closet. "And there'll be no more TV."

"I guess not," said Dylan. He went over to the telephone.

"Who are you calling?" I imagined he was going to call one of his friends and go out and lean against walls. Or watch TV in someone else's house.

"Okay. Adult behavior," he said. "I am calling Grandfather. I'll take him up on the art school number."

"Just like that?" I said.

"Just like that. Snap decision. Like we moved to Connecticut, like we've always done everything. Think about it too long and you might not do it, why just react when you can overreact." He paused by the phone. "Not that it isn't going to be a real bummer, taking the train every day, for years." Oh, that was Dylan, and that was me. The instant reaction, the right reaction and then the fear coming in, the doubts quickly masked as hostility.

"Well, don't ask me to drive you down there when you miss your train," said Brynn.

"You won't be able to because you'll be in college," I said. "And," I added, for Dylan, "you can start working on your negative attitude right now. Life is the same for everyone; it's only good or bad depending upon how you come at it. Practice liking something, such as a refrigerator full of goodies. It gets better. End of speech."

"Where do we send the honorarium?" said Brynn.

I swept up the broken glass. Then I rolled the TV out the front door and pushed it flying down the driveway, where it spun and careened into the garbage cans. I dusted off my hands. "Today I am a mother," I said to myself. "Tomorrow an adult." I'd planned to watch *Wuthering Heights* tonight. Plan A is always what you think everyone else should do. Plan B is doing what you should do.

It would work, of course, for a day or two, this spirit ignited by uproar. It always worked. Sergeants had known that for centuries. But sergeants came round every morning to shout at the troops. I would have to be my own sergeant. And theirs. And I would have to try to remember on days when no one mobilized at all that that did not mean the whole plan was shot, so what the hell, don't bother trying again tomorrow. That is how their lives had slipped into this doldrum.

Everything had been put away. The giblets were simmering in a pot; fruits and vegetables were washed and ready for chopping. I was propped against my pillows, reading background material on a new rock composer I'd be interviewing next week, and I'd ask him probably if he'd heard the new Headmaster and the Class group. And I'd hope Hedy would be listening and hear me asking and know I was asking so he'd know I was thinking about him. Brynn walked in wearing one of our Lanz nightgowns. It had a pattern of tiny blue, green and red hearts, each one centered with a little cottage with a heart-shaped door. Brynn sat on the foot of my bed. She looked angry, eyes brimming, needing the anger to keep from crying. "Don't I have a choice?" she said.

Trying to do what I preached, I put down my papers and pencil to look at Brynn when I was talking. "You have a choice of colleges to go away to."

"I've been away," she said. "I showed I could do it."

"A trip to Europe is hardly running the gauntlet, Brynn. I wish I had the freedom just to go off like that . . ."

"Well. You do it. I'll stay here."

"I'm not getting off here onto me, Brynn." I was tightening. "I don't want to watch you just plodding through. I hoped you'd see something you'd want . . . to excite you . . ."

"I'm not saying I'm not grateful for the trip. But that's different than when you're goin' where you're expected to be; thinking what they want you to think, when they want you to think it. You never really did college. You never even did Europe. You hid out in your marriages. I'd rather even do that."

Don't pick that up. Let it go. Did I hide?

"You think there aren't expectations in marriages? That you don't have to be there in a job?" I was too fast. Did I fill those expectations? Even?

"Mom. You know what I mean. Just a job. Where I show up. And do it. And go home."

This was too hard. For Brynn? For me, actually. "I suppose you could stay home and commute to college." And that, I hoped, was what Brynn would choose to do.

"I just know college won't work, Mom. And I need to be here." Her eyes filled. "I almost lost my brother. I liked Bill. It's been a lot for me. I just need time, Mom."

"Time." I remembered St. Cheri telling me, long ago, it seemed, that it takes time. All of it.

It was too hard for both of us. Brynn had taken up the challenge of caring for me during the bad years; she was too exhausted for another challenge. I reached out over the coverlet, leaned forward and touched Brynn's hand. A tear dropped down and Brynn pulled her hand away. Does there come a time when the touch of your mother's hand only reminds you of how much you're wanting, wanting that other touching?

"Brynn. If that's what you think you want to do, then you can do it, but only if you get some counseling to find out why college is so threatening."

"You sound exactly like one of those informed mothers on soaps. 'Would you like to get a little help, dear?' " She imitated one of those soapy motherly voices. "They're euphemisms for 'the child is troubled.' I'm not troubled. I want to work. Is that a problem for your image as the competent mother?" The tears came down now. "I'm sorry, that wasn't fair. I just don't want to be signed up for anything right now. I just don't, don't want to."

Is this letting go? Why can't I ever understand what that means exactly. If this is it, keeping back, being so cool and direct, I cannot bear it. I crawled over the bed and held Brynn, who sat rigid, at first, in my arms. Then she eased, and I held her tight and put my face down to her head. And I thought, it is like holding a woman. Then: it is not "like"; Brynn *is* a woman—tender, frightened, unready. The choices would have surely alarmed me. When I was Brynn's age, the easy choice had been: get married. It had seemed so much simpler. But look how it had worked against the time to come.

Brynn patted my arm. "I know I can't just hang out here. But a lot of people don't go away after high school. I can work in the bookstore, sell records. I can take some courses so next year I could go away to a better school, you know."

I tried to remember what I'd wanted from my mother at that time—not what I was telling myself now that I'd wanted, and what I remembered getting, and not getting. I'd actually had everything I thought I wanted. My parents had not wanted life to be difficult for me. In fact, they expected it would be easy. That was perhaps their only mistake, and such a forgivable one; and I believed in that expectation, that it would be easy. And if life has any universal characteristic it is not ease. How would it be interesting if it were easy? Look how those few who start out with the facilities for ease drive their lives into troubles and complexities, how else to feel one is alive without the frustrations and challenges to urge one through to the moment of triumph and release.

I thought of the story of the Little Mermaid learning to have legs, feeling it was like walking on razor blades. You would rather carry the child than watch her have to walk. You have to let go first, so she can. That again.

"I have to get back to work," I said, picking up my pen. I must practice making the first move. "Do you have something you want to read? Look in my stack of books there."

"Swift not to suggest I watch an old movie on TV."

"I almost did; stopped myself just in time." I smiled. I wished we could sit together and watch an old movie. Screw changing.

"I've got a paperback."

"There's a wonderful new novel," I started to say.

"I don't want to read anything wonderful," Brynn said; "it's like some days you just want to look at dinosaurs you know."

Of course, I thought. It's probably about love. Everything was for me when I was Brynn's age. I never knew what to do with myself when it wasn't. Did time really change that? You simply want someone to love. It's called feeling blue. And all the goals, the drive, the challenges in the world don't make that go away, when you're young. Or when you're older. I thought of Hedy. My temper, the rapidly justified rage. How much of that was the cover-up of loneliness, missing him before he even had been really here, missing the notion of him at the Thanksgiving table. I reached my hand again for Brynn.

"Jennie told me this thing. She was in the laundromat. She pulled four socks out of her dryer, and no two matched. She decided that's what life's about, the socks never match. Then, after she folded everything, someone was starting to put her wash in another dryer and that woman said, 'Hey, there's some socks in here.' And there they were, the four other socks, all four of them. Matching. Brynn, sometimes we're looking too hard, too fast. If I just give it a while, the answer will come when I'm not looking." I could have, of course, told the same story to Hedy. But maybe that was what I liked. "Maybe, Brynn, a year from now, we'll both find matching socks, and we'll know; we'll be glad we didn't force it."

"It is not about socks, Mom. Sometimes what I really don't want you to do most of all is try to understand."

We had gotten up early; Jennie had come over with Reilly to help. The giblets were chopped now and into the gravy; the pumpkin pies ready for the oven; the cranberries cooling on the screened porch. I was chopping celery; Dylan chopping onions, laughing at the tears he said he wasn't having, as the tears fell. Brynn had gone off in her car in a huff to Kimmie's house, to be consoled because Freddy had come home from college and had not called.

"I can't bear it for her," I said, scraping the bits of celery into the big wooden bowl. "She does exactly what I did not choose to teach her. I've fought so hard—well, recently, anyway—I've tried not to show either of you that this obsessive thing does any good for life." Tears now fell from my eyes too.

"Damn!" I said. I crushed juniper berries in oil to pour over the string beans.

"Since you're crying anyway, why don't you do the onions?"

"Oh. I'm impossible."

"You have got to stop having guilt about Brynn's disappointments. They're hers, you know, Ma. You can't take credit for everything that happens to us—even the bad stuff. We have a choice; we don't just repeat—I can't believe that."

"I can't accept it, Dylan, that no one is responsible for anyone else; I absolutely hate it. I know that if I had had another emphasis in my life—on something academic, on excellence or order or . . ." That was my limitation, that it was difficult for me to think of what might have been better. "I meant to try to do it the way a parent should. I would have made life maybe not simpler, but richer for you." I gave Dylan mushrooms to chop and put butter in a pan on the stove to melt. This may—I snuffled—be the last time we will be doing this together. Oh, go put yourself in a condo near Disney World or knock it off, I told myself, and wiped under my eyes, getting butter all over my face.

"The only thing, Ma, I don't want is the guilt. A lot of my friends don't even want to go home. We have trouble leaving. You make it very interesting."

I stopped and, hands shining with butter, embraced Dylan, kissing his head, getting butter on his hair now. "That's beautiful."

"Let's drop it now. I went through my trouble, now Brynn has to go through hers."

"Oh, relationships," I said. "And I never can think of another word to call them. I hate them all for everyone."

"You're just mad at this thing you almost got yourself into."

"I'm not," I said. "I am over it. Not to worry." Every time

the subject came up in this fashion of not really coming up, I got very brisk.

"You shouldn't get over it all, Ma," Dylan said. "You'll meet someone right. You can't wind up, you and Brynn, like some *Grey Gardens* scene." My mother started encouraging me when I was Dylan's age. "You'll meet someone." How many times to try? And to run. Would my grandchildren fix me up with spacemen?

"No. Because we both hate cats. Don't worry about that. Actually"—and I had forgotten about this as I, cataloguing disaster in the family tradition, always forgot the hopeful things—"I did see a man last week going by in a Jaguar. I liked his blond hair and the car. I could always have it traced."

"You do real well tracing guys in cars," Dylan said. "It's going to be easy for you, Mom. You are successful, you have bucks, you know who you are, and you're not so old. But I don't know what women want. They want you to be macho, strong and take care of them, *and* they want you to be sensitive, passionate and soft." He talked of going out on Alison, of sleeping with a girl he didn't want. "I found her tender little slip in my car. I woke up at eight-thirty," he said, "and took a shower. You know what I mean."

I leaned over the counter, watching Dylan making little cross cuts in the chestnuts so I could roast them. How many years, how few years, it had taken for the children to learn automatically what was done, to learn so they could one day do it in their own homes. "So if I can—I guess that's what I'm sayin'."

"Mom, watch your g's. God!"

"I'm watching. There they go," I said.

"Very cheery of you. I don't think you really believe it's over with Hedy," he said.

"I do," I said. "It's just I'm not yelling, not crying, not having car wrecks. Maybe the only easy answer isn't easy."

"I'm going to give Alison a call, if you don't need me for a minute."

"No, I'm fine." I had pulled more from him than any mother could reasonably expect. The time had come when I could not be their refuge and I could no longer expect them to be mine. The tension has to build in order for them to break away: we will all need to find anger to use as the energy. This summer had been the practice, the test run. Now they would have to find a safe place to go, a place even more alluring than home. So perhaps what I had taught them about the urgency and interest of that search was not wrong after all.

22

In the very early morning, before it was really light, I had gone out with Spike into the woods over the hill. I imagined Captain Medwin, brushing past here. I hummed to myself, *Come ye thankful people, come*, and looked for acorns to make the stuffing authentic. I picked armfuls of weeds and vines and rushes and garlands with bittersweet; I had come home, sniffling, rosy-cheeked and covered with burrs and mud. Now Brynn had returned, and she helped me arrange everything in copper urns, brass pots and baskets.

I looked around my glowing dining room with its warm wooden walls and arching beamed ceilings and imagined Mrs. Medwin stuck with everyone in a small wooden ship for two months. What if the ship sank, and her children were not in her arms? She would not have gone up on deck without them. Mrs. Medwin must have been a solid sort of survivor: in that ship, watching her husband lose his mind. They were surely of stronger stock, all of them in the ship praying to get through this day, praying to hold on, praying to find the New Land. I go mad when the heat goes off. Wrong thought—that evening when Hedy came to rescue me. It was so dark, so cold, and he was so gay, so cheery. Don't.

Brynn pulled some branches out of an urn and balanced them on the beams. We draped some bittersweet around the front door. Brynn smiled, cocked her head, the way I remembered my mother doing it when she was checking out a design for a fabric.

I remembered how Brynn had screamed at me when Bill left: "You did it. You chased him away with your crazy ways. You always want more."

Now the turkey was already stuffed and roasting in one oven. Cranberry bread was baking in the other with dozens of cornbread muffins studded with kernels of corn. Mince and pumpkin pies were ready to be baked. The gravy was fragrant with sage, tarragon and basil, and crushed garlic. Watercress and parsley were wrapped in white terry cloth towels in bowls of ice. Tiny purple and white pearl onions were blanched and waiting to be cooked in pure cream. Half gallons of fresh cider were keeping cool on the front porch.

Reilly brought over folding tables and chairs, borrowed from the Theodore's church. I covered the tables with Indian print bedspreads in pumpkin and scarlet print. Deborah brought Poppy and Dana without Mark.

"I miss Mark a bit," I said to Deborah, "but if Mark were here, I'd look at you and wonder how he doesn't drive you crazy."

"I know," she said. "I miss him myself today; it's like the old joke—but what are you going to do for aggravation. Our family doesn't know how to have a holiday without some exasperation."

"We'll think of something."

I showed Poppy and Dana how to arrange long festoons of fruits and nuts, bright Indian corn and sprays of wheat and bittersweet up and down the centers of the tables.

"These long narrow tables," Brynn explained to her cousins, "are like the wide planks the Pilgrims used to put on trestles down the centers of their meeting rooms, and they'd also put aside after the meal is finished—the difference is ours go back to the rental place."

The girls looked at her, followed her, watched her. I remembered her watching me. And me watching my mother, maybe not in a dining room, but surely with that expectation as she strode about her factory and her showroom. I started to think, God forbid to say, that Brynn would be a splendid teacher—the irony. But Brynn would be whatever Brynn would want.

She looked at me watching her. "You're planning." She laughed.

"I'm planning not to." I wanted to rearrange this one heap of fruit Dana had sort of landed on the table. Don't.

I placed candles all over to soften the gray November light, then, with Deborah and Brynn and the little girls, I set twenty places around the table, tying squares of red, gold, orange and cinammon calico with sprigs of ivy, wheat and bittersweet for napkins at each setting. This Thanksgiving was going to be perfect.

Alison's parents called me to ask if Dylan could come to their house for dessert. I thanked them and said that was really up to Dylan, and that I was sure he would call shortly. I decided not to say he had already called.

"It's your decision," I repeated to Dylan.

"But you don't want me to go," he said.

"Well, later, after you've had dessert here. I have all your favorite pies, and look," I said, taking out containers of cream to be whipped, "chestnut puree and whipped cream. Your favorite."

"I'll tell them I'll be there later. Don't worry, Mom."

I poured the cream into a chilled bowl and began to whip it.

My father called from the city and said my mother needed to hear some show on television that a protégée of hers had done the costumes for. "I want to be sure your TV will be working," my mother said on the extension.

"It's been smashed," I said. Things were not going to be perfect. I kept on whipping with the phone cradled under my chin.

"That's impossible," my mother said, "and extravagant."

"I liked the feeling," I said.

"You sound like Deborah," my mother said. She hung up the phone.

"Millicent!" said my father.

I mixed the chestnut puree into the cream and tasted it with my fingertips. My father called back to say he'd bring their portable TV and that he was going to talk to Dylan about coming back to spend the weekend in the city. "There are some people I'd like him to meet." Which meant probably someone influential at the Art Students League.

"He'd love that," I said. "But he also plans to drop over at Alison's." So. Margot, stop. "Why don't you work it out with Dylan, and it's fine about the TV thing," I said, "but she'll have to listen upstairs in my room. I'm not having a TV on downstairs."

"Margot, don't be cruel," he said. His voice was soft.

"You're right," I said. "It's okay." I wanted my parents to be comfortable this year. I hoped it was for reasons beyond the suspicion that I lived partly to impress my inspired version of my parents with how much better I had done in my own conception of their roles than they had.

I poured the chestnut cream into a blue pottery bowl, decorated it with slivers of dried apricots and blanched almonds, and set it in the refrigerator. Dylan, having talked to my father, came bounding downstairs. "Mom, you will not like this, but I'll have to do Alison's during dessert so I can get back in time to go with Grandfather. I'm going to pack now."

"No, of course, I think it's terrific for you—don't be crazy —go!" And don't ask him if he needs help packing.

Reilly announced, bringing in firewood, that this kid, Skip, just out of the hospital, needed a place to come to, so he was going to bring him.

"Of course," I said. Mrs. Medwin would surely have opened her robust arms, all twelve of her arms. I ate six ladles of cranberry sauce. Ample bosom. Mrs. Medwin would have clasped them to her ample bosom. I would work on that today.

I was peeling gingerroot when George called to report that their friends who owned this drying-out place had had a ferocious fight. "So what else is new?" I said. "They're sexy when they fight."

"This one was not so sexy. She went off yesterday to be a cook on a cargo ship bound for Hong Kong," George said.

"That's kind of sexy, I think" —I laughed—"and crazy. I love it!"

"Thought you would," said George. "Well, he is despondent and ready to kill."

"All at once?" I started cutting tiny splinters of ginger to put in the carrots, which I should have done last night.

"By turns, actually," said George. "I told him to come down for Thanksgiving with us, but he's got the kids. And then Helena—"

"George. Stop. He can bring them," I said, "of course; don't worry. I'm just so glad Helena can make it."

"She is, too," George said, "but she's having a rough time."

"I know." There was a long pause. A silence.

"Well." He cleared his throat. "I've made some extra pies I'll bring, and a whole rice pudding for you."

Deborah now was peeling potatoes for me to mash with Monterey Jack cheese melted on top. Jennie arrived to help, reminding me she adored creamed turnips, and Deborah quickly said, "Fine, you can peel them and get them ready."

Our father called again. "This is difficult, I know, but your mother just reminded me she hates turkey and hopes you have a steak around."

"I already took care of that," I said, taking the steak out of the freezer.

The doorbell rang, and I sent Poppy and Dana to answer it. They returned carrying a bushel basket full of glowing, polished apples all tied up in red ribbons.

"From Daybreak Orchards, wow," said Jennie.

"Put it on the coffee table," I told the children.

"Aren't you going to see who it's from?" Deborah asked, handing me the card.

"You read it to me," I said.

" 'If apples were kisses, Hedy.' "

I looked at the card.

"They're from Hedy," said Dylan.

"Isn't that sweet?" said Brynn.

"Really thoughtful," sighed Deborah.

"Never would have thought he'd do that," said Jennie.

They all looked at me. I was the cool heroine in a western musical comedy, brushing my hands on my apron, going over to look at my surprise. I touched my hand to the tops of the apples and perked the ribbons. I saw his face, his hair, his eyes and his hands and wanted to feel the rush, to run to him, to cling to him the way I would have yearned for Bill. I wanted to need Hedy for what he could give. Without wanting more.

"I'll be back in a minute, Jennie. Watch the onions; don't let them boil dry."

I went upstairs. I showered quickly. I stood in my room. I looked out over the river, the mist swirling in. The colors were soft, rose, gray and taupe, smaller touches now of russet, as if the sun, unseen, was glancing off the hills. I thought of England all across the entire ocean. I thought of Hedy. I saw him there alone, walking through the moors there, in his velvet jacket, with his muffler flying behind him in the wind. His hair would be curlier from the fog, and he'd be thinking of me now. But then he'd see London, all the clubs, the girls with faces like roses, and rock stars living in real castles with stone walls and town houses with places to go dancing right next door.

It really had run its course. One day we might be friends. We'd laugh about how we almost bought that crazy estate together and nearly ruined each other in the process. We'd never remember who stopped it in time, and I would never remind him. Oh, damn. I do want to be loving and fighting, pulling it apart and patching it up again. I put my clothes on. I went downstairs.

I looked at the long glowing table. Brynn would sit at one end, and I would be at the other. Blanche surely ought to have a place of honor, and so, of course, should my father. But what about Helena? I just wanted to make some special place for—I will figure it out when the time comes.

There was such a bustling, such commotion, from this far end of the living room, all the way through to the kitchen where Brynn and Deborah were presiding and Jennie was happily complaining, "Another mystery Thanksgiving."

"What's the mystery?" said Brynn.

"What I'm supposed to be grateful for."

"You got Reilly," said Brynn.

"Oh, Reilly," said Jennie, and through the windows I could see him still raking up leaves from the front porch which Poppy and Dana were putting in a wheelbarrow with an equally concerted, and contrary, effort from Spike. Spike! I thought of Sundance, Binky and Madge—of Ivan and Stan. I should have invited Ivan and Stan. Of course. Too late.

Helena and George arrived with Fitz. Helena had the Liberty print scarf that I had given her on her head and a new cocoa silk dress. "It matches," she fussed. "I'd never show up with my colors wrong." I hugged her. We looked in each other's eyes just long enough to have to swallow, look away and grab on tight.

"The table's actually set. You're organized!" George exclaimed.

"It's an effect," I said. "All surface. My mother will say the forks are wrong. I did them that way so she has a little something to correct."

Fitz was wearing a brown beaver hat, his tweeds, a foulard vest and a scarlet paisley ascot. "The country squire," I commented. He gently walked Helena to the wing chair near the fireplace.

The mists were settling, lowering. I went to close the front curtains. I saw Blanche emerging from the mists, coming down the path with a long walking stick. Then Spike darted out at Blanche, his ears flying like banners. I ran out, shouting at Spike. Reilly ran and hung onto him by the collar.

"Salutations," said Blanche, perfectly calm. "They loathe sticks. Sorry, Spike." She patted the dog, held now by Reilly. "I'm glad to see you here, Reilly." She looked at him softly, as she paused there, scanning his face.

"Are you, ma'am?" he said. He kept his head down.

"Yes. I am. It should be a splendid dinner. I hear our friend Margot is a fine chef."

How nice of Blanche not to say any of the things someone else—I—might have said—such as "I hear you're doing better," or "We'll have to talk," or anything. It was enough for now, and she knew that, just to share one meal together. Blanche then reached out her hand. Reilly dusted his hands on his jeans and he reached out his right hand to Blanche. "You have a firm handshake. Sign of very good character," she said. She turned just briefly, and touched his shoulder lightly and repeated herself, "I'm glad to see you." Blanche repeating herself! I would hope to hear that whole story one day.

Dylan went out and up the walk to greet my parents; he took the TV from my father, who put his arm around him. My mother was wearing black taffeta with the elaborate diamanté belt which had belonged to Elsa Schiaparelli. "I remember standing in your dressing room and trying on that belt; you are amazing—the tiniest waist," I said.

"She has the same figure she had when we met," my father said, and kissed her.

"It's too bad," my mother said, "it wouldn't fit, or I'd let you borrow it for parties." Don't bite, I thought, not today.

Dylan looked taller today than my father, but they had the same graceful bearing, a light angle to their walk. I held my father tightly in my arms. I paused. And I kissed my mother. Her cheek felt like velvet. I kissed her other cheek.

Helena and George's friend John sauntered in next with his new recruits: a sad-looking boy; an attractive man, still ruddy and cocky and not off the sauce for long; a fragile young girl who pulled her black cardigan tightly around her still shaking body. John also had his kids with him, down from school.

Deborah introduced herself to the man with the ruddy face, brought him a cup of coffee and sat beside him talking, her hands using all the angles of expression, the way she did when she was eager.

My mother looked around the room; stood back from the table, peered through her dark glasses at a place setting. "The table is very nice. You still have your good silver. It looks lovely. I suppose this is the new way to place the dessert forks?"

Jennie was putting up the coffee urn and the tray of sodas, while Brynn and I were organizing the food on the round breakfast table and the kitchen counters. "With our friends here who are still shaking," I said, "I'm not sure buffet is going to work."

"Well, I'm not serving anyone," said Jennie.

"I am not asking," I said. Yes, I would ask my father to carve the turkey at the table and then everyone could go up and help himself.

"You know," Brynn said, "a lot of people have been figuring out how to feed themselves before they met you." She kissed me very fast. "Don't worry, it's going to be fine," Brynn said. She set down a platter of vegetables. "Oh, yes." She paused.

"What?" I said. I could tell by her expression she thought I wasn't going to like it.

"I told Freddy I'd go up to the mountains to Vermont with him this weekend; a bunch of our friends have a cabin and if we can't ski we're going to hang out and relax."

"That's a terrific idea," I said. I stirred up the gravy with the ladle quickly to smooth it out again.

"I didn't think you'd feel that way," Brynn said. "Thanks."

"For what?" I said.

"For being easy about me going!"

"Well, of course," I said. I swallowed hard.

My mother looked at the buffet; she picked up a carrot and tasted it, then put it back on the platter. "You have a lot of food here. Is your doctor friend coming? I was going to ask him about this show I'm crazy about, all medical people. Was Ivan able to get you on TV yet?"

"Yes, I'm starring in a soap about a designer who is a closet roller derby queen."

"That's very interesting," said my mother; "they will never teach you to skate. You'll wind up as a patient on *General Hospital*."

"Could be worse," said Deborah. The phone rang. "Saved by the bell," she said, picking it up. "Long distance for you." She looked at me. "Take it upstairs."

Hedy.

I did the steps two at a time.

"Hi," I said. I looked in my mirror quickly, checking out my hair. Idiot!

"Hi. Do you have one hundred and eighty people there?" he said.

"Yes," I said. "I like the apples a lot."

"Look," he said. Long pause. "Here's the deal. You got a passport?"

"Yes!"

"Okay. That's all you need to tell me. Turns out I'm not going until tomorrow. I want to take you to England. Look at it this way," he said, edgy. And I understood. "If nothing else it will be a dynamite show . . ." He paused. "A real limousine will pick you up around midnight, so we take off in the mornin'. And so when the limousine comes back to New York you will be in it or not in it."

"That simple?"

"That simple. I'm hanging up now."

"Oh, Hedy."

"No oh. In it or not in it."

We hung up. I have never hung up a phone so slowly, so softly. And I looked in the mirror and I opened my closet door.

Then the phone rang again. "Yes?" I said.

"Yes?" said Cleo. "What kind of way is that to answer a phone?"

"Strange way," I said.

"True. Listen. St. Cheri did not go to Texas."

"Wonderful! Bring her."

"No—she's doing a dinner here for everyone in the world. Sort of what you're doing there, except she's sending out to La Grenouille."

"Cleo. I'm going to a rock concert tomorrow. In England."

"Anyone I know?"

"Yes. But I'll be back for Monday."

"Fine. We have a chef coming on with recipes from Gold Rush days. Chuck wagon."

"I did not forget," I said.

"Who could forget? I am just considering how well it will go with the interview with the American rock singer just back from England."

"Cleo, how can you be so cynical!"

"You just practice," she said; "a day at a time."

"Never," I said.

Last year, even this summer, I would have looked down this table, looked at these faces with their holiday expressions, squinted slightly to mute the colors in the glow of late day sunlight, the gleaming spots of candlelight, and I would have clasped my hands together with such a sense of completion.

But a twist again of time, and I looked down through the mirrored shaft to the colors, the shapes, the images, and this is a picture of individuals poised on the brink of change, hanging on, just for this night, all of us.

Dylan brought the huge golden turkey to the table on its ironstone platter. He placed it in front of his grandfather and sat down at my right. My father said, "Thank you, my boy," and stood up and, with such a flourish, honed the knife and began to carve the turkey. "A perfect bird," my father said, and my mother smiled up at him. "No one does a turkey like Sylvan. Whatever he touches is art."

"That's my girl!" said my father, and my mother added, "But not such big slices so there will be enough perhaps to go around." And Dylan looked at me and grinned and Deborah caught that look and said, "It should never just be perfect."

Any one of us around this table would notice a different part of the pattern, would pick up a small exchange of an expression and hear it, see it in quite another way. And so there were hundreds of images and thoughts catching light here in this moment; eyes stealing glances, Deborah's children looking at the man she was sitting next to, learning about that new kind of pleasing-him-for-her that our kids of divorce do pick up. Jennie looked at Reilly, who passed a plate to Blanche with a smile which she briefly answered before returning to a conversation she was having with Brynn. "So if you're interested," Blanche was saying, "you should come up and we'll talk."

"I think I'll do that," said Brynn.

Now Reilly turned back to Jennie, who passed the cranberries to her father, and George put his arm around Jennie for an instant. Fitz reached over to Helena, who was having chills and shaking. "I'm okay, Fitz," she said. "Margot keeps the heat down to spare her plants the slightest discomfort."

"Yes," Fitz said, "and a penny saved is a dollar more to spend at the florist."

Helena looked at Jennie, who had avoided her mother all evening, and Helena said, "Oh, Jennie, would you get me another cup of tea?" and Jennie, released, said, "Sure, Mom; lots of sugar?"

"Lots," said Helena. And Helena winked at George as Jennie got up.

And I'm already somewhere else, imagining myself backstage watching Hedy as he watches the guys set up for him as he stands there in the dark, the lights on the control system flashing like a spaceship about to take off, and he hears the sounds of the throng waiting for him. I watch him leap onstage, his hair lifting like wings, wafting out on beams of pink and orange and green and cobalt light; like Captain Medwin imagining spills of ribboned waterfalls, jungles beyond the next forest, and I'm going to be there. Just for that.

I looked at Brynn and I looked at Dylan. They will have to go up onto their own empty stages, jump into open pairs and pairs of arms, go down their own odd winding roads: I wanted to reach out, to hold them tight, to tell them more.

I did not want to know what I knew: I had reached out; I had held them tight; I had told them more. And more. And now they would go down these roads and they might take the wrong turn, and they might be somewhere they didn't mean to go and they would invent a better reason to be there and they would do that often enough and know they were survivors.

"Applesauce!" I said to myself. "They already are."

"Let's say grace," I said, "and, Daddy, would you lead us?" I took a deep breath, bowed my head and followed along as he led us in prayer, and I sensed the hopes and heartbeats and I felt my own leaping pulse as I imagined the purr of the real limousine coming up the hill and I tried to invent the idea again that it would be wonderful, that tomorrow would be wonderful and that I could believe in that forever.

A Note on the Type

The text of this book was set on the Linotype in Janson, a recutting made direct from type cast from matrices long thought to have been made by the Dutchman Anton Janson, who was a practicing type founder in Leipzig during the years 1668–87. However, it has been conclusively demonstrated that these types are actually the work of Nicholas Kis (1650–1702), a Hungarian, who most probably learned his trade from the master Dutch type founder Dirk Voskens. The type is an excellent example of the influential and sturdy Dutch types that prevailed in England up to the time William Caslon developed his own incomparable designs from them.

Composed by Maryland Linotype Co., Inc.
Baltimore, Maryland
Printed and bound by
The Haddon Craftsmen, Inc.
Scranton, Pennsylvania

Typography and binding design by
Virginia Tan